I0598695

A Cache of Trouble

A Cassidy Callahan Novel

by

Kelly Rysten

CCB Publishing
British Columbia, Canada

A Cache of Trouble: A Cassidy Callahan Novel

Copyright ©2011 by Kelly Rysten
ISBN-13 978-1-926918-87-7
First Edition

Library and Archives Canada Cataloguing in Publication

Rysten, Kelly, 1960-
A cache of trouble : a Cassidy Callahan novel / written by Kelly Rysten.
ISBN 978-1-926918-87-7
Also available in electronic format.
I. Title.
PS3618.Y78C33 2011   813'.6   C2011-906419-7

Cover artwork by Kelly Rysten: www.kellyrysten.com

Publisher: CCB Publishing
              British Columbia, Canada
              www.ccbpublishing.com

This book and all of my books should be dedicated to my husband, Gary, who stands beside me and behind me, through thick and thin, believing in everything I do, and helping me all along the way.

Other books by Kelly Rysten

Triple Trouble

Read about Cassidy Callahan's first
tracking adventure with trouble at every turn.

Published 2009 – ISBN 978-1-926585-41-3

Car Trouble

Car troubles abound as Cassidy sets her sights on Police Academy.
With a serial killer on the loose determined to send the police
department a message, Cassidy's attendance is in question.

Published 2010 – ISBN 978-1-926918-03-7

Chapter 1

Time was running out and it was late in the evening. The sun was fading fast, the trail endless. I'd been on it for two days and I would have killed for a piece of cheesecake. I was cold, wet, hungry and getting very worried that I wouldn't find Angie Grey in time. It had rained twice since starting this trail and with each drop her footprints faded more. She had been happily camping with her family at Piney Point when, in typical teenage fashion, she'd gotten mad at her parents and stomped off into the woods. Her parents had wanted to stay another couple of days but Angie wanted to go home to see her boyfriend. She left camp to sulk, or maybe, they thought, to try and walk home and they hadn't seen her since. So her parents called the police, who called search and rescue, who then called me. I'm Cassidy Callahan, tracker. My search team is good and we have a very good record. Our guys are dedicated and give their all to each case but sometimes they need a little help, and when they do they call me because I have a handy knack for seeing people's footprints. It's just something I grew up doing and somehow I got pretty good at it. Good enough that I'd been sent off to police academy and gotten my handy little badge and my stiff uniform. Then I began to help out the police, search and rescue, or anybody who would call on me. Mostly I worked with a team under Lou "Strict" Strickland. We were becoming a tight group, able to work well together and follow the toughest trails.

Right then I could really identify with Angie. I would have liked to just walk right out of there and join my boyfriend too. I thought this search would be a simple matter of following Angie until she got tired, but she didn't get tired. Not only that, but she had left the trail and headed up a canyon that pointed towards the city. I hoped she wasn't really trying to walk home, but I knew how irrational teenage girls could be. They can rationalize any wish into a simple solution, which later turns out to be more difficult than imagined. So there I was, two days up a fading trail chasing down an emotional teenager.

Victor wasn't much help. He was along for two reasons. One, because they wouldn't let me go out alone, and two, he knew how to use a first aid kit. EMTs are handy that way, but this call was more my area of expertise. I doubted Victor could have followed this trail. He tried keeping track of the footprints for a while, but after many attempts to see what I saw and getting left behind, he gave up and followed me. His job would come later.

"Cassidy, do you ever slow down?" Victor gasped, short of breath.

"Do you see these tracks?"

"Barely."

"In an hour you might not. One more rain like we had this afternoon and the trail will be gone."

"Neither rain, nor snow, nor dark of night..." Victor said.

"Nope, that doesn't work for tracking. Can't track at night. And rain is murder on tracks. We need to find Angie before it rains again. The only good thing about rain is that maybe she was able to get enough water to stay alive. As far as snow goes, I've seen my share of snow for a lifetime. How many times did we go after lost skiers this winter?"

"Me, or you?"

I'd just joined the team in January, so I guess I couldn't complain about the snow trips. I'd only gotten two months worth and then the snow had melted enough to make the snow birds stay home. Lou, Victor, Landon and Rosco sure had their share of snow shoeing even before I came on board.

"Aaaangie!" We called out as we tracked along. Time was getting critical. At first we hadn't called her name because following her trail seemed sufficient. However, as we thought we were getting closer and Angie's time was running out we started calling her by name, hoping for a response. So far, the hills had been silent. When darkness finally stopped our search I became torn. Another night out in the open and I would put the chances of Angie's survival at almost zero. Nights were still cold. We'd woken up to frost on the ground the two nights we'd been out. Angie's family had slept snug and warm in a motor home but she was a city kid out to get her yearly dose of the outdoors. She'd taken off without water. I needed to find that kid and I needed to do it yesterday.

After we made camp, ate some dinner and cleaned up, I put a headlamp on and walked a circle around camp. More than one lost person had spotted headlamps and then called out to us, so I wanted to give Angie a chance to spot us too. Two circuits around camp and still no response. I went to bed dejected.

"Up at first light," I called out to Victor as I crawled into my tent.

The next morning the trail was noticeably fainter. Frost again covered the ground. I called out to Victor as soon as I got up and then I started my little one burner camp stove to heat water for hot chocolate and breakfast. I was tired of oatmeal and so determined to not eat it again that I made a pouch full of powdered eggs, then couldn't eat it all. Victor looked at it and went to his pack and pulled out a sweet roll, gooey with glaze and begging to be eaten.

"Where'd you get that?" I snapped. It wasn't cheesecake but it would do in a pinch.

"The grocery store."

"You're lucky it isn't cheesecake. I'd do anything for a piece of cheesecake!"

"Anything?"

"Well, almost anything."

"Sorry, I don't have cheesecake."

We hit the trail and I could hear little sweet rolls whispering to me from the bottom of Victor's pack. I wasn't going to ask for one, though. Nope, I would be tough. I'd ignore the call of the sweet roll.

The only way I knew I was still following Angie's trail was the fact that her tracks were the only footprints around. All distinguishing marks had been erased by the rain. The one thing that kept me going was the fact that Angie was not experienced in the woods. She didn't walk carefully and she was tiring. She dragged her feet a lot now and she was growing unsteady.

We finally caught up to her around mid morning but the sight of her was so disturbing I had to stop, taking a second to let things register. Not wanting to rush into this all panicky, I calmed myself and then walked over to her. Victor was still several steps behind me. She was lying on her side out in the open. She was covered with muddy raindrops, so she had been lying there for a long time. I felt for a pulse and almost fainted with relief when I found one. I ached for her, though. Victor stepped in, handed me the radio, and started his work. Still feeling overwhelmed, I contacted base camp and arranged for pick up. Missing person found. Condition serious. Send airlift. Stat. Lou could tell just from my voice that I'd been hit hard this time. I was glad he didn't know why.

After a seemingly endless wait the helicopter clattered overhead and lowered the basket. Victor and I lifted Angie's still form into the basket and strapped her down. Victor rode up with Angie and then the basket was lowered again and I hopped in. I rode the basket up into the helicopter and found a place that was out of the way. I sat beside a very still Angie all the way to the hospital, Victor and Nathan monitoring her vital signs as we flew along. Dehydration and hypothermia were the main concerns. She didn't appear to have been attacked by animals or have any broken bones from a fall. She'll be okay, I kept telling myself. One good thing I noticed, we were headed towards Joshua Hills. If Angie were in real danger Victor and Nathan would have sent the helicopter to L.A.

At the hospital Angie's family found me, clapping me on the back and thanking me profusely. I was embarrassed. They were thanking me for taking three days to find their daughter and she'd lain out in the open for close to a day unconscious. How could they be thanking me when I felt so guilty?

I should have called Rusty and gotten a ride home, but I was still so disheartened that I shouldered my pack and started walking towards the condo. A half mile from the hospital a big, white, older model car pulled up and a little old lady tottered around to the sidewalk. She pressed a bag of fast food into my hand and handed me a flyer about her church's upcoming revival.

"God bless you," she said pleasantly, tottered back to her car and drove away. I guess she didn't notice the 9mm still strapped to my thigh or she would have kept driving. I was puzzled. She either knew about the search or thought I was homeless. I was going with the homeless theory. Backpack, dirty clothes, no bath for three days, walking through town... Oh well, who could blame her. I opened the hamburger and ate it as I walked. Even fast food cheesecake would have been an answer to prayer right then, but I only found a burger and fries.

I entered the condo hot, tired and discouraged. My dog, Shadow, raced around, happy to see me. I petted him until he calmed down then I dropped my pack by the front door and went upstairs to shower. The warm water went a long way toward perking me up, but I still needed a warm hug, a slice of New York cheesecake with something gooey on top, and a good report about Angie to make me feel like my old self again. I put on a tank top and shorts and stretched out on the big, soft bed and was out like a light.

I didn't sleep long before I felt the bed move and an arm came around me. My hug had arrived. I really needed that hug. I turned over and put my arms around Rusty's broad shoulders.

"I missed you," he said, "Why didn't you call?"

"I rode in with the helicopter."

"I know, Strict told me. He was as puzzled as I was about why you weren't at the hospital, though."

"I'm sorry, I was discouraged and I thought a long walk would help so I just walked home from the hospital."

"You spent two days hiking those rugged mountains and you still needed a walk? What could have you that discouraged?"

I got a big lump in my throat. I really needed that hug so I snuggled closer.

"Oh, Babe," he said pulling me close, "okay, we'll talk later."

"Would you call for a report for me, later? I know she'll be okay. I just can't shake the sight of her. But I think she'll be okay."

"Sure."

Now that I was home, had my hug, and Rusty was there I relaxed enough to think about other things. My mind wandered to other questions. Questions that had popped up from time to time but had never been answered.

"Rusty?"

"Yeah?"

"This seems like kind of late to be asking but, with a wedding to plan, do you have a family? It seems kind of strange to think we're getting married and I don't even know if you have a family."

"Of course I have a family. I have two brothers and a sister. My parents live in San Diego."

"Do you ever visit them? Can I meet them? Do they know about me?"

Rusty pushed himself up onto one elbow and looked down at me, eyes smiling.

"You really want to meet them?"

"Of course! I'd love to. Do they all live in California?"

"One brother lives in New York, the rest live in the San Diego area. Why so many questions all of a sudden?"

"All of a sudden? I've been wondering these things for months."

"Why didn't you ask?"

"I am."

His eyes smiled again. He lay back down and started telling me about his family. He was the oldest of four kids. I could have guessed that he was the oldest. He just acted like an older brother. His dad was a cop and his mom was a dispatcher. They were retired. The next younger brother worked for a big sports magazine based in New York City. He had a long-standing Yankees/Dodgers rivalry going with his brother. His sister was close to my age. She designed store displays for a big department store. The youngest brother would finish college this semester and liked the beach more than work. Rusty spoke of them with detached fondness.

"Did your dad inspire you to go into police work?"

"Not exactly. It kind of ran in the family. It was the talk at the dinner table so as I grew up it was all familiar to me and I just followed what I knew. The other kids were more creative, I guess. They did their own thing."

"Do you think they will come to the wedding?"

"They'll try. If it doesn't work out, though, there will be no hard feelings one way or the other."

"Do they know about me?"

"A little. They know I met someone I love very much and I've never been happier. That's enough for them."

"You didn't warn them about me being a trouble magnet?"

"Cass, no one is a trouble magnet. You've put yourself in some sticky situations, but trouble doesn't go looking for you. You could avoid getting into trouble if you didn't go looking for it."

"I don't go looking for it. I didn't ask to be carjacked. I didn't ask to be hunted by drug dealers."

"Poking around drug labs hidden in the mountains is asking to be hunted. Going after Patrick when Peccati took him was asking to be hunted. Driving around in a marked car was like asking Trent to kidnap you. I know you don't do these things on purpose. But you do them accidentally with frightening regularity."

"The search went okay," I said, changing the subject to something safer. "I wish I'd known how hard it was going to be from the beginning... I was looking for a fourteen year old girl. Her parents thought she'd be close to camp. They thought she ran off to sulk and ran into trouble. Instead, she'd tried to walk home not knowing how far it was, not taking anything with her. We had two rainstorms in the search and every time it rained the trail got harder to follow. When we found her she'd collapsed. She was unconscious and she'd lain out in the open for close to a day. When I found her I saw what could have happened to me so many times and no one would have known to look for me. No one even knew I was out there or where I'd gone. It could have happened a dozen times but I always managed to come home again." I paused, waiting for the lump in my throat to go away. "I felt guilty that I took so long to find her... And her family thanked me for it. How could they thank me for leaving their daughter out in the wilderness while I patiently followed a bunch of tracks? I couldn't understand it. So what if I found her, I almost found her too late. I still hope I wasn't too late. Can you find out for me later?"

"You know I will. But you can't blame yourself for any of this. You did what you could. You have to remember that, no matter what the outcome of your search. You can only do so much. The outcome is not in your hands."

"I keep telling myself that I could have tracked faster. I could have gotten there sooner..."

"Shhh, don't do that to yourself. You did what you could and you probably saved a life. Who went with you?"

"Victor."

"And could Victor have followed the trail?"

"No. He tried. He watched the trail for a while but I kept leaving him behind so he had to quit."

"There, you see, no one could have gotten there any sooner than you did."

I snuggled up close, still worried.

"I need a cheesecake fix. I've been craving cheesecake. Victor brought sweet rolls on this search and it was all I could do to keep from stealing his pack."

His eyes laughed again. "Come on," he said rolling off the bed, "let's go find that elusive cheesecake."

I changed into jeans, t-shirt and moccasins. I always felt underdressed when I was with Rusty in his detective clothes. We went to a restaurant that served dinner and dessert. Rusty ordered dinner. I ordered cheesecake.

"You have to eat more than cheesecake," he said.

"What's wrong with cheesecake? Milk, cheese, eggs, flour. I don't need meat every day."

"Cass."

"Okay," I said looking up at the waitress, "with strawberries on top. I'll add fruit, it's healthier than caramel sauce. Is that better?" After the waitress left I turned back to Rusty. "I won't need another cheesecake fix for a couple of weeks. Besides, some lady thought I was homeless and handed me a hamburger while I was walking home from the hospital."

He shook his head grinning. "My poor homeless fiancée."

"I have a homework assignment for you." I said over dinner. "I need you to make a list of everyone you should invite to the wedding. Family, relatives, friends, co-workers, anybody who would want to be invited. And I will need addresses for all those people, too. I need to get a head count so I can find a place to have the wedding."

"Can't we keep it simple?"

"We could try, but I doubt if we'll succeed. Just make the list and you'll see how impossible that is. Think of how many people there are just at the station and it's already a big wedding. Plus, my mom will be in her element with this. She didn't get to go all out the first time around. She basically just showed up for the ceremony and Jack and I wore our dress uniforms. She's going to have fun with this. But the first step is getting a head count. Then, with the count in mind, we look for a location. After we have a few places in mind we can try for a date."

"I thought the date was up to us."

"In a way it is, but we also have to work with the schedule of the person performing the ceremony and the site where the ceremony will take place. So what day would you like to shoot for? It takes at least three months to plan a wedding. At this point we are looking at July, but we need to avoid holidays. Everybody at the station is going to be busy over Independence Day Weekend so that's out."

"This is going to be complicated, I can tell already."

"I'll make you a deal. I'll make your assignments short and easy if you'll have patience when things get crazy. The list of addresses will probably be the toughest one."

"What else?"

"You might be thinking about who you want for attendants. I hope it's a short list because I don't know anybody besides my sister who would be a bride's maid. I suppose I could talk Rhonda into it if I had to. After that I draw a blank. I think Steve and Randy would feel pretty silly standing up there. So, if you can, think of two people that would work and I'll talk to Rhonda."

"What else?"

"That's all for now. You'll have to get fitted for a tux later."

"That can't be all."

"I told you I'd keep your part easy."

"What if I want to help?"

"If you want a really tough assignment then plan the honeymoon."

I could tell this idea interested him. Where would a cop and a tracker go on their honeymoon?

"Where do you want to go?"

"I don't know, surprise me."

"Well, what do you want to do?"

"I want to spend time with you."

"Do you want to rough it or go easy?"

"To be honest, I don't want to spend my whole honeymoon in a tent. And I definitely don't want to eat oatmeal for breakfast. And I'd prefer to avoid all kinds of backpacker food except trail mix."

He smiled at me, glad to see my outdoors fix was over for a while. Maybe, if people would watch where they were going in the woods, we'd have a few days to ourselves.

After dinner Rusty excused himself, "What's the patient's name?"

"Angie Grey."

Rusty went outside to make the phone call so I wouldn't try and read him during the conversation. He knew me too well. He came back looking somber.

"We'll try again in the morning," he said when he got back to the table. "It was good news, just not the news you were hoping for."

It was going to be a long night. Rusty's cell phone rang and he got up to answer it, wandering off again. I always made a point to not listen to his work conversations.

"That was Strict," he said on his return. Lou Strickland, Search Commander. "He just wanted to know how you were doing. He said we should go do something fun tomorrow. You've been running yourself ragged."

"I am not, I'm just wishing this last one had turned out more positive."

"Nope, Strict is right. You do need a break. Let's start a different search." I looked at him quizzically. "I have something I want to show you. Tomorrow."

Chapter 2

In the morning we called the hospital again to check on Angie. She was conscious now. Things were looking up. I was able to relax a little.

We drove up into the hills and wound around on some back roads. Rusty pulled up into the driveway of a ranch style home. The yards were landscaped and the house looked freshly painted. A welcome sign was nailed to the wall beside the front door and pots of flowers lined the porch. We walked to the front door and Rusty rang the bell.

The door was answered by an older woman, maybe seventy-five years old. She brightened when she saw Rusty. She was dressed in slacks and a polyester blouse with flowers embroidered all over it. Her clothes were immaculately pressed, not a wrinkle in sight, well, not on her clothes anyway. She walked with a delicate grace as she led us into her living room.

"Mrs. Morgan, this is Cassidy."

She looked me up and down and gave Rusty a sly look. "I'm pleased to meet you Cassidy," she said politely.

"It's good to meet you too," I replied, curious about why we were there.

"Cass, Mrs. Morgan is trying to sell her home. I've been looking around in my spare time while you were out with the team and so far this is the first house I found that I've wanted to show you. I don't know exactly what you are looking for in a house. I just know the condo is not a good long-term solution for us, so I've been watching for a house that you might like."

He'd been looking at houses? He never said anything about looking at houses! He looked at me uncertainly. Okay, so I'd look at the house. What I'd seen so far I liked. Mrs. Morgan had obviously taken very good care of it. Everything was tastefully and carefully decorated which made me wonder what it would look like with Rusty's old brown couch sitting where the pink, mint green and white Victorian floral couch was. The front windows opened onto the landscaped front yard and beyond that were rolling hills with neighbor's houses far enough apart to be private yet close enough to see. The kitchen looked freshly remodeled with oak cupboards and glass inserts. Everything was clean and sparkling. The den was warm and cozy. I walked around the house timidly, not wanting to intrude. Mrs. Morgan took over, sensing my hesitancy.

"The house has nice big bedrooms," she said brightly, leading us down a hall. "Here's the bathroom. There's another one off the master bedroom. There's three bedrooms but I don't use the rooms for bedrooms, since it's only me here now. I love the master bedroom. My husband built the house and he loved the outdoors. He put a bay window in the bedroom and he would sit for hours watching the birds. Sometimes deer come down out of the hills." Uh oh, she'd hit the nail on the head there! "The master bath is a bit odd. My husband was in a wheelchair in his later years and we needed the bathroom remodeled. So the doorway is wider than most and the shower has been replaced and expanded. We had this bench put in so he could sit and shower." I blushed, thinking of creative ways to use that bench in the shower.

I looked out the bay windows and paused. There was a small barn, a corral, an open area of dirt and Bermuda; not a pretty site but there was space for an agility course. It was obvious a horse hadn't lived there for years and the area needed some clean up. Mrs. Morgan led us through the house showing us all the little things her husband had done to make life easier for her while also explaining that she was waiting for the right buyer for the house. Someone who would take care of it and liven it up again. She talked about the horses her husband had kept and told us she was moving into town, closer to conveniences, downsizing to ease the workload.

I was still in shock when Rusty and I climbed into the Explorer again.

"What do you think?" he asked.

"Rusty," I said, "it's too much. It's a wonderful house. But it's too much."

"Too much what? Too big? Too fancy? Too expensive? You grew up in that mansion at the ranch but this house is too much?"

"Even my old house was more house than I really wanted, except for the yard. I always wanted more of a yard for the agility course. If you took the condo out to the hills and plopped it down where Mrs. Morgan's house is I'd be fine with that. I don't need a fancy house, just a little place, close to the hills."

"I get the feeling we are back to the issue of not liking to wear a dress. Anything that is fancier than plain old jeans is uncomfortable to you. You think of this house like you think of a dress."

I thought for a moment and realized that he was right on. Bingo. How did he do that?

"So," he continued, "take out all Mrs. Morgan's fancy furniture and years of accumulated knickknacks. Take away the flowers and the embroidered towels. What are you left with? It's just a house. You make a house into what you want after you buy it. Tell me what you don't like about the house once you mentally pare it down to size. The only things I can really place in it that dress it up are the bay window in the bedroom and the cupboards in the kitchen. Everything else is just a nice, big open house. You could bring Shasta down. Set up an agility course. If it closed in time you could even have the wedding here. Did you see the yard beside the house? There's a big grassy area that runs from the house right up to the tree line."

"You like the house, don't you?" I asked.

"I do, but I won't make you live there if you don't want to. I picture waking up in the morning and finding you sitting in that bay window, watching the deer come out of the hills. I think about standing in that window myself and watching you out in the corral area with the horses. I picture a house full of friends, not often but occasionally. I picture a Christmas tree in the front window."

"You do? You picture all that when you see that house?"

"I do, and more."

"Would you go riding with me?"

"If we started out slow. I could take you around and show you some of the houses I looked at before I went to Mrs. Morgan's house. That might show you a thing or two. The problem is that, after seeing this house, other houses just don't measure up."

"Let's see. Let's go to a realtor's office, tell them what we are looking for, and see what they come up with. If we haven't seen anything we like by the end of the day I'll be convinced."

So that's what we did. We looked at five more houses that the realtor thought were exactly what we were looking for and Rusty was right, they just didn't measure up.

What would I do with a house that big? Did I really want two horses to take care of? Who would take care of them if I got stuck on a three day search? Horses needed daily care. They needed feeding and brushing and shoeing and exercising. I battled with myself back and forth over the house, thinking about how much furniture we would have to buy to make it presentable for a wedding. Ironically, finances didn't enter the picture much. I had life insurance money left. After my house had burned down I got some compensation for that. Then my neighbor had bought the lot from me to add to his own yard. I was sure we could come up with a sizable down payment. I just wasn't sure if I wanted the house. But why wouldn't I want it? It was a beautiful house, near the forest, with a barn, with room for an agility course. I could set up a regulation size course out there and train Shadow to compete in obedience and agility trials. Round and around I went. I would keep arguing with myself until the wedding at this rate. Then I remembered I could have the wedding there if the house closed in time. And we didn't have a date yet so maybe we could schedule the wedding for after the closing.

"Cass, your ears are smoking. You're burning off your brain cells. What's going on?"

"I've got a million piece puzzle and I'm trying to put it all together at once. Let's stop for lunch and look at some numbers."

We looked at the numbers, assigned a furniture allowance and it was doable. Oh dear. Then I drew out the floor plan and where things were on the property. I drew out a possible set up for a wedding. It was doable, too. Hoo boy. Umm, okay. Rusty watched the smoke billow out of my ears with amusement. I was trying to talk myself out of the house but the longer I tried the more it looked like the house for us.

"Houses never close in three months. If we want to have the wedding there we will have to choose a later date."

"Let me talk to Mrs. Morgan. I think she has to move out sooner anyway. She's moving into a retirement home and if she doesn't take the apartment when it's available she'll lose her chance at it. Maybe she will rent the house to us until it closes."

Rusty looked at the figures again. I didn't know if I was dreading this or celebrating it.

"Cass, are you sure this is what you want?"

No, yes, maybe, give me a year to get used to the idea. I didn't know. The house was everything I wanted, plus. This just felt like an awfully big step to take even though he was right, the condo was not right for us either.

"I think I need to talk to my mother."

I dialed the phone wondering what in the world I was doing. I could handle being stalked, shot at, chased by lunatics and I could brave the woods and wilderness, but I couldn't make a simple decision that would affect my happiness for the next ten years or so.

"Hello?"

"Hi, Mom? Do you have a few minutes?"

"Cassidy! Of course! Oh dear, what's happened to you this time? Are you in trouble again? And how bad could it be this time? You didn't call when your house burned down..."

"Mom, I'm fine. I just need some help deciding something."

"Oh, okay, well what is it?"

"Rusty found a house."

"Cassidy, that's wonderful!"

"I'm still trying to decide if it's wonderful. I was hoping you could help me decide if it is really wonderful or not."

I described the house in minute detail and it still sounded wonderful. I told her about the layout for the wedding and it still sounded wonderful.

"Cassidy, why are you so worried about this decision? Everything sounds perfect for you."

Sigh, maybe that was why I was being so wary. I wasn't used to things being perfect. I was used to things turning into trouble.

"Okay," I told Rusty, "go ahead and see if Mrs. Morgan will sell us the house and let us move in early."

He glanced up from his study of the floor plan I'd sketched out. "Are you sure about this?"

"I'm trying really hard to be sure." I saw the mixture of hope and uncertainty in his eyes. "Okay, I'm sure. Go for it. Just remember that if we have the wedding there the date depends on when we move in. I need time to get the house furnished and ready."

Chapter 3

Strict waited four days before calling me out again. I wondered how they did the searches when I wasn't there. Did they still try to track the missing person? Or did they just send out a bunch of people to do a broad search of the area? That was one thing tracking was very good for, saving manpower. It narrowed the search down to one trail. I hadn't lost a trail yet but if I ever did, tracking would still save time because there would be a more specific starting point to the search. This time the search worked the other way. They had searched until they found the last visible evidence and then I needed to figure out what had happened from there.

When I arrived at base camp Landon was there ready to take me in. He was in full backpacker and mountain climbing gear complete with harness, ropes and pitons. What had they been up to while I was gone? I put on my pack and pulled the shoulder pads down snug. I fastened the Fastex buckle and was ready to go. Rosco and Victor appeared with packs ready and side arms. I looked at Landon. He was armed too. I was used to these guys carrying but for some reason their attitudes clued me in that this was no ordinary track. Four officers joined the group and I became even more wary. Rosco, Victor and Landon were all EMTs. As long as they were in the group it was a rescue. Add the officers and it was now an apprehension involving possible injuries. I looked around for Strict. He stood with a group of men who were bent over studying a map. He glanced up and motioned me over.

"Cassidy, will you promise me to listen to the guys up there?"

"What's up?"

"It started out as a simple traffic stop on the highway. Drugs were found, the driver was arrested. Two passengers took off into the forest. That was yesterday. Backup was called in and a search was started. It's going to be a fast hike to the last visible sign. After that we are stumped. There's tracks all over those hills. Two of them belong to our escapees."

"Will I get a chance to see some examples of their real tracks before I get up there?"

"The guys will do anything they can to help you. Don't try and be a hero. Find the end of the trail and back off."

"Okay, I'll try. Does Rusty know what you are doing up here?"

"I'm sure it's made the rounds of the station by now."

"Oh great, if he calls keep the answers nice and general."

Strict laughed at me, "You're more concerned about worrying Rusty than you are about getting shot at. Take care up there."

"I will."

I went back to the group. "Okay, first things first. I need to see these guys' tracks. Anybody know where a good example of them can be found?"

We headed up the mountain cross-country. It was rough going. These mountains are pretty much all up and down. To get some place out in the middle of them by trail could take days on foot. I hoped there was a quick way to reach the last known sign. I didn't want to spend the day hiking and *then* start the track.

The officers went first, fanning out in front of us. A mile and half from base camp they stopped. One of the officers approached me and he held out his hand.

"Kent Jacobsen," he said. "In case you need to know, I'm your senior partner today."

"Cassidy Callahan," I said shaking his hand.

"Here's the best set of tracks we can give you. They only hit this trail for about fifty feet but it'll give you a feel for the chase."

"Give me five minutes," I said, getting out my sketchbook. I made a quick sketch of all four tracks and noted irregularities on the soles of their shoes, wear marks and general shape. The guys all waited patiently. Victor and Landon were used to this by now. The others paced nervously. I did a quick measurement of the men's strides and made a mental note.

"Okay, let me read the trail and then you can take over again."

I followed the trail absorbing as much information as I could in fifty feet. These were young men, lightweight and fast. They were running and in some haste. It wasn't a panic run, I concluded. These men knew where they were going. When their tracks headed off trail I let the officers take over again. They led me up a steep canyon. The top of the canyon was lined with rocks. So that explained Landon's climbing rope. The officers suddenly stopped and fanned out.

"Here's where we lost them."

"Did you have a visual?"

"Nope, look here."

I followed and Jacobsen brought me to a spot where the men had scrambled up into the rocks. Shoot. Rock is the worst thing to track over. I went back to the footprints leading to the rocks. The two men were still together and definitely headed up the rocks just like Jacobsen said.

I stood at the spot where the last footprints were left and studied the rocks for the easiest way up. The guys stood in a knot talking amongst themselves about how best to tackle the rocks at the end of the canyon, which gave me space to work. I appreciated them backing off, but at the same time they weren't aware of what I was likely to do if left to my own devices. I noticed Landon glance my way every once in a while, just keeping tabs. If any of them knew my tendency to take off on my own it was him.

If the men we were chasing were on the run, they wouldn't attempt a difficult climb that could result in a fall. They'd look for the easiest way up. They didn't have ropes, which meant I shouldn't need ropes to track them. I chose a likely path and carefully examined the rock in the direction I thought they may have taken. I was looking for anything that confirmed my choice; scratched rocks, scraped lichen... I could see why the guys lost the trail, but it wasn't hopeless. I pictured myself being chased up this canyon, looking in desperation at the rocks before me. It was a puzzle so I fiddled with the pieces until something clicked. Okay, I thought, if it was me I'd run straight for that crack, chimney climb it to the top and take off running. I walked up to the crack and began my ascent. Maybe there would be tracks at the top. I was nearly to the top when Landon noticed that I was climbing and rushed to the bottom of the rock.

"Cassidy, what are you doing?"

"I'm taking the easiest route. The guys we are after didn't have ropes so they climbed out of here without them. If I find the trail up here I'll let you know."

I finished climbing the crack and paused, knees locked at the top to get a look at where the men would have come out. Bingo. I didn't see tracks but I saw definite marks that looked like a person had scrambled up the loose dirt at the top. I looked down and spotted loose dirt on the rocks below. I was sure I could pick up a trail somewhere around the top of the canyon. I climbed over the top and found the first set of tracks. The gravely soil up here didn't help at all. I looked closer. Damn. I cast around in a broad arc around the top of the rock. Oh damn it again. I could only find one set of tracks up here. I started around the side of the top of the canyon finding a spot where the other guy could have come up. I didn't find any sign so I tried the other direction examining closely the dirt around the top of the canyon. No sign. These guys hadn't tried to hide their tracks before so I doubted they would start now. Nope, only one guy had made it over the top. Should I follow him? Should I concentrate on the more present danger? I was just lowering myself into the crack to rejoin the group and get some advice when I saw a slight motion to the side of the canyon. I stayed up top, eyes glued to the spot. I didn't know what to do, I needed some advice but Jacobsen would be put in line for a bullet if I asked him to climb up to me. And if I climbed down I could lose my visual.

"Jacobsen, 10-66, eight o'clock," I called out. Suspicious person behind you at eight o'clock. I saw them all freeze and find Jacobsen's eight o'clock.

I had a clean view of everybody from up there. I felt the gun on my belt. Could I shoot the guy if I needed to? I knew I could hit him, but could I bring myself to shoot him? Shit yeah, I could do it. If I had to protect my team, I could do it. Please, I thought, please be unarmed. I found cover and aimed my gun at the suspect, ready in case I was needed. Jacobsen hadn't spotted him yet. I saw the guy get up like he was going to run but he fell almost immediately. My mind was working a mile a minute piecing together his actions. Then I realized the guy was hurt and hiding out in the brush. He couldn't climb the rocks and had been left behind. If he had been abandoned in the chase and was armed, he would be forced to shoot. No, I thought, please don't! I changed my hiding place to keep the guy in sight. Jacobsen noted my movement and followed my line of site, down my arm, down the barrel of my pistol and down to the floor of the canyon. There was brush between the team and the suspect. They fanned out, surrounding the area. The suspect backed away, a desperate look in his eye. He reached into his pocket and pulled out a gray object. My vision narrowed to the object. Gun? Nope. If I didn't know better I'd say that thing looked an awful lot like a hand grenade. What would a civilian be doing with a hand grenade? And what kind was it? There were all kinds of hand grenades these days. Teargas, stun grenades, explosive devices that sent shrapnel flying in every direction... He reached for the pin and instinct took over. I pulled the trigger and felt the gun jump in my hands. I saw the suspect jerk upwards and then fall backwards.

"Get back! Hit the dirt!" I yelled. I hit the dirt too. If the guy was going to blow himself up I sure as hell didn't want to watch. After several seconds an explosion rocked the mountain and caused a couple of small rock slides around the little canyon.

After the noise subsided, the team stood warily. A stark silence told us our suspect was no longer a danger. Victor Gomez and Mike Townsend cautiously parted the branches and Victor signaled to the others that it was safe to move about.

"Cassidy, are you okay?" Landon called up the cliff.

"Yeah," I replied, "I'm okay."

"Get down here!" barked Jacobsen.

I lowered myself into the crack and worked my way back down.

"Discharging your firearm without permission?"

"Yeah, I guess so," I replied, "I'm glad *you* get to write it up. I didn't want to have to do it for you." A short pause. I really needed out of here. The thought of what I had just done was sneaking up on me. I needed action. I needed to put the scene in the canyon behind me and fast. "There's a trail up top. Do you want me to follow it?"

I waited while everybody got their orders straightened out. We had to call in reinforcements to investigate the scene in the canyon, and that meant splitting up our group. Jacobsen and I, followed by Landon and the three other officers, set out. I climbed the crack again, a little shakier this time, and waited at the top for the group to catch up. I found the tracks and settled into tracking mode again. Our suspect definitely had a destination in mind.

The ground was hard in this part of the forest. I could see why the team had given up. Tracking was slow. I puzzled over the ground gathering all the clues I could find.

"Can you give me a description of our fugitive?" I asked, making conversation. "From the trail I know he's young, slender, lightly built."

"Latino, black hair, brown eyes, black t-shirt with a rock band logo on it, blue jeans, tennis shoes."

"Skater shoes," I corrected. "Any weapons?"

"We're supposed to consider them armed but so far the grenade is the only confirmation of that."

The tracks were puzzling. If we weren't in a hurry I would have found them interesting. It would have been a fun challenge. With an armed fugitive out running us it was just plain frustrating to slow down.

"This guy could be home watching a ball game by the time we see where this trail goes," I complained.

The forest thickened. The soil changed from rock and hard pack to something more porous. At the same time the vegetation in the area grew up and shed leaves and pine needles obscuring the ground completely. Large trees loomed overhead, blocking the light and making it even harder to distinguish tracks. We startled a deer resting in the underbrush and I wished I'd been alone so I could try stalking it. I'd rather stalk deer than fleeing suspects.

I kept to the trail until something cued me in to look at my surroundings. I couldn't pinpoint what it was. Something triggered a memory. An almost forgotten memory and I looked around suspiciously. What it was, I still couldn't say. It was so faint.

"What is it, Cassidy?" Landon asked.

"I don't know. Something is familiar to me in a bad way. Something doesn't feel right."

I continued on, looking around more carefully while I tracked the footprints before me. Landon was wary. He'd never quite seen me like this but he seemed to trust my instincts.

The feeling came back. A smell? Was it a smell I was perceiving? I licked my finger and held it up to the breeze. The footprints were leading into the wind. I sniffed the breeze like an animal but I still couldn't quite identify it. Something was niggling at the back of my mind.

"Cassidy," Jacobsen said, drawing me from my thoughts.

"Wait," Landon told him, "This could be important."

Niggle, niggle, I could feel the thoughts churning but they were coming up empty. Then, with a disappointed, if silent, curse it fell into place. I looked at the land ahead.

"Guys, we need to proceed very carefully. Let me scout ahead. I can keep out of sight if I go by myself. If we have to stay as a group we could stumble on something we don't want to stumble on. We have to see what we are getting into without being spotted."

They all looked at me as if I was nuts. They weren't going to let me go out there alone.

"Jacobsen? You can hold onto my gun if you want to. I'm just looking."

He started to object.

"Landon, tell him I know how to stay out of sight. Tell him how it took a whole team hours to find me when Trent was after me. I could lose the whole lot of you in five minutes if I wanted to."

"Cassidy, you're serious, aren't you?" Landon asked.

"One person can sometimes do what six people can't. I know what I'm looking for. I've seen it before. I've observed it and kept out of sight before. I've dealt with the people before. We are close. We are close enough to smell it. Give me ten minutes."

"Michaels wouldn't give you two," Kent Jacobsen said.

"He knows I can do it though. Who else thinks they can do it? Who knows what we are looking for? Who can stay out of sight, not leave a track and not make a sound? Anybody?"

They all *thought* they could stay out of sight but I knew I had them when it came to staying quiet. Tracking with them was like tracking with a herd of elephants behind me. Not one of them would bother hiding their tracks.

I shed my pack and started removing my pistol but Jacobsen shook his head. I took that as permission to use it if I needed to. I took off my boots, then turned and got a bearing on the trail. Heading quickly in the same direction the footprints led, I ducked into the trees and within a few steps I was invisible to the men behind me. I went into stealth mode hiding my tracks and creeping up to some unknown danger before me. I knew what I was looking for. I'd been in this situation before and was looking for cabins, or small buildings hidden by trees. I was looking for a field of marijuana plants, keeping a sharp eye out for movement of any kind.

Ten minutes wasn't much time to scope out a drug lab. My main goal was to locate people. I needed to find our suspect.

I crouched low making myself small, and continued forward hiding from view, hiding my tracks. It all felt so natural. Like stalking deer except I was stalking people; unknown, unknowing people.

The field was just as I had remembered, and I was glad it confirmed the niggling in my head. I wasn't imagining things and really had identified the smell correctly. Circling the small compound, I could identify two people at the site and made mental notes about their locations. I made sure to remember what each person looked like, cataloging their features like a list so I could recite it back if needed. Not liking what the guys would be walking into, I was careful to take special note of exactly where things were, to provide them with as much information as possible. Then I slipped silently back into the woods and circled around to my nervous team. I made sure I came back to the group silently and gently appeared beside them without startling anyone. It's not wise to surprise a wary group of cops. They were all anxiously looking down the trail I'd taken until I stepped out of the brush beside them as if I'd been standing there all along.

Removing the sketchbook from my pack, I quickly made a map.

"Okay, listen up and listen fast. Here we are." I drew an X. "If you go the direction you saw me head you will come to a field of cannabis. There's a small building, almost a shed, on the far side of it. When I was there our suspect was standing just inside this building. Another man was over here." I said drawing another X. "Short guy. Short black hair, very dark complexion, baggy oversized blue jeans, white muscle shirt. Tattoos. I only saw the two men. Of course they may have moved some since I was over there. I don't like the looks of this. If we get one man the other will escape. We don't have enough firepower to get both. I'm leaving the rest up to you. They are probably armed. They were last time I dealt with a group like this."

"When did you deal with a group like this before?" Landon asked.

"When I tracked Kelly Green. I ran into a compound bigger than this one. This is a small operation, but it doesn't mean it's safer. I don't like it. It's going to take more than the six of us to get both these guys."

"You've done your part, Cassidy. You've done more than you should. Michaels is going to lynch the whole lot of us when we get back."

I sat down by my pack and started putting on my boots. The guys went into a huddle. I heard radio talk. We waited, the tension growing.

Jacobsen approached and watched me for a bit while I finished tying my boots. He then sat down on the ground beside me.

"How far is it to the fields?"

"Maybe a hundred yards. The field's maybe a quarter acre. The building is on the far side."

"Find a place where you can stay out of sight."

"I can stay out of sight within six feet of these guys."

"You know what I mean. I don't want you in on the raid. I'm in deep enough as it is."

"You didn't do anything wrong. I'll write up the report and I'll tell the truth. I really did fire my weapon without permission. You won't catch any flack because of me."

"It's not Schroeder I'm worried about."

It was Rusty.

I heard a helicopter off in the distance and was relieved that the guys would have backup. Four officers wouldn't have been able to surround that field and someone would have gotten away. I saw them spread out, covering the near side of the field in case the helicopter scared the suspects this way. They closed in.

"I'm going to try and get you a lift out with the copter. You scared of heights? Will you ride a cable up?"

"If I have to. And, no, I'm not afraid of heights. I've done the cable thing before."

The helicopter clattered in closer. Jacobsen called the helicopter pilot over the radio and got me a lift. I started walking toward the helicopter, giving the compound a wide berth, stalking around it in stealth mode. The officers came rappelling down cables, unclipping their harnesses and fanning out to surround the field. One of the first down tossed me a harness and I worked my way into it. A cable was handed off to me and I clipped on grasping it tightly. Half of me was disappointed to be left out and the other half was relieved to be free of it. The place was going to turn into a war zone. I'd have been okay down there and would have done my job, but I could only get into trouble by staying and so far trouble had been nice to me lately. No sense in tempting it. When the cable reached the top I grabbed the handle and pulled myself to a place where I was able to stand. Unclipping the cable I let it go, then found a bench and made myself comfortable. I didn't know where the helicopter was going, but I was sure it would be a quieter place than the one I had just left.

Tension filled my little niche in the helicopter as the realization of what I had just done began to expand, filling my head, starting the old memories and emotions to churning.

The helicopter came to rest a short distance from base camp. When the doors opened I sprang out like a caged animal, looking around. I then made my way over to see how things were progressing. Everybody was tense and focused. I picked up my packet of report forms from Strict, took them to a car, and sat quietly filling them out.

Trying to condense the scene at the canyon into a few sentences was eating at me. The more times I replayed the scene in my head the more it saddened me. It was an emotional rollercoaster ride that varied between tears and a sad acceptance. I'd killed somebody. So what if I had a good reason, I had still killed somebody. Strict walked up. I hadn't intended for him to see me like this and I needed to vent. I needed a punching bag. I needed a four mile run. Anything to work off the feelings boiling inside me.

"Strict, I can't do these runs without some warning. I have to prepare myself if there's going to be violence. I have to. I can't shoot someone without it leaving scars. I just can't. You have to remember that. I can track. I can deal with things as they come up, but Strict, I killed somebody today. I'm never going to forget that. Never. I wasn't put here to shoot people."

I finished filling out my police report and shoved it through the open window. He read it.

"You're good at covering your trail in the woods but you're lousy at it on paper."

"I told Jacobsen I'd tell the truth. I'm not going to lie."

Strict looked worried. He jogged back to rejoin the others. I saw him pacing with the cell phone to his ear.

I got out of the car and did my own pacing. I wandered into the woods and wandered back. I found a game trail and followed it until I came to a place where deer had bed down. I sat in the spot letting my emotions wash over me. They rolled over me, beating at me, wearing me down and I lay in the bed of leaves trying to still them, trying to still myself. I pretended like I was waiting for the deer to come back, but I knew the deer wouldn't come back if I was fretting. It would sense unease and stay away. I had to still myself for the deer to come. I tried, I really tried but it was no use. Nothing was helping. I got up and walked back to base camp. I was sorry I did. I could hear Rusty's voice long before I could see him.

"...can't do these things to her! She's not a cop. She's a tracker. And her heart is as big as the all outdoors. You can't ask her to be a cop. Where'd she go?"

I couldn't hear Strict's answer.

"You called her out here on an apprehension, to fill in the gap between the bottom of a rock and the top?"

Strict's calmer, quieter voice answered.

"It amounts to the same thing. Anybody could have climbed that rock. Even I know if the trail ends at the top of a canyon there's bound to be a way up and there's a trail somewhere up there."

Another quiet response from Strict. Strict was good at self control; I'd give him that. He didn't raise his voice to Rusty. He didn't get defensive.

Rusty turned, running his hands through his hair in frustration.

Watching Rusty angry was like watching a big storm. I never wanted to get caught in that storm.

I moved and he caught the movement. Our eyes locked for a second and I ran. I didn't know why I ran. I slipped into stealth mode. I just wasn't ready to face him. I could hear him tromping around in the woods behind me.

"Cassidy?" he called.

I couldn't answer him. Not yet. I stayed out of sight, dodging from tree to tree, silently. My emotions were so close to the surface. I could have wrestled a grizzly bear, but I couldn't face Rusty like this. He searched and searched. I was never more than twenty feet from him but he couldn't find me.

"Babe, please don't do this to me."

"I'm sorry." He spun around and zeroed in on my voice.

"Come out and talk to me."

A sob escaped. "I can't. Not yet."

"What did I do?"

"Nothing, it's not something you did."

"Cass, I know what happened on the search. Please come out."

"No, I need to hit something. If I come out you're going to stick me in the truck and take me home and I'm going to go nuts. I'm fine out here. I'll run or clobber a tree or cry until I can't cry anymore or maybe I'll just wander until I need to come home."

"You can't beat yourself up over this. It wasn't your fault."

"Don't! Don't talk me through the logic of it. You think I haven't done that a hundred times?"

"Okay, then come out. Let's go to the station. You can take it out on the punching bag. You can cream it if you want to. It's used to it. It's had hundreds of cops in the same state you're in beat it up."

I was tired. I was frustrated and angry and sad. I couldn't believe how miserable I felt. Finally, it all came crashing down on me and I couldn't carry it by myself anymore. I sat down in the dirt and leaves and started crying. Rusty followed the sound through the trees and found me sitting at the base of the tree where I'd been hidden. He sat beside me and placed his arm around my shoulders. When my crying didn't ease he picked me up and just placed me in his lap and held me like a child. I didn't feel like a little child though. I felt dirty. I felt evil. I felt very guilty. But most of all I simply felt sad.

"Oh, babe, you had to do it. I know you had to. It would be worse if you hadn't." A long pause. "This is one of the reasons I love you so much. You have a big, kind heart. And people who have a heart get it broken a lot. It'll mend. I promise."

"No it won't. It'll never go away."

"Shhh, but it'll fade. You'll do other things that'll push it into the background and some day it'll be almost gone. Maybe I can help put some good memories in there. Push all the bad ones away."

The touch was helping. Having Rusty close always helped and his deep voice was relaxing. When the crying finally eased he still held me close.

"Okay, that's better. Now, think of something more positive to talk about. If you can't think of anything then tell me a story. I love to hear you talk about what you did as a kid."

"You do?"

"Yeah."

I thought for a minute. Nothing was coming to mind. I needed a little more calm. I waited for it, afraid the bad memory would show up first. Calm. Cass, think of a story, any silly little story. Finally, I said, "Remember the wood where I pinned down Peccati?"

"Yeah."

"I used to track foxes in that wood. One day I tracked a fox and she led me to a den there. I came back later when the mother wasn't there and she had three kits in the den. I was laying at the front of the den watching the kits. They would toddle up to the front and see me and fall over themselves trying to get to the back again. They were so cute, I wanted to hold one but I knew better than to try. They got scared and started a racket and the mother fox surprised me. She was afraid of me too, but in one big burst of bravery she rushed forward. I was still on my hands and knees and she rushed in right at my face. I thought I was going to lose my nose."

"Did she bite you?"

"No, but it's just because I was quick and she was scared. She was a terror! That's when I learned to stay back from baby animals."

He laughed, the sound of it easing the sadness.

"I wish I could see a baby fox."

"If we go the ranch at the right time of year I'll show you the den. Maybe that fox's grandkits are using it now."

"How old were you when that happened?"

"Oh, I'm guessing thirteen or fourteen. Foxes are not the easiest animals to track so I had some experience by then."

"What age do you think would have given you the experience to find Kelly?"

"Do you mean, just follow his trail? Or do you mean, complete the track the way it really happened?"

"Either."

"Well, I could have followed his trail by the time I was fifteen. He was hiding his tracks and that part would have given me trouble. As far as doing the whole trail, dealing with the bear and Peccati's men, I would have died without my Marines training. The bear would have got me. And when Peccati's men were after me I wouldn't have shot back and so they would have brought me in."

"I'm sorry, Cass, I didn't mean to bring up those memories again. I was just wondering how young you were when you had learned enough to be a real tracker."

"It's okay. You just proved to me that what you said was right. The memories fade. I don't even think of that as a bad experience anymore. There are parts of it I laugh at now."

"You ready to go home?"

"No." I stood reluctantly and offered him a hand up. We walked back to base camp. "What made you come up here?" I asked.

"Strict called."

"What did he tell you?"

"Not much, then when I got here he was busy so he just handed me your report."

"Guess I need to think about who might be reading my reports."

"Cass, why did you go on such a dangerous call? Did you know what you were walking into?"

"Yeah, once I got up here, I knew it wasn't a lost hiker. Strict sent the normal team, Rosco, Victor and Landon. I wondered about the search at that point. Three EMTs? It seemed excessive. When the four officers joined us I knew. And when Jacobsen introduced himself as my senior partner I knew I could be in for some police work."

"And you went anyway."

As we were walking back the helicopter took off again. Base camp was buzzing but the tension had eased. Strict noted our presence and walked over. He looked me up and down. He reminded me of a combination between a drill sergeant and my grandfather. He was in uniform so more of the drill sergeant showed through. I had trouble settling on a name for him. To most of the guys he was Strict, short for Strickland and a reflection of the drill sergeant half. With me he leaned more towards the grandfather side and when he did he was Lou. When he was on the job and all business he was Strict.

Lou asked, "You okay?"

"Will you remember what I told you?" I replied.

He nodded.

"Then I'm okay."

That day bothered me for weeks afterward. I relived the incident night after night in my dreams. Sometimes my mind would play tricks on me and I'd find myself involved in a capture gone bad. It hurt to see the worry in Rusty's eyes as night after night I woke up shaking either with sadness or fear. I wondered if he had called Strict, because I didn't get a call to go out on a search for over a week. Part of me said that tourist season hadn't really started yet, that a week was nothing unusual this time of year. The other part of me said Strict was giving me time to heal.

I spent the time doing happier things. I talked to Rhonda about being in the wedding. She was surprised that I would ask her because we didn't know each other well. I explained how I really didn't know any women in the area and I only had one sister. I also pointed out that Kelly was most likely going to be best man so she wouldn't be sitting with him anyway. She agreed to it, so we pored over a bridal magazine for hours and marked a few pages of dresses that we both agreed would work for her. Then I emailed Jesse and asked her to go buy a magazine and choose one of the dresses that she liked.

I looked at wedding invitations, but I couldn't buy any until I had a wedding date. They all looked too stiff and formal. In fact the whole wedding felt stiff and formal. I didn't want it to feel that way. To me the wedding should feel like a natural extension to the relationship Rusty and I already had. We had grown closer so naturally and comfortably that I wanted our wedding to be the same, but I knew it was also a show of sorts. It had to be what people expected it to be. All the wedding invitations I saw had flowers and diamonds and lots of white. I wanted something more personal.

One day I sat down with paper and watercolor pencils and just started drawing. It was a simple landscape with pine trees and mist and a trail. I liked the effect so I then used real watercolor paper and tried again, more carefully, drawing pine trees and a few aspens and leaving the background in mist. I widened the trail and drew two sets of footprints that came together. I also used water to soften the lines and fill in open places with a little color. Then I wet down the misty center of the picture, where the words would go, to give it some texture and character and make the words easier to read once I added them on the computer. I left the painting on Rusty's desk to dry and checked my email. Glancing down my list of messages one in particular caught my eye. Oh yay, I thought, Jesse chose a dress!

"Hey Cass! Please choose page 75. I went to a bridal shop and tried on page 75. Mom agrees, rule 642 applies. Let me know. Love ya, your sis."

Rule 642 was in the Shopper's Law. It said that, if you found a dress that was perfect for you, and somebody pointed that out, you had to buy it. Mom and Jesse adhered strictly to the Shopper's Law. I tended to bend the rule a little bit. My version said that you only had to buy the dress if you were intentionally looking for it. If you accidentally stumbled on it you were exempt. I called Rhonda and arranged a shopping day

After dinner I went upstairs to see what Rusty was working on. He held up the painting I'd completed earlier.

"Did you do this?" he asked.

"I was just putting ideas down on paper. All the wedding invitations I find are so general. I was hoping for something that was more personal. I think that's too simplistic, though. I should ask a real artist to do one for me."

"No, it's not. It's great. I didn't know you could paint."

"I like to draw. I have a sketch book up in the hideout, but I was never much good at it."

"Don't put yourself down. Scan it and print out some copies in the right size and play with the pieces. You might find something that clicks."

Creativity was not my strong suit but I promised to give it a try. I was glad I did because once I printed the picture on vellum it softened the look and made the picture appear more romantic and less childish. I put the vellum over parchment paper, added a ribbon to the side that matched the wedding colors and left the card on Rusty's desk.

I never had a chance to hear Rusty's opinion of the card or go shopping with Rhonda because trouble tracked me down on my next search. How many different ways could trouble find me, I wondered.

Chapter 4

It was a simple search, a lost kid. How dangerous can a search for a lost kid be? The trail was fresh, the kid hadn't gone far. Searchers should have been able to find him but Victor and I had been the only ones available that day on short notice. The boy had been gone five hours and only planned on climbing a hill near his parent's car at a pullout. He'd climbed up the hill, disappeared down the other side and was still gone. The dad had climbed the hill and circled around. Trevor had to be close. He wasn't known to just take off. It should have been a quick track over a hill, maybe a short hike down the other side. We were afraid the reason Trevor hadn't returned was because he was injured somewhere so Victor was along for medical support.

I was glad to have a fresh trail, but set out irritated at being called for something so simple. I followed Trevor's footprints up one side of the hill and down the other side, and then down a wash to an old shack. I followed his trail in, out and around the old building and then into an abandoned mine. Behind the shack I found creaky timbers supporting the entrance of the old mine.

I hadn't brought my big pack because the track didn't look like it warranted it. So I was only prepared for a daylight search.

"Victor, did you bring a headlamp?"

"No," he said, "but I'll run back to the car and get one."

The trunks of the search vehicles were packed with an odd assortment of tools, ropes, weapons, climbing gear and flashlights. We usually found what we needed in there, but had to guess what we would need.

Victor took off and I looked around outside the mine trying to locate a trail leading away from the area. I didn't find one. Trevor was definitely in the mine somewhere.

I spotted Victor jogging back down the hill when suddenly the earth came alive beneath my feet. There was a rumbling like a heavy train going by. I saw Victor lose his balance and tumble down the hill as I fought to keep myself steady. Earthquake! I heard a startled scream from inside the mine and dashed in. I collided with Trevor, grabbing him to keep from bowling him over. I was going to make a run for the mine entrance, but it started crumbling so I headed deeper inside. There was a deafening roar followed by a cloud of dust which engulfed us and made us cough. Not knowing how much of the mountain would fall, I just kept going until the noise settled down. We were enveloped in pitch-blackness. We couldn't even see our hands in front of our faces.

"Trevor?" I gasped.

"Who are you?" he cried in fear.

"It's okay, we'll be okay. I'm Cassidy. Your parents got worried about you and called me to find you."

"Why'd they call a *girl*?" he asked.

"They couldn't find you when they looked for you and they were worried so they called the police. The police called me because I know how to follow tracks."

"I got lost in the tunnel. It's cool back there but then it got too dark and I couldn't find the way back."

The ground shook again and in fear, Trevor nearly dove for cover. I wondered how stable the mine shaft was but figured it had withstood many earthquakes in the past.

"It's okay, I know earthquakes can be scary but my search partner is outside. He knows where we are. He'll call in help and they will dig us out soon."

"I don't like this dark."

"I know, that's why I sent Victor for a flashlight but he didn't get back in time. It's a good thing he's out there, though, and not in here, or nobody would know where we are."

My radio crackled.

"What's that noise?"

"It's my radio. It's probably Victor trying to contact me but the signal won't go through the rock." I pushed the button on the radio. "Strict? Victor? I found Trevor. We're in good shape. When can you get us out of here?"

Nothing, maybe a little crackling. They didn't hear me. Hopefully they at least got a little crackling back so they would know I tried to respond.

"We might as well get comfortable. It's going to be a long wait." I took off my pack but kept it in easy reach. "We'll be all right in here. I have enough food and water in my pack for an over night search so we won't starve to death. Have you ever eaten back packer food?"

"No."

"It isn't the greatest but it will have to do. How old are you?"

"Ten. I'm in fourth grade."

"Are you from California? Have you ever been in an earthquake before?"

"No, my family was visiting from Texas."

"So, are you from the tornado part of Texas or the hurricane part?"

"The tornado part."

"Have you seen a tornado?"

"Only from a distance but my uncle's house got torn apart by one."

"So, what's scarier, earthquakes or tornadoes?"

"Earthquakes, I think. I'm glad this didn't happen when I was on the roller coaster yesterday! What do roller coasters do in an earthquake? Do they go flying off the track? I always thought they would fly off the track."

"No, they don't fly off the track. If they did, they wouldn't have roller coasters in California."

We talked for hours. Trevor was talkative, which was good because it distracted him from being scared. My radio crackled again. I sent a probable crackle back to let them know I could respond.

"What are all those numbers you said?" Trevor asked.

"They are codes that the guys out there understand. You're our 10-65, our missing person. And you're 10-45A. That means you're in good shape, not injured seriously. 10-01 means I don't have good radio reception."

"How do you remember all that?"

"If you use it a lot, you remember."

I wondered what time it was. It was hard to tell without light. I'd set out after Trevor about two in the afternoon. I wondered if it was night yet and if I should cook up a packet of food.

"Trevor, tell me when you get hungry, okay? I don't want to cook until we need it but I don't want you to go hungry either. So you let me know, okay?"

"Okay, right now I need to go to the bathroom. How long are they gonna take?"

"Well, don't wait on a rescue to go to the bathroom. Just go back down the tunnel a little ways and go there."

"I'm not going with you here!"

"I won't look when you go if you won't look when I have to go. I can't see you anyway."

"There's no toilet paper here."

I fished around in my pack and handed him a half roll.

"Conserve it. That's all we've got."

Trevor went down the tunnel and in a few minutes he came dashing back.

"There's a funny noise back there!"

I listened.

"Sit down," I said, "I think it's bats. Just stay low. They are used to coming out of this tunnel at night so they aren't going to be happy that it's blocked."

The bats flew overhead to the end of the tunnel.

"What are we gonna do? I don't like bats. They give me the creeps!"

"Hey, I'm the girl. I'm the one who's supposed to get creeped out. The bats won't hurt you if you just stay out of their way. And they will go away soon. This might mean it is nighttime out there, though. I wonder how the bats know it's night if they live where it's dark all the time."

After a while Trevor said that he was tired and hungry, so I located the pack and got out my stove.

"Hey, Trevor, we'll have a little light while the stove is on. Choose a backpacker meal from the pack."

I took apart the pots and the stove by feel and set it up. I felt around in the pack for the lighter, pumped up the stove and lit it. I put the lighter in my pocket so it would be easier to find next time. Trevor chose spaghetti. Not my favorite, but they all tend to taste alike after a while anyway. I rationed out just enough water to cook the spaghetti, heated it to the boiling point, and poured it in the pouch. I folded the top over to keep the steam in.

"How do you cook the spaghetti? Doesn't the plastic melt?"

"It's cooking right now. It absorbs the hot water and stays hot until it gets done. Then you just eat it."

I opened the pouch and stirred the spaghetti judging the doneness by the feel. I dug in my pack until I found my only fork and handed it to him.

"Just eat it right out of the pouch. If you do that we don't have to wash dishes. We don't want to have to wash anything because we don't have enough water to waste it."

"What about you?"

"I'll finish off whatever you don't want. If I need to, I'll cook another packet." I wouldn't, but let him think I would. I didn't want him to skimp on his meals.

Trevor ate most of the spaghetti and pronounced it on the bland side. I agreed with him. That's what I always thought about backpacker spaghetti. Trevor left me a little spaghetti so I finished it off. Time stretched on. We ran out of things to talk about and eventually we both fell asleep. Trevor was cold as he slept so I dug out the extra clothes I had in my pack and laid them on top of him as he slept. I drifted off again.

"Miss, miss," Trevor said, trying to wake me without touching me. "Are they ever going to find us? It feels like we've been in here forever."

"Sure they will. We just don't know how much of the mountain came down in the earthquake so we don't know how much digging they have to do. They won't just bring in a tractor to dig because they will worry about hurting us if the rocks buried us. So they are digging carefully, and careful digging takes time. I wish I had a way to tell them we're safe in the tunnel."

We got bored so we played car games. We played the old suitcase game to keep us thinking.

"I went on a trip and in my suitcase I packed an apple, beach ball, cat, dingbat, egg, frog, golf ball, headlamp… are we on I or J?"

"J"

"Ice cream cone and jump rope."

"I went on a trip and in my suitcase I packed…." It went on and on. Trevor did pretty well at it. We played I Don't Spy because there was nothing to see. We felt more aftershocks and I prayed they didn't knock more rocks down.

We only ate when necessary, and I measured time by how many times we ate and slept. We'd gone through three backpacker meals, two sleep cycles and had no idea if it was day or night. The tunnel was getting pretty ripe but there was nothing we could do about it. Eat, play mind games, sleep, talk… We were on the sleep part of the routine when I was awakened by noises.

"Hey, Trevor, I think our rescuers are close! I hear noises."

"Hey!" he yelled, "We're in here! Hey!"

I heard excited voices, more scrambling and digging.

"Hey, Trevor, when you get out of here be sure and smile real big. You may be on TV. You can tell all your friends back home you went to California and became a TV star."

All those rescue vehicles within sight of the highway had surely lured in the press. It was usually a pain to work with the press hanging about, but I was willing to bet Trevor was ready for his spot in the limelight.

"Cassidy?"

"I hear you," I called back.

I started digging from our side, pulling rocks out of the way. I would have been digging all along but I wasn't sure our food and water would hold out and I didn't want to push it. A stab of light blinded us and we both stumbled back shielding our eyes.

"Ouch! It hurts my eyes!" Trevor wailed. I covered his eyes with my hands so he could relax. I closed my eyes and turned away from the light. When a large enough sized hole was opened I sent Trevor through first.

"Cover his eyes," I called out. "He's been in the dark too long."

Then I crawled out of the mine. The light hurt even with my eyes closed. The rush of fresh air was wonderful. I felt firm hands lift me to a standing position and guide me away from the mineshaft, then strong arms enveloped me. Rusty's worried hug. I'd recognize that hug anywhere whether I could see or not. After burying my face in his shoulder I tried looking around, but quickly hid my eyes again. Hands patted me on the back and jubilant voices filled the air. Rusty clasped me like he'd never let go. His sleeves were rolled up and his shirt was dirty. I peeked out again and realized he'd been digging. Okay, time to tough it out. I placed my hands over my eyes and cracked my fingers. Just a little light at a time.

"Point me at the truck."

It took him a while to let go but he finally turned me and I started walking, feeling with my feet just like I did in the woods when I was stalking. My toe gently hit a big rock and I felt my way around it. The ground went down and down and down some more and finally leveled off to where all the emergency trucks were parked.

"I swear, Cassidy," said Landon, "you're a cat. You have nine lives or something. Let's check you out."

"No, Landon, I'm fine. As soon as my eyes adjust I'll be back to my normal self. We had food, water, nobody got squashed or cold or hot or anything. The worst thing that happened was boredom. And bats. Trevor didn't like the bats."

When my eyes adjusted to the light I looked around. I picked out Kelly and Rhonda, all my search team, Lou, Schroeder, Trevor's parents, and Paul. There were a dozen people in hard hats. I could hear Trevor off in the distance, "And there were bats in there! Real live bats!"

I looked back at the mine. The shack was gone. The wash was gone. Part of the hill was gone. A huge section of the mountain above the mine was gone. How long had we been stuck in there?

"Hey, Cassidy," Victor said, a big grin on his face, "I'm glad you made it."

"I'm glad I sent you back for a headlamp!" I replied.

"We didn't know what to think when you didn't answer your radio. It looked pretty grim there for a few days. Then we started hearing faint voices when we used a listening device. Everybody got a second wind right about then."

"A few days? I made a backpacker meal whenever Trevor said he was hungry but we only cooked three or four of them. We couldn't have been in there two whole days."

Trevor, his parents and a flock of reporters converged on me.

"This is Cassidy," Trevor told the TV camera, "she tracked me down to the mine and when the earthquake came she saved me from the mine caving in. We didn't know the whole mountain fell 'cause of the earthquake. She's a good searcher. She brought food and water and a stove. The only thing she forgot was a flashlight. But we did good in there, didn't we, Cassidy?"

"Hey buddy, we sure did. You were a real trooper. But I'd really like to thank the rest of the team. I'm sure things were a lot worse for everybody on the outside of the mine than it was for me and Trevor. You put your all into the rescue and I want to thank you for that. We're in good shape here. Trevor can go back to Texas and tell about his exciting trip to California."

"When is the wedding?" one reporter shouted over the crowd.

"The wedding?" I asked

"Yeah, we all saw the invitation. When's the wedding?"

Someone else shouted, "July twenty seventh. That's what the card said." What card?

"Were you scared being buried under tons of rubble?"

"No, I knew the people on the other side, and it was just a matter of time. We were in good shape in there. I wasn't scared at all."

"What did you do for three days in the dark?"

"We talked, played games, cooked a backpacker meal when Trevor got hungry and slept when we got tired."

"I bet your family is relieved to know you are safe. How do you think they will react when you talk to them?"

"They'll be glad I'm safe. But they are used to my misadventures."

"What are you going to do next?"

"I'm going to go home and take a hot shower. I'm sure I'm a mess after camping out in a mine all that time."

"You seem awfully calm considering what you've been through."

"This was nothing compared to the other things I have been through. If you want to know who it was hard for talk to this guy." I said looking up at Rusty. Then I ducked under this arm and disappeared into the crowd.

"Is she always like this?" a reporter asked Rusty.

"Always. You were lucky to get two minutes. Remember the L.A. bridge story? That was her too. We gotta go."

"Why did you do that?" I asked him when he caught up. "That's like tossing one steak into a cage full of lions."

"It'll keep them busy. Besides, I thought it was better than telling them you were the one who took down the bank robber at the mall. That's still an ongoing mystery."

"And what's this about an invitation?"

"I'm sorry, Cass, when Strict called me about the avalanche I had just picked up the card you made and I dashed off to the truck with it still in my hand. Then once I got here and the digging had been going on for a while they kicked me out off the site. I went to the Explorer to rest up and I was looking at your card when a reporter spotted me and dragged out some back-story. They really blew up the engagement part of this as a human interest thing. This has been big news nationwide for three days. They've been looking for everything they could get their hands on to fill time between digging shots. They cornered Strict, Victor, and Landon. Trevor's parents were on TV several times. I think Rosco escaped."

"He would. He's not a very social person."

It was late in the evening before we got home again. There were six messages on the answering machine, all from my family. I gave them a quick call back so they could hear for themselves that everything turned out all right. Then I started up the stairs to take a shower.

"Cass, come here first. Please…"

All the worry from the past three days was catching up to him and I hadn't seen it. I hadn't spent days worrying about my safety. It was just a dark camping trip to me. I forgot that it was something truly different for him. I walked down the stairs and he embraced me so tightly I couldn't breathe. He scooped me up and carried me over to the couch and sat down.

"Just a few minutes, babe," he said and then started crying quietly. I snuggled down into his arms and oozed comfort his way. "Three days… three days I didn't know if you were alive or crushed. People say all kinds of things about you. Steve says you're made of rubber. Wilson says you're a cat, you have nine lives. I can't buy any of that. You're human. Things can hurt you. No matter what people say, I know things can hurt you. And I can't stand even the thought of something hurting you. When I saw all that rock…the only thing that made me feel better was digging, but they wouldn't let me stay. Everybody else felt the same way. When the guys were told to leave and go rest they would just think about you in there and they'd be right back. Guys came in to help that weren't called. Off duty officers, firemen, Kelly, Paul…they dug because they cared about you. If guys came by and there were too many people digging they would go away and come back with food for the people who were working." I let him talk. Something told me he needed to, which was unusual for him. "When I came home I had news for you. June first. We can move June first. I was glad because it seemed like it would work in well with our plans. I was standing here, invitation in hand, admiring your work, happy about the moving day. Strict called and asked if I felt the earthquake. I was at the station when the earthquake hit so I felt it a little bit. Then he told me about the avalanche. All he could say was that he didn't know. He didn't know if you'd made it far enough in. Victor thought you had. Victor has a lot of faith in you. He knew your reactions would be right. He trusted you to analyze the situation and respond correctly. But I saw the pile of rubble. The rocks, the trees, and I… all I could do was dig and hope."

The doorbell rang.

"It's probably Kelly," Rusty said.

"Should I let him in?"

"Yeah, he knows, he understands."

I got up and answered the door. Kelly looked at me seriously, which was unusual for Kelly. Kelly Green. Green Lite was what he'd told Jesse when they met. But tonight he was struggling. Rhonda stood behind him but he wrapped me in a hug anyway. Embarrassed, I gave Rhonda a hug too. They came in and I returned to the couch, sitting beside Rusty. He shook his head, held out his arms.

"Rusty!" I said, embarrassed.

"It's okay, I just need you close. It's okay."

I climbed back into Rusty's lap. Kelly looked worried.

"I think it's going to be a tough night," I said.

"Cassidy, what did I tell you the first day we met?" Kelly said, finding a seat on the other side of the L-shaped couch.

"You said lots of things," I answered. "You told me about your family. You said you were going to kill Rusty for letting me go out there alone…"

"And I told you that Rusty needed you. Do you remember? Not just any girl, I said, he needs you."

"I remember."

"I'm glad I was right."

"I saw you at the mine. Thank you, both of you. Whether you were there for Rusty or for me, thank you."

"We were there because we needed to be there. They couldn't have driven us away." Kelly spoke while Rhonda nodded in agreement. I looked forward to knowing this couple better. I could use a few friends like them.

I could feel Rusty withdrawing. He needed alone time or a distraction.

"Did Rusty tell you he found a house? We're moving in June, so we can have the wedding there in July. Tell them about the house, Rusty."

He shook his head no. He was still struggling. "You tell them, the more I hear you talk the more alive you feel to me."

I started describing the house to them and Rhonda began asking questions. What style was I going to decorate in? What colors? As the talk flowed back and forth Rusty gradually relaxed.

"What do you like best about the house?" Rusty asked.

I blushed, "I'll tell you later."

This got a curious look from everybody. Oh gee, I should have just made something up. The kitchen tile. The open space for an agility course. The fact that deer visit there…anything. Rusty looked at me, waiting for an answer. Oh, okay…

I whispered in his ear, "The shower."

Another curious look. "What's so special about the shower?" he whispered.

"It's… different, you didn't notice?"

"I barely even glanced at the bathroom."

Kelly and Rhonda were really curious now.

"Then I'm not going to tell you. I'll save it as a surprise for June first."

"Cass…"

"You have to see it for yourself."

He gave up with a defeated sigh, but at least he wasn't thinking about the mine any more.

"You two staying for dinner?" Rusty asked.

"Nah," Kelly answered, "I think you two need some time. We were just checking up on you."

After Kelly and Rhonda drove away I led Rusty up the stairs.

"Now, why did you have to go and remind me about that shower? I can't think about that shower without seeing both of us in it. And I really need a shower before dinner."

"So, tell me about this shower. I must have missed something."

I started stripping down.

"It's big enough for two." I dropped my filthy clothes in a pile. "It's got big clear glass doors, so you can see *everything*." I unbuttoned his top two buttons. "It's got this big bench across it." A couple more buttons.

"Oh yeah?"

"Yeah."

I unbuckled his belt.

"It's got two shower heads. A regular one and a handheld one."

He dropped his pants and followed me into the bathroom. I reached for a second bar of soap from under the counter and handed him the big bar.

"I couldn't help it. When I saw that shower I saw both of us in it. Finding interesting ways to use that bench. Giving soapy, steamy massages. Trying out different positions…"

I stepped into the water and rolled the smaller bar of soap around in my hands until they were slick and sudsy. He stepped in and I moved over so he could get under the water too.

"This shower will do for now. But June first… June first I want to try the other shower." His soapy hands found my body, caressing and teasing, washing away three days of dirt and grime with shivery, delicate touches. And my hands found him and eased away the cares of the past. Two bodies slipping and sliding. Kisses, lots of kisses. Deep passionate kisses. Delicate playful kisses. A celebration of another day together.

Later, as we were lying lazily in bed he asked quietly, "Can I just take you away? Can we just go somewhere for a few days? Would you come to

San Diego with me?"

"You know I will."

"I'll see what I can do."

Chapter 5

Mission Beach was busy with beach walkers, tourists and kids. Rusty, decked out in swim trunks and a loose t-shirt, was scanning the crowds. I was trying not to study the ground. Ignore the tracks, Cass, just enjoy the day. I'd started out this morning in shorts and a t-shirt over my swimsuit but the beach beckoned and I'd left my clothes in the Explorer. The sun felt good and the beach stretched out in front of us.

"Let's see if the water is cold," I said.

Rusty smiled, continuing his search. Rusty was on a mission at Mission Beach. "We will, but first we need to make contact, then we can do whatever we want."

"What are we looking for?"

"A grown up kid on a red bike, or a worn out skateboard, or a yellow surfboard or talking to a group of girls, who knows. You won't recognize him until you meet him once. Let's try the taco stand."

We walked over to the taco stand and the old man at the booth smiled broadly.

"Rusty! Long time no see! Where have you been?"

"I'm looking for Cody. Any idea where he can be found these days?"

"Good luck. I think he lost his job at Belmont Park but last I heard he was trying to get on at Tacky T-shirts. There was a cute girl working the morning shift. He was trying to decide if she was worth getting up at eight o'clock for."

Rusty smiled. All this sounded normal to him. We walked down to Tacky T-shirts. I looked around and saw a few tacky t-shirts that I liked. I'd have to remember this place on the way back to the truck. Rusty approached the counter.

"I'm Rusty Michaels and I'm trying to find my brother, Cody. Sam said to check here."

A girl in short shorts, a Hawaiian shirt and a flowered name tag that read Alissa answered, "He's out for his tenth break of the afternoon. He should be back any time. He didn't tell me he had a brother."

"He's got two. What time does he get off today?"

"Four."

"Tell him not to leave, we'll be back at four."

We left the shop and headed for the water.

"It's always like this finding Cody. At least all the locals on the boardwalk know him. I'm surprised the t-shirt shop hired him except that he draws in customers. Well, when he's there. He gets a kick out of having his picture taken with young tourists, makes a point of maintaining a surfer dude look just for the pictures. I think he makes more money off the pictures than he does at any job he's had."

We waded out into the water. It was cold but not too cold. After an hour of getting nearly soaked in the surf we figured we might as well just get wet so we swam. It was so pleasant to have a day with no one's life hanging on the line, no searches, no uniforms, no work pressing. After swimming we walked the beach and ate tacos. Sam had worked the taco stand for twenty-three years and would have told me all about Rusty's wild childhood at the beach but Rusty suddenly found something else to do. Late afternoon rolled around and we were laying on the beach soaking up the sun. I'd dozed off, and the voices above me were faint.

"It's not four o'clock yet. Go finish your shift."

"Aren't you going to at least introduce me?"

"She needs the rest." Rusty gave me a kiss on the shoulder. "I'll be right back." He got up and followed Cody back to the t-shirt shop, talking as they walked. "…seen the news lately?" He was going to tell Cody about the mine. Maybe that's why I was so tired. Maybe my days and nights were still mixed up. I turned over to keep from frying my back. When the skin on my front felt toasty I thought I'd had enough sun for the day and headed for the water to cool off. I came up out of the water after a wave washed over me and noticed Rusty standing on our towel looking up and down the beach. I hoped that wasn't a worried expression on his face. He worried too much and I hadn't been gone five minutes. When I waved my hands so he would see me a younger version of Rusty came up behind him and pointed me out. Wow, I thought, he's a Coppertone model, a Hawaiian cruise poster boy. I hoped Jesse's marriage was stable. They met me halfway up the beach. Rusty handed me a bag.

"I never would have taken you for a camouflage girl," Cody said.

"That's because you've never seen me in the woods," I answered.

"Cassidy, this is my brother, Cody. Cody, this is my fiancée, Cassidy Callahan."

Cody flashed me a toothpaste commercial smile.

"It's good to meet you," I said.

"Where's your bike?" Rusty asked.

Cody looked around. He walked over to the boardwalk and pulled a very worn skateboard out of a corner. It had a strap attached to it and he slung it across his back. Then he walked off down the beach and came back with a red bicycle that looked like it had been made for a ten year old kid.

"Want a ride home?" Rusty asked.

Cody looked me up and down.

"Sure. I usually bike home to make a few social calls but I guess I can use a lift today. So," he said turning to me, "what do you do in the woods that you need camouflage for?"

"Thanks to Rusty, I've kind of become Joshua Hills' official tracker."

"What? You mean like Chase Downing does? You're kidding."

"Chase was the tracking teacher at academy. He didn't teach me much. He seemed to know what he was talking about though. I'm sure the rest of the class learned a lot more."

"Chase is an interesting guy. I go surfing with him sometimes. He walks the beach and tells me what the people did as he walks along, describes them to me, it's like watching people without them knowing."

"Rusty hates it when I do that. I was nice today. I don't think I did that once, out loud."

"Nope," Rusty said, "you showed good self control. Notice anything I should be aware of? Any drug dealers making a hand off? Any potential purse snatchers or carjackers lurking in the parking lot?"

"I've been trying to remain oblivious to all that. I just wanted to enjoy the day."

"That's my girl," Rusty said, then turning to Cody he continued, "Cassidy tends to see things that other people don't. She's somehow tuned in to odd behavior. She spots crimes before they happen, reads tracks and knows more about the people than if I had met them and talked to them myself. I don't know how she does it."

"So, if there was a troublemaker in a crowd you could spot them?"

"I'm not going to say I could for sure. I wouldn't just do it to point fingers at people. What if I were wrong? But I have spotted odd behavior and been right a lot."

"Well, what about this crowd. I happen to know that there is one troublemaker in this crowd. Can you see who it is?"

I studied the people around me and ruled out all the families, all the older couples, all the little kids. Of course any of them could have been the one but I didn't think so. There were bike riders out for exercise; nope, not them. There were roller bladers and skate boarders. I was looking for someone with nothing better to do than get into trouble. My attention kept coming back to one older boy on roller blades who glanced at every tote bag and purse he skated past. He was followed by two other boys who were watching and waiting for him to try something.

"The boy in the green t-shirt, tan shorts and roller blades," I said, "he skates by open purses and tote bags and pulls things out that look interesting."

"Bingo," said Cody.

"You figured that out in five minutes observing a crowd of people?" Rusty asked.

"I can see him doing it. It isn't hard to guess when people are openly looking for something to steal. They stand out to me. How do you think I spotted that bank robber? Let's get out of here before the kid steals something and you have to run him down."

"That kid gets caught every other day," Cody said.

"Are you ready to go?" Rusty asked us both.

"After we get to the truck can you give me five minutes? I don't want to meet your parents in a wet swimsuit."

I opened the back of the Explorer and found my shorts and t-shirt. I looked in the suitcase for a hairbrush, found it, and then trotted off to the restrooms to change and freshen up a little. Looking in the mirror I was glad I'd spent so much time outdoors. The sunburn wasn't too bad. I dried my hair with the hand dryers and then brushed and shaped it a little. I really needed to wash and dry my hair properly but there was no time for that. Well, they'd just have to take me for who I am. I changed clothes quickly, avoiding the sandy puddles on the floor and in five minutes I was back.

"Okay," said Cody, "she's a keeper. Any girl who says five minutes and keeps her promise is a keeper. I always figure a half hour for every five minutes they ask for."

"Look out everybody!" Cody announced as he busted in through the door of a two story Cape Cod beach house three miles from the ocean. "Rusty brought a girl home!" He carried his bike up the stairs, disappeared into a cluttered room and dropped the bike and skateboard.

"We don't go much on formalities here," Rusty explained.

Rusty's mom appeared from behind the stairs. "Rusty! What are you doing here? You didn't tell us you were coming. And what's this I hear?"

"Mom," Rusty said giving his mother a big hug, "this is Cassidy."

"Oh my," she said when she saw me. "It really *is* you. We were so afraid we would never get to meet you. We caught the news program by chance and recognized Rusty in some of the shots so we started recording the news. When they aired the story about your engagement we were stunned. We didn't know."

"Nobody really knew. We knew we wanted to get married last fall but decided to wait until I finished academy to announce our engagement. That was in January and then I started work with the search and rescue team. It's only been recently that we have had a chance to make any wedding plans."

"Well, we taped it all. If you'd like to see…"

"Mom, we came here so we could forget it. We need to just clear our heads while we're here. Cassidy has had one tough track after another and I just got her back out of the mine. I don't want to watch her be lost to me again. We just need a couple of days to regroup."

"Well, regrouping is our specialty. Your dad will be home in an hour or so and dinner will be ready shortly after that."

"Can we have the attic?"

"I don't know if you want the attic. Cody has been having friends over at all hours of the day and night."

"I'll talk to Cody."

Rusty took the suitcase and started up the narrow stairway. At the landing he knocked loudly on the first door he came too. Loud rock music blared out as the door was opened.

"I'm taking the attic over for two days."

"But…"

"It's just two days. You'll survive."

"Hold on…" Cody dashed down the hall and up a set of pull-down stairs at the end. We heard scuffling, bumps, furniture being moved around and the sound of bare feet coming back down the stairs. Cody reappeared carrying a pile of clothes and assorted odds and ends, then disappeared back into his room.

Rusty carried the suitcase to the pull-down stairs and then clunked up to the top. The attic was a long narrow room that ran the length of the house from front to back. Double doors overlooked the backyard. The floor under the lowest part of the roof was lined with odds and ends. There were a couple of mattresses, board games, beanbag chairs and low coffee tables. A small TV was hooked to an electronic game system and there were bookcases filled with paperbacks in every imaginable genre along with Nerf balls and piles of bedding. The center of the room was dominated by an ornate pool table. The floor had plush carpeting to cut down on noise and the finished undersides of the roof were lined with posters of young people doing adventurous stunts: surfing, motorcycle racing, skateboarding, freestyle skiing and more. Rusty opened double doors that led out onto a balcony and dragged a mattress to the doorway. Then he went to the pile of bedding and found several comforters and put them on top of the bare mattress.

"It's not a posh hotel but I've found it's one of the most pleasant places to sleep."

I went out onto the balcony and looked down into the backyard. There was a flagstone walk all the way around a small swimming pool. A tiny patio stood between the back door and poolside. How they got the equipment in that small area to dig a pool I'd never guess.

"Are you finding everything you need up there?" Rusty's mom called up the stairs.

"Yeah, Mom, we're fine." Then he turned to me and asked, "Ever played pool?"

"I haven't played in years. I used to play a lot when I was living at home. The ranch hands have an old pool table in the bunkhouse and we'd play in the off season."

"Your dad let you go in the bunkhouse?"

"The guys were considerate. They kept things clean when Jesse and I were around. I learned how to play poker there, too. I lost a lot of pocket change to them, especially Old Frank and Steve. They'd never take more than pocket change from me."

"You want to try it?"

"Nine Ball or Eight Ball?"

"What?"

"What version do you want to play? I'm used to Nine Ball, where you have to shoot the balls in order. Most people play Eight Ball. But we can do either. I just think Nine Ball forces you to think more and provides more of a challenge."

"I think I better wait until after dinner to take you on."

I had more luck at Nine Ball than I did skill. I was not very good at leaving the ball set up for the next shot and so the target ball always ended up hidden behind a higher numbered ball, forcing my opponent to try complicated bank shots to get at the target ball. It was one of the things that made Nine Ball interesting.

I found the rack and then set the balls: one ball at the point, nine ball in the center and balls two through eight in a diamond shape around the nine ball. I slid the rack to the marked spot and then carefully removed it.

"Okay," I said, "you break."

Rusty chose a stick from a row of them on the only flat wall. I chose one too, after rolling a couple to make sure they were straight. Rusty was amused watching me, but then traded his stick when he discovered how warped it was.

He broke. His shot scattered the balls all over the table and two fell into pockets in the confusion. I think they got scared and dove for cover.

"Okay, now you have to hit the one ball, or you can also use it to hit any of the other balls in. First one to sink the nine ball wins. If you miss the lowest numbered ball or sink the cue ball, it's ball in hand."

He studied the table. He took careful aim at the one ball and almost made it. He might have sunk it if he'd been a little more gentle. It clung to the edge of the pocket begging me to sink it, but to just shoot it meant I'd scratch and it would be ball in hand. I bounced the cue ball off the side of the pocket barely nudging the one ball over the edge. The two ball lay across the table. There was a lot of green to cover and the seven ball was guarding the logical pocket. I used the two ball to sink the seven ball.

There was a bump and some thumping downstairs, talk drifted up the stairs and we heard footsteps coming up to the attic. Rusty's dad made his way up the stairs and across the room.

"Uh oh," he said, "who's stripes?"

"Nobody, Cassidy's creaming me at Nine Ball."

"I am not. You got two in and then I got two in. But the two ball is a tough shot. It's almost hidden behind the five ball. I can hit it but I can't sink it. Or I can maybe try a bank shot and try for the side pocket, but that's a long shot."

I decided just touching the ball was a better move defensively. I gave the cue ball a gentle tap and it slid between the five ball and the eight ball, just barely tapping the two and leaving Rusty with the cue ball, eight ball and two ball in a nice, neat row. They were all lined up in front of the corner pocket except for the lousy eight ball in the way. My luck was holding out.

"I'm Bill," his dad said giving me a firm handshake.

"I'm Cassidy," I replied, "it's good to meet you."

"Likewise."

Rusty was forced to make a bank shot to hit the two ball. He studied the angles.

"You're right, it does force you to think. Instead of choosing the easiest shot on the table you're stuck with the toughest one."

"Not always. It's good practice. Once you play Nine Ball for a while you will think Eight Ball is too easy and too cluttered."

He tried a bank shot but missed. I lined up on the two ball.

"I missed," he admitted, "it's ball in hand."

"Are you sure you want me to do that? I usually just keep shooting unless the cue ball goes in."

"Go ahead, it's your rule. It's my miss. It's ball in hand."

"Okay," I said, "you asked for it."

I picked up the cue ball, placed it on the table with the two ball and nine ball neatly lined up on the corner pocket and sunk the nine ball on an easy combo shot.

"It was your own fault," I said, "if you'd have just let me shoot you probably would have won."

"Do the games always go that fast?"

"No, usually you end up sinking the balls in order until you finally get to the nine ball. Combo shots that make the nine ball sinkable are hard to spot. So the games are usually longer."

"Bill?" Rusty's mom shouted up the stairs, "Find out what people want to drink with dinner. I'm putting it on the table now."

"Got beer?" Rusty asked.

"Just ice water for me," I added.

"Got it," said Bill and headed for the stairs.

The table for six nearly filled the small dining room behind the stairs. Beyond it was a small kitchen painted in a cheery blue with white trim.

"I'm sorry to drop in on you for dinner." I apologized, "I know you weren't expecting us."

Cody laughed.

"Nonsense," Rusty's mom answered, "I never know how many to expect for dinner. If it wasn't you it would probably be a group of people Cody brought home from work. You *are* still working, aren't you?"

"Barely," answered Cody.

His mom shook her head.

Rusty passed the roast and I took a small piece. "Take another one," he said. "Cassidy never eats right when she goes out on a call. She ends up eating backpacker food and giving most of it to kids who go do damn fool things like exploring abandoned mines."

"Well, you have to admit the boy did look remarkably well for being trapped in a mine for three days," Rusty's mom countered.

"Trevor did great. I told him to let me know when he was hungry. There was no way to tell time so I didn't know if he was eating only once or three times a day. I had only two days worth of food in my pack but cooked a meal whenever he was hungry. I can't believe a ten year old boy only went through four backpacker meals in three days."

"And what did you eat?" Rusty asked.

"I finished off whatever he left behind," I admitted.

"So," Rusty said, "take another slice, there's plenty."

I humored him by taking a second slice but then skipped the potatoes. My appetite worked the other way around. I hadn't eaten much for days so I needed to build back up slowly.

The doorbell rang. Rusty's mom gave Cody a glare.

"Set another place," she said in a firm tone and then got up to answer the door. She opened it and I heard footsteps on the hardwood floor as someone followed her through the living room. They turned the corner around the stairs and there stood Chase Downing, my tracking teacher from reserve academy. He was definitely in a more informal setting now because his wavy hair was dark salt and pepper and fell over his collar in disarray. He wore a holey t-shirt, baggy shorts, and flip-flops.

"Well, well, well, look who's here," he said to Rusty. "And with the only student I've had some respect for, too. Callahan, how have you been?"

"Busy," I answered. "Will it ever let up?"

"It's got its ups and downs," he said.

"It's had a lot of downs lately. But it's still busy. You haven't talk to Strict lately, have you?"

"I stay to myself down here. I don't take just any case. They know when to call me. I used to take a few calls up in the desert but I haven't gotten any lately. Maybe I have you to thank for that." He took the last chair and Cody handed him a plate, fork and knife. Cody went to the refrigerator, pulled out a can of Bud Lite and handed it to Chase. He popped the top with one hand. "So, what have you done that's interesting, lately?"

"How much of the news have you seen?"

"None. I try to pretend the news doesn't exist."

"Well, that wasn't the most interesting thing I've done lately anyway. I was sent on an afternoon's search that turned into a three day track. We had two rainstorms that nearly wiped the trail. It was slow reading and tough terrain."

"You find your man?"

"It was a fourteen year old girl but yeah, I finally found her. Last news we had of her she was doing well."

"That's good, I guess. I've developed a cynical attitude towards these searches. Sometimes I think stupid people should pay the consequences."

"What kind of cases do you take then?"

"I like to do clean up work. Rid society of people who plague it."

"They should have called you on this latest raid then. I tracked two guys up out of a canyon, well, one of them left the canyon. When I got up top there was only one trail. The other guy was down in the canyon. The guy that made it to the top was tracked down and the apprehension was made."

"And the guy in the canyon?" Chase asked.

I looked at Rusty. I couldn't say it. I just couldn't tell them about it and then it all came back to me. I'm surprised I didn't jump when the shot went off in my head. I bolted from the table and ran up to the attic.

After a while I heard footsteps on the stairs but it wasn't Rusty. I'd know his footsteps anywhere. It was his dad. I sat on the balcony, my feet hanging off the edge, legs through the wrought iron rail surrounding it, hands tightly gripping the supports, trying not to cry, trying even harder now that Bill was beside me.

"How long ago did this happen?"

I swallowed hard trying to control my voice, "Two weeks ago."

"I don't want to sound cruel, but I'm glad this is tough for you. We see it the other way too often, where it's a macho thing to be able to bring down a man. It should never be easy. But if it's the right thing to do there's nothing you can do about it, and in the canyon it was the right thing to do. Everybody downstairs knows that. You're allowed to mourn for criminals, too. I'm glad to see you're one of those who does."

"I don't even know who he was."

"It doesn't matter. He was a person and every life is precious. Don't let it be any other way."

"Did you tell Rusty that the first time he…"

"I even told him that before he became a cop. I told him that when we was six and wanted to be a cop. And as I tried to get him to value life I also told him that some day he'd find a life so precious he wouldn't want to let it go. And when he discovered that life he should hold onto it with all his heart."

"He has. I haven't made it easy for him but he listened to you, and he did what you said."

"I know, I could see it in his eyes when you came out of the mine."

He came and sat with his feet hanging off the balcony too.

"Thank you," I said, "you've been a good dad for Rusty. Nobody else could have stuck with me through the things he has. He has been nothing but patient and kind even when I fill his life with grief."

"I doubt he sees it like that."

"The first time he saw me I was in danger. I'd been carjacked by a bank robber. I've been stalked by a crazy murderer and attacked by animals. I've been in a car wreck and an avalanche. Seems like every time I turn around something bad happens to me and Rusty takes it all in stride. I don't know how he does it."

"How do *you* do it?"

"I'm too busy dealing with whatever happened to worry about myself. I just do what I can whether it means running or stalling or fighting or hiking for the Jeep. When Rusty proposed I almost said no. In a way I did, but he was crushed and I couldn't stand to see him like that. I just thought it wasn't fair to put him through all the trouble that happens to me. But then, when I saw his response, I knew he'd be there whether we were married or not. I knew putting any more distance between us would only hurt more. So I said yes. And I love him with all my heart... I feel like I've doomed him. But I'll try, I'll really try to stay out of trouble."

Just like Strict and Schroeder, he had that look about him. It was a mixture of sadness and wonder. They seemed to wonder how an innocent looking kid like me could cause so much trouble. They worried about what that might mean for the future, for their jobs. And yet they always sat back and marveled as I came through each and every crisis that befell me. Now I saw that same look on Rusty's dad and he had barely met me.

"Since I graduated from academy things have been better. An emotional roller coaster, but better. The mine was rough on Rusty. You know the story from the news. It was easier for me. It was just a dark camping trip with a kid for me. But Rusty's had a hard time with it. That's why we came here. We both needed a break. He needed to do something fun. We went to the beach today and had a blast. That was good for him. I could see the worry fading away while we were at the beach. He needs more days like that."

"How does Rusty respond when you have these things happen to you?"

"While they are happening he does everything by the book. He knows the drill. Afterwards, when we are finally alone, he just needs to hold me close. He says he just needs to…"

"…feel you be alive," he said, finishing my sentence for me.

"Yes, exactly."

"I used to have the same response when I was in uniform. Something would happen, a bad car wreck involving a woman, or a violent crime against a woman, and I'd come home and just hold Bev and be thankful everything was really still okay. I didn't know it wore off onto Rusty."

"Maybe he just takes after you."

"Maybe. Are you ready for round two of dinner? Come downstairs and tell the family a little about yourself."

The mood was rather subdued when we got downstairs. Nobody knew how to act. Everyone was still sitting around the table, just talking until Bill and I walked in. I took my plate, microwaved it, then sat down and started eating again, waiting for the conversation to begin.

"Cassidy, I'm sorry," Chase said.

"There's no need to apologize. You were just making conversation. I'm sorry I reacted badly."

"So," said Bill, "tell us a little about yourself. Where did you grow up? Do you have any family?"

So I told them about growing up on a quarter horse ranch, raised as a boy, hunting, tracking, camping, cowboying.

"I can rope, flank and tie a calf almost as quickly as the ranch hands. They are better at it because they are big guys and handle the horses day in and day out. Every once in a while we will have a friendly competition and I hold my own when they challenge me. I'm pretty handy on a horse."

"But I can't watch her do it anymore. I watched her get thrown once, and the horse fell on top of her. I thought I'd lost her right then and there. But she got up, dusted herself off and got back up on the horse again."

"Ranch procedure, you know that."

"Yeah, but I'll never understand it. One of my favorite things to do is watch Cassidy stalk deer. There is a place where we like to go camping and nearby is a meadow where deer graze. She can get into the herd and lay there with the deer all around her. She has taught me how to do it a little but I'll never be as good at it as she is. And she knows how to be invisible in the woods. A time or two I've looked for her when she was trying to stay hidden and she is impossible to find if she doesn't want to be found."

Chase followed all this with interest.

"Rusty asked me to teach him how to track and we spent two days out in the hills by the ranch, me walking, him tracking. He's getting better at it. I tend to hide my tracks without thinking about it so it has been good practice for him."

"Cassidy, do you mind me asking? How old are you?" Rusty's mom interjected, "You don't look old enough to have done all this. When I first saw you I thought you were fifteen."

"I'm twenty-five. Eighteen years on the ranch, four years in the Marines, one year of marriage, no kids, no messy divorce, one ugly plane crash, six months of…of, well, and then I met Rusty."

"It took me forever to get her to go out with me," Rusty said.

"No it didn't, we went out the very first day we met."

"That wasn't a date, that was an interrogation."

"An interrogation over pizza."

"If she was a date she was the sorriest looking date you ever saw. Black eye, ripped up clothes from being roughed up, tape marks from being tied up. After she went through all that, we lost the guy and she tracked him down for me. I didn't even know she could track. There she was all bruised and beaten and she takes off after the guy that did it to her, leads me to a mobile home park, finds the trailer he's holed up in, almost got her head blown off."

Rusty's dad watched us with professional detachment. The others looked like they were listening to campfire stories. I ate and talked. Rusty's mom didn't say much but she listened carefully. Cody and Chase enjoyed the stories. I think Chase was trying to piece together just how a girl like me could have come about. He knew how hard it was to make a good tracker and to have one, especially of the female persuasion, land on his doorstep was particularly intriguing.

Slowly night settled over the house.

"You aren't really going to make Cassidy sleep on the floor in the attic, are you?" Bev said.

"No, I'm going to make her sleep on a mattress on the balcony. She's used to tents and worse. In the mine… What did you do in the mine? I never thought to ask."

"I only had my day pack so we just slept on the ground." There was that worried hug again. "The mattress will be fine."

We climbed up to the attic and Rusty pulled up the stairs from the inside. He wrapped me in a warm hug, hands straying, but more as a comfort to him than anything sensual. He was still feeling the worry and the stories over dinner hadn't helped. He led me out onto the balcony where the night breezes were blowing lightly. The pool shimmered below in the starlight.

"If you wake up in the night and you can't sleep, wake me up too," he said with a gentle kiss.

"Okay, why?"

"I chose the attic for a reason."

We lay on the mattress out on the balcony, snuggled close, watching the stars. Now I was too curious to sleep. The breeze tickled my skin. I watched as the lights in the surrounding houses slowly went out one by one until we were finally in the dark.

"Darkness doesn't bother you after the mine?"

"No, it didn't even bother me when I was in the mine. It's like I tell kids when I speak at schools. If they are lost in the forest, the place where they are is no more dangerous than the place they intended to be. So many people get scared and panic when they get lost, but there is no need to. Wherever they are is just as safe as where they wanted to be. When it's dark all the same things are there that can be seen in the light. If there's nothing to fear with the light on, then why worry when it is off?"

"You can't sleep?"

"How do you expect me to sleep when you've got me curious about something?"

He smiled then got up and looked over the railing at the downstairs windows. All dark. He went to the little window facing the front of the house and looked out. All dark. He put his ear to a wall in the corner of the attic. He smiled again.

"You? Curious?' he said. "You never get curious."

"Ha," I said, "you know better than that. You probably did this to me on purpose just so I wouldn't go to sleep."

He smiled again. He went to a corner of the balcony and pulled out a rope ladder. "If the house catches on fire, and you're stuck in the attic, climb down this ladder to the backyard and run, through the gate to the meeting spot. That's what my dad always said when I was little. What *I* heard is, this ladder is your easy access to the pool. The ladder's nice and quiet and, if we go down this way, the stairs won't creak and the porch light doesn't flash on like it would if we went out the back door. Follow me."

"I don't have my swim suit. It's drying downstairs."

"Who needs one when nobody's up?"

Skinny-dipping in Rusty's parent's pool? My heart rate suddenly doubled. We stepped silently down the rope ladder and padded over to the pool.

"It's been warming in the sun all day. I hope it's not too warm. I've come out here at night and found the pool bathwater temperature."

"You really think I'm going to swim at your parent's house in the nude?"

"You don't have to," he said taking off his t-shirt and teasing me with it. He took off his boxers and eased into the pool. He gave me a pleading look.

I glanced around at all the windows I could see before slipping out of my tank top and panties. I slipped into the pool, delighting in the cool caresses, scared to death the porch light would come on. Rusty motioned for me and I swam towards him, trying not to splash. It's amazing how noisy the water was even though we were trying to be quiet. Each little drip and splash seemed magnified. I put my arms around Rusty's neck and he waded out to deeper water. He stopped when the water became neck deep. He laughed at me as I dunked myself trying to stand up. Then he caught me around the waist and pulled me to him so I could hold on.

"Arms around my neck. Feet around my waist. Now, if you want to float just let go with one or the other."

"If I stay like this, do you really think we will last ten minutes in the pool?"

"It depends. It's your choice."

Gulp, okay. I took that to mean he wouldn't mind rushing up the ladder and making love until we crashed out. I had to admit, it was one of the more pleasant ways to get to sleep. I let go with my hands, laying back in the water.

"Mmm," he said softly, "I think ten minutes is stretching it."

I looked up into eyes full of longing. I felt hands encircle my waist, then fingers wandering up my front, fingers teasing my nipples. Shivers ran down my body and my legs tightened around his waist. Oh yeah, I thought ten minutes was definitely stretching it. He put his hands under my back pulling me up for a kiss. It was deep and sensual, with a lot of tongue. His hands on my back tightened. I wrapped my arms around his neck, hugging tight, skin to skin. I lay back again, the water lapping around my breasts, the cool breeze causing my nipples to contract.

"Oh, babe, you feel so good to me," he said, hands roving.

I reached down behind me under the water and felt his hardness. I rubbed the end gently against my bare backside. I gave it a gentle squeeze and he tensed.

Some invisible something above caught my attention. A noise? A movement? There were some disadvantages to being constantly in tune to my surroundings. I filed it away as harmless, hoping the distraction hadn't brought binoculars.

"What is it, Cass?"

"Nothing, nothing we need to worry about anyway."

His hands, those wonderful hands drew me back.

"Are you ready to go back upstairs?"

I glanced at the balcony and busted out laughing, quickly stifling the noise.

"What?" Rusty asked, wondering what could be so funny under the circumstances.

"The ladder is gone," I answered still laughing quietly. "I thought I heard something."

He looked.

"Cody!" he whispered loudly.

I looked more closely, it wasn't gone, it was very carefully left just out of reach. We weren't stranded completely.

"It's okay," I said, "we can get it back. He was only trying to have some fun."

"I'll kill him," Rusty said.

"No, no you won't, that's what he expects. You won't go storming after him. It's not that big a deal. Leave it to me."

"Not a big deal? Now you'll never come out here with me at night again."

"Voyeuristic little brothers are not what I was worried about. I think it's funny." I found the rescue hook on the back wall of the yard and tried to hook the ladder. Rusty took it from me and tried, too. He had an extra foot or two of reach, but it didn't help. "I think you're going to have to boost me up," I suggested.

I stood in Rusty's cupped hands and he boosted me up over his head. I almost cracked up again as I thought about the view he was getting. I hooked the ladder and started pulling.

"Too bad my hands are busy," Rusty quipped.

I laughed, "If the top of the rope comes down too, then you can kill him."

I pulled the ladder down and Rusty lowered me, my breast brushing against his cheek on the way down. We were both laughing as we started up the rope ladder. I remembered our clothes left by the side of the pool and dashed back for them. Rusty checked the attic to make sure we really were alone and we tumbled back onto the mattress, laughing at our predicament.

"Now where were we? Oh ya, I remember. I was right about here. And, let's see, my hands were busy so that only leaves…"

Oh, yeah, whatever he had in mind was fine with me. It sure felt good, gentle flicks sending pleasure every which way until I could hardly stand it anymore, then those tantalizing hands. Oh wow, my back arched as the feelings took over everything. It was like being tumbled in the surf except it was good. Instead of water it was electrifying sensations rolling over me. I reached for him, a lifeline in the sea of feeling and he came to me all kisses and the sensations rolled over me again. He rejoiced in it, feeling me be alive and in love. The worry was erased and all the cares in the world fell away for just a moment while everything was just us.

Chapter 6

We awoke late the next morning, but it seemed like this household wasn't in a hurry to get going. I took my time getting ready, putting on make-up and curling my hair. I wore my best jeans and a spaghetti strapped top. The straps were decorated with beads that crossed in the back and made me feel cute.

Coffee was brewing when we came downstairs.

"I'm still going to kill him," Rusty said.

"No, don't do that. It'll be more fun to see what happens if you don't."

"Why?"

"You just have to wait for the right timing. I'll take care of it. What were you planning on doing today?" I asked, trying to plan my response to Cody.

"Shopping."

"Does it involve swinging by downtown?"

"It could, why?"

"You'll see. Why are we going shopping?"

"To meet Sandy. We go to the beach to meet Cody. We go shopping to meet Sandy."

As we made our way through the city center's one-way streets Rusty asked, "Where are we going, downtown?"

"Hooters," I answered.

"You want to go to Hooters? That's a new one."

Rusty drove to Hooters not needing an address. He pulled into a parking garage, parked, and then we walked across the street to the restaurant where we were promptly greeted by two girls in neon orange short shorts and white tank tops.

"Welcome to Hooters!" they called out in unison.

I purchased a gift card at the gift shop.

"Are you hungry?" I asked, wondering if Rusty wanted to stay for a while.

"If we catch Sandy at the right time she'll go out to eat with us."

"Okay."

"What are you going to do with the gift card?"

"I'm going to give it to Cody."

"What? After what he pulled?"

"He's going to be my brother-in-law. I want to make him squirm and still stay on his good side. He'll respect me for it if I do it right."

At the mall I bought a thank you card. Inside I wrote: *Cody, thanks for the practical joke last night. You made our evening more interesting. Cassidy.*

"You're thanking him for doing that to us?"

"Yeah, and I'm going to have your mom or dad give him the card. That way he'll have to open it in front of them and they should be curious enough to read it too. Then he'll have a little explaining to do but I bet he comes out of it squeaky clean. And I bet he thanks me for it in his own way."

"It scares me to think how devious you can be."

"Well, am I right or am I wrong?"

"Nope, you're right."

I dropped the Hooters card in the envelope and wrote Cody's name on it in big block letters.

Finding Sandy at the mall was similar to finding Cody at the beach. We walked around the store from one department to another and finally asked at the service desk. The girl called Sandy's extension and pretty soon Sandy hurried through some double doors, her high heels clicking across the linoleum floor. Sandy looked polished in a designer pants suit. Her hair was styled with dark curls tumbling down her back, and she wore diamond earrings which sparkled as she walked.

"Rusty!" she squealed with delight, "I haven't seen you in ages! Kendra, look, this is Rusty, my big brother."

Kendra blushed, a natural reaction to meeting Rusty.

"I brought someone for you to meet," he said, putting his arm around my shoulders. "This is Cassidy. Cass, this is my sister, Sandy."

"Oh my," she said, "does this mean what I think it means?"

"We're planning our wedding for the end of July," he said.

"Rusty, this is so sudden."

"It's not sudden for us. We've known each other for a year. We came to see if you would go out to lunch with us. We're hoping you will."

"A year? And I didn't know. Let me get my purse."

We walked down the mall and decided to eat at a big, noisy Mexican restaurant. Rusty appeared uncomfortable but listened while his sister thoroughly grilled me. Seems like every time we turned around something reminded us of the heart wrenching times we'd been through. I tried to avoid it but also wanted to answer her questions honestly. Despite the discomfort Rusty apparently knew Sandy needed this time, and if he sat back and allowed it to happen everything would pay off in the end. Gradually Sandy relaxed and started seeing me as a friend and not as someone who appeared suddenly to steal away her big brother.

As we were talking I noticed a man at a table nearby. He was alone, eating slowly and appeared distracted. He was watching another table close by where a mother sat eating lunch with a toddler and a sleeping baby. The little boy was impatient and the mom was hungry so she grew short with her son and admonished him to sit still and be quiet. Every time she scolded the boy the man tensed. Irritation lined his face but it didn't appear to be the irritation of a distracted diner. This man had an emotional connection somehow, and when his irritation turned to anger I became worried and started keeping tabs on the man. Something wasn't quite right about him. He seemed like a normal guy except for his focus on the other table. Other diners glanced at the mother and kids but only seemed mildly annoyed. I tried to figure him out as I talked to Sandy.

"Cass," Rusty said interrupting the conversation, "you're not all here. What's up?"

"I'm sorry, I got distracted," I replied.

"No, tell me."

"Rusty I don't want to tell you. I don't want to pursue it. I just can't help but notice it. Maybe it's nothing."

Sandy looked at us with interest.

"You know it's something or you wouldn't be so focused on it."

"See the guy with the brown slacks, green tie and bomber jacket?"

"Yeah."

"If he follows this mom out, keep him in sight."

Rusty also started watching 'Bomber Jacket'. After a while he looked at me.

"How do you do it? Now that you point it out I can see it but how do you do it?"

"It's just obvious to me. I can't help it."

"You two lost me somewhere," Sandy said.

"I'll explain later," I said, "just keep talking about the wedding. Now that Rusty's got it covered I can think again. I'd have kept quiet and handled it myself but I'm not armed. I don't like to carry my gun unless I'm on a call. Have you seen any wedding dresses that made you think 'that looks like something Skipper would wear'?"

"Skipper?"

"Yeah, people tell me I look like Skipper. Barbie's little sister? And I'm kind of a fashion klutz. Usually I have pretty good luck with outfits that look like something Skipper would wear."

"Skipper's too young to get married. But, yeah, I've seen one."

"I was hoping for something quietly elegant, simple, but classy. No billowy skirts, no ruffles. Lace or beadwork are nice. Long, so I don't have to wear heels, I hate heels."

"Maybe Rusty can walk the mall for a little while and I can show you."

I looked at Rusty, still keeping tabs on Bomber Jacket.

"You know, normally I would think it was really strange for someone to mention guns, Barbie dolls and wedding dresses all in one breath but for you it doesn't seem strange at all."

Rusty smiled. It didn't seem strange to him either.

The mom paid for her lunch and started gathering the baby's things together, packing a toy and a bottle into the mesh basket on the stroller. Bomber Jacket fished out his wallet and pretended to look through it. The mom walked out and Bomber Jacket gave them a head start, slapped a twenty on the table and followed. Rusty looked at me.

"See that security guard over there?"

"Okay."

Rusty got up and followed Bomber Jacket.

"Be careful." I said as he walked past.

I went over to the security guard and explained the situation, identifying who each of the people were, and what had transpired. The security guard followed, hand on his radio.

"I hate when that happens," I said to Sandy as I returned to the table.

"When what happens?" she asked.

"People who are thinking about doing something bad stand out to me for some reason. And it seems like every time I turn around I see someone acting suspiciously. Did you see the guy Rusty followed out? He was abnormally focused on that woman and her kids. When she left he didn't even wait for his check. He paid for a ten dollar lunch with a twenty and followed her out."

"Will Rusty be okay?"

"He'll just follow unless the guy tries something. He's armed and knows what to expect so he has an advantage. I just hope it turns out to be nothing."

"But Rusty knows it's something or he wouldn't have followed."

"Things like this just happen when I go to the mall. I normally avoid malls because crooks wait for me to go shopping to try anything."

"Is it safe to go look at the wedding dresses?"

I laughed, "It should be now. I've never run into two suspicious characters on the same shopping trip."

Half an hour later Rusty was still gone. After checking to make sure my cell phone was still on, I paid for lunch and walked with Sandy back to her store. She led me to the bridal section. She looked me up and down, then took a dress off a rack and held it up.

"There's only one way to find out," I said.

She led me to a dressing room.

"Don't you need to go back to work?"

"As long as I'm in the store and checking things out I'm working. They don't ask me to help with customers, but if I happen to be on the floor I try to."

I tried on the dress. It was too fussy.

"Back home I always go to the same store and look for the same sales clerk. She always helps me find something I can use. She brings me armloads of things to try on and we narrow things down until finally something just fits right."

"It's the same with wedding dresses. Here, try this one."

"Strapless?"

"Sure, you never know. It might be just the thing. Rusty would like it."

I stepped into the dress and worked my way through two dozen tiny buttons up the back. I stepped out and looked in the mirror.

"Oh my," said Sandy, "you look stunning!"

I looked at the dress. Bands of silver thread and tiny, sparkly rhinestones went up and down the bodice.

"It's not too much? You have to understand, Rusty has seen me in more camouflage than jeans and I only wear dresses for him. All these rhinestones seem like…"

"I don't know, it just suits you for some reason. Do you like it?"

"Yes, surprisingly, I do."

"Look, here's the one that has Skipper written all over it."

It was strapless too, but was almost informal in its appearance. The whole outside layer was made of lace. Soft lace, not stiff, formal lace. And the inside layer added just a hint of classic elegance. I tried it on.

"Oh, you look so cute!" she announced as I stepped out of the dressing room.

Hmm, was cute what I was going for? Not with most of the police force in attendance. Of course, most of them described me as cute behind my back, something I wasn't too proud of. The lace one *was* cute. I had to admit that. It would be even cuter when it was actually in a wedding. But the silvery one was stunning.

"Should I ask Rusty which one he likes?"

"No! You can't do that. He can't even see the dress until he sees you walking down the aisle."

"That's silly, I don't care if he sees the dress before the wedding."

"Trust me. He can't see you in that dress. I haven't seen him cry since he was ten years old and I don't want to see him cry until the wedding."

"Sandy, it's just a dress."

"No, it's not," she insisted.

"Well, which one do you like? I like them both but the silver one seems like it's more appropriate for a big wedding. If it was a small wedding on the beach I'd go for the lace one but it's going to be a big, formal one."

"I agree, stunning is better than cute. Are you sure about this? You have to be sure."

I put on the silver trimmed dress and stood in front of the mirror.

"Hand me a veil."

She chose one with silver trim to match the dress.

"Oh, yeah," she said, "that's the one. I don't think you're going to find a better fit than that. It looks like it was made for you."

Uh oh, she had said the magic words. Rule six hundred and forty two was now in effect. I was glad she hadn't said that about the lace one, though, and that sealed it. I had to buy it. I turned this way and that watching the dress sparkle, watching the short train move around behind me.

I paid for the dress and Sandy hung it up in a solid white garment bag so Rusty couldn't see it.

"I wish you could get it home without him knowing about it," she said.

"Oh, he's not that curious. He won't peek."

"Then he's changed a lot since he was a kid. He was always the one to tell me where the Christmas presents were hidden."

"It must have been the detective in him."

"Are you staying at Mom and Dad's house?"

"Yeah, we'll be there today and tomorrow and then we'll head for home."

"Maybe I'll stop by tonight. I'll call Mom and tell her if I get a chance."

"Okay, it was really good meeting you and I'm sure you'll see Rusty again before we leave."

I was walking down the mall with the garment bag held over my head to keep from dragging it on the ground or wrinkling it when I heard quick footsteps behind me. Rusty took the garment bag from me and gave me a questioning look.

"It's a dress and you can't see it. Sandy would be mortified if you saw it."

The look widened and then turned to smiling eyes. He kissed me right there in the middle of the mall. "Every little step that brings us closer to July twenty-seventh makes me want to celebrate."

I laughed, "You always want to 'celebrate'."

He slung the garment bag over his shoulder and we continued down the mall.

"That was a good call at the restaurant."

"Do I want to hear about it?"

"No, just know it was a good call."

We had to drop the wedding dress by the house where Bev hung it in her closet until we packed to go home. She was really curious about it so while her curiosity was already going I asked her to give the card to Cody.

"It's nothing personal, you can read it if he'll let you."

Rusty and I left again to run errands, hoping Cody would return home while we were gone. We were back in time for dinner and Sandy and Cody were both home. They barbecued dinner on the tiny patio and we ate around the pool. Then we played a very rough and tumble game of volleyball and I got tromped on, being the shortest of the bunch. Whenever we rotated and I was in the deeper part of the pool I was useless. I couldn't move fast enough to get to the ball. I got a lot of kidding but it was all in fun. Later while sitting with Bev and Sandy I listened as she told her mom about the dress I'd bought. It was funny watching her quietly describe it in detail, all the while stealing glances at Rusty to make sure he couldn't hear. I was trying to pay attention, really I was, but I kept getting bits and pieces from the guy's table and found it to be more interesting.

"You're going to have your hands full with that one."

"I know."

"And you're looking forward to every minute of it. I don't get it. Why'd she… I expected a thrashing out of you and nothing happened."

"She wouldn't let me… said she knew a better way… she had to do something so I'd be satisfied you got what you were asking for but she wanted to do it in a way that you'd still like her for it when it was over."

Cody laughed.

"Why Hooters?"

"Maybe she thought you didn't see enough last night. You have to admit she has a sense of humor. I went with her plan so you'd see what you were up against."

"I can deal with you. Mom didn't appreciate my little joke."

"Can Mom see it?… Cassidy…" Sandy asked.

"I'm sorry. Sure, if you want to show it to her. I don't really want to put it on with wet hair, though."

The two disappeared into the house. I jumped in the pool to make sure my hair stayed good and wet. I swam the length of the pool along the bottom, picking up two coins from the bottom of the deep end.

Cody continued, "I can't play jokes on someone who will only be nice to me."

"Maybe that was part of the plan, too. She can take anything you dish out but don't expect it to boomerang on you like it will with me."

I found two more coins on the bottom of the pool. Now that I looked, there were a lot of coins on the bottom of the pool. I put the two coins on the side of the pool with the others and dove again. I picked up as many as I could in one breath.

"Aren't you guys a little old to be diving for coins on the bottom of the pool?" I asked after coming up with four more.

"Coins?"

"Yeah, there are coins all over the deep end of the pool."

I gathered up the ones I'd collected so far and looked at one. What in the world? It looked like a buffalo nickel. I looked at another, a wheat penny.

"Anybody missing a coin collection that you know of?"

I handed the coins up to Rusty and dove again coming up with three more. Cody jumped in and swam to the bottom joining in the hunt.

"I think I better go talk to Ted Iverson," Rusty's dad said. "He's got grandkids and a coin collection. I've caught them in the pool before. It's dangerous for them to swim alone over here. He's got to put a stop to it."

By the time Cody and I were finished we'd gathered up close to thirty old coins ranging in size from pennies to silver dollars.

"How do you do it?" Cody asked. "Everywhere you go interesting things happen to you."

"If you find everything interesting, it isn't hard to find interesting things," I answered.

"You go to the mall and foil a kidnapping. You swim in a pool that I swim in every day and you find a rare coin collection. You look at a group of people at the beach and pick out a pickpocket."

"Just teach yourself to be observant. If you practice keeping an eye on your surroundings you'll notice interesting things too. I bet you already do, you just have different interests. I bet you aren't looking for pickpockets at the beach."

"And you are?"

"Not exactly, my observation skills are way too finely tuned for my liking. I don't want to see kidnappers and pickpockets when I go places. I wish I could be oblivious to them. I wish I could just swim without asking myself what all those dots are on the bottom of the pool, but I can't, I'm too curious."

Chapter 7

We went back to the beach the next day spending slow time, just walking, swimming, laughing together. I tracked, silently noting who had been down the beach before us and what kind of people they were.

I bought a plastic raft and blew it up, hoping to sunbathe on the water. I towed the little blue raft out to open water and settled in. It was peaceful just floating free, feeling the sun on my skin, hearing Rusty splashing close by. Every once in a while he would swim up and drip cold water on my hot skin. I closed my eyes, not quite dozing. The sea was particularly calm that day so I didn't have to worry about being tossed onto shore by the surf. The last thing I remember of my day at the beach was glancing up because I'd heard a motor and had always wanted to try waterskiing or parasailing. I looked up to see the boat *whoosh* past, then glanced around looking for the skier. I found him swiftly bearing down on me, two hard, wooden skis pointed directly at the small raft, a shocked expression on his face. He must have pictured a skewered sunbather because he just had time to raise the tips of his skis enough to miss me. The undersides, though, crashed into the raft, which promptly folded in half, trapping me inside. Water and plastic closed around me. Our tangled mess got dragged through the water and then the world went black.

Water isn't the best place in the world to be knocked unconscious. It tends to be slightly dangerous when that happens and you are submerged in water, so I found out. I came to on the beach. No, it wasn't the beach. It was close to the beach but it wasn't sand. It was something hard. The rescue workers were strangers to me and I missed Landon and Victor. I guess it means I get into a lot of trouble when I miss my usual rescue workers. I was used to them talking to me and knowing me a little. These guys were all business and they weren't having fun. They weren't shaking their heads in amazement that I'd come through another disaster in one piece. These guys were still wondering if I had survived, and that scared me a little. I felt sick. I felt like I'd been run over by a train. I tried talking, but all I could do was cough. A subtle yet gripping fear began stealing my thoughts. Usually when something happened, Rusty was right there. Even as I coughed up the sickeningly salty water I was wondering what happened to Rusty. He'd been right beside me. He was swimming next to the raft. No! Stop! Make the world stop! Make the water go away! I needed to see Rusty so badly. I needed to know he was okay. The fear overcame all else, and I tried to get up, but pain exploded, nearly knocking me out again. I was gently pushed back down, my body straightened.

I couldn't speak. I couldn't move. It was the closest I'd ever come to panic in my life. He could have been run over too. He could still be out there. And the stupid water wouldn't let me talk. I coughed up some more. The coughing hurt too. My chest burned and my side flashed with needles of pain every time I coughed. I was miserable, mentally, physically, emotionally. I had to know.

Calm down, I told myself. Panic isn't going to get you anywhere. Calm down enough to get past this. I stilled myself. When semi calm had returned I tried talking again, but every attempt just brought forth more coughing. Things started getting fuzzy again and I could feel the rescuers working feverishly but everything was becoming dull and muffled around me. No! At least show me Rusty's all right.

When I woke up again it was in a hospital. Still no Rusty. Oh please, somebody tell me something. A nurse came in. She was all business. She took my pulse, wrote it on a chart, took my blood pressure and wrote that down too. She checked the IV.

"Rusty? Where's Rusty?"

"Hon, just lay quiet. It'll be okay."

"No! Please, I need to know."

"I don't know anything about a guy named Rusty, but I'll ask around."

Time crawled. All I could do was lie there and cry quietly, and when they noticed I was upset they gave me a shot. I thought it was a good sign that they would give me a shot. It meant they had figured out that I was okay. They wouldn't give me a shot if they were in doubt. But how could they do that to me? How could they take away my only link to the one thing that mattered? As I was fuzzing out again an officer stepped into the room. I didn't recognize him, but he stepped to the gurney.

"Cassidy?" he asked.

I nodded and he looked relieved. "Please," I mumbled as urgently as I could, "where's Rusty? What happened to Rusty?" He spoke into his radio and settled into a chair. I phased out thinking *stupid shot.*

I heard a door slam open, urgent talk, some calmer talk, the door closed more quietly. I felt a kiss on my forehead. I tried to open my eyes in the haze, but it didn't work. I felt his hand in mine and I could rest. Calm settled over me and I drifted. I woke up slowly, little bits of awareness growing. A hospital. Noisy halls. Heavy limbs. Why did everything feel so heavy? Even my eyelids felt heavy. Somebody please tell me. I need to know. What did I need to know? Rusty.

"Rusty…" I mumbled in my half sleep.

"Shhh, babe, it's okay. Be still. Be still. Quiet." I felt his fingers brush the side of my face. His fingers, Rusty's fingers, Rusty's voice. I reached for him and pain immediately stopped me. He was here and I couldn't even reach for him. "Quiet, just be here with me. It's okay. Just be here." Words I'd heard so long ago, when we hardly knew each other. Just be here with me. I felt the relief and the pain in them just like I had the first time. "Can you hear me?" he asked.

I nodded. "Rusty, I was so scared. I didn't know what happened to you."

"Shh, it's okay. Nothing happened to me. I just couldn't get to you. The boat stopped and hauled you in. I was swimming for it, but they took one look at you and the other guy and they sped off looking for help. I had to swim for shore and then figure out where the boat had taken you. It was gone by the time I got to shore. And when you arrived at a hospital nobody knew your name. I called Dad and he had the station check all the hospitals. It took us hours to find you. Almost all the hospitals in San Diego had someone fitting your description in the emergency room."

"My promise didn't last very long."

"Your promise?"

"I told your dad I'd try to stay out of trouble. And I did try. I really did."

"He was here earlier. He sat and talked for a while."

"Has anybody told you anything? I've only talked to one nurse and she wasn't very helpful."

"You'll be okay. It's going to feel worse than it is. They'll probably release you tomorrow. But you're going to be laid up for a while… This was a close call. Babe, how do you do these things? How many ways can you find to cheat death? You almost drowned this time and I wasn't there. I wasn't there for you. I tried."

"Shh, I know you tried. It wasn't your fault. I'm glad you didn't have to watch it. It was scary."

"I talked to the doctors. They said you've got a minor concussion and several cracked ribs. I'm guessing it's going to mean bed rest. And it's going to be hard to carry a backpack for a while. You're going to have to be very firm with Strict. Only take on what you know you can accomplish. Will you do that?"

"I'll try. You know it isn't easy for me to stay down. Was the skier hurt?"

"He's got a broken leg and a big fine for venturing into the swimming area."

"You didn't do it, did you?"

"No, but I would have."

"Rusty, he was just out having fun like we were."

"He nearly killed somebody. Don't worry about it. Just rest."

Cody came to visit me in the evening.

"Hey, little sis," he greeted me.

"I'm older than you are. But I don't mind if you call me that."

"You gotta quit this. Rusty's going to have gray hair before he turns thirty-five."

"It wasn't my fault this time. I was just lying on a raft at the beach."

"Since all the cops in town were out finding you, I robbed a bakery," he said producing a piece of cheesecake. I took it with my left hand.

I smiled. How did he know? Everybody from San Francisco to the Mexican border brought me cheesecake when I needed a picker upper.

"Did you get one for yourself too?"

"I got a whole cheesecake. This is what's left."

"Yeah, right. Did you happen to steal a fork too?"

"No, but I'll go steal one from the nurse's station."

"No, that's okay," I said looking around. "Do you have a pocket knife?"

He pulled a small penknife from his pocket. I found the bed controls and raised the head of the bed until my ribs complained.

"Hand me that plastic cup," I asked.

I held the cup in my right hand and cut it with my left.

"You're going to kill yourself with that. What are you trying to do?"

"A wedge shape will work well as a spoon. Just cut an oval piece out of the side of it," I said, handing him the cup and knife. "Backpackers are resourceful people. I end up making a lot of things when I am out in the woods."

He cut the cup and handed me the wedge, throwing the rest of the cup in the trash.

"What kinds of things have you made?"

"I've made various kinds of snares when I went out on survival trips. I made a still to collect water. I tried to make a bow but it wasn't powerful enough to hunt with. I was only able to shoot a squirrel with it and then I felt bad because I like squirrels. I ate it anyway. Once it was dead it didn't care anymore. Squirrels make good camping companions, so I hate to kill them. I was pretty hungry by the time I killed that one. Once, I made a whistle from a willow branch just for the fun of it."

"Does Rusty know about all this?"

"Some. I've learned to be careful what I tell Rusty. When I told him about the survival trips he didn't take it particularly well. So he doesn't know a lot of the details. He just knows they happened. All that happened after Jack died and before I knew him. After we met and got to know each other a little bit I started being more careful. I showed him where my camp was so he'd know where I could be found, and now I do most of my camping with the search and rescue team so I'm not alone out there as much. As long as I stick to just tracking I think I'll get into less trouble than I used to. Camping at the hideout is pretty safe, too."

"The hideout?"

"The hideout is a permanent camp I made up in the mountains. You can't tell it's a camp. It just looks like a part of the forest. It's pretty well hidden. If I disappear for more than a day Rusty knows to either call Strict or look at the hideout."

I ate my cheesecake slowly, left-handed and very awkwardly. A nurse brought in dinner and looked at the cheesecake with disapproval. I set the cheesecake aside and saved the last of it for dessert. Dinner was something with pasta. Angel hair pasta. How was I supposed to eat pasta left-handed? She left and I looked at the plate with dismay. Okay, so I'd try to eat it. If all else failed I had cheesecake, right? And I had a real fork now. I took the fork in my left hand and tried twirling it in the noodles losing my grip within a few turns of the fork. I lifted my right hand to try but it wouldn't even go high enough to get to the plate. Pain shot down my side. I took a moment to gather my wits.

"Cody, can you take the tray away? Just for a bit?"

He wheeled the table away and I hunkered down in the covers holding my right arm close so the pain would ease. I tried not to cry. He was patient, waiting for me to come back on my own. I thought that if he would settle down and find his niche he'd be a lot like Rusty. He was just not in his niche yet. He was still looking for it and enjoying the search. I thought his practical jokes were a part of that, finding his place by testing people. I couldn't help but like him, jokes or no jokes.

The pain eased up, and I straightened back up gradually.

"You're going to take it easy when they let you out of here, aren't you?" he asked.

"Unfortunately I'll probably be out on a search long before I can carry a pack again. I'll just have to limit myself to day searches and warn Strict I'll be packless for several weeks."

"Weeks? Cassidy, it's going to be months before you can backpack again. Eight weeks minimum. Those ribs are going to give you fits."

"I don't have eight weeks to sit around. Ask Rusty. I'll be back to normal in four. I rolled a car a month before I started reserve academy. The doctors and the police called it a miracle if I made it to academy at all and I trained enough to pass the physical test before I ever got to academy. I was at the gym running before my stitches came out. Okay, I'll take the tray back.

Where's that cup I was using before?"

He wheeled the tray over and handed me the piece of cup. I used the curved end of it to cut up the pasta and then scooped it up with the makeshift spoon.

While I was in the middle of my meal Rusty walked into the room.

"Cass, what are you doing?"

"Eating dinner, what does it look like?"

"Do you want some help?"

"No, I got it. Just don't let them throw this thing away," I said, holding up the piece of cup. I cut up more pasta left-handed. He stepped forward and gave me a light kiss, then pulled the other chair over to sit beside Cody.

"Are you feeling better?" he asked.

"As long as they lay off the meds and I don't move. If the pain medication is working I can't think enough to spell my name. I don't know which one is worse."

"I talked to Schroeder. When do you think you can handle the trip home?"

"I'll tell you by the time we get back to your parent's house. I know we were supposed to go home tomorrow."

"Tomorrow?" Cody asked, "You're not going to make her sit through a long car ride tomorrow! No way!"

"Cody," I said, "He won't force it. I'll do it if I can."

"No, you won't," he countered, "you'll try whether you can or not and then it'll be too late."

I had to admit he was right there, but I didn't say so. I didn't want to be left behind if Rusty had pressing matters at work.

The next day the ride to the Michaels' house was painful. Every bump of the Explorer started my ribs to aching all over again, and there were a lot of bumps. When I walked into the house Bev gave a startled gasp. Rusty helped me up the stairs and into the second bedroom. I looked in the mirror over the dresser. Yikes! No wonder Bev was startled. I had ski tracks across the right side of my head, big red welts and purple bruises. A big lump on my head made my hair stick out weird.

"I sure wish you'd tell me when I look like this," I told Rusty as I settled onto the bed and straightened out to ease the pain. "No wonder your mom was startled to see me."

Rusty gave me time to get settled. I looked around the room and realized I hadn't seen it before. Everything was a dark, shiny wood, including the bed, the dresser, and the bookcase. Pictures of Rusty and his brothers and sister hung on the walls. There was a formal anniversary picture of a much younger Bill and Bev. I tried to determine which of his parents Rusty took after, but I couldn't decide. He seemed to take after both of them, but he was taller than both parents, as was Cody. The third brother, the one in New York, looked a lot different. He definitely took after Bill. He was shorter, stouter, and there seemed to be an intensity about him.

Rusty came in with some medication and a glass of water.

"What is it?" I asked.

"Doctor's orders," he answered.

I took them obediently but I knew I wasn't going to like what they did. He sat next to me, each shift of the bed sending stabs of pain through my body. He ran his fingers gently through my hair.

"Tell me about the pictures," I asked.

He took them down one by one, talking about them, telling me little family stories that I didn't want to miss. These were first day of school pictures. Those were a family vacation. I started fading out. His voice grew further and further away. I knew this would happen, why did I let him do this to me? I slept.

I heard people come and go, short, quiet conversations in the hallway or next to the bed. Finally, Rusty's deep voice and gentle touch.

"Cass, you there? I don't want to shake you, babe. I know it would hurt. Come on, try to wake up." Gentle strokes. Gentle strokes until he got to my right arm. The pain shot through the fuzz like lightning. I tensed against it and that hurt my ribs. He backed off. "Cassidy, you need to eat something. Wake up."

I opened my eyes slowly but couldn't shake the fuzzy feeling. I hated feeling fuzzy. It seemed to take over everything. I was used to being very focused and aware, so fuzziness didn't fit with the plan.

"Everybody's downstairs. Do you think you can eat something?"

I shook my head.

"Babe, you need to try. Mom fixed something you can eat left handed. I can bring a plate up, but they really need to see that you're okay."

Fuzziness. Go away fuzziness, let me think. "Can you find my brush? I can't go downstairs to dinner looking like this."

It was true, but I also wanted to attempt standing by myself so I could deal with the pain while he was gone. He left the room and I tried rolling out of bed without sitting up. I caught myself with a leg and pushed up with my left arm, so far so good. It hurt, but not as much as it could have. Rusty came back and I brushed my hair left handed, which didn't work very well.

"Don't worry about it," he said, "they know how hard it is."

I looked in the mirror. I was a mess, brushed hair or not.

"Rusty, I look awful."

He came up behind me. Wrapping his arms around me, he gave me a gentle squeeze. White-hot pain took over everything. I froze, shocked to immobility by the pain and then my knees buckled. He stopped me from falling head first into the dresser but it meant another jarring. He picked me up and it bent me all wrong. I cried out. He laid me on the bed. I was drowning again. I was downing in pain. I rolled back and forth knowing I was just making it worse, unable to stop, needing a position that didn't hurt. Finally he saw what I needed and settled me back against the bed. He pulled my right arm gently down and straightened me out, just physically moving my parts to positions he had seen me resting peacefully in.

"Cassidy, I'm sorry," he said, "I'm so sorry, babe. I didn't know. I didn't know it hurt that bad."

I just lay there, unable to move, unable to comfort him. Fuzziness, please come back. Please come back. I thought it would hurt forever.

Bev stuck her head in, alarmed. To his mom he said, "I just hugged her. I wasn't thinking and I hugged her."

"You big oaf," she said, "what do you think it feels like with all those cracked ribs? And you, never knowing your own strength."

"It's okay, it'll settle down in a minute." I wasn't sure if I was speaking to Rusty or to myself although it seemed like I needed to hear it too. Give it a minute, Cass, it'll ease up.

As the pain subsided I remembered that other people were waiting for me downstairs, so it was time to try again. Okay, easy does it. Roll off the bed, catch the floor with a foot, push up with the left hand. I was standing. Don't even look at the mirror, Cass, it doesn't matter that much. I stood cradling my right arm, waiting for Rusty to gather himself. He was really shaken. His mission in life was to keep me from harm and he'd nearly knocked me out with just a squeeze.

"Let's try again."

It even hurt to walk until I put myself into a kind of stealth mode, placing my feet gently and quietly, feeling my way forward, down the hall, and then down the stairs. Everybody looked up, worried, as we entered the room. I eased myself into a chair and Rusty followed, looking dejected.

During the meal I kept forgetting to use my left hand. Every time I raised my right arm to try and do anything, pain stopped me. I had to rethink everything I did. I couldn't pass bowls. I couldn't hold a bowl and scoop with the other hand. This was going to get old very fast.

Dinner was good. Bev had gone to some trouble to figure out something that was easy to eat with just a fork. It was a casserole of sorts and I spent some time trying to figure out what was in it. The talk flowed, everybody careful to avoid sounding too worried but at the same time curious what exactly had happened. I wasn't sure myself.

"All I know is I was run over by a very surprised water skier. My raft folded in two and I woke up half drowned on a pier or boardwalk or something. There were tall buildings and lots of flashing lights, lots of uniforms, lots of worried faces. I couldn't talk. All I could do was cough. I woke up at the hospital but nobody would tell me anything. I asked about Rusty and nobody knew anything. They gave me a shot to calm me down and I remember a policeman calling me by name right before the shot made everything blank out."

The doorbell rang and Bev glared at Cody again. They went through the same routine, Bev answering the door, Cody getting another plate for his uninvited guest. In walked Chase Downing again.

"I made an exception and watched the news last night. Didn't know what made me turn it on. Thought I better come over and see how things were going. I see you survived, Cassidy. Did anybody tell you the tracks are supposed to be on the ground?" He looked over the side of my head. "Hmmm," he said "Hydroslide Deluxe. I can tell by the pattern of bruises. Tracks look a day or two old..."

"Very funny. I would laugh but it hurts too much. How did you know it was me on the news? The hospital didn't even know who I was until Rusty showed up."

"It was pretty graphic. Some discussion about safety at the beach."

"Oh, great. Please tell me it was just local news. It must have been just local news or my mom would have called."

Chase joined the group and dinner went smoothly. I started getting the hang of eating left handed and as long as I used patience and took my time, making sure the food was firmly stabbed, I managed to eat the rest of my meal with relative ease.

Chapter 8

In the morning Rusty started loading the truck for the trip home. I wasn't sure I could manage the journey. I remembered the pain driving from the hospital, and that had been only a fifteen-minute trip. This was going to be three hours, at least. I began to wonder how long the fuzzy pills lasted. When everything was ready, I gave hugs all around. Cautious, left handed hugs. Everyone was careful to give right-handed shoulder hugs. I thanked Bev for the hospitality. Thanked Bill for his understanding and willingness to help out when Rusty needed it. Thanked Cody for his practical joke and the cheesecake. Made sure we had the wedding dress, we didn't so Bev ran upstairs and retrieved it from her closet. More hugs all around.

I climbed slowly and carefully into the Explorer and we took off. Rusty watched me, worried, and finally, when he couldn't stand watching me hurt, he pulled off at a convenience store, bought a soda, and handed me my relief. He knew I'd fight taking any medication that wasn't absolutely necessary, but I really needed it, so I took them reluctantly. He waited in the parking lot, talking, giving me a rest and time to get drowsy before taking off again. After a while I heard distant music, old rock and roll music and Rusty singing along. I'd never known him to sing before. He seemed too macho to sing along with a radio. I enjoyed it so much. His deep voice was calming, and as long as he was singing I knew he was close. I wanted to hold onto the moment and capture it, but time stood still and the bumps and jostles became less and less until I faded away.

He must have been extremely careful, because I didn't notice when we got home and he carried me up to the big, soft bed. I awoke in wonderful, familiar softness. Familiar smells. I reached for Rusty, but he wasn't there. I heard voices downstairs, Rusty's voice and Kelly's voice. I wasn't ready to face Kelly so I dozed. The voices grew louder and I realized they were coming up the stairs. They peeked in the bedroom and then went into Rusty's office.

"Every time I come in here," Rusty said, "I wonder why Cass chose this gift for me and it reminds me of her. When she's away on searches and gets tied up I come up here and just sit in this room."

Sleep came again, a more natural sleep, and when Rusty woke me for dinner I wasn't fuzzy and my ribs had had a long rest so I was in pretty good shape. He'd gone out and picked up Chinese food so I could eat it easily with a fork.

"Did anybody tell you skis go on your feet, not your head?" Kelly asked.

"I can't remember any time when I've gotten more ribbing from one of my trouble attacks. Actually, I would like to learn how to water-ski but I don't know anybody who can teach me."

The two guys looked at each other. I don't know which of them knew how to ski but they weren't sure they wanted me to know how. One more way for trouble to strike.

The night was miserable. I couldn't turn over or sleep in the only pain free position I had. When I did fall asleep I'd turn over but the pain would set in, and then Rusty would gently wake me so I could start the cycle all over again.

The next day while Rusty was at work my cell phone rang. I was afraid to pick it up but I did anyway.

"Hello?"

"Cassidy? Lou. I talked to Michaels already but I wanted to get the rundown from you."

"Okay, that's appropriate. I was run down."

"What happened?"

I gave him the basics of the story. "I can do anything I feel up to doing. Right now it means I can walk. I can do things left handed. I can't backpack. I can't camp. I can't even shift the Jeep. I'm moving very slowly and very carefully. If you looked at me you wouldn't send me out. I've got ski tracks across my head and four cracked ribs."

A long slow silence flowed over the line.

"What?" I asked, knowing he had a job for me but wouldn't ask me to do it.

"Nothing," he answered, "I'll send out the guys. I just hope they can do it."

I hung up, worrying. What if the guys couldn't do it? They were great at searching. They were experts at taking care of the medical aspects of a search. But they couldn't track well. I tried to tell myself that they had done without me for years. I tried to tell myself that Landon wouldn't allow me to go if he took one look at me. I told myself a hundred different things until I was nearly pacing the house.

Rusty called a little before noon to check up on me.

"Hey, babe, how are you doing?"

"Okay."

"Do you need anything?"

"Yeah, but you won't do it."

A cautious pause.

"What's that?"

"Take me to the base camp."

"No, I told Strict you weren't tracking for a week at least. He shouldn't have called."

"He didn't. He sent the guys out. But if I go to the base camp maybe I can talk them through the rough spots. I talked the cadets in academy through their rough spots in class. I can tell them what to look for. And if I go up there Lou will see I'm not fit to go out. I can't get into any trouble just sitting at base camp talking into a radio."

"No," he said again.

"Okay, but Strict will keep calling. At least, if he sees how bad it is, he will lay off for a little while."

Rusty was battling with himself. He knew I was right but didn't trust me to stick to the radio. I couldn't blame him. If I'd felt even a smidgen better I would have gone on the search. But it wasn't the wise thing to do at this point. I reminded myself that even the drive up the mountain would be hard on me. But nothing I told myself gave me any peace.

Rusty came home with dinner and I paced some more.

"Cass, you need to rest. Come, sit with me."

"I can't."

"I'll call Strict in the morning."

"You will?"

"Yeah."

"What if he needs help? Will you take me up there?"

"No promises."

"Do you know what they are doing up there?"

"Yeah, the guys should be able handle it. Give them a chance."

"Are they searching or tracking?"

"They started out searching and they found a trail. That's the last I heard."

"So you already called Strict?"

"Yeah."

"So you were considering taking me up there?"

"I was feeling out the situation."

I felt better knowing Rusty was keeping tabs on the situation.

"I still can't sit. It hurts to sit."

"Well, come here then. Lay down. You need to rest. You're more likely to get a ride up there if you can rest."

He got me on that one. I'd rest as much as I needed to, if he'd drive me to that base camp.

What was wrong with me? Was rescue work getting into my blood or something? Why would anybody want to go up and listen to a bunch of guys search the mountains for a missing person? It was worse than reality TV, but I had to know. I had to know we did all we could. If we didn't do all we could, and I could have helped, I'd be miserable. If I could have helped and they failed, I'd be even more miserable. I'd do anything I could to get a ride up there.

Rusty knew I was determined to get up to base camp when I willingly took my medicine that night. No constant turmoil, no waking up in pain, just blissful rest. He rested better too.

He rose early and got ready for work. He came and kissed me goodbye before leaving.

"Rest," he said, "I'll call Strict and come by later with the news. I just need to take care of a few things this morning."

I was still fuzzy but I gave him a kiss back and drifted away.

The next thing I knew Rusty was back.

"Cassidy?"

Noises downstairs barely making it through the fog. Footsteps on the stairs.

"Cass? Are you okay?"

Noises in the closet. Things being hung up and taken down. Changing clothes noises. The bed moving. Gentle arm rubs.

"Cassidy, babe this isn't like you. I thought you'd be up and dressed and standing at the door with the car keys."

The fog. The never-ending fuzziness that I had to fight through. Okay. I can do this. I shifted position until I could see Rusty and that brought on the pain. If I could just stay still there would be no pain, but I had to move to get up to the mountain.

"Cass, are you okay?"

"Yeah, I'm just still fuzzy headed. I need something to break through the fuzz."

He looked concerned.

"Give me half an hour."

I rolled out of bed, pausing to let the pain die down. I took a quick shower, which was hard to do left handed. I had to twist and turn and everything hurt. I couldn't even dry off completely without my right hand. I lay on the bed to let the water evaporate. My half hour was nearly up and I could barely move.

"Are you sure you're okay?" he asked. "I'm about ready to call this off. Look at you. You're even more bruised than you were two days ago."

I almost let him. I almost gave up, but I knew I had to do what I could. I had to try. I knew that despite the pain I couldn't really do anything to hurt myself worse. The pain would stop me. I went to my drawer and chose clothes I could get into with one hand. It wasn't easy finding things. Everything had buttons or zippers. I had to settle for baggy gym clothes, pull on shorts and a loose t-shirt. I couldn't get my arm up through the sleeve. Rusty shifted it around and brought my hand gently into position.

Spoken like a mother hen, Rusty reminded me, "You need to eat something before you go."

"Let's drive through and get something I can eat with one hand. If we get three or four soft tacos I can eat them throughout the day, one handed. And I want to stop at the drugstore to buy a sling. It'll remind me not to use my arm and it'll clue people not to hug me. I don't know why it seems like everybody wants to hug me."

"Because you're very huggable," he answered. "I guess I'll have to settle for kisses."

Lou Strickland's bright smile promptly vanished when he saw me hobbling towards base camp. He took in the half brushed hair, the loose clothes, the sling, and as I grew closer, the colorful bruises across my head. His expression softened to one of concern and he changed from strict commander to friend as we drew near. Rusty took note of the change in him. He knew that feeling well. Lou held out his arms to me. I knew it wasn't politically correct to let the guys hug me, but it just seemed to be the natural thing for them to do. Even the cops that barely knew me hugged me now.

I was scared to step forward because I didn't want to feel that pain again.

"Lou, it hurts. Just gentle shoulder hugs, okay?"

"Okay, what are you doing up here like this?" he asked. He stepped back. He ran his finger over the lump on the side of my head. I flinched. "Sorry."

"That's okay, it's not the worst of it."

"Go home," he said. "You're not going anywhere near that trail."

"I know. I just had to see how things were going and yack at the guys through the radio. If they get stuck, maybe I can talk them through it."

"They always think they are stuck. But so far they have pieced it together pretty good given their experience. I know if you'd started this track you'd be a lot further along."

"Thanks, I wish I could."

"We need to find this guy. It's important. The whole force is counting on us."

"The force? Who are you looking for?"

"Big John."

"Jankowski?"

"Yeah."

I turned to Rusty. "Did you know this? And you let me sit at home?"

"I told you, the guys should be able to handle it."

"Big John should be the easiest guy in the world to track. He leaves a clear trail wherever he goes. It's like tracking a bull elephant."

"When have you ever tracked Big John?" Rusty asked.

"Remember when we were bringing Trent Senior out of the canyon? Big John was the guy that helped bring him out. I know this guy's tracks. I know some of his mannerisms. What was Big John doing up here by himself?"

"Endurance run."

"On a trail?"

"Yeah, three days ago. Something caused him to leave the trail."

"Do we know what?"

"No, but he left the trail in a bit of a hurry."

"How far is the point where he left the trail?"

Both men looked at me seriously. "You are not going down that trail," they said in unison.

"It could be important to know why he left the trail."

Incredulous looks.

"It's just a trail," I said, "How far is it?"

"You are not going down that trail," Lou repeated. "Michaels, you better get her out of here before she does some damn fool thing."

Shoot, I knew I shouldn't do it. But my mind was way ahead of my capabilities.

"Was he armed?" I asked.

"Yeah."

I paced the camp, restless now that my mind was on the trail.

"At least let me say 'hi' to the guys."

We walked over to the radio. I looked at it wondering how they got connected at all. All the dials and switches were bewildering to me. I was used to being on the other end with one button to push.

"Hey, guys!" I said brightly into the radio transmitter.

Crackling, then, "Cassidy! Get your butt up here. We need you," came Victor's voice.

"Sorry guys, no can do. Strict and Rusty have me hog-tied to the camp. How's it going?"

"Rough and slow."

"Are you tracking or searching?"

"I'm tracking, Wilson is searching."

"What's that mean?"

"It means I haven't given up on the trail but Wilson is scouting ahead hoping to find another part of it."

"What have you got in front of you now?"

"Almost nothing."

"And you can't see where it goes next?"

"Right."

"Make the one track you have more defined. Push on the soil where you know the track is so you can see it really well. It will force you to analyze the track and decide what is or is not part of the track. When you have the track as clear as you can make it, it should point you in the direction of the next one. Big John has a long stride and he comes down hard on his heel, so a heel print will be the first thing to show on his tracks. Did you measure his stride?"

"No, the terrain makes it impossible for him to just walk normally. He is weaving in and out of brush."

"What made him leave the trail?"

"We don't know."

"You didn't see any other tracks where he left the trail?"

"Not that we could see. Of course we didn't think it was important at the time."

"Not important? Guys, it's all important. Has he been running?"

"Can't tell."

"You guys need some lessons. It's important to recognize a run. Do you have the track to where you can see it?"

"Yeah."

"And?"

"I'm looking. There's all these little plants and they sprung back up."

"Any broken leaves? Look for where you think the track should be and gently bend the plants aside. There may be distinct tracks under the plants. Also, when branches almost hit your head, look at the leaves. Big John has a habit of swatting things when they are near his head, so you may notice torn leaves overhead if he has passed that way."

I thought I was probably giving him too much information at one time. He was losing focus.

After a few minutes Victor said, "Got it."

Rusty looked relieved that I'd found something to do that didn't include trekking off through the woods.

"I'll be back before dinner," he said.

"Wait a minute, you're not leaving her up here," Lou announced.

"She needs the time up here. She won't leave camp. If she so much as ventures out of sight, she'll be under house arrest for a month."

Gulp. Okay.

"Victor, you guys have a consultant up here for four or five hours, so if you have any questions ask away."

"Will do. We're okay for now."

I walked Rusty back to the Explorer.

"If you need out of here early, just call. And don't leave camp," he said.

"Okay, I won't."

"Take care of my girl," Rusty admonished me gently as he climbed in.

I walked back to camp and eased myself onto a picnic bench. Lying with my back flat was the only way to be pain free. I kept an ear on the radio a few steps away. I watched the trees swaying overhead and soaked up the peacefulness of the woods as much as I could.

"You got run over by a water skier?" Lou asked.

"Yup. Hydroslide Deluxe according to Chase Downing. He read the tracks on the side of my head when they were still fresh."

"What did you think of Chase?"

"He's an interesting character. He's friends with Rusty's brother, but he needs an attitude adjustment."

Lou laughed, "That's an understatement. Did you go out tracking with him?"

"No, the first part of the trip I was trying to forget about tracking. And the second part I was laid up. I was lucky again, Lou. Someone on the boat knew CPR. I was knocked out and got tangled up with the skier and nearly drowned. I came to on the land somewhere. The rescue crew was all business. I learned a thing or two from them. They might have saved my life, but they could have saved my sanity, too, while they were at it."

"What did you learn?"

"That if someone is trying to talk it might be wise to listen to them, either for their sake or because they might be trying to tell you something important. I can tell you I'll be more inclined to listen to the people I track down, now."

Radio crackle. "Cassidy?"

I rolled off the bench and Lou walked over to the radio. "Hang on, she's coming," he said.

I waited for everything in my body to line up right so I could walk easily.

"Hey Landon, what's up?"

"What do you do if the trail suddenly ends? We're seeing nothing."

"Where was your last sign?"

"I'm standing at it."

"Describe it to me."

"It's a partial track, just the outside edge of it."

"Is it a soft line or a deep cut?"

"It's deep and sharp and slightly twisted." I pictured Big John making a deep, sharp, twisted track. Only a few actions like that came to mind.

"Look at the vegetation around. Is any of it squashed or broken? It sounds like the type of track you get when someone twists their ankle, so look for signs of that. If he fell, he might have taken off in an unexpected direction."

"Okay."

There was a longer wait for the next call. Each wait left me tense and wondering if my four or five hours were going to be enough. If I could only have a glimpse of what they were seeing... I wanted so badly to hike up there, but I was tiring just sitting in camp. I wouldn't last an hour on the trail.

"Cassidy?"

"Yeah, Landon, go ahead."

"I think we are seeing bear tracks up here."

"Are John's tracks on top of the bear tracks or vice versa?"

"They don't over lap so far, but it looks like he might have followed the bear."

"That's bad news. Bears are unpredictable. How old is the track? Can you still make out details of it?"

"It's about the same age as John's as far as I can tell."

"If they overlap you know the one on top is the most recent, right?"

"Right."

Well, at least they got something out of tracking class.

"Shit," Landon said, "things are getting rocky up here."

"Put yourself in their shoes. If you think John's following the bear, put yourself in the bear's shoes. Where would a bear go? Where would a bear go if it thought it was being followed? Look at your surroundings and think like a bear. Remember, bears are not going to go rock climbing. They will go for the broad way where it is easy to walk. If you think you are following John, then put yourself in John's shoes. Imagine him making the footprints. Imagine the actions involved in making that kind of print. Twists represent turns. Bulges in the soil can indicate turns, too."

"We're not talking a few stones, Cassidy. It's a whole field of nothing but rock. A half mile of rock with no soil over it. He could have gone any direction."

"Is it flat or are there outcroppings?"

"Both. We can walk on it fine, but we'll have to detour to go around the outcroppings."

"Your best bet is probably to circle the rocky area and find where the trail comes out the other side. Watch the dirt where the rock meets soil. Usually there's a buffer zone where it turns from rock to dirt to vegetation. That's the kind of place the tracks will show up."

"It'll take all afternoon to do that."

"No, it won't. You and Victor can split up and each do half. Just keep a sharp eye out for that one track that landed in the buffer zone."

"One track?"

"Hopefully more, you can usually count on one or two. Can Victor hear me?"

"No, but I'll talk to him."

A couple of hours went by. I lay on the bench. I paced the camp. I was getting antsy.

"Lou, I know if I was just up there I could find it. What if they miss it? What if they can't find where he left the rocks?"

"You just have to trust them."

"I hate being like this. I can't even move enough to hike up there, but in my mind I can see what needs to be done. I can see the possibilities. I know what to look for if one thing pans out. I know what to try next if it doesn't. If they tell me they didn't find a trail out of the rocks, I don't know if it's not there or if they just missed it. I know they are being careful, but they still miss a lot that I know I would catch."

"Cassidy?" Victor, this time.

"Go ahead."

"We don't see John's tracks leading off the rocks. We each walked half of the circle and then we continued on around and examined the other half. We found the bear's tracks but no sign of John's."

"And you both agree on where the bear's tracks are?"

"Yes."

"Go back to the bear's trail. Examine it as close as you can for about fifty feet. Do you have a magnifying glass?"

"No, I don't think so. Do you carry one?"

"Not usually, only when I know things might get sticky. You are looking for John's tracks, hairs, bits of fur, threads, blood, any itty bitty sign that tells that John might have met up with the bear or is still following it. Get down on your hands and knees and look carefully."

This waiting was going to drive me nuts. I'd much rather be up there doing it myself than down here trying to lead them through it. I paced nervously. Lou reached out to stop me and I ran into his arm. Pain shot through my side and I staggered back, tears in my eyes. I hugged my arm to my side. I would have been doubled over in pain but I knew to bend would make it worse. I lay back down on the bench waiting for the pain to subside.

The radio crackled.

"Cassidy?"

"Lou, can you get it? I can hear them."

"Victor?"

"Where's Cassidy?"

"She's right here. What's going on?"

"There's no sign of John's tracks following the bear and we don't see any other signs in the bear's trail."

"Ask them if they are still at the bear's trail."

Lou relayed the question.

"Yeah."

"Tell them to go back to where the bear left the rocks. Oh hell, let me get up."

I rolled off the bench, still stifling my reaction to the pain. I took over the radio. Lou looked worried. If one little bump did that to me, how long would it be until I could go out on a search?

"Go back to where the bear left the rocks, just the first few tracks. Find the front paws. They are the wider, rounder looking ones. Pick up the top layer of dirt from the track and sift it around in your hand. Look for anything unusual, particularly anything human related. Examine it closely. Rub it between your hands when you think you are done with it, and notice if there is any moisture making the soil pill up. If it pills up try and decide what made it do that. It could just be damp soil but it could be…"

"Blood, it's blood."

We all went silent for a minute.

"Are you sure?"

"It's dry, but it's definitely blood soaked dirt. Just little bits of it."

"And you're sure Big John didn't leave the rocks?"

"Cassidy, we can't be a hundred percent sure."

"How sure are you?"

"Sixty, seventy percent?"

"Okay, well, look back at the rocks. Pick out the rocks that look like the most likely place for John to hide if the bear turned on him. Where would you go to get away from a bear? If nothing jumps out at you from this trail, go back to John's trail and do the same thing."

I felt them conferring amongst themselves.

"Okay."

Half an hour later the radio came alive. It wasn't questions for me. It was orders and codes and the base camp came alive. Big John had been found. My job was finished. I'd done what I could and had to hope for the best. I didn't like the sound of the orders being fired back and forth, but I knew Big

John was alive and I knew more help was on the way. I found a lean-to that was set up for searchers to rest in and lay down in the shade. Sleep came quickly. Recovering from this accident felt like it was weighing me down. I craved sleep.

I heard voices, felt Rusty's familiar presence.

"Did she follow orders?" Rusty asked Lou.

"To the letter," Lou answered.

"How did she do?"

"She's still in an awful lot of pain. You should try to keep her home."

"It would be easier to do that if you'd quit calling her. Even if you don't have her do the search she feels like she has to do what she can."

"She's a good kid. She probably saved the guys three or four hours of searching. Three hours can make a big difference in some cases."

"I hate to wake her up. As soon as I do the pain will catch up with her again. You can't imagine the sight, watching that guy plow into her, watching her get dragged under the water."

"I don't know how you do it time and again. Seems like you'd be a basket case by now."

"No, never. I can't stay away from her. I tried to let her go. She wasn't ready for a relationship after Jack died. I tried to back off and I couldn't. I just couldn't. She delights me and terrifies me... She bought a wedding dress in San Diego. When I saw the accident I thought I'd never see her in that dress... She surprises me every time I turn around, and I'm always scared to find out what it's going to be next. She saved a kid from being kidnapped at the mall. She just noticed some odd behavior and it turned out she was right. I followed the guy, mall security stepped in. He didn't know he was followed and tried to snatch the kid. Three guns were on him before he could think, all because something looked odd to Cass. We had a great time at the beach. When she is having fun she is so fresh and alive. When she is tracking she is in her element. When she is stalking she is so graceful. No one knows how to live life to the fullest like Cassidy. I *ache* for her when she is laid up like this."

His words touched me and I felt guilty listening when he thought he was only speaking to Lou. I tried moving and my ribs screamed at me. I stiffened against the pain.

"Cassidy? Wake up, babe, time to go home. You okay?"

"I can't move."

He removed the tarp of the lean-to so I wouldn't have to bend and gave me a hand up. Oh, but it hurt. He put his hands on my shoulders, gently steadying me while the pain eased up.

"Cassidy," Lou said, "Thanks for your help today. Stay home and take care of yourself. Stay out of trouble. We need you back, but you'll have to let me know what you are ready for."

"Okay. Tell Landon and Victor I'd like to know what happened."

"Will do. Don't expect to hear from them today. It's going to take them all evening to get back to town."

"I know."

I stared at the Explorer, but didn't want to get in it. With my ribs like this it would be a torture box. I climbed in awkwardly, then sat uncomfortably and rode home all tense from the bumps and movements. When we reached the condo I eased myself along the walk, then up the stairs and finally onto the bed. I waited an endless period of time for my body to relax and the ache to subside.

"Eat something before you fall asleep," Rusty said.

"I can't think about food. All I can do is ache. It wears me down."

I fell asleep without dinner again.

Landon came by the next morning. I still couldn't manage most of my normal clothes and I felt self-conscious answering the door in boxer pants and a tank top. I invited him in, moving slowly.

"Can I get you anything? Coffee? Breakfast?"

"You can sit down. Cassidy, what were you doing at base camp yesterday? You shouldn't have done it."

"That's not what you said yesterday."

"If I'd have known, I wouldn't have accepted your help. What happened to you?"

"Don't worry about it. I lucked out again, that's all."

"This is lucking out?"

"Yeah, I'm glad you weren't there for the worst of it... No, Landon, I guess I can't honestly say that. It was scary. It wouldn't have been as scary if you had been there. But I'm glad you didn't have to see it this time."

He smiled. There was a time when I wouldn't have given Landon even a smidgen of encouragement. However, since he'd come to the conclusion that Rusty and I were together forever he'd backed off, and so I had eased up, too.

"Sit down," he said again.

"I can't yet. The angles are all wrong for my ribs."

"You're telling me you spent yesterday standing at the radio? Like this?"

"No, I lay on the picnic table bench in between calls. That's why I was a little slow answering. Tell me what happened. How's Big John?"

"First I want to know how you did it. How could you tell what we needed to do without seeing the trail?"

"You and Victor told me what the problem was, what you could see. I just needed something to trigger my imagination to picture something similar and then decide what I would do in those circumstances. It's like talking someone through any problem. If I called you and asked you how to change a flat tire you wouldn't have any problem telling me what to do. You can picture the things that need to happen, the pieces of the car... I just did the same thing with a trail."

"A trail and a car are two different things. Trails change. Every one of them, every piece of one, is different."

"But the process is the same."

"Big John will be okay. He got roughed up by the bear but it happened very close to the rocks." He laughed. That was a good sign. "I don't know how he did it, Big John was nearly as big as a bear but he managed to wedge himself back in the rocks far enough that the bear couldn't reach him. He was so packed in there I thought we were going to have to grease him or chip away the rock to get him out. He was unconscious so he was no help at all. Victor and I couldn't get him out of there. It took four of us and a lot of ingenuity to get him out. If he'd have had broken bones we'd still be up there puzzling it out."

"Why was he unconscious? What had the bear done to him?"

"He got a couple of good swipes from the bear's paws. I don't have much experience with being cornered by bears. So I don't know how long he was pinned down in there. I'm guessing he was unconscious from a combination of a loss of blood and dehydration."

"The time I was treed by a bear they hung around for three or four hours, but it was a very angry bear."

"When was that?"

"When I was searching for Kelly Green. Maybe Big John was just stuck, even after the bear left."

"Could be. We had a hell of a time getting him out."

"Did Big John shoot the bear?"

"He at least tried. We didn't see the bear anywhere. There's a guy hunting it now."

"Oh, no, don't tell me that."

"Maybe it was the same bear that treed you."

"I wouldn't shoot it anyway. She was only protecting her cub."

"How long is it going to be until you can track again?"

"A few weeks, anyway. You could tell me more than I can tell you. How long does it take for cracked ribs to heal?"

"Depends on how they are cracked. Normally I'd say six weeks, maybe a little more. But this is you we are talking about. I give you two weeks to hit the trail and four weeks to be back to normal."

"Will you do me a favor?"

"Sure."

"You don't know what it is yet. If I get called out before I can carry a pack, and the search goes into another day, don't get all bent out of shape if I don't have a tent. It's no big deal to me. If I had my choice I wouldn't pack one in the summer and I've slept in the open many times."

"Cassidy…"

"Please?"

"I can't promise. No guy could."

"I know, you'd have to break one of those macho guy rules. But really, it doesn't bother me to sleep without a tent or a sleeping bag."

Chapter 9

Three days later I'd had enough. This was the pits. I wanted out, and I wanted to be in the mountains again. I needed my mobility back, so I began exercising my right arm, slowly lifting it away from my body. Fire raced down my side with each attempt but I tried anyway. Ten times, then later, twenty. Gradually I could move my arm further. So far so good. I tried strapping on my day pack and wearing it around the house. It hurt like crazy to put it on but it wasn't too bad just wearing an empty pack. I added things to the pack: my camp stove and backpacker food, since those were the most necessary of my tracking gear. Gradually, over several days, I added my other tracking tools, measuring tape, sketchbook, matches, a change of clothes. When I could wear the pack in relative comfort around the house, I tried backpacking on a walk around the block.

My bruises started fading and, with my improved mobility, I could wear normal clothes again. Yes, progress was what I'd needed. When I saw progress, I kept trying. Rusty was encouraged to see me working to get better, although he hovered like a mother hen as I tried new things that hurt my ribs or tired me out.

Finally a noteworthy day occurred. Rusty came home from work and I hugged him without even thinking about it. He paused, almost startled by it, and wrapped his arms around me gently, still afraid to squeeze. It felt wonderful. I didn't want to let go.

"Can we go to the firing range some time?" I asked Rusty.

"Sure, you can use the firing range as a reserve deputy. You knew that, didn't you?"

"Can I use the gym, too?"

"Yeah. You mean to train? Just go in through the women's locker rooms."

"I usually just go to the fitness center, but they don't have a punching bag. I just want to see what kind of movement I can tolerate. If I can still shoot and can take a jarring, I'll call Strict and let him know I'll take calls again."

"Are you sure? It's only been two weeks."

"I can carry the day pack with the basics in it."

It felt good to get back to the shooting range. I definitely needed to work on speed, but speed was rarely a factor when I was tracking. I needed to work on my stamina, too. If I got my shot off in time, my accuracy was right on, but if I delayed, my arm tired and I lost my edge. Rusty was satisfied I'd be able to hold my own if I needed to use my gun.

The punching bag was a little tougher. My movement was good but the impact hurt like crazy. Still, it was better than it had been.

Two days later I was back at the punching bag when an officer walked in and watched for a minute.

"You need to work on your right."

"I know, that's the whole purpose."

"You want an opponent?"

"You? Want to box with me? This is going to sound awfully bad, but, do you know who I am?"

"No, why, should I be scared?"

"Not of me. I doubt anybody else here would box with me though."

"Why?"

"Well, one, I'm engaged to Rusty Michaels, and two, I'm trying to get back in shape after an accident. That scares off almost everybody."

He smiled. "You need a moving target. Come on, just tag boxing. You try for me till you tag me, then I try for you."

"Don't you have something better to do?"

"No, not that I can see."

"Okay, just keep your fingers crossed that Rusty doesn't walk in."

We both pulled on gloves. Just having the glove on my right hand weighed it down.

"See the circle on the floor? Stay in the circle."

"Okay. What about feet? Can I use my feet?"

"Sure."

We stood in the circle uncomfortably.

"Try and hit me," he said.

I put up my fists. I worked my way around him, looking for a break. I feinted with my left and watched his reaction. I feinted with my left and swung with my right. He jumped out of the way easily.

"What kind of a cop are you?"

"I'm not a cop, I'm a tracker."

"You?"

"Yeah." I swung with my left and barely tagged him. Keep him talking, Cass. He gets distracted when he's talking.

He came at me with a left and then a right. If I'd done this a month ago I might have given him a run for his money. Now I'd be lucky to last ten minutes. I stayed out of reach and he advanced. I ducked, avoiding another swing.

"What's a kid like you doing tracking?"

"It's what comes naturally to me." Duck again. "And I'm not a kid." Tag. I was glad it was to my left shoulder. Okay, Cass.

"How'd you become a tracker? We send guys to school for that and they come back with the knowledge but no eye for it."

Feint with the left, kick with the right. I tried a quick right, left, right. I knew he wasn't trying. If he wanted to, he could have had me down in two swings, but he knew better.

"I told you, it just came naturally. I was tracking when I was six. I'm trying to get back on call for Lou Strickland. Two weeks ago I couldn't move, much less box."

"You're not boxing now." Tag.

"Gee, thanks."

"What did you do to get laid up?"

"Got run over by a water skier, nearly drowned, cracked four ribs."

"Ouch. Two weeks ago?"

"Two weeks and a few days."

I dodged two quick swings.

"You shouldn't be doing this."

"I told you."

He tagged my shoulder and I quickly tagged him back. His hits were getting harder, but I doubted he knew it. It made me wary. A good solid hit to my right side and I'd be out for good. I heard doors open and close, but I couldn't find where they were without getting tagged. I dodged another jab to my right side and ducked under a hard left. I got back in position just in time to jump back from another right. I reacted wrong and left an easy opening for his next hit.

"Okay, enough of this. I want you to really try this time."

"No tagging? Just boxing?"

"Yeah."

"No. You'd flatten me in two hits."

"Aw, come on. What are you afraid of?"

"Being grounded from this place, getting laid up for another two weeks, seeing Rusty pound you."

He took a jab at me and I jumped to the side.

"Rusty's not going to pound me."

"How do you know? The last guy that hit me almost got flattened."

"Because he's standing right behind you."

Yikes! I turned around.

"Don't turn your back on your opponent," he said and hit me square in the right side. I went down.

"Damn it, whoever you are, I told you! I'm just trying to get my mobility back."

"Tom. My name's Tom. Are you mad yet?"

"No."

"Too bad," he said. I got up. "Now, hit me, whoever you are, hit me."

I took my stance, guarding my right side.

"Cassidy," I said, swinging hard with my left, stepping into my swing. He took the hit to his jaw. "My name's Cassidy."

"That's better," he said stepping back. "Now with the right."

I took a swing, but he jumped out of reach. I went after him, feinted with my right, since he was expecting it, and caught him with another left. He came at me and I ducked under his arm, then rounded on him with a right and a left. Rusty came up behind him and grabbed his arms before he could come at me again.

"Tom, I think we need to talk," he said.

"Rusty, he was just helping me," I quickly added, afraid I wouldn't get a chance to back Tom up if he needed it.

"Cass, are you really worried I'd hurt him?"

"Yes, no, I don't *think* you will but then I saw what you did to Trent Senior. And all the guys I work with won't let me do anything because they don't want to get on your bad side. So what am I supposed to think?"

"You don't have to worry about that. Have you talked to any of these people that are so worried about getting on my bad side?"

"Only enough to know they don't want to do it."

"Maybe they don't want to see you get hurt and they use me as an excuse. Maybe you managed to stay out of trouble because of them and there was no reason for me to be mad at them. I'm not unreasonable. If anybody knows how hard it is to keep you out of trouble, it's me. If some other guy can't manage it, I'm not going to fault him easily. It's usually your own doing that gets you into trouble, and these poor guys think they are going to get the fallout. Have I ever been mad at you?"

"No."

"Have I ever been mad at *anybody* that you know of?"

"Yes."

"Who?"

"Strict. You were mad at him for sending me on an apprehension."

"Okay, I'll give you that one. I was mad. And I hope he learned his lesson. I never want you to be put in that spot again."

Tom was watching all this with interest.

"Tom, I see you met Cassidy. Next time she says no, listen to her. She usually takes on more than she can handle, so if she says no, she means it. In a month, if you box with her, I wish you luck. For now, lay off."

I thought it was time to change the subject and give Tom an easy out if he wanted one. "I'm going to call Strict and tell him I'll take calls again."

"No, it's only been a few weeks," Rusty said. "You need to give yourself time to heal."

"I've been working at this. I can carry a pack, I can hike, my shooting is accurate and it'll improve. Getting out in the woods again will get me moving and back in shape."

"Will you let me go too?" Rusty asked.

"You want to go tracking with me?"

"Yeah."

"If the team will let you go, I certainly will."

To Tom he said, "You should see this girl track."

"Strict won't send out just the two of us because we need some medical know-how on hand."

"Let me call him then. He'll let me go if he thinks that's the only way he's going to get a tracker."

While waiting for some careless person to wander off in the woods I finally arranged a shopping day with Rhonda. We went to Betty's Bridal and asked to see the dress on page seventy-five of my bridal magazine. Rhonda tried the dress on, and several others that she had marked in the magazine before finally declaring page seventy-five to be a good choice. I wondered if she did it to humor Jesse or if she really liked the dress. I liked it, but rule six-forty-two definitely didn't apply in her case. I wished it did since she rarely had the opportunity to own a nice dress. I would have preferred she have one that really was made for her. I convinced myself that Jesse really liked it and Kelly would like it as well. We purchased one in her size and made an appointment for her fitting closer to the wedding date. Another step in the long process was accomplished. I emailed Jesse to let her know she could order the dress too.

I found a printer who would produce my wedding invitations the way I had designed them.

I bought a veil and shoes.

I spoke to a florist to get some ideas, then needed to go visit the house and look at the yard to get an idea of the layout for the wedding and reception. My to-do list seemed endless.

I called Steve, Randy, Zack, and James to see if they would be ushers. I taught Shadow to carry a basket so he could be the flower girl. It took several days to teach him to hold the basket, but once that problem was overcome he carried it happily.

I shopped around for a caterer but needed to talk to Rusty about food before making a decision.

I was sorting through my to-do list feeling overwhelmed when my cell phone rang. It was Rusty.

"Hey there!"

"Strict has a job for us, and we need to get out there."

"Details."

"Marital dispute. Guy took off suicidal. The wife called, worried about him. He took off into the hills."

"Is he armed? How long has it been?"

"Yes, but she doesn't consider him to be a danger to others. We'll talk to the wife before we take off. Put the tent and my sleeping bag on my backpack. Pack for a two day search although we don't expect to be gone that long. Only pack your sleeping bag and tracking tools in your pack."

"Okay."

"I'm on my way."

I went to the garage, pulled out the packs, and emptied both. I located all the basic camping gear: tent, stove, two days worth of food, water, a change of clothes, tracking tools, and the sleeping bags. I felt guilty making Rusty carry everything. I couldn't carry two days worth of gear yet, but I'd pack my share. I added stuff to my pack until it bothered me to wear it and then took a few things out. I changed clothes. I was supposed to wear my uniform but something told me I might need stealth, so I wore camouflage and moccasins. I strapped on my 9 mm.

I was preparing the trail mix when Rusty hustled in the front door. He gave me a kiss, then looked at me seriously, taking in the pistol strapped to my leg.

"Are you sure you're ready for this?" he asked. He hefted the packs. They weren't heavy. He opened my pack and took out the stove and a couple of bottles of water and put them in his pack. Then he went upstairs and changed into hiking clothes. He came downstairs looking like part of a swat team.

We dropped Shadow off at the kennel just to make sure he was taken care of in case this stretched on. I called ahead to make sure we could do a quick drop off.

Base camp was set up when we got there. Lou met me as I was getting out of the car.

"Are you sure you're ready for this?" he asked.

"Yes."

"How are the ribs?"

"I can carry my pack, I can hike, I can track. If I need to slow down a bit I'll still track faster than the guys."

"You're not going to like your team."

"Oh yeah?"

"Yeah."

"Okay, I'll stick to my job and let them stick to theirs. Why won't I like it?"

"City slicker."

He was right, I wasn't going to like it.

"What's up?"

"You're looking for Jamal Jacobs. His wife's name is Tamara. She insists Jamal will come home if their priest can just talk to him. So all you have to do is find your man. You'll have Rusty and Rosco there for backup."

"Why Rosco? He has the social skills of a potato. He'll work out great if Jamal follows through but he's useless in crisis negotiation."

"It was Rosco or Thez. Thez lacks the medical skills that might be needed."

"At least he'd keep the priest busy."

I went and spoke with Tamara, who was mad and upset. I thought Jamal better watch what he did when he got back.

It was handy having base camp at Jamal's house. I asked to see a picture of Jamal. He was a tall, good looking black man, athletic and fit. He looked like he could take on anything that came at him, except maybe his wife. Tamara had an attitude problem and I tired of her excessive bad humor. I examined several pairs of Jamal's shoes. Size eleven. This shouldn't be too tough. I found some of his tracks outside the house and got a feel for how he walked. I noticed he drove a Corvette but couldn't afford one. The inside of the house was ill kept. The furniture was worn beyond recognition. There were dishes stacked on coffee tables and stacks of old magazines next to every sitting place in the living room. The smell of smoke hung in the air.

"Does Jamal smoke?" I asked.

"Hell yeah, he's a freaking chimney," Tamara said.

"Can I borrow a pack of cigarettes?"

Tamara, Rusty and Lou looked at me strangely.

"Even a suicidal man wants to have a last smoke. If he ran out maybe he'd like some more. They might come in handy."

They couldn't argue with me.

An older gentleman dressed in black slacks, black suit coat, and a white shirt with a priest's collar strolled in peacefully from the back of the house. He was going to roast alive before he got a half mile from the house with that tight collar and all that black fabric and layers of material. I could picture the smoke coming out of his ears already. He was fiftyish and balding, but seemed like a pleasant enough person.

"Father," Tamara said, "these are the searchers who will take you to Jamal."

"I'm pleased to meet you," he said. "I am Father Dominic."

Lou stepped forward first, always the diplomat. "Father, this is Rusty Michaels, Rosco Lansky, and Cassidy Callahan. They will lead you to Jamal. And I am Lou Strickland. My job is to stay here and handle the other side of the search if it becomes necessary. Cassidy, do you have everything you need?"

"Yeah, all set except for a starting point."

We all went to the cars and strapped on our backpacks, except for Father Dominic. He waited, patiently amused by our preparations. He seemed particularly intrigued by me but I didn't think it was in an approving way.

"Young lady," he said quietly, "you mustn't carry that heavy load."

"I'm fine. I do this all the time and it isn't a burden to me. If we get stuck out there overnight I'll need this stuff."

"Overnight? Surely not."

"I've had searches last three, four days. You have to be prepared for anything. Everybody ready? Where's Tamara?"

"She's inside watching her soaps."

"Lou," I asked, "do we have a start to the trail?"

Lou led us to a spot in the backyard where it looked like a bear had charged through the vegetation. I got a fix on Jamal's footprints and started out. The men followed along behind me. Jamal was not hard to track. He was angry and that anger showed in every move he made. His footsteps were stomped into the ground and shoved in odd directions. The vegetation was torn and bent in his wake. After about a quarter mile Father Dominic started dragging.

"Excuse me," he said, "but I'm afraid I must ask a question. I don't wish to pry but I am accustomed to the man leading the woman."

"Father, we follow Cassidy because she knows how to find Jamal," Rusty said. "If I knew how to find him, I'm sure she would be satisfied to follow us. Right now the trail is plain, but it may not always be that way, and Cassidy can see the footprints when other people can't."

He nodded, not quite satisfied.

Rosco gave the group a Moose Miller look and I knew one of his rare gems was fixing to burst forth. "Father Dominic, the Lord has given Cassidy a discerning eye. The Bible tells us all to walk circumspectly. Cassidy is using her talent from God to do His will. We are simply allowing her to be used of God. You must trust her to do God's will."

Where in the world did *that* come from, I thought.

Later Rosco said quietly to me, "You just have to know the right words. He can't stop God from using you if He wants to."

I pressed on waiting for the smoke to start billowing out of Father Dominic's ears. It was hot out, even in jeans and a t-shirt. That suit must be like an oven.

Jamal's footprints continued to weave in and out of the junipers and sagebrush. At least Jamal chose good tracking soil when he went off in a snit.

"Cass, are you doing okay with that pack?" Rusty asked.

"Yeah, but it doesn't matter. I'm pressing on no matter what."

"Don't push yourself. There's no need."

"We're looking for an armed, suicidal man and we will have to deal with the wrath of God if we are caught out here after dark. I don't have anything against priests, but I don't see how he can expect to get through this search in a black suit, with no water, no gear. And if I'd known this was going to happen, I'd have picked up a marriage license on the way out of town so he could marry us."

"Marry us?"

"What do you think he's going to say if we have to stop for the night? Two tents, three guys…"

"He can spend the night with Rosco."

"With no sleeping bag. And where does that leave us? And I am not going to sleep with celibate Father Dominic!"

He laughed at me silently. "Okay, press on. Just don't hurt my girl."

The trail started up into the foothills and continued up, ever upward. I eyed Father Dominic watching for signs of exhaustion. He appeared tired and hot, but so far no smoke billowed forth. I was impressed and would have welcomed a chance to track him for a bit. His steady stroll ate up ground slowly but surely. His peaceful demeanor never faltered.

The going got tougher. Behind me I heard huffing and puffing.

"Here's where Cassidy begins her work, Father. If you look at the ground you see very little of Jamal's trail, yet she leads us on. She sees what others cannot discern." What happened to Rosco all of a sudden? It was like somebody flipped a switch on him or something.

Father Dominic nodded looking at the ground. I wondered if they could even see my footprints, and if Rusty was practicing tracking me. This could be fun, tracking Jamal's footprints while hiding my own. The track turned into a game of sorts and I was soon rewarded when I heard from behind me, "Cassidy, stop it. You're playing with me." I quit hiding my trail and then gradually faded it out again to give him exercises in tracking. In the meantime Jamal was giving me problems of my own. We had been on the trail for hours and he continued walking at a frantic pace. I didn't like what I was reading. He was still angry and appeared to be running from some internal turmoil. I decided it was time for a break. I stopped in the shade of a large juniper, opened my pack, took out a bag of trail mix and passed it around. I got out a new bottle of water and handed it to Father Dominic.

"Oh, thank you, my dear," he said.

"Father," I explained, "the reason I stopped is because I can see in Jamal's footprints that he is still upset. I wanted you to be thinking of what might be bothering him. It will prepare you for the time when we find him. Usually when I follow a trail like this the person gets tired and slows down, but Jamal is still rushing off in anger. Normally I can figure a person traveling cross country is walking about two miles per hour, but Jamal is covering much more ground than the average person. What this means is that if he keeps up his present pace we could be in for a very long hike. Are you prepared for a hike of this magnitude?"

"My dear, I am prepared for anything the Lord leads me to."

"But you have no food, one bottle of water…"

"See," he said, "the Lord provides."

"You have no shelter if we stop for the night."

"I am unconcerned."

Okay, this was getting frustrating. Strict should have forbid it and never let him come so unprepared. I looked to Rusty, but he wasn't offering any help. There wasn't much I could do about it, so I continued on.

All this uphill tracking was taking its toll on my ribs. The pack bumped and pressed against my ribs with each step.

Three miles later the trail topped out and Jamal stopped. I was glad he needed a rest and hoped maybe he would slow down now. I looked at the mess of tracks, pacing, stopping. He was thinking. It was distressed thinking, lots of sudden twists and toe jabs. His trail continued across the top of the hills until he came to a rock outcropping. I followed the footprints through the yellow grass. Trees sheltered the rocks ahead and I was suddenly sure we were nearing the end of the trail. I looked behind me, thankful it hadn't gone into a second day, wondering if Father Dominic was ready for the challenge before him.

A shot rang out and we all hit the ground. One shot, from a suicidal man. What could it mean?

"Rusty, take Father Dominic to cover," I said.

I wasn't too worried about Rosco. He was trained for this. Rusty was trained for this. Father Dominic was a sitting duck.

"Cass!" Rusty called, afraid I was going to do something dangerous.

"I'll be okay. I'll be right with you."

I just might do something dangerous but I would take stock of the situation first. I had to pinpoint exactly where Jamal was in the rocks. I crouched and ran in stealth mode to the closest group of trees. After looking around I found the rest of the group sheltered behind some trees further back from the rocks. I prioritized. The group had to stay together. If we were stuck up here tonight we would need to pool our resources and my pack contained a lot of what would be needed. The pack, at least needed to stay with the group. I crouched and made a dash for where the others were hidden.

Now we were in a bind and our mission had changed perspective. It wasn't a search and it wasn't a rescue. Rusty was the senior officer. In the city it would have required backup, and lots of it. But there we were, the four of us, a detective, two reserve deputies and a priest, five miles from the nearest road. If Rusty hadn't been with us I would have had a plan. However, I knew that he would handcuff me to a tree before letting me attempt it so I kept quiet. I let him fiddle with the puzzle from a detective's point of view and I fiddled with it from my own perspective. I couldn't really say it was from a reserve deputy's point of view. Sure I'd follow orders, but I suspected he wouldn't give me any besides staying put. I didn't want to hear that so I tried not to draw attention to myself. I took off my pack and dropped it next to the tree.

Rosco got on the radio, explaining the situation to Strict. Rusty took over. I fiddled with the problem. I tried to tune out the radio talk. Rusty didn't like whatever was going on as he listened to the radio and stalked back and forth. He was clearly distressed. My heart beat double time. Only one thing would do this to Rusty and it was clear what should be done. Rusty had to lead the operation. Rosco was needed for medical backup. Father Dominic needed protection. That left me to scout out the situation. It was precisely what I wanted to do, and had been my plan all along, but the question was would Rusty send me? Would he go by the book or go with his heart?

"Cassidy?" he asked. Using my whole name might have been a formality, but I thought it showed the level of stress he was under.

"Yeah?" I answered, trying to sound unconcerned.

Long pause, "I can't. No matter what Strict says, I can't."

"He wants me to go scout out the rocks, locate Jamal, and find a place we can begin negotiations from."

He looked at me seriously.

"I can do that. Rusty, you know I can."

"I just came down on him because you were put in this spot before. Now I have to do it to you."

"You're not doing anything to me. It's what needs to be done. You know that. I'll just be looking. We don't even know if Jamal was firing at us yet."

I looked over the situation, found the rocks where Jamal was holed up, and examined the location of the trees and brush surrounding the area. There were plenty of open spots where he could get me if he was careful. I'd have to be very cautious. First things first, find Jamal so I'd know what I was hiding from.

"Don't watch me," I told Rusty, "watch the rocks. If you watch me you might miss something important. And don't worry about time. To be really careful I have to take my time."

"Cassidy…"

"I'll be safe. I promise to do everything I can to stay safe." Father Dominic was looking at us very strangely. I turned to the priest and said, "Father Dominic, you have to understand, Detective Michaels and I are engaged to be married." He put two and two together and I saw understanding. "Okay, so watch the rocks, not me, and don't worry about time," I repeated.

All Rusty returned was a worried look, but I knew what he needed. He wanted that hug. Shoot, who cares who's watching, I thought. I stepped into his arms and felt that familiar, passionate worry. It radiated from him with an intensity that made me stifle the emotions welling up within me. He pulled me into a long kiss. Father Dominic blushed while Rosco pretended to be watching for Jamal.

"I'll be back," I said, and placed myself in stealth mode right from the start. I chose my destination and raced to the next tree, closing in on the rocks. I pressed myself against the tree, then glanced around the thick trunk, examining the rocks before me. I was looking for any place Jamal could be, but not seeing any, I continued around the area. The rocks turned out to be a larger area than I had originally thought they would be, and as a result I ran into trouble. I had to either go down the mountain on an impossibly long detour or climb up onto the rocks and become a target. I remembered my promise to Rusty and returned the way I came. Coming back into view I could see Rusty from the corner of my eye. He stood alert, wondering what I was doing. Tree to tree I scouted around the other side of the rocks. Tree to bush, bush to rock, I stayed out of sight of the rocks until I finally came to a cleft in the rocks where I caught a glimpse of the top of Jamal's head. Needing to get closer, I waited until his back was turned and crept up to the rocks. I inched around, peeked over the top of the rock. He was pacing, gun in hand, rolling the barrel of the gun over his hand, listening to the clicks. He paused, then set the gun on the rocks. There was some serious thinking going on in there. I eyed the gun on the rocks. If I could just get to that gun. I examined the layout of the rocks and decided I would have to come at him from the back side of the rocks. I backed off and inched around, finding a place I could climb up easily. The climbing was easy, but staying out of sight might be tricky up here. I used my lowest stalking crawl to move over the top of the rock. It was low. It was quiet. It made me look like a tailless lizard. Anybody watching would think it couldn't be done but I'd used the position to stalk animals and it came quite naturally to me. It was good exercise for my right arm. I crawled over the top of the rocks until I found the opening in the rocks where Jamal still paced. I spotted the gun laying on the rocks in a different spot. I inched closer, very aware how easy it would be for him to grab the gun and pull the trigger if I frightened him. I only moved when his back was turned. I froze to the rock when he moved. I placed each hand and each foot with extreme care, making sure every movement was silent. I only moved a foot at a time, but my patience was paying off. I could see the gun just a few feet away. I picked up a stone in my crawling. When I was close enough to make a grab for the gun I checked the shadows to be sure I wouldn't cast one in Jamal's sight, then threw the stone where it would cause a distraction. He glanced up, walked in the direction of the sound and I silently picked up the gun and inched back. Jamal decided the noise was nothing and turned back. He noticed his gun was missing. He turned this way and that certain nobody had entered the cleft the way he had come. He charged up the rock. I cocked his gun, pointing it at him. The guy wasn't too smart. I could have blown him away. He was shocked to see his foe was a young girl, well, what he thought was a young girl. His expression softened.

"You don't know what that gun can do," he said, "hand it to me before you hurt someone."

"Yes, I do," I said calmly. "But I don't want to shoot you. I didn't come out here to do that. We just came out here to talk to you. I'm part of a search party."

"You?" he asked.

"Yes, me. We were told you were suicidal and since they wanted to find you as soon as possible they called in a tracker. That's me."

He just looked at me weird, like he thought I was high on something.

"When I saw you leave the gun on the rock I thought I could prevent you from killing yourself."

"Did it ever occur to you that you could have gotten yourself killed?"

"Did you see me take it?"

"No," he admitted.

"Then it wasn't too much of a risk. How about if we go down the hill and talk this over? You'll get your gun back eventually, but I'm afraid you'll have to talk to the police about it first."

"The police?"

"These search parties usually consist of reserve deputies. We have to go by the book, and the book says you don't get the gun back while you could be a danger to others."

"So there's a bunch of reserve deputies waiting for me down there? And they sent *you* in after me? What are they, nuts?"

"No, I'm actually a pretty good scout. I've been looking over your situation here for some time without you seeing me. I got the gun without you seeing me. I was the logical choice. And I do know how to use the gun. I could take it apart, clean it, and put it back together before you figured out I have my own here ready to use. But actually I was only supposed to find a place for negotiations to be held. When I saw how careless you were with your gun, I thought I'd eliminate one of the risks."

"Negotiations? What are we negotiating?"

"How to get you off the mountain peacefully. Your wife sent a priest up here and everything."

"Aw, shit. Somebody needs to tell that old woman that I like to get out in the hills when I'm mad. I shoot at tin cans and broken tree limbs and stuff like that until I calm down. I'm not killing anybody."

"You shouldn't just go shooting around in the mountains. You could hurt somebody," I said.

"Yeah? Who? There's nobody up here."

"What about me? I spend a lot of time in these mountains. I wouldn't appreciate a stray bullet. The search team is in these mountains weekly, on more serious searches than this one. They would not take kindly to shooting either. You'd have the cops down on you in nothing flat. You almost did today. I was supposed to scout out the situation and decide if we needed backup. Look, I'd love to stay up here and chat, but I've got a detective, a deputy and a priest worrying about me. If we don't do something soon, at least one of them is going come marching in here to find me. He's going to assume the worst, so you don't want that to happen."

He rose to follow me out.

"No sudden movements," I warned, "and don't walk behind me. They might assume you caught me and have me at gunpoint. It might help if you show them you have nothing in your hands."

Jamal walked out, hands exposed, and I followed closely behind. When we got to the group I handed Rusty Jamal's gun.

"Cassidy, how did you...? Never mind. I don't want to know. Are you sure he's unarmed?"

"Well, I didn't frisk him."

Rusty checked Jamal over quickly.

"Cass, you need to follow procedure. What if he had been armed?"

"We had a nice chat, he doesn't want to hurt anybody. He just wants to hike in the hills," I replied.

"Then what was that shot all about?" Rusty asked

"I don't know. Jamal, what were you shooting at?"

"That pinecone," he said pointing at a tree limb overlooking the rocks.

"You missed," I observed.

"Yeah, I never was a good shot."

"If you're going to play with guns you need to take a safety course or something."

On the way back Jamal seemed amused to see me in full gear, camouflage, backpack, gun. Skipper meets GI Joe. I bet the sight seemed even more strange when he saw me next to Rusty and Rosco. Father Dominic used the time on the hike back to talk to Jamal. I passed around my trail mix. By the time we got back to Jamal's house Tamara was in more trouble than Jamal. The police did not appreciate false alarms and Jamal took great satisfaction in seeing Tamara squirm for a change. I was just glad to have the situation behind me. I used the search to gauge my fitness for the next one. I could do it, I was sure I could.

When we got home again and settled down I felt the aches and pains catch up to me, but it just slowed me down enough to rest.

"Rusty, did you just come along on this search to pack my gear for me?"

"No, I went to see for myself that you were really ready. But I was glad to make the hike easier for you. Now, tell me what happened up in those rocks. How much of a risk did you put yourself in this time?"

"Not much?"

He looked at me askance. He wasn't going to buy that for a second.

"Jamal left his gun on a rock. I just snuck up on it and took it while he wasn't looking."

"Just like that. You just snuck up on it. What if he'd seen you? He'd have shot you."

"By the time he saw me I was ready for him."

"And how did you end up bringing Jamal back?"

"When he saw his gun was missing he charged up the rock, and when he saw me he thought I was a little kid. So he tried to talk me out of the gun, thinking I was dangerous with it. We started talking about what I did and what was going on, and he said he just liked to shoot stuff up in the hills to work off his anger, that he wasn't shooting anybody."

"You are too trusting. What if he had another gun?"

"He wasn't a criminal, Rusty. He was just a guy out in the hills trying to get some space from his crazy wife. After meeting her and seeing his house, I didn't blame him one bit."

"How do you think Father Dominic fit into all this? Why would she send her priest into the search if she didn't think it would accomplish something?"

"Maybe she was just mad at Jamal and wanted to teach him a lesson. Speaking of priests, who are we going to get to perform our wedding ceremony? Do you have any favorite judges?"

"What about Father Dominic?"

"Very funny, plus I think he only does weddings for church members."

"Since we expected to be out on a search tomorrow, why don't we go get that marriage license and look at rings."

"Rings?"

"Yeah, rings. You never even got an engagement ring. Some girls wouldn't even consider themselves engaged without a big rock on their finger."

"You know I'm not like that."

"I know. You're about the least materialistic person I've met. But you should have one anyway."

Chapter 10

So that's what we did. The next day I wore a dress so I'd feel more like Rusty wanted me to feel. It may sound silly but it works. My attitude is determined a lot by my clothes and I wear jeans and t-shirts most of the time. When I'm feeling serious, as I do on a big search, I wear my uniform. When stealth is required, I wear camouflage. When I want to feel pretty, I'll put on a dress, but that is rare. Maybe it was the rarity of it that always made Rusty smile when he saw me in a dress.

"I can tell you right now, I'm not going to consider any large diamonds or high settings, and nothing flashy. This isn't an easy thing for me."

"What was your old wedding ring like?"

"It's just a gold band with a little decorative etching along the edges. I was in the Marines. I was thinking about what would be practical to wear through training exercises, crawling around in the desert, working on machinery. I wasn't thinking about style or even whether I liked it. It was necessary for the ceremony, so we got rings. That's all. I don't even remember going into town to get them. I think we bought them on base."

"Well, you're going to find something you really like this time."

We looked and looked, but it was like buying shoes. When I bought shoes, everybody wanted me to pick shoes with high heels. This time everybody wanted to sell me diamonds. Big diamonds, lots of diamonds. I thought wearing a dress was a mistake and I should have dressed down for this occasion. People who walk in wearing camouflage don't buy big diamonds. People who walk in wearing dresses do. Finally we ended up at a little mom and pop jewelry store off by itself in the parking lot of a larger discount store. I was sitting there trying harder to place the owner's accent than I was in selecting a ring.

"I got jus' the ting," he said over and over after hearing me say the usual, too big, too fancy, too flashy...

He showed me a set that consisted of two slim bands of gold intertwined around a simple setting of two small heart shaped diamonds. I was intrigued by it. There was nothing ostentatious about it. Something just clicked. The winding bands reminded me of the roundabout way Rusty and I had grown to this point. They reminded me of the trails I so often followed, winding around in the hills. Rusty could tell we'd finally found something special.

"What about you?" I asked. "We've been to a dozen jewelry stores. Did you see any ring that you really like?"

A man walked in the front door causing the little bell to jingle cheerfully. He walked around, looking at nothing in particular. A door opened and closed in the back of the shop. The hair on the back of neck stood up.

Cassidy, I thought, stop imagining things. You are not a trouble magnet, you are not a trouble magnet. Ignore it. Just ignore it. But the more I tried to ignore it the more I noticed little things that didn't seem to add up, including sounds that didn't belong in this setting.

"What is it, Cass?" How could he tell these things? I knew he watched me like a hawk but I hadn't done anything.

"My trouble radar is going off," I said softly.

"Why?"

"I don't know."

"Yes, you do."

"Okay, this guy isn't here to look at jewelry and the guy in the back is snooping around like he's not supposed to be there."

"The guy in the back?"

"Yeah, came in just after this guy."

"Maybe it's just the jeweler's wife."

"If I were the jeweler's wife I'd come in and at least say hello. I'd see if everybody was being helped out front, and I'd know what was in the back room. I wouldn't need to go rifling through stuff."

"Half of me says you're being paranoid and the other half says you haven't been wrong yet."

"Me too," I almost whispered and then more loudly I said, "so, did you see anything here that you like?"

"Let me look around a bit."

"One moment pliz," the jeweler said and rose to help the man who wasn't shopping.

I started fiddling with the puzzle. Did the store have a silent alarm? Where would they put the switch for it? If I had a jewelry store I'd at least put a switch by the cash register and the most popular items. I'd put one by the wedding rings because people sit there for longer periods of time looking.

I wished I was armed. I didn't like Rusty taking on two guys from different directions. He didn't like it either. His movements were guarded. He kept his sidearm in easy access at all times and pretended to be looking at men's rings.

I could see the man in the back now. He stood watching the inside of the store. The guy posing as a customer was trying silently to corral everybody between the two gunmen. It reminded me of Shadow working the deer when he went stalking with me. They didn't know they were being herded, so they didn't react right. Well, I wasn't going to be corralled either. I was a rebel. I wandered to the end of the display case and noticed that the area in back of the display case was not visible from the front. There were locked cabinets back there where jewelry was kept. I glanced across the back of the cases looking for an alarm switch.

The jeweler walked over to the man and I expected him to say "May I help you?" Instead, he looked the guy in the eye and said, "You! I give you five seconds to get out my store! Tree times past year you rob me! I not put up wit it. Dis time I prepared! You not get away!"

He pulled a sawed off shotgun from behind the counter and pointed it at the "customer". Rusty pulled his Glock aiming it at the man in the back of the store. The jeweler turned, surprised. I hoped he wouldn't mistake Rusty for being one of the robbers. Rusty went through the whole police act that you see on TV. "Police! Freeze! Put your hands over your head…" I always felt so fake doing that when I was at academy, and never did it with much authority. Rusty didn't have any problem, though. When he spoke, they listened. Hell, I almost froze too. He had the guys spread eagle on the floor and searched before I knew what had happened. Then he took the sawed off shotgun away from the shopkeeper.

"Cassidy?"

"Yeah?"

"Hold my gun while I check the back room."

I took his gun, feeling silly standing there in a dress and holding the big Glock on the two robbers. With the shotgun in hand, Rusty checked over the back room quickly.

I heard sirens wailing and two black and whites pulled up to the front of the store. They hustled out of their cars like they were planning a raid. They were a little disappointed to find their thieves already caught. Tom walked in with another officer I didn't recognize.

"Well, well, well," Tom said, "if it isn't the little boxer."

"He's new," Rusty explained, then turned to Tom. "Get used to it. This happens a lot."

Another officer walked in and said, "Hey, Suzie Homemaker! When do we get more cookies?"

"Cookies for you guys is no small order."

The officer who wanted the cookies cuffed the two men and led them away.

"Tom, wait! I have another one for you, but I have a transaction to make first."

Rusty turned to the jeweler.

"We'll take this one," he said, pointing to the ring I'd chosen. "What do you think, Cass? What about this one for me?" He pointed to a simple man's ring with a couple of small diamonds in a deep setting. It was simple, yet classy. Why weren't women's rings made like that?

"Do you like it?" I asked.

He put it on and looked at it.

"Yes, and I'd like to get one here. It'll have a story behind it, a reminder I can look at every day to tell me to always listen to you."

I looked at the selection in the case. The one he'd chosen seemed to suit him the best. After the transaction was rung up, Rusty informed the poor shop keeper that he would have to find a different way to defend his shop, and he also had an illegal weapons charge to deal with down at the station.

Chapter 11

"It's time to restock the hideout," I announced one morning at breakfast. "Do you mind if I pack the stuff up there this week while the tourists are all at work? Maybe if I go up there on Tuesday and come out on Thursday I can do it before Strict calls."

"If you wait until the weekend I'll go with you," Rusty replied.

"If we wait for the weekend we probably won't get to go."

"I don't want you carrying your big pack yet. If you're stocking up it's going to be heavy."

"I'm not stocking up that much. I'll pack in a sleeping bag, stove and backpacker food, a few books, and the lantern. The lantern is the only thing that makes the trip a pain. But I need it inside the hideout. The branches block all the light so there isn't enough light to see when I'm inside. I will only have trail mix and water on the way out because I leave all the other stuff up there."

I got out my big pack and filled it with all the necessary items, including a change of clothes to leave up there and one to wear on the way out. The lantern wouldn't fit into the pack and that was the glitch in the system. I liked this lantern, though. It was florescent, so it wasn't a fire hazard in the hideout. One scary flare-up was enough to convince me not to use a gas lantern inside the hideout. I thought about trading the lantern for a flashlight, but that wouldn't do on days when I was stuck inside due to bad weather. I needed something that would just stand there and light the whole place. Besides, the hideout wasn't exactly cheerful in dim light and it really needed the light this lantern gave. So I was stuck with it.

I hefted the pack. Hmm, I hadn't packed something this heavy since the accident. I put the pack on, ribs complaining at the squirming I had to do. The old ache started while the pack was hanging from my shoulders, but once I fastened the hip belt and settled the pack firmly into place it was tolerable. I walked around the condo in the full pack then picked up the lantern and toted it around for a while. I'd definitely have to carry the lantern in my left hand.

I, too, questioned my readiness for this trip, but I needed to test myself in the mountains without the pressure of a search on me. I could come home whenever I wanted or back out if it proved to be too much. This test would tell me if I was fit.

Tuesday morning dawned clear and bright. I was at the trailhead shortly after dawn trying to get the main part of the hike in before it got hot. I had assured Rusty this was just a trial hike and I'd come back early if necessary. He wasn't satisfied, but he knew better than to try and stop me. I looked around the parking lot to see how busy the trail might be. One old yellow van had been parked there for a few days. It didn't have an adventure pass on it, and there was a ticket on the windshield. I made sure my adventure pass was hung on the rearview mirror of the Jeep.

Shadow paced nervously beside me as I struggled into my pack. He was ready for this trip. He had missed the mountains and been cooped up in the condo for months while I went out on searches without him.

"Are you ready, boy? Ready for a long hike?"

He woofed loudly.

"Okay, heel!" I said and started out. Shadow fell into place at my left side, competing for trail space with the lantern bumping along beside him. He kept a sharp eye on the trail, watching for squirrels and rabbits. He wouldn't chase them unless I released him, but became excited when he spotted them nonetheless. He enjoyed the familiar smells of the woods, knowing much more about the comings and goings of the animals here than I did. I had to go by sight. His nose told him volumes.

We hiked quickly if clumsily down the trail, stopping at the creek when my hand got tired of carrying the lantern. I thought of tying the lantern to my pack, but that would put more weight on my shoulders. The first two miles went in spurts; quick hiking, short rests. When the turn off to the hideout came up I was tempted to ditch the lantern and come back for it the next day, but that would mean setting up camp without light. Shoot. Okay, I'd press on. Next winter I planned to leave the lantern at camp rather than packing it out and back in again. Nobody would know it was in the hideout anyway.

I picked my way up the canyon, taking Shadow's route that didn't require rock climbing. If I wanted to, I could rock climb tomorrow. Rock climbing with the lantern held no appeal. It would be awkward and dangerous, and I couldn't chance a fall.

The canyon was still green from the winter rains. The creek was flowing swiftly. I hiked with my eyes on the landscape before me, keeping an eye out for animals. I hadn't stalked the deer in a long time and looked forward to spending some time at the clearing. Unfortunately, I was thinking of stalking when I should have been thinking about tracking. I was over a mile up the canyon when I noticed footprints. Footprints in my canyon. Of course, I knew it wasn't *my* canyon any more than it was anybody else's, but I still felt possessive about my home in the woods. I thought only a few people knew about it, only people I trusted. I examined the tracks. Men. Men with very old, worn out shoes. Not hiking boots. The tracks were a few days old and that made me wary. I remembered the yellow van. Surely the people who came in that van hadn't headed for my canyon. Why would anybody do that? Hikers usually came up the trail and stayed on the trail. Off trail hiking was rare in these mountains and usually resulted in lost people that I had to go in and find later. I felt the 9mm on my side. I'd learned to hike armed after several brushes with trouble up here, all of them man made threats. I wasn't concerned about wildlife. Wildlife was predictable and would hide before attacking. Men and their citified pets were another story, so I hiked armed.

I tracked my way up the canyon and discovered three sets of tracks of differing patterns and ages. The tracks went up and down the canyon, telling me people had been coming and going.

I was starting to wish that I hadn't brought Shadow. If I needed to stay out of sight it would be easier to do by myself. Shadow's bold black and white coat stood out in the predominately green and brown landscape.

The further I followed the tracks the more dejected I became. Would I even be able to stay up here? I wouldn't stay overnight if there were others in the canyon. I followed the tracks right up to my camp, but the tracks kept going and my camp seemed to be fine. Only the footprints in and around camp appeared odd to me. The hideout remained well hidden as always. No footprints went up to the entryway. I looked carefully at the trees and brush around camp and examined the canyon walls, looking for any signs of life.

I found the flap of the hideout buried under months of forest debris. After lifting it I slid my pack in and then followed it, dragging the lantern behind me. I lit the lantern and arranged the camping gear I'd brought. I restocked the ammo box with backpacker food, then put the sleeping bag in a protective trash bag, stashing it in a corner. After unpacking the books, a collapsible water jug, and my little one burner camp stove, I was all set up again. My home away from home. My home away from home that had seen some unwanted visitors.

It occurred to me that Kelly could have come up here, but I didn't think so. I had seen enough of Kelly's tracks that I would have recognized them up here. If Kelly had used the hideout he wouldn't have worn shoes like the ones that made the tracks outside. He would have worn hiking boots or ranger boots, so I didn't believe it was him. I began working through my options. With Shadow along my options were limited. I made sure to carry all my survival gear on my person: the 9mm, just for emergencies, my hunting knife, and a magnesium stick for starting fires. I stuck my cell phone in a pocket by itself. With these essentials I could live up here no matter what happened at camp. I could hike to a place where the phone would work if needed and could live off the land if necessary.

I fed Shadow before venturing out, then I found a set of tracks and followed them up the canyon. When they went a mile past the hideout I decided they were harmless. While in the area I checked the meadow at the top of the canyon for deer and looked over the place where the dog had attacked me the year before. There was no sign of dog or deer. I hoped to find deer at the lower meadow tomorrow. I then followed the footprints back down the canyon to camp.

After examining the footprints around camp I came to the conclusion that someone knew about the hideout. They didn't know the exact location but they had looked for it. Only a few people knew about the hideout: Rusty and Kelly knew where it was, and Cody only knew that it existed. I crossed all three men off the list and was left with one more. Trent. Trent knew the hideout was somewhere near the camp and he knew the landmark. He also knew who came and went from it. And he was very dangerous. Trent Senior fit the circumstances perfectly except for the fact that he was now serving time behind bars. None of these footprints belonged to Trent.

Thinking furiously, I continued to track. I wanted this solved in my mind before nightfall and had to decide whether or not to stay. I wished Chase would suddenly appear. Maybe he could help me puzzle this out, not that I needed help. What I needed was his bad attitude and his quick reaction to trouble. The tracking I could handle. I circled the camp looking for fresh footprints leading away from it. After picking up a trail, I followed it down canyon. It led me downhill and then deviated to the side of the canyon and up a small cleft in the canyon wall that I hadn't discovered yet. It led up out of the canyon, through the woods, and back down another small cleft. A worn trail led down and down some more until I realized it was leading me to Trent's cave. Alarmed, I leaped off the trail and hid in the bushes. I needed to think. If the trail was leading me to Trent's cave, who would be staying there? Who could possibly know it was there? Either Trent or someone he trusted. Anybody Trent trusted was no friend of mine. Possibly the location of the cave had been passed along to other criminals who needed to drop out of sight for a while. I didn't like this. I didn't like it one bit. This was dangerous ground I was tracking. But I was curious. If the cave was being used, what was in there? Was it being used *now*? Or was this a sporadic thing? The footprints I found had been a few days old. But then what about the yellow van? Where were those people? I have *got* to be more careful, I told myself. Had I examined the ground around the yellow van before taking off, I would have recognized those footprints up here. Round and around I went.

I wouldn't be able to hide my tracks if I ventured into the cave. I'd been there before and knew there was too much open sand. I crept out of hiding and carefully examined the tracks, trying to determine the age of them and get a feel for the people I might be dealing with up here. I put the tracks at two days old, but that didn't convince me that the cave was safe. Nope, I wasn't going to venture there, but I was convinced I'd be safe at the hideout for the night.

I went back down to camp and circled it again, finding two trails leading out of it. There was one more somewhere. There were multiple sets of tracks going up and down the canyon. The freshest of them went down canyon towards the trail. I was worried about counting that as the third set. What if I was wrong? It appeared as though the camping spot had been thoroughly investigated, but it was also devoid of other people and so far the hideout remained undiscovered.

Not wanting to draw attention to the camp, I cooked dinner and went to bed early. I lay in my sleeping bag, stewing over the events of the day. I had planned to stalk deer tomorrow but something told me the canyon was not entirely safe. I decided to hike out in the morning and tell Rusty about my findings. Then, if he thought it was worth the trouble, he could bring a team up to investigate the cave. It bothered me that just having the cave in close proximity to my camp might make it unsafe for an indefinite length of time. If Trent had disclosed the location of the cave to other criminals, half the crooks in southern California could shelter there whenever they wanted. If that were the case, the hideout would never be safe. There would always be a fresh crop of criminals to pass the word along to.

I fell asleep with my mind drifting in uneasy circles. Tossing and turning, I awoke often, listening for noises outside the hideout. In the morning I was disappointed to find that my chipmunk friend was no longer living in my roof. I knew chipmunks didn't live long in the woods and it may have been dinner for a hungry hawk or owl. For some reason, though, I thought it had more to do with human activity than anything else. Before leaving the hideout I checked for my gun, knife, magnesium stick, and cell phone safely hidden away on my person. I packed trail mix, and water, then headed down the canyon. This time I kept a careful eye on the ground and weaved back and forth across the main part of the canyon floor where hiking was easier. Should I run across a fresh trail, it would be where the walking was easier. Criminals didn't come up here to rock climb, stalk deer, or hand feed chipmunks. They came here with serious issues on their minds. Reaching the clearing where the deer usually stopped to graze, I was disappointed to find all the deer gone. No chipmunk, no deer. This did not bode well for the future of my canyon.

I took my time hiking out. I wanted to learn what I could on the way, so I studied the ground as I went along. There were lots of old, worn out footprints going in and out when I reached the main trail, but very few that would have been left by tourists. Tourists out for a day hike wore tennis shoes or hiking boots. These footprints were old boots, old work shoes, worn by men who felt older than they were.

Once reaching it, I kept to the side of the main trail. For the most part I thought the men up in the canyon were just hiding out. However, they must have been told something or they wouldn't have been exploring my camp. If they had been told about my camp, it would be safer to assume they also knew about me.

I walked all four miles down the canyon, then down the trail, and with a sigh of relief set my pack inside the Jeep. An eerie stillness engulfed the campground making it feel threatening. I felt eyes watching me and froze, looking around. Nothing seemed out of place until my gaze settled on the yellow van still parked in the trailhead parking lot. Two sets of tired eyes stared back at me. The two men were looking, talking quietly, and pointing at me.

Chapter 12

Shadow leapt into the passenger's seat and I closed the door, then rushed around to get in the driver's side. It was locked, and I'd stuck my keys in my pocket. I was fumbling around for the keys when a large man came up behind me. I spun around drawing my gun, but a kick sent it flying before I had a good grip on it. Large hands closed around my arms and lifted me off the ground. I squirmed, kicking and making a pain of myself. Shadow barked frantically.

"Very handy," the smaller man smirked as he picked the gun up.

I dug my feet in when the big man dragged me to the van. When they tried to stuff me in their vehicle I braced my feet against the door.

"Damn it!" I yelled. "What do you people want with me?"

"Just hold still!" the big one bellowed as he wrestled me into the van. He placed a knee in the small of my back, then tied my hands together. I gritted my teeth against the pain in my ribs.

"The least you can do is tell me why you are doing this."

The smaller man answered, "We were just told to bring you in alive. So you better stay that way for a short while."

I kicked out at my captor, catching him in the chin. I was sorry I hadn't worn hiking boots. He was trying to get both of my feet together so he could tie them up. I tried kicking out with both feet to send him tumbling out the back of the van, but he was so big I just ended up pushing myself further into the vehicle.

"Would ... you ... just... hold... still!" he said, anger growing.

The younger, smaller man handed the larger one the gun. He pointed it at me.

"The other end, stupid. We're supposed to bring her to Troy alive, remember?"

He turned the gun around and brought it down with a solid blow to the back of my head.

I felt the van moving. How long had I been out? How far from the trailhead were we? I opened my eyes but only saw dirty white. There was a pillowcase tied over my head. No blood stains on it. I was glad of that. My hands and feet were tied. My arm was asleep from being laid on so long. I guessed that meant we were a half hour or more from the trail. In a moving van we could be fifty miles away already. I started thinking. Rusty wouldn't worry about me until tomorrow night. Then Friday morning he'd hike to the hideout. No, I corrected myself. He would check the Jeep and see Shadow inside. He'd see the gear was gone and know I'd made it in and back out. He'd know something happened after I got back to the Jeep, but he'd assume it happened on Thursday. I could be a long ways away by Thursday. Or I could be within a few miles. I didn't know where they were taking me. It felt like a long drive, though, and it felt like we were moving fast.

I thought about trying to call for help but I couldn't risk using the cell phone, that was if I still had it. Had the phone been seen they'd have taken it away. Same with my knife. I felt my leg under my baggy camping pants and was relieved to feel the hunting knife was still there. How had they missed feeling that in all the struggle? I was glad I had thought to hide everything as well as I could, although it also made it harder for me to use to get loose.

We had been on the road for a long time. It was hard to tell time but the jostling, bumping and turning seemed to go on forever. One thing bothered me and that was the lack of slowing down and turning. If we were on city streets there would be a lot of turns and stops. There wasn't. It was just go and go some more. When we arrived I'd be totally lost and at the mercy of my captors.

Finally I felt the van slow down. I heard the click, click of a turn signal. I felt bumps and jostling as the van pulled over somewhere. The van stopped and I heard both doors open and close. I waited, listening. I heard voices, a loud stereo, and short beeps like the sounds from an ATM. I got up on my knees and felt the back door of the van. I felt for the window and looked out, even though I couldn't see through the pillowcase. I was hoping a Good Samaritan might see me. A woman screamed. Okay, maybe someone had seen me. I shouldered the door knowing it wouldn't budge.

"There's some one tied up in that van!" the woman wailed.

The men took about ten seconds to stop the gas pump, stick the gas cap on, jump in and peel out of the gas station, throwing me against the back of the van. Well, I thought, that little plan worked. Would I see any results from it? Would I see anything at all besides the inside of a filthy pillowcase?

One of the men moved to the back of the van and pulled me around to face him. I thought it was strange for him to do that since we couldn't see each other. Psychologically, though, I could still feel the piercing stare come through the cloth.

"Cause more trouble like that and you might not make it to our destination," he said, backhanding me. My head snapped back. He shook me, angry. He shoved me back. My head hit the side of the van and I rolled around trying to find a stable position. He yanked me back up and sneered in my face. "No one says we have to bring you in at all. In fact it might be easier on you if we just kill you before we get there. We'd probably do a quicker, cleaner job of it than Troy. Troy isn't a nice guy and he already doesn't like you." He released me and I fell back, angry, frightened, and determined to get away. Then I heard noises that sounded like the guy climbing back into the passenger's seat. Troy? I never met a guy named Troy, but I didn't like what this was adding up to. The only person I could think of that knew about the hideout and didn't like me was Trent Senior. Trent had one son named Tyrone. He could very well have another one named Troy. This did not look good for me. What was it with this Trent family? Did they all have an agenda against me?

I brought my feet up close to my body, then pulled my hands over them so my arms were in front of my body. They'd probably be mad at me for doing it, but a girl's gotta do what a girl's gotta do, and I needed my hands if I was going to get out of the van. I worked at the rope that bound the pillowcase around my head. It wasn't tied tight, just secure enough so that I couldn't see. I pulled at the knot. Then I felt the van turn and immediately start climbing uphill, steadily uphill. This might be good news for me. Uphill meant trees and forest and a place to lose an enemy. The van then slowed like it was having trouble with the grade. Slow was good too. I worked frantically at the ropes binding my feet and finally pulled them free, then worked the pillowcase loose. I glanced out the window, but stayed lying down. I wanted them to think, for as long as possible, that I was still tied up. All I could see were trees, huge, tall trees.

Slow, uphill, tall trees, things were looking brighter to me. Next I studied the van door. A good pull would open it. A hop and I'd be out, albeit out going down the road at thirty miles an hour. If I was lucky, there would be a drop off on the downhill side of the van. It would be a risk, but one I didn't think my captors would be willing to take on themselves.

I waited for the van to get higher. The farther I tumbled down the hill, the less likely they would be to follow me. I couldn't wait too long, though. Wait too long and we'd top out or reach our destination. I silently got up and looked out the back window. Yes! I was ready to risk it. I would risk almost anything rather than face another Trent. There wasn't a window on the sliding door, only the back, so I wasn't sure exactly what I'd be jumping out to. Hitting the asphalt in moccasins at this speed was going to hurt, so I found myself wishing I had worn boots again. However, I was prepared for the impact, so maybe I could work with it. I crept up to the sliding door, counted silently to three and yanked it open. Not waiting to hear a reaction inside the van, I leapt out, rolling with the impact. I was right, it hurt. It hurt like hell, especially when my sore ribs met the road. When I finally stopped rolling and looked around, the van had stopped and the men were getting out. No time to think, I rolled to my feet, ignoring the pain, and glanced at the drop off. The mountain went on forever. I looked for my captors. They sprinted toward me, ready to make the grab. I took a few running steps then dove from the drop off, holding my bound hands over my head to protect my skull if I hit a tree on the way down.

I rolled and rolled. The mountain felt endless. I took out small trees, snapped branches, and still I was tumbling. I saw a rock outcropping. Oh, shit! Not rocks! I spread eagled as much as my bound hands would permit, trying to slow my descent, rolled over the rocks, and came to an abrupt halt. My bound hands felt as though they were going to be ripped right off my arms when the ropes caught on a rock. I was bound, hanging from a rock, a hundred feet over a raging river. I was feeling dizzy and sick, but there was no time to dwell on it. I couldn't move. My beaten body was in shock. I looked an impossibly long way up to the road. Had I really made it that far in one piece? No matter my situation, it was worth it to avoid meeting Troy, whoever he was. If the men saw me go over this rock there was no doubt they would believe that I was dead. If I saw somebody tumble down a mountainside and fall off a rock outcropping, I'd put their chances of survival at zero. Fortunately, I wasn't watching. I felt alive, that's for sure. Death should mean the end of pain and I sure felt plenty of that. I stuffed it aside. No use worrying about that if I couldn't do anything about it. Better to concentrate on something I could do something about and that was my predicament. My hands were killing me, but I was afraid to move before the men left. I peeked around the rock, exposing as little of myself as possible to the men above me. I saw two tiny heads turn and leave. I waited until they had a chance to get down the road, then checked once more to be sure. I grasped the rock with my hands and pulled myself up to the little ledge that had almost launched me off the mountain to my doom.

Okay, Cass, you made it. You survived. Now it's time to get out of here.

I looked around. These woods were foreign to me. They were much older and greener than the woods I had just left. The mountains were different, too. And now I was lost. Not totally lost, but lost nonetheless. I wasn't worried, though. There was a road close by, and a river below me. We had turned off a major road and onto this smaller one. That was maybe fifteen minutes ago. Fifteen minutes at thirty miles an hour meant the main road was seven or eight miles away. I could walk that. I thought about climbing up to the road but rejected the idea. I'd rather deal with anything else in the woods than chance running into the yellow van again. I wasn't worried about the woods, so that option easily won out.

Still sitting on the ledge, I set my priorities. First, I needed to untie my hands, and then I could climb down to the river and follow it to the main road.

I pulled up my pants leg until I reached the knife strapped to my leg. I'd be forever grateful to the guy at the knife shop who had talked me into an extra heavy-duty sheath for it. If I had bought a lightweight one my leg would have been cut to ribbons in the tumble. I unsnapped the strap and pulled the knife out. I sawed through the ropes. It took work and patience but the cords finally parted and I was free. I kept the small pieces of rope in case they were needed for making a snare.

Next I tried my cell phone. Nothing. No surprise there. Okay, Cass, you are hereby in survival mode. You have your knife. You have your magnesium stick. I felt for it; yup it was there. You have your useless cell phone. You have a river. You ought to be in good shape. Time to analyze the situation. I was stuck on a rock. I didn't want to go up, so that meant climbing down. Down was a long way. I examined the rocks and found them to be sturdy. I didn't want a hand hold to come loose a hundred feet over the river. I looked over the ledge. After about twenty feet of rock there was a steep mountainside sloping down to the river. I could hold onto brush on my way down. I could make it, I decided, but there was only one way to find out.

I eased myself over the lip of the ledge and found footholds. I examined the rock and found handholds. I was glad Rusty couldn't see me. I pictured him at work, safe in his office, or at home. I never pictured him in a standoff somewhere or in a shootout. I always pictured him somewhere safe in spite of his dangerous job. Now, here I was hanging off a rock on some unknown mountain looking for a way back to him. And back meant down, for now. Down I climbed, carefully and ever so slowly, until I met dirt. The dirt slid under foot and at first I thought I was in for another tumble but the sliding stopped and I was able to grab a bush and turn myself around. I scooted down the mountain, careful of my speed, keeping to the brush so I could grab something if I slid.

I watched the river get closer and closer until finally my feet met rock again and I could stand. Yes! I'd made it!

I looked at the sky and saw that I didn't have much daylight left. A four mile hike and riding in the van for several hours had used up the day. I wished I knew where I was. I made my way to the river. It was one very rough river. Rocks bordered each side and the water rushed by with a deafening roar. I hoped I could find a spot to sleep that was well away from the noise of the water. Following the river downstream, I realized that the water was leaving me less and less room between the hillside and the rushing torrent. Soon I would have to cross over or go back upstream. The water seemed icy cold and the river was so fierce I was sure it had claimed a life or two. I'd come close enough to drowning that I wanted to avoid that feeling at all cost.

Just then a white water raft appeared on the river above me. It floated quickly down to me and the people inside were staring, obviously alarmed. I made a move to cross, but the river guide in the front of the raft was glaring at me with a frantic "No! No!" written across his face. I heeded his warning. If it was swift and deep enough for rafts I didn't want to try and ford it. I started back uphill knowing that the rafts had to have started from somewhere.

I walked uphill, ever uphill, climbing over rocks and boulders, getting hungrier by the minute. There wasn't any sign of another raft, a raft landing, a ranger, or even a camper. When the light started to fade I headed away from the water, trying to find a quieter place to curl up for the night. The sound of rushing, tumbling water echoed off the boulders everywhere I went, and finally I gave up my quest for a peaceful night. I found a place where I could lie down out of sight and made a bed of leaves under some brush. I lay in the woods, totally alone, longing for Rusty. I wondered what he was doing and knew he expected me home tomorrow. I hoped to be there. There were no guarantees of that, though, and then what? I had to find a way to contact Rusty before I was due home. I didn't want him to worry.

Who was I kidding? I had no way to contact him and not worry him. Hello dear, I'm going to be late getting home. I was kidnapped and fell down a mountain and spent a day lost in mountains I've never seen before, but don't worry. Yeah, right.

What had happened to Shadow? Was he still trapped in the Jeep? Questions. I had too many questions and no answers.

The night was cold, and I didn't sleep well. As the darkness closed in the chill seemed to seep all the way to my bones. I curled up tightly to conserve my heat. Morning dawned late because of the big mountain to the east and it was still cold. I got up and continued my climb upstream, hoping the activity would warm me up. By midmorning I was getting shaky from hunger and exhaustion. I began watching for edible plants, but these were different mountains than I was used to. I considered building a trap to catch fish but didn't want to do it. In the time needed to make the trap I could find civilization. I kept an eye out for Jerusalem artichoke and dandelions. Both were usually easy to find in most of the United States and had kept me from starving before. Flowers and rabbits were the staple of survival but I didn't want to take the time to catch a rabbit either. When I found a dandelion I ate the younger leaves from the top of the plant. When I found a Jerusalem artichoke I pulled it and ate the tubers. I didn't worry about the taste or the dirt. In survival you can't be too picky.

In the afternoon, while making my way from rock to rock, I spotted a large gopher snake. It was slithering amongst the rocks looking for small animals. I stalked it quietly, then caught it with my bare hands. I dragged it away from the water's edge and cut off its head, then gathered twigs, small dead branches and pine needles to build a bed for a tiny fire. I shaved off some magnesium filings and struck the steel with my knife. When the fire was going I fed it more dead sticks and quickly skinned the snake. I roasted it over the flame, one small section at a time, until the meat was cooked. The cooking tried my patience. It was taking up a good portion of the day and I still needed to find a way to contact home. Finally I deemed the snake done and ate as much as I could, knowing there might be a very long wait until my next meal. After I'd eaten I took a few extra minutes to scrape the snakeskin clean then rolled it up and put it in my pocket. A souvenir from an unplanned trip. Maybe I'd sew it on as trim next time I made a pair of moccasins. The pair I had on was quickly wearing out on all these rough rocks. I put out my fire completely and erased as much sign of my meal as I could, then took off again.

Upwards and onwards I hiked and climbed. The river felt never-ending. It was late Thursday afternoon when I finally heard voices. Kids playing by the river. Where there were kids there should be adults close by.

"Where's the campground?" I yelled across the river.

They pointed up stream and behind them.

"Is there a bridge?" I yelled.

"No," they yelled back. I looked at the river. If kids were playing here maybe it was fordable. I took the cell phone out of my pocket and held it out of the water. The kids all watched in surprise as I waded across. The water *was* cold. Icy cold. The water became knee deep, then waist deep and still I waded. The rocks were slippery and my moccasins didn't help. I almost lost my footing but caught myself in time. I felt my way across, finally landing on the other side. I sat exhausted, dripping wet, freezing, with the kids looking on in wonder.

A mom ran over, angry with me. "I have been telling those kids all day to stay out of the water and then what do you do? You wade right through it. How am I supposed to keep the kids out of the river when you show them it's easy?"

"It isn't easy," I said, "I was desperate. I've been following that river for a day looking for a place to cross but it was too dangerous. I need to find a ranger or a policeman. Do you know where can I find a ranger station or a police station?"

The mom looked at me in disbelief.

"I need to get to a station. Can you at least point the way?"

She brought me to their camp and then her husband took me to a little store near the campground. They called the local police and I drooled over chips, candy bars, fish bait, and bottles of soft drinks while I waited.

The squad car pulled up and an officer got out.

"Can you just take me to the station? I have a report to file and a phone call to make."

He looked at me like I was nuts.

"Look," I said impatiently, "I'm from out of town. I got kidnapped and escaped yesterday and I've been looking for civilization ever since. I need to call the Joshua Hills Police station and let them know I'm okay. These guys stole my gun so they are armed. Can you, please, just take me to the station?"

It was a half hour drive to the nearest police station. They had never heard of Joshua Hills but my cell phone worked from there so I was in business. I hit the speed dial on my phone and within a ring Rusty was on the line.

"Cass, what happened?"

"What do you mean, what happened? I'm not due home until tonight."

"You know what I mean. Something happened. Kelly was sent out to check on a report. Some lady was worried about a dog locked in a car in the hot sun. Kelly recognized your Jeep and Shadow so he called me. We've been in a panic since yesterday."

"It's a long story. Call off the search. They aren't going to find me. Hold on, let me find out where I am."

I asked a passerby what city I was in. Visalia.

"I'm in Visalia."

"How'd you get there?"

"I don't want to talk about it over the phone. Don't let anybody go to the hideout. Warn Kelly. I need to talk to you when I get home."

"Too late. Kelly and Chase went in to the hideout this morning. Chase told me right away that you weren't up there but he wanted to track you in to get the full story. He came out with a lot of information but nothing that would help us find you."

"Can you pick me up from the ranch? It's only two or three hours away from here. I'll call there for a ride."

"Are you okay?"

I paused. I wasn't sure. "Yeah, I'm okay. I'm bruised and starved but I'm okay."

"Cass…"

"I'm okay. But I miss you…I really miss you."

"I'll come right now," he said urgently.

"I know you would, but I need something to eat, and the ranch is closer. I'll call there. I wanted to let you know I was okay."

Chapter 13

"Hello, Mom?"

"Cassidy! It's so good to hear from you!"

"Thanks, can you do me a favor?"

"Of course, Honey? What is it?"

"Can you send someone to the Visalia Police station? I need a lift home."

Silence on the other end.

"Mom, I'm not in trouble. I just got stranded here and I need a place to spend the night. Rusty will be up to get me in the morning."

"Of course, dear. I'll send someone right away."

While waiting for my ride I filled out a report on the kidnapping. I described the two men and their van, writing everything that had happened in detail. I reported the stolen gun. The officer read my report, noticing the block letters and vocabulary.

"You've done this before."

"Yup, you get lots of practice at these things when you're a trouble magnet. Plus, I've filled them out from your point of view, too. I work search and rescue. Do you have a sketch artist handy? I can provide a pretty clear description of the men and the van is very recognizable."

"Are you sure you don't need to get checked out by a doctor?"

"I'll be fine as soon as I get a real meal and a real bed to sleep in. I'm expecting a ride in an hour or two."

He led me to a room where an officer brought up a computer program. We started out identifying the larger man by height and weight and changed the physical features on the screen until he appeared close to how I remembered him. The procedure was then repeated for the second man.

They had a similar program for vehicles so we began by identifying the van by model and year, then added features such as the odd yellow color, the distinctive brown stripes, and the placement of windows. I sat back when we were finished, hoping I never saw that vehicle again.

With all the reports filed and the descriptions complete, they allowed me to leave, so I went to the lobby to wait for my ride. I was hoping Mom would send Steve. He understood these things and there would be no long storytelling with him. If it was Randy who came I'd have no peace tonight. It seemed a little odd, though, that I wasn't even expecting Mom or Dad. When my ride walked into the police station my wish had come true and it was

Steve who swaggered in to collect his little misplaced charge. He was ready to tease me about getting picked up from the police station but changed once he saw me; then his smile turned to concern.

"It's okay. I'll be fine. I just need a meal and a place to crash."

"Looks like you already crashed," he said.

It was a long drive to the ranch. I tried to find a position that didn't cause something to hurt but it was impossible. Cuts stung. Bruises ached. The bump on my head was tender.

It was well after dark when we got to the ranch. As I walked into the kitchen, Martha was washing the dinner dishes. Her days were long and busy and she hadn't been expecting me. She became alarmed when she saw me so I gave her a hug. Then I scrounged some leftovers and microwaved them on a paper plate so Martha wouldn't have more dishes to wash. She finished the dishes and ran off to talk to my mom. Later she settled next to me at the table and we talked while I ate. When Mom came in, she took in my torn clothes and shook her head.

"Cassidy, when will you learn?" she asked with dismay.

I went to my old bedroom, stripped and then showered. After climbing into bed I tried sleeping but I was still in survival mode. Having nothing else to wear, I put on my dirty, torn clothes and brought my blanket to the barn to sleep in the hay. You'd think after the van and the woods I'd want a soft bed, but it just didn't feel right.

In the morning I visited with my mom and dad. My sister, Jesse, came over to join us for breakfast and to catch up on the news. She confirmed that she had bought her bridesmaids dress, but informed me that I needed two more ushers for the wedding. The ranch couldn't afford for all the hands to take off at the same time. So ushers were added to my long to-do list again. My mind wasn't ready to take on wedding plans yet. I didn't want to clutter it back up this soon. When you find yourself in a survival situation, bridesmaids' dresses and wedding ushers kind of get pushed from your mind. I was tuned to one sound. When I heard that sound I knew everything would be okay again. I thought I'd have a long wait, but it was still early when I heard tires crunch on the gravel outside. I looked out the window and there it was! The Explorer! I was whole again. Rusty was here and I was whole again. I could breathe again. I opened the door and flew down the steps into his outstretched arms. Mom, Dad and Jesse filled the doorway, looking on, but I didn't care. Chase and Cody got out of the Explorer. I couldn't let go. I just couldn't. He wrapped me in comfort. The only comfort in the world that I needed and it was right here. I felt his chin on the top of my head, felt his arms wrapped around me. A hand strayed to my head and he noticed the knot on the back of it. I felt a shift in his feelings.

"Oh, babe, it's okay. It's all okay again. Come on, look at me."

I looked up into his eyes. I saw smiling eyes lined with worry.

I heard the gravel crunch again and James pulled up to the house. Patrick and Wyatt jumped out of the pickup truck. Patrick gave me a high five.

"Aunt Castidy," Patrick said, "are you going to tell us more stories?"

"Sorry, sport, I have to go home today. But here, I have a souvenir that will make your mom scream. Do you want it?"

"Cool!"

I took the snakeskin out of my pocket and unrolled it.

"Maybe your dad can make it into a hat band for you. I had to kill it for lunch when I was stuck out in the woods. Have you tagged your first rabbit yet?"

"Almost! I tagged the dogs, though!"

"In your boots?"

"Naw, I can't sneak good in boots yet. Mom got me some moccasins."

"All right, that's what I like to stalk in, too."

"Cassidy, how could you do that?" Jesse asked.

"Do what? Give Patrick the snakeskin? It'll make a good hatband for a little kid. You know how he likes my stories. He'll get a kick out of telling Ricky that his aunt eats snakes in the woods."

"Ewe! You really ate that thing? And to think I meant how could you carry that awful thing around in your pocket all this time!"

"When you get hungry you aren't as picky about what you eat. I was going to save the snakeskin and use it in my next pair of moccasins. But Patrick can have it. And you might as well get used the idea of finding weird things in his pockets. This kid will bring home worse. Just give him time."

"This is an interesting little family," Chase said.

"Chase, I'm probably the strangest one of the bunch. All the rest are pretty normal. Except Patrick. We're still wondering about him. This is my dad, mom, sister, Jesse, and brother-in-law, James. The two kids are my nephews, Patrick and Wyatt. Everybody, this is Cody. He's Rusty's little brother. And Chase Downing, my tracking teacher at reserve academy. What are you doing here anyway?"

"Rusty called me to figure out what happened to you when you went missing. From what I saw in the canyon, I didn't teach you a thing at academy. You followed the right trails. You came to the right conclusions. You showed a lot of wisdom and skill. You were right to get out of there when you did. And it's a cool little camp you've got there. Now I want the rest of the story. I told Rusty you'd been taken. All I could tell was the vehicle was old and it had been parked there a long time and was used by many different people. I could tell you'd put up quite a fight but you didn't have much of a chance. One guy was big, over six feet tall, nearly three hundred pounds, and the other guy was smaller and didn't get involved much."

"Guys, it's a very long story and I don't want to tell it all here. You and Rusty need a totally different version than my family does."

"Then tell us our version!" Patrick said enthusiastically. "How did you catch the snake? Did you shoot it?"

"No, my gun got stolen. I just followed it until I could pick it up and then I chopped off its head with my hunting knife."

"Cool! You picked up a live snake? What did it taste like?"

"Gopher snake."

Jesse cringed at the thought of picking up any snake, much less eating it.

"What if it bit you?"

"It was harmless. I wouldn't have caught a poisonous one."

"How'd you get up in the mountains?" This kid was all questions, another thing that made him more like me.

"I was kidnapped and the kidnappers were taking me somewhere. I got away, and when I escaped I was way up in the mountains." There, that ought to do for the family version.

After giving the guys a tour of the ranch, I had Steve saddle Shasta and then talked them through the basic riding commands before letting them ride. Zack and Randy came out to see what was going on.

"Hey, Trouble!" they greeted me. "Frank! Get out here! Trouble's home!"

Frank came hobbling out of the office. I'd called him Old Frank ever since I'd been a kid. Every time I saw Old Frank he seemed older. They all gathered around me and there were hugs and handshakes all around. I braced myself with each one.

"He just calls me Trouble because he wins so many bets from my little ranch disasters," I explained.

"Sounds like an appropriate name to me," said Cody.

"No," said Old Frank, "we call you Trouble because you've gotten into trouble as long as we've known you. Shootin' coyotes when you were six. Trying to drive the tractor when you were seven. Riding green broke horses before they are trained. Trackin' and stalkin' and ridin'. I think you got into trouble every which way was possible."

"Nope," said Rusty, "she's still finding new ways to do it."

"So," said Chase, "this is where trackers are born? This is where you grew up?"

"This is it. Ride out the back of the ranch and you'll see why. There are miles and miles of hills full of critters back there, and there were more when I was a kid. I'd get on this horse and ride until I found tracks, and then track the animal. When I found it, I'd stalk it. There's a clearing where I stalk deer. It was a great place to grow up. See all the dirt? I knew each ranch hand by their boot prints, each horse by the curve of its shoe, and each dog by its track. Do you want to go? Or should I unsaddle Shasta?"

"I'll be back in a few," Chase said and rode Shasta around the side of the barn and out the backside of the ranch. He was comfortable in the saddle and had obviously ridden many times before.

"Cass, have you ridden since you got here?" Rusty asked.

"No, I better not, but Shasta likes to be ridden so I thought the guys could give it a try."

"That's not like you. You always ride if you have a chance."

"I know. I would, but I don't think it's a good idea this time."

He stepped back and looked me over. I was still in the same filthy khaki hiking pants and t-shirt I was wearing when I left home. I was scratched and bruised. The tumble down the mountain had made my ribs start hurting again. The trees I hit on the way down hadn't stopped me from falling but they sure tried.

He fingered the bump on the back of my head.

"How'd you do this?" he asked softly.

"Rusty... don't ask unless you really want an answer, okay?"

Cody looked at us.

"I know I'm not going to like the answer, but I need to know."

"It'll go away soon. And I'll be fine."

"Cass..."

I tried to answer him but it stuck in my throat. Why did he always need to know the worst? Why couldn't he take me for what I was? Or at least what he thought I was? I didn't want to see that worried look one more time. I didn't want him to feel sorry for me. I was so tired of being a trouble magnet. I just wanted to be normal. Couldn't I just be normal? But then I remembered a time in the not so distant past when I needed to hear what Rusty had been through, not so he would be forced to talk about it, but so I could deal with the situation in my own way, so I gave in.

"They hit me with the butt of my gun. They knocked me out so they could tie me up." There, it was out.

He reached out to me, just a reflex action he always had when something touched his heart. It reminded me of someone jumping to the rescue, taking a bullet for somebody else. He wanted to pull that pain away from me. Take away that terrible memory.

"There are some more important things you need to know though. The police station in Visalia has a sketch on file. They've got a description of the men and the van. There's a list of possible plate numbers. We need to look up whether or not Trent Senior had another son named Troy. Did Kelly and Chase go to Trent's cave?"

"I don't know. I know Chase tracked you all over the canyon. I sent him in because I knew if you were in trouble I'd never be able to see your tracks. And I stayed where I could act on any leads he might give me. If Chase called on the radio, I wanted to be able to take off quickly and easily."

"I didn't go to the cave. I'd decided even the canyon was risky after reading all the tracks there."

"Chase was pretty impressed with your abilities. You read the signs right, you reacted right."

"Walked into trouble right... I was just getting out of there to avoid trouble, but they were watching for me. I was going to go to the station and tell you what I found so a team could go in and verify what I thought."

"And what was that?"

"That Trent had leaked the location of the cave to other criminals so they could use it to hide out too."

"That's exactly what it looked like," Chase said behind me.

"If he did that then my camp will never be safe again. People will keep passing the cave's location on, and I'll always run the risk of meeting a dangerous person up there. The hideout is... is gone. I can't go there again. That hurts worse than all the bumps and bruises. My canyon is gone. When I was there the deer were gone, the chipmunk was gone. The chipmunk that would eat out of my hand. The deer that would let me lay in their meadow and graze all around me. It was the first place I ever stalked a deer and touched it."

It was strange that criminals had destroyed my city house, and many thousands of dollars worth of possessions, and I had barely blinked an eye. Then they made a worthless tarp and a few camping supplies inaccessible and it left me heartbroken.

"Do you know where you were when you escaped?"

"No, although I might be able to make some guesses if I saw a road map and a topo map. I know it wasn't very far from Visalia. I was tied up in the back of the van and couldn't see anything until a few minutes before I got away. We had traveled for hours on highways and I remembered we had just turned off a main road and started going steeply uphill. We'd been going like that about fifteen minutes when I jumped out."

"Jumped out?"

"Yeah."

"Jumped out of what?"

"The van."

"Cass, you didn't… do you know what happens to people who jump out of moving vehicles?"

"Yes, I do. But I expected it. I bent my knees and rolled with the impact. And you're right; I don't recommend anybody try it. But that wasn't the worst of it. They stopped the van, and they were coming after me, so I jumped off the drop off."

"No…" It was just a reaction. A quick denial. A refusal to believe the picture in his head. It was unimaginable to him. It was beyond reason. Cody and Chase stared at me. Rusty couldn't. I shouldn't have told him that.

"Excuse us, guys," I said and led Rusty to the house and to my old bedroom where we could be alone. "Come on. Lay with me. Just hold me. Rusty, it's okay. Come on. Just be here with me."

He lay down and I snuggled in next to him, feeling hard emotional walls go up. He lay there, guarding his emotions, still trying to maintain the tough strong guy.

"I'm sorry," I said softly. "Rusty, I'm so sorry. I had to. I knew what I was facing and I couldn't face someone else like Trent. There was less risk this way."

"How far? Babe, how far did you fall?"

"It wasn't a cliff. There wasn't much falling involved. It was a steep slope and it was forever. But I'd sort of planned it that way. I needed it to be far enough that they wouldn't risk coming down after me. And they didn't. They probably assumed I hadn't made it. They probably told Troy that I was dead."

"And you could have been. Cass, one wrong move and you'd have died. I don't see how you made it. I can't imagine you surviving all that. While Chase was tracking you, you were way up here jumping out of moving vans… Do you know the forces involved in jumping out of a moving vehicle? You shouldn't have survived even that."

"Don't do the math, just see the reality. I'm here and talking to you. What you imagine is textbook stuff. It's what they told you in police academy."

"And to jump off the mountain… one rock or one large tree in the way and you would have died. All these cuts and bruises…"

"Are from small trees and brush. And the rock probably saved me. I left a pretty good trail. But I made it. Rusty, just remember, I made it in good enough shape to survive in the wilderness another day. I found food. I had water. I had everything I needed to get by."

"How far did you have to walk to find help?"

"I don't know. I tried going downstream first because I thought the main road was closer, but I couldn't follow the river without crossing it and it was way too swift to cross. So I had to turn around and try upstream. It was a rough climb, rougher than the canyon to the hideout. I spent an hour or two Wednesday and then most of Thursday following the river. But, Rusty? I was more worried about you than I was about me. I was doing okay. The woods are a friendly place to be. They provide for me when I need it. It's not the woods or the wilderness that hurt me. So, I wasn't worried about me. I was wondering what you were doing. I missed you. The mountains felt huge without you there." I talked and talked, letting him hear my voice, letting him feel me close, letting his worries relax.

There was a light knock on the door. I gently slid away to see who was there. It was Jesse.

"Cass, here. These are all clothes I've out grown. I thought you might be able to find something to wear home."

I opened the bag. "Are you sure? You don't want these anymore?"

"I can't wear them."

"Thanks, I'll feel a lot better in clean clothes."

I closed the door and brought the bag into the room with me, then sat back down on the bed.

"Jesse gave me some hand me downs, so I'm going to shower and change clothes. Is that okay?"

"Can I watch?" he asked playfully.

I didn't answer, just leaned down to kiss him, knowing he'd watch. We were nearly married and had been living together for some time.

I slipped out of my dirty clothes and was heading for the shower when he stopped me. His look went from playful to guarded in an instant. I had big bruises on my knees from the impact of jumping out of the van. Then more bruises across my back from the roll across the asphalt and little cuts from my neck to my ankles from the tumble to the river. He took my hands and fingered the rope burns around my wrists.

"It'll all heal," I reminded him. "In a few weeks they'll be gone. My only complaint is that my ribs hurt again. That's why I didn't ride. The motion would hurt, and a fall would lay me up again."

I showered and put on the fresh clothes, going commando instead of wearing the three day old underwear I took off. Most of the jeans in the bag were too big for me. I found a pair that came close, probably from Jesse's high school days. And I found a low cut top that Rusty would probably like. There were even old socks in the bag.

"Is it okay if I wear this in front of the guys?" I asked Rusty.

"Sure, why?"

"If you need to ask, I don't need to worry about it. Okay, I feel better.

How are you?"

"Come here," he said. I sat down on the bed and he drew me down, wrapped me in that familiar worried hug, and just soaked up some peace. After a while we heard the dinner bell and he sighed, "I guess we better go join the real world again, and see what trouble Cody got into with Shasta."

"I hope he didn't get into trouble with Jesse."

I poked my head in the dining room on our way out to retrieve Cody and Chase.

"I'll be back in a minute. I need to put Shasta away."

I found Chase still in the saddle. Cody and Jesse stood talking along the fence.

"See?" I said to Rusty. "Hey guys, that bell meant lunch is ready. We need to wash up and go up to the house."

I took Shasta's bridle and led him to the barn. The girth strap gave me trouble. It was hard to pull up enough to undo it. Each yank hurt my ribs. Rusty looked on, taking mental notes, and stepped in. He pulled up and released it easily. I started to pull off the saddle and blanket but he stopped me.

"How did you saddle him up if you're this sore?" he asked, hauling down the heavy western saddle.

"Steve did it for me."

I tried pulling Shasta's head down so I could slip off the bridle.

"How do you do it?"

"Just pull the straps over his ears and then it slides off easily."

I took the bridle from him and hung it in the tack room. I closed the stall door and we headed for the house.

"So, Cody, are you ready to trade your surfboard in for a horse?" I asked.

"No thanks, life is too quiet here," he answered.

"Yeah, and you'd develop a farmer's tan."

He shuddered. "Give me the beach anytime."

"Chase, did you find any interesting tracks in the hills?"

"Coyotes, foxes, deer, horses. It was good to ride again. You have a nice horse."

"Thanks. I chose him from a ranch up north when he was young. I named him Shasta because he grew up in the shadow of Mount Shasta and I liked the fact that the name could be spoken quietly if I was stalking. He took me on many tracking trips into those hills. I'm glad you got to go there too."

"Who trained him?"

"I started his training when I was a teenager. When I went into the Marines, Randy took over. I'm better at gentling horses than I am at training them. So I saddle broke him. Randy is very good at fine tuning, working out problems. Last I heard he was getting Shasta used to gun fire. I don't know how that little project is going."

"Gun fire? When would he ever hear gunfire around here? It's so peaceful."

"Last year. He dragged me down the road after a shot scared him. I bet Randy rode Shasta when he went deer hunting last fall. He should be fine now."

The dining room was busy with hungry cowboys when we walked in and took our seats.

"Aunt Castidy, tell us the story of the coyotes!" Patrick yelled across the table.

"What coyotes?"

"I told him about the time you shot the coyote because it was after my lamb," Jesse said. "I meant it as a lesson on why little kids can't have BB guns but he took it wrong. He thinks if you could do it he should too."

"Then I think Grandpa should tell you the story about the coyotes. He sure told me!"

Patrick turned to my dad. I smiled, thinking this should be interesting. Big Wayne Gordon looked around the table uncomfortably. He started out slow with his western drawl. He didn't really have an accent, but he adopted one for storytelling and I thought it was funny.

"Waaay back in the dark ages when Cassidy was your age, I gave her a BB gun. It was the first gun she ever had, and it made her feel all growed up," he drawled. "Now you know how much of a tracker she is. Even when she was six she knew a coyote's track from a dog's track, and she knew this ranch inside and out. She knew the comin's and goin's of everybody, and knew when things were running right and smooth, and when things were off in some way. Weeell, one summer things seemed off in some way to Cassidy. Every morning she saw fresh coyote tracks at the back of the barn, and every evenin' I'd find her staked out in the loft, waitin' for the coyotes to show their faces. And every night I made her go to bed before the coyotes showed up. One night she got tired of being sent to bed, so she waited until everybody had gone to sleep and then she did something you should never do."

"What?" asked Patrick. He wanted to know what this forbidden activity was, so he could watch for a chance to do it.

"She snuck out. She took her BB gun down to the barn and stalked around the side of it and laid in wait for those coyotes and when they finally came…"

"Yeah, what?"

"She shot one of them, BAM! She was a good shot even then and it scared the coyotes so bad they hightailed it for the hills. She was lucky they didn't turn on her. Nobody was there. Nobody could have helped her if they had."

"What happened to the one she shot?" Patrick asked.

"A BB gun won't take down a coyote. The poor critter hightailed it into the hills and probably has a BB gun pellet in his shoulder to this day. Cassidy got in big trouble for doing that, just like you would get in big trouble if you ever used a firearm in any irresponsible way."

"What did you do to her?" Patrick asked, wanting to know what terrible thing would happen to him.

"Well, first off, she got the lecture of her young life. Then I taught her how to clean guns. I made her clean guns until she was doin' it right. Even at six she was good at cleaning guns, and when she was eight I started her on a twenty-two, and now she's an expert with a 9mm. But you give her any gun, you name it and she uses it carefully, accurately, and responsibly. And you won't get to use a gun, even a BB gun, until you display the same responsible behavior."

Patrick's eyes got real big. What Wayne Gordon said had made an impression, and Patrick realized he'd have to shape up to get a BB gun.

"Tell me how to stalk a deer!" Patrick said. Everybody at the table rolled their eyes. They were tired of hearing how to stalk deer and I didn't blame them.

"When you tag your first rabbit, I'll take you out stalking deer. And I'll teach you all the right moves. If you can tag a rabbit, you'll be ready to try deer."

"The rabbits always leave the yard, and I'm not allowed to leave the yard."

"Maybe you need to learn to be both quick *and* sneaky. Or do it while your mom or dad is outside so they know where you are. If they see you are stalking, they will let you finish your stalk because it is good for developing observation and coordination, and your mom and dad know that's good for you."

"Gee, thanks, Cassidy," Jesse said.

"Martha, the lunch is wonderful," I said, "I'm glad to eat real food again."

"What did you eat after you escaped from the kidnappers?" she asked.

"Dandelions and Jerusalem artichoke, it's like a sunflower. It grows from a tuber and the tubers are edible."

"And snake," Patrick added. "Martha, can you cook snake for us some day?"

"If you catch enough snakes to feed everybody, I'll cook them," Martha promised.

"Martha! No, she will NOT cook snake for us. I forbid it!" Jesse shrieked. "And you will NOT go catching snakes. You don't know one from another, and you could get bit," she said to Patrick.

"What if I learned how to tell them apart? Then could I catch them? When I learn to read I'm going to study snakes, and I'll know which ones are good and which ones are bad."

"That's a good idea Patrick," I said, "work on your reading. When you get good at that I'll buy you some books that tell about outdoor survival."

Chapter 14

After lunch it was time for us to go home. My mom went on and on about how we visit so seldom, and I reminded her that we would all be together for the wedding.

"Chase, do you remember the way?" asked Rusty.

"Yeah, why?"

He tossed Chase the keys and got in the back seat. I threw the bag of clothes in the back and got in, too. Chase drove. Cody rode shotgun.

"Interesting family," Chase observed once we were on the road.

"Yeah, they are all okay. The ranch hands are like brothers to me. Old Frank is like a substitute grandfather. He was the one who kept my mind going when I got stuck tracking. He can't track, but he can sure think, so he taught me to think."

Chase was a thinker too. I wondered if he thought he had me figured out now that he'd been to the ranch. I wasn't an easy person to figure out. I seemed to have a normal side to me and a side that was twisted somehow. I don't see things the way most people see them. I was glad I was one of the good guys. I didn't want to think about what I might be capable of as a bad guy.

It didn't take long for discomfort to settle in. The movement of the truck caused my ribs to ache. My cuts and scratches began to itch. I shifted this way and that trying to find a comfortable position. Finally, I scooted to the middle seat where I could snuggle up against Rusty. He put his arm around me and talked quietly as we rode along, telling me what had happened in the mountains while I was off riding around in the yellow van. I was going to catch hell from Strict and Landon.

"I wish it was just you and me riding home so you'd sing," I said.

"You don't want to hear me sing."

"I remember the ride home from San Diego. I enjoyed hearing you sing along with the radio. You have a good voice, and it was comforting to me."

"I thought you were asleep."

"I almost was, and I tried to stay awake so I could listen to you, but I couldn't."

"Can you sing?" he asked me.

"Only along with the radio. I can't carry my own tune, but I can follow somebody else. Never ask me to do karaoke. They'd throw me out."

"What else can you do that I don't know about."

"I can make a whistle out of a willow branch. I can make illegal traps for catching fish. Is it illegal to use a fish trap in a survival situation?"

"Yes, but I think anybody would overlook it if they were convinced it was really a survival situation."

"I thought of making a fish trap when I was at the river, but they are complicated to make. I'd have wasted most of a day and I needed to concentrate on finding a way home."

"How long do you think you could have survived out there if you had to?"

"If I had to? In good weather, with the river nearby, I could get along okay for three weeks. There was plenty of food if I wanted to catch it. It's just taking the time to set things up that is hard. Most of the time it isn't worth the trouble unless you are going to be out there for a few days. To make a snare you have to find strong, pliable plants that can be used for rope. There are so many things to be gathered, but first they have to be found. All that takes time. You have to look for just the right sized tree, or just the right shaped rock. You have to know what to watch for to build the different types of snares. Then you need to locate a well used game trail that meets all your requirements for building a snare. Then, since you took all that time to set it up, you don't want to take it down, so to get food you are stuck where the snare is. I needed to keep going and didn't have time for all that, so I opted for snake. But if I knew I was going to be in that area for a week and had to live off the land, I would have taken time to make snares and fish traps. I would have done just fine... I make my own moccasins. I'll have to make a new pair soon since I've worn holes through these."

We talked while I squirmed and he enjoyed the closeness. The miles went by and eventually we drove into town. It felt like ages since I'd last seen it. I could have sworn it had grown while I was gone. I walked into the condo and it felt foreign to me again. I knew it was home, but lately I was more used to the ground than a bed. I was used to open skies above me.

"What's wrong, Cassidy?" Rusty asked.

"Nothing, this always happens to me after I've been in survival mode. I feel claustrophobic; it's hard for me to sleep indoors. I tried last night. I couldn't sleep in my room, so I slept in the barn. It takes me a while for all the clamor of city life to become comfortable again."

Chase gave me a strange look. "You can have the hammock if that helps," he said.

"You slept in the hammock when you were here?"

"I chose the hammock. I know how you feel."

"Chase, why did you come up here? You didn't have to. I know you don't drop everything and come up here for just any old reason."

"You. You're important to me. It's not everyday a person like you comes along. You're needed up here. You're needed in the Michaels family and they're important to me too. And even though I didn't find you, I got a lot of answers to questions that had been bugging me. You're a puzzle to me, but now I've put a few more pieces in place."

"A puzzle. You're not the first person to tell me that. Thank you for your help."

"No problemo, kid."

"I just came up here to go someplace new," Cody said. "I thought Mom and Dad could use a few days alone. They can go skinny dipping in the pool at night without worrying about getting caught," he added with a wink.

There were four messages on the machine. Two were from Strict, one was a caterer that I'd talked to, wanting to know if I'd made a decision, and the printer had a question about the wedding invitations. The messages stopped and I turned away dejectedly. I wasn't ready to deal with any of them.

I went to the kitchen. Dinner for four. And I didn't even know what we had in the house. Cooking involved so many decisions. I was wishing for a helicopter to whisk me away and drop me in the mountains again. All my decisions would be made in the mountains. Find anything to eat. Watch for animals. Look for water. So simple. No worries about comfort. No endless lists of details. No telephones. Rusty came up behind me.

"Put on some clothes you're comfortable in, and let's go out."

"Okay." One decision made. That helped a bit.

I went upstairs and took a quick shower. I blow dried my hair and made a point of putting on make-up and finding an outfit that would help me feel better. I put on a pair of jeans I'd found that fit just right and one of the tacky t-shirts from the shop where Cody worked. I almost dressed up, thinking it would make me feel more civilized, but then I remembered what all the guys were wearing and decided tacky was more appropriate. I looked at the soles of my moccasins. I'd definitely need to make new ones after a search or two. Time to look for a leather shop.

Rusty knew where to go for dinner to make me feel better. We went to a restaurant we'd been to many times. It had a big open patio and bands played there. I had the sky above me, a lot of distractions, good food, and good company. The busyness grated on me a little but I let it flow around me. I ordered some fruity drink and something small to eat. I couldn't eat big portions yet. The guys sure could, though. They'd been living on the run, grabbing meals when they could. They were ready to settle down with a plate of real food.

"What was Strict's role in all this?" I asked.

"I had to call Strict to check up on you. When he found out you were missing he questioned me thoroughly. Then, when he got the story, he said we were doing everything right. Chase and Kelly were searching. I was basically filling Strict's shoes. He told me to call if he needed to take over, but there was nothing more we could do. Victor and Landon would have gone out but we couldn't think of anything for them to do. We had nothing to go by until you called. I questioned the campers who were there but they hadn't noticed anything unusual."

"I know it's not something you thought about because the van was missing when you got there, but when I saw it there was a citation on the window. I wonder if that citation is something we could look up. Surely the police have the other copy on file somewhere. It would give us the plate number."

"Do you know what the ticket was for?"

"I didn't read it. I didn't go near the van. But I'm guessing it was for being parked there without an Adventure Pass on it."

"Every little bit helps," Rusty said.

"So Strict knew I'd gone missing, but he never got personally involved in things?"

"You know he couldn't just sit back and wait for days to find out what happened to you. You're like a daughter to him. But there really wasn't much he could do."

"Does he know anything more?"

"He knows we found you."

"But he doesn't know anything about what actually happened."

"I called him after I talked to you, so he just knows I went up north to pick you up and bring you home. But even I didn't know what had happened until I got to the ranch."

Sigh, so I was going to have to tell the story one more time.

"I should call him when we get home."

"And?"

"And let him know I'm okay."

"And when he asks if you can track, what will you tell him?"

"Rusty, I'm fine. I can track. But I do hope he doesn't need me soon."

Chase ate and watched the band. Cody took his plate and made his way to the bar where he sat down to chat with two girls. After a while I looked over and he had put on a sombrero. One of the girls was taking his picture and giggling. I smiled and pointed him out to Rusty. He just smiled and shook his head.

"Have you ever looked him up on the internet to see how many girls have his picture plastered on their blog sites?"

"No," he answered, "I don't want to know."

"It would be funny to do an image search for 'Cody' and find out half the pictures in there are of him."

When we were back home I called Strict.

"Cassidy!"

"Hey, Lou, I got your messages, and I'm just returning your call."

"That sounds nice and polite after what you put me through. You're just returning my call?"

"Yeah."

Long pause. "I was just checking up on you." That was Lou saying, what in the world happened to you this time!? And where have you been and why haven't I heard anything?

So I told him, "I'm fine."

"Cassidy…" This was Lou repeating what he'd just said, except louder.

"Lou, it's a very long story. I'm fine."

"Fine for you is debatable. Tell me the truth. Before this happened you were barely getting healed up from your last accident."

"Yeah, and I didn't help matters much in this last little escapade either. But I can track. I haven't put on a pack yet, but I'd say I'm good for two days."

That was bad news to him. That was me saying, I'm battered and bruised, but if you really need me I'm capable of a two day track.

"When am I going to get the full story?"

I tried to think of who could go through it all, but Chase hadn't heard everything. Cody would embellish too much, and I wasn't going to ask Rusty to recount it. I sighed, settled back on the couch, and started from the beginning. The beginning was a long way back because he didn't know about the hideout or Trent Senior. He only knew I went camping and when I got back to my Jeep something happened. He listened silently. I knew he was trying to figure this out from a search commander's perspective.

"Cassidy…" he stammered when I'd finished, "What could we have done? Can you think of anything?"

"Nothing, unless one of the campers had some clues for you, but Rusty said he questioned them. Nobody noticed the yellow van. Nobody thought anything was out of the ordinary."

"What could you have done to prevent what happened?"

"Well, if I'd been smart, I would have read the tracks around the van and the tracks on the way up the trail so I'd have more information. But I was carrying that crazy lantern, and it was awkward hiking. When I got back, I shouldn't have put my keys in my pocket. I should have had them handier. I should have thought to pull my gun as soon as I saw the men were focused on me so I'd be ready. But you know me. I'd be worse off now if I'd have shot them. I'd rather go through all the physical stuff they put me through than shoot them."

"It would have been self defense. Two men against one woman. Anybody would call it self defense."

"Anybody except me, and I have to live with myself."

Chase stood in the kitchen, watching me carefully, putting puzzle pieces together.

"I'm not going to tell you how much danger you put yourself in. I'm sure Michaels has been through it all with you. I'm sure you weighed your options before acting. When will you be ready to track?"

"I'm ready. Rusty's not. He'd say to give me a week."

Chase stepped in front of me, "Tell him I'll be in town on business this weekend. If he needs you, I'll go out."

"Chase…" He looked at me like I shouldn't talk back. I thought I really ought to find out what his official title was so I'd know if I *could* talk back to him.

"Lou? Chase says if you need me this weekend to call him instead. He says he has business up here, but I don't believe him."

"He's just watching out for you. Let him."

"I know. Put me back on the on-call list Thursday."

"Will do."

"Thanks, Lou."

"Take care."

"I will." I hung up. "Chase, you didn't need to do that. What are you going to do in Joshua Hills for two more days?"

"I told you, I have business."

"I could have gone out if Strict had called."

"I'd rather you didn't. Rusty would rather you didn't. Give yourself some time to acclimate and heal. If you keep at this outdoor stuff, pretty soon you'll be like me. I don't want you to be like me. You need to stay the way you are. A valuable and useful part of society. Too much of the wilderness gets in the blood. Pretty soon society grates on you until you can't stand to be in it, and then you get like me. Look at me. I'll never marry, never settle down, never be complete. I don't want you to end up that way."

I was thinking I needed to put a few of the Charles "Chase" Downing pieces together. This guy was quite a puzzle too.

The bedroom walls felt so close. I lay there feeling them crowding around me. Having Rusty near helped, but I still felt trapped. I knew if I got up he'd notice and then he'd be awake, too. I didn't want to go downstairs and bother Cody who was sleeping on the couch. I couldn't leave the condo without alerting Chase. So I laid there and finally, after what felt like hours, I felt myself slip closer to sleep. Awareness slipped away and the walls closed in. The walls closed in, and my mind drifted. I could feel the walls, the metal walls, and they were moving. I was in the van. I could smell the dirty automotive grease and the old spare tire that was back there. I fought the ropes until I was free. I could see the two men in the front seats, my gun on the console between them. I crept across the filthy van floor until I stood behind the passenger's seat, crouched low. I made a grab for the gun and the man in the passenger's seat made a grab for me slamming into me and knocking me into the driver. The van veered. I was forced into the back of the van. The man was furious; he beat me with the butt of the gun. Blow after blow.

"Cassidy, Cass, hon, wake up, wake up, babe, it's okay." He reached out to hold me and I saw a swing coming. I raised my hands instinctively to protect myself. "Hey, it's okay, you're home again. Nothing's going to hurt you here. Come here. Come on." He gathered me into his arms, my hands still shielding my face. I hid, pressing myself into him, hiding from the blows, knowing it was a dream but still feeling the fear. His hand came across the lump on the back of my head and I flinched. "Oh, babe, it's okay, shhh." His deep thundery voice calmed me until I could cry. I felt him gradually tense up, anger building at the men who had driven me into such a state. Gradually I relaxed, but he kept me close. I lay hidden in his arms all night. I don't know if he slept. I did a little and when morning came he was still there. I woke up, but I still didn't want to move. They couldn't see me here. I was small and invisible and safe. Rusty shifted. I found a new hiding place.

"I'll be right back," he said with a light kiss.

He put on some clothes, opened the bedroom door, and I heard him pad downstairs to check out the activity or lack thereof below. He opened the refrigerator door, checking out the breakfast options, and closed it a little too loudly. I heard him climb the stairs, followed by the sound of running water. A few minutes later he climbed back into bed and gathered me up again.

"You okay?" he asked.

"Yeah, I'm just comfortable. I feel like I can hide in here."

"What are you hiding from?" he asked, gently amused.

"Nothing, invisible is just comfortable to me."

"What were you hiding from last night?"

"The men in the van. But it was different this time."

"Have you been having nightmares every night?"

"No, they usually don't start while I am in survival mode. They start when I shift out of it, when my mind is freer. When I am in survival mode, I am focused on what is happening to me even when I'm asleep."

"I hope, some day, you won't have to worry about survival. I hope, someday, you will feel safe forever."

"It sounds boring."

"Oh, I don't know, there's plenty of ways to make it exciting."

We lay in bed, just enjoying the peace. The walls didn't feel close anymore. The warmth seeped into me and I was able to relax. I luxuriated in Rusty's presence.

Finally hunger drove us to the kitchen. I started the coffeemaker, made toast, fried up some sausage, and scrambled a dozen eggs, adding onions, peppers and cheese to the mix. Cody awoke to the aroma of breakfast wafting into the living room. I transferred all the food to serving bowls and platters and set the table for four, then went to the backyard to wake Chase.

"He's not here," Cody said. "He told me he had business to do. It's normal for him to suddenly vanish. He doesn't like hellos and goodbyes. He likes to just fade in and out. He only knocks when he arrives to be polite."

"Well, I hope you're hungry then," I replied.

Cody went to the coffeemaker and poured a cup of coffee for himself, dumped in more sugar than the coffee could hold, then added cream. He scooped out a plateful of scrambled eggs and took a couple of sausage patties. Rusty waited for me to take my portion before helping himself to another big scoop. We ate breakfast quietly.

"Chase is an interesting character," I observed. "He isn't an officer unless the dress code is a lot different in San Diego. How does he fit into things down there? When he came to academy to teach tracking he looked like a typical officer, short haircut, uniform."

"He's been retired for several years," Cody said. "He might look like a misplaced hippie but he's at least sixty. He put in his time. He's been through a lot, serving in some of the toughest parts of San Diego. His heart was always in tracking, though. When he retired, he concentrated on it. He helps the police and the border patrol. He's a people hunter."

"Why does he teach the classes if he has so little respect for the cadets?"

"He watches for people like you. He feels like tracking is a fading art. You give him hope that it's not dead. When he saw you and Patrick together he saw the torch being passed. It gives him hope."

"I never would have guessed he was sixty. And he surfs?"

"Yeah, you'd be surprised how many old people surf. You have to remember the times they lived through. They were our age in the sixties and seventies. Surfing was very popular back then."

"I wonder what I am going to do with Patrick. I don't know if he'll ever be a tracker. So far he leans more towards stalking. He hasn't noticed tracks much. I bet once he gets into stalking and finds out he can find the animals by tracking them that will help. I'm not sure my family wants another tracker up there, though. They're all thinking, oh no, not again! And Jesse is a lot stricter than my mom was. She isn't going to let him go off in the hills by himself and learn on his own. I'm not up there enough to teach him. Tracking people and tracking animals are very different. Animals are harder to follow but people make decisions that show in their tracks. It's the decisions you need to read, not the tracks. They teach people to read the tracks in academy. They don't teach them to read the decisions behind the tracks. There isn't enough time."

Late Saturday night the doorbell rang and Rusty answered it. Chase came in without a word, looking like his business involved hacking his way through a jungle.

"Did Strict end up calling you out?" I asked.

"Nope, just taking care of some personal business."

"Did you get dinner? I can warm something up for you."

"I got it."

He took a shower and changed clothes. Chase then turned on the TV, and everybody gathered in the living room, wondering what Chase could possibly want to see on the late night news. This was the guy who had just told me he made a point of never watching the news.

The anchors began with several announcements regarding the situation in the mid-east and commented on a recent speech given by the governor. The news narrowed down further and further until it got to one interesting story in particular. "Authorities are baffled by a mysterious explosion in a remote area of the Angeles National Forest." They displayed a map of the mountains. A large red circle showed the area where the explosion had occurred. They compared the explosion to a minor earthquake and asked several experts for their opinion, but nobody had any real answers.

"I bet the area's crawling with curiosity seekers next week. I hope they don't wander off and get lost," Chase said. "I bet they drive out anybody who might be trying to hide up there. What do you think Cody?"

We all looked at Chase, including Cody.

"Oh, yeah, umm, right," Cody said.

"I bet this time next year it'll all be forgotten and nobody even goes up there anymore," Chase added.

"Chase, you wouldn't happen to know anything about this, would you?"

I asked.

"Me? This is the first I heard about it. Sounds like some outlaw in a cave somewhere misplaced some dynamite and it accidentally got set off."

I didn't believe him for a second. "Oh yeah, you really think that?" I asked sarcastically.

"Sounds plausible to me."

"Me too," said Rusty.

"Give it some time to blow over before you go back up there," Chase advised.

"We will," answered Rusty.

Chapter 15

I tried to give it some time to blow over, but Strict didn't let me. People were flocking to the area, and they needed deputies out there for crowd control.

"I know you didn't want to go out until the weekend but this is minor stuff. No camping, no packs. Just wear your uniform, look official and encourage people to let the authorities do their job. You'll be out of there by nightfall."

"How many days do you think we'll have to do this?" I asked.

"Through the weekend. I'll give you your own radio in case anybody wanders off and gets lost up there."

"Can Rusty go if he wants to?"

"Sure, we can use all the help we can get. I'll show you the area on a map when you get up here. It's going to be a two mile hike to the location and then we'll have to cover a large area off trail."

"Where are we meeting?" I asked, trying to sound ignorant.

"Creekside Trailhead."

"Okay, I'll be there as soon as I can."

I went upstairs and started changing into my uniform. Rusty came out of the shower and gave me a reprimanding look.

"You weren't supposed to get a call until Thursday."

"I know, but it's not a search, it's the result of Chase's work, and it's just patrolling the area. You can come, too, if you want. We just have to hike around and discourage people from going up there. We'll be home in time for a late dinner."

And so I found myself up at Creekside Trailhead again, in uniform, pretending to know very little about the area, and hoping to be assigned to my very own canyon so I could see my camp.

"Here's the trail," Lou said, pointing out the most familiar trail in the country to me. "Hike up two miles. You'll come to a place where the two creeks merge. You can patrol this section of trail and the lower portion of the canyon. I don't want you going more than a mile up this canyon. It's rough. If this had happened next week I'd send you to the top, but I don't want you roughing it. Just a mile. You can work a T-shaped circuit covering the trail on either side of the canyon and one mile up it. Here's the area the authorities are working in. They should all be recognizable to you."

So close and yet so far, I thought. Maybe tomorrow I'd ask to do more of the canyon. Today I had to remain as ignorant as possible. I pulled the pack out of the Explorer and Rusty took it from me.

"It's just snacks and lunch," I protested, but I let him carry the pack anyway. I'd been operating on automatic, getting ready for work, but after a few miles I'd appreciate not having to carry it.

"Cass, how do you put these things behind you so fast? The bruises haven't even faded and you're taking off into the hills again. Less than a week ago you were jumping out of vans, rolling down mountainsides. You need to learn to slow down."

I checked the gun at my side, a police issue version of my own gun. Rusty took note of it.

"Let's go," I said.

We took our time hiking the trail. No need to rush, this was patrol. Just keep up a steady pace. When we met hikers I was glad to let Rusty do the talking, taking note of what he said so that when he had to go back to work I'd know how to make it sound official.

"Good afternoon, out for a hike? Stay safe. Don't get off the marked trails."

While we were alone I said, "I figure the waterfall near the deer clearing is about a mile."

"Sounds about right."

"I wish we could go look at the camp."

"I know, you showed real self control when you didn't push Strict to let you go further."

"I figure I can do that tomorrow. I can tell him I liked the canyon and want to see more of it."

"You're coming back up here tomorrow?"

"Lou thought we might have to patrol through the weekend but I know you will have to go to work."

"I'll talk to him. I don't want you up here by yourself."

We hiked and talked to other hikers and when we reached the canyon we made our way up, discouraging people from hiking off trail.

"The trail's just down the canyon. We're asking everybody to please stay on designated hiking trails. It's for your own safety."

It was a long, hot day. When we stopped for lunch by the waterfall I checked the clearing for deer. I knew they'd be gone but was still disappointed to find the little meadow empty. Early in the evening the radio crackled with Lou informing us that we were now off duty. Halfway back to the trailhead the radio crackled again.

"Cassidy?"

"Yeah Lou?"

"Put Michaels on."

I handed the radio over to Rusty. Lou reverted to talking in codes. He only used the basic codes when he spoke to me. I think he still had a hard time thinking of me as a deputy. I was still just Cassidy, his little tracker. I didn't care as long as he let me track. Unfortunately, I could still understand the codes and didn't like the ones I was hearing. He was warning Rusty about a suspicious vehicle. There was only one suspicious vehicle that I knew of that we'd be warned about, and the drivers of it thought I was dead. I preferred to leave it that way.

A quarter mile from the trailhead I couldn't resist melting into the forest. In a minute Rusty stopped and looked around.

"Cass, don't hide from me."

"I'm not hiding from you. I'm hiding from the yellow van. They think I'm dead. I don't want them to know otherwise."

"We don't know that it's the same yellow van."

"I know, but how many yellow vans hang around this trailhead? How many yellow vans are curious about what happened to Trent's cave? Meet me in the campground. I'll check out the van from the woods and let you know if it's the right one."

"If it's the right van do you really think they'd drive into a campground full of deputies?"

"If they believe I'm dead they might think they are in the clear. We don't know who these guys are except hired thugs for a guy named Troy."

When we got close enough to see people moving around at the trailhead, I took off around the parking area and made my way to a vantage point. I observed the men at the trailhead. Lou was standing with a group of deputies and I watched as Rusty joined them. Lou looked at him with a questioning stare. Pretty soon Lou looked around at the trees, didn't see me but winked anyway. I examined the vehicles from the safety of the trees. Most of them were county cars driven by reserve deputies. There were several privately owned vehicles belonging to the hikers we had encouraged to leave. Then there was the yellow van. I froze. Just any old yellow van wouldn't cause the feelings that boiled inside me: helplessness, anger, fear. I made my way back to the other side of the parking area, hiding in stealth mode, and crept up on the group where Rusty was talking to Lou. More deputies joined them as they returned from their patrol. With seven burly deputies and an SUV blocking the view I stepped out from the trees.

"It's the same van," I said. "What happened to the people inside it?"

Three of the deputies turned suddenly, surprised by my abrupt appearance. Lou and Rusty were used to me coming and going silently. Even if I surprised them, they rarely let on.

"We played it safe. Three men from the van have been detained and are on their way to the station. You can identify them without being seen."

"Three?"

"Yes, they put up a good fight, too."

"Were they armed?" I asked, hoping to get my gun back.

"There are still officers over there if you care to ask."

"No, if they found it, they need it for evidence. I'll be contacted later."

"Then go on and get it over with."

Rusty pulled up and parked in the station parking lot, but I couldn't force myself to leave the truck. He got out and waited for me. I glanced his way and pulled the door latch, but still couldn't move. He leaned over and peeked through the window, then walked around to my side of the truck.

"What's wrong, Cass?"

"I can't go in there."

"They'll never see you. Haven't you ever seen a lineup before?"

"Even if they don't see me word will get back to Troy. I want to know who this Troy character is before I do anything. The only connection I can make between Troy and the hideout is Trent Senior. It's certainly not you, Kelly, Cody or Chase so it has to be Trent Senior. Do you know if Troy is another Trent? I don't want another Trent after me."

"Come to my office. We can look up Troy Trent and see if he's in the computer. All three of these guys could be wanted for something if they are hiding out in Trent's cave. All you'd be doing is adding to their charges. We can talk to Tom and see what he's found out."

"Tom?"

"Yeah, he's got the case. He'd like to talk to you about what happened, too. I told him everything I could. It gave him something to go on. He requested the files from the Visalia police and he's been working on the case, but he still needs to hear it from you."

"Great," I said sarcastically, and slid out of the Explorer. I followed Rusty into the station, then to an office a few doors down from his. He knocked loudly and waited for Tom to answer before opening the door and showing me in.

"Cassidy, you've been busy since I saw you last. Do you always keep the station this active? Catching jewel thieves, following false alarms, getting kidnapped."

"Yeah, unfortunately, I do."

"Let's go take a look at these guys."

A long pause, "I don't know if I can do that, Tom." I stood up and paced the room. "I need to have some questions answered first."

"Okay, like what?"

"I need to know about a guy named Troy and how the men from the yellow van are connected to him. There's also a link between them and a guy I call Trent Senior. I'm sure Rusty knows his first name but to me he's Tyrone Trent's dad. This guy, Troy, doesn't like me for some reason. He sent two kidnappers to fetch me. They didn't succeed. They think I died jumping off the side of a mountain. If I ID them for you, word will get back to Troy, and possibly back to Trent, and they'll know I'm alive and well. That means I'll be a target again, and I don't like being a target. It's slightly stressful and very boring. Rusty puts me under house arrest and I end up baking cookies all day. I don't want to hide out and bake cookies. So I really don't want to identify these guys even if they are my kidnappers. I'd rather have two kidnappers on the loose than have a psychopath after me."

"What if we need to catch the kidnappers to bring in the psychopath?"

"I don't know that you could charge him with anything even if you did. He didn't actually do anything to me yet. I escaped before we got to wherever he was. All I can say is he had two guys pick me up and bring me to him. They did it against my will and rough enough that you could pin a kidnapping and assault charge on them, but you may not be able to touch Troy."

"What made you take a chance like you did? They must have said or done something to make you decide you didn't want to meet this Troy character."

"They got mad at me and told me they didn't have to bring me in, that Troy was not a nice guy, and it might be better for me if they just killed me. They said Troy didn't like me, and that they'd do it quicker and easier."

"Why'd they get mad at you?"

"They stopped for gas and a woman saw me trying to get away. I was tied up and had a pillowcase over my head. She made a scene and they ended up running for it because of all the commotion."

"Where was the gas station?"

"I don't know. It wasn't far from the turn off into the mountains. The street the gas station was on was a straight shot through town. I don't remember any twists and turns. It was just pull in and pull out and keep going."

The questions went on and on. How'd I get away? What exactly did each of the two men do to me? It wasn't such a bad kidnapping, as far as kidnappings go. Sure, it could have been worse, but I thought I'd come through it rather well. If we didn't have this Troy character mysteriously hanging around out there I'd identify the kidnappers, no problem. But... and that was the sticking point. I paced back and forth while they went to Rusty's office to talk. I paced some more and then thought my excess energy could be put to better use so I went into the gym area and attacked the punching bag. This time the punching bag's name was just Trouble. I was tired of it. Sure, I didn't mind it in small quantities. A little of it made life interesting, but this life endangering, bone crunching trouble was grating on me. I was tired of it. Bam! I struck out at trouble. I kicked out at violence. I pounded fear. I punched hurt and worry and nightmares. Whatever bad thing trouble had brought my way I imagined it on that big punching bag and killed it. No more worry, no more fear. Bam, bam! Stupid kidnappers! Bam! Stupid psychopaths! Bam!

"I think she's mad," Tom said.

"Nope, not quite," said Rusty, "just a little frustrated."

"Your right side is feeling better, I see," Tom said.

"No thanks to the kidnappers." Bam! "Okay, I'm ready."

"You're ready, just like that."

I sat down on a bench against the wall.

"A year ago a guy named Manuel Silva robbed a bank and used my Jeep as a get away car. Unfortunately, I was driving it at the time. He forced me to take him to my house. When we got there I told him I wasn't letting him in. He pointed out a mom and two kids down the street and offered to take them instead. Aside from the fact that he wasn't going to let me go that easily, I couldn't let him do it. I couldn't let him one step closer to those people. These guys you're holding aren't any different. If I can keep them away from other people I'll do it. And I'll take the fall out from it, just like I did with Silva. Rusty?"

"Yeah?"

"I want to file for a permit to carry concealed."

Both guys looked at me seriously. They took me to a room with a big window in it. Tom disappeared and after a while a light came on in the room on the other side of the window. A uniformed officer escorted six men into a line up. I didn't need them to line up. I turned away as soon as they had all entered the room. I knew they couldn't see me, but my heart leaped in my chest. I kept my breathing in check. I wanted to run. I needed to run. Rusty read my every movement and put his hands on my shoulders steadying me. He knew he was my anchor. His hold on me oozed stability. I could feel it seeping in through my shoulders. Where was that hug? The hug that only Rusty could give me that made everything okay again. Before I could get it Tom stepped back into the room. I couldn't turn around. I couldn't meet those gazes. I knew I had to. I could identify the kidnappers without turning around but I had to look for the third guy. I had to really look. To me the third guy was more important than the kidnappers.

"The big guy and the guy in the plaid shirt," I said.

"They can't see you. Turn around and be sure."

"I'm sure. I don't even need to see their faces to be sure."

I turned around, looking for the third guy. I took note of their dress, especially their shoes. Two of the men had newer shoes with tread that definitely did not match what I had seen in the canyon. One wore sandals. The three remaining men wore older shoes. Shoes that had seen many miles, with worn tread and stories behind them. The three men included my two kidnappers. The third man... he interested me more than the two I knew. I watched for any signs of a Trent about him. It was hard. Trent Senior and Tyrone Trent were very different looking people. I looked for Tyrone's piercing eyes, his attitude, his mannerisms. I looked for Trent Senior's powerful build, his expressions. The men were lined up standing straight and looking directly ahead.

"Who's the guy in the gray pants and black shirt? Do we have a name?"

"Unfortunately we have four, none of them are Troy."

"Have you questioned him? How is he linked to the other two?"

"Friend. You're only identifying two men here. How does the third guy fit into the picture?"

"Friend. That could mean anything. I could tell more about them if they were moving around. I wish I could see the soles of their shoes."

"That can be arranged."

"Do you have a piece of paper and a pen?"

Rusty pulled out a sheet of paper from a notebook and a pen from his pocket. Tom spoke to the men next door. I quickly sketched the sole of a shoe for each of the three men and mentally ruled out the others. Only the three had shoes that could possibly match the tracks in the canyon. Then I drew a crude map of the canyon, including Trent's cave and the path leading to it. I thought back to the tracking I had done at the hideout, picturing the tracks as I had seen them. They matched up, I realized. All three. Using different kinds of dots I marked each man's trail on the map. The big guy had been the one who hiked to the top of the canyon. The other kidnapper had gone to Trent's cave. The third guy had searched the area around the hideout and then left. I was convinced the third guy was not Troy. But if he were released he would be the one to contact Troy. Now, how could I tell Tom about my findings without letting on that I knew something about the explosion in the mountains?

"Okay," I said, "the guys in the line up can go."

I watched as they all filed out, taking note of the way they walked and who grouped together with whom. Behavior quirks had always stood out to me. Nothing came to mind as I watched but maybe someday, if I ran across one of these men again, some tiny piece of observed behavior would catch my eye.

Tom and Rusty sat down at the table.

"What's this?" Tom asked.

"It's a map of an area I tracked recently." I explained about the camping spot I had up there, carefully leaving out any mention of the hideout. I told him about Trent Senior's cave and how he'd been watching my camp last year. I told him about going camping up there and seeing all these footprints in the canyon. I explained how I thought Trent had leaked the location of the cave to other criminals so they could use it as a hideout. This interested him in particular because of the recent explosion up there.

"Do you think they had explosives in that cave?"

"Trent didn't when I was there. He just had a forty-five, a little ammo and odds and ends of groceries. There's no telling what people have brought up there since then. After tracking these guys all over the canyon I wasn't going to risk a trip into the cave. If there were explosives in there, they'd be buried under tons of rock now. There's no way anybody would be able to get in there again."

"Why didn't you mention this possibility when the inquiry into the explosion first started?"

"First of all, I thought it was a scientific investigation. If the police were involved in anything but patrolling the area I didn't know about it. Second, I want to keep as much distance from these guys as I can. That's why I didn't stick around when I went camping up there. Anybody linked to Trent was someone to avoid so I came out early and got kidnapped by them instead."

"So, you could lead investigators in to this cave?"

"I doubt it. Well, I could try, but I don't have much hope of actually reaching it, if that's where the explosion occurred. The cave is very well hidden under a boulder field. When the explosion happened those rocks probably would have filled any access to the cave. But, yes, I know a route that would bring me as close to the cave as possible."

As we drove home in the Explorer Rusty said, "You know what you're going to be doing tomorrow, don't you?"

"I hope not."

"You're going to be leading a group of investigators in to the cave."

"They won't dig it out will they? It's impossible. You know how much rock is up there. Hopefully some of those huge boulders blocked the way."

"Hopefully Chase knew to cover his tracks."

"Well, if I see any I'll be sure to walk all over them."

"How would you recognize Chase's tracks after all those other people have been tromping around in the woods?"

"I'll know. Hopefully all the other people obliterated his trail, but I doubt he left one. I'm more interested in seeing the hideout, or at least the outside of it."

"For wanting to save you from one weekend of searches, he sure caused a lot of work for you to do."

"Chase's real goal was to give my hideout back to me. If the cave is really, truly gone all the work will be worth it. Besides, these day jobs are just what I need to get me ready for a real search."

Chapter 16

Six o'clock the next morning the phone rang and I picked it up knowing it would be Strict.

"Cassidy? How are you?"

"I'm fine."

"I've had a request for your services from the higher ups."

"Okay, it's what I expected after talking to Tom."

"Can you be at the trailhead by nine o'clock?"

"Sure, earlier would be better but I can be there at nine. Which hat am I wearing this time?"

"You're guiding in a group of people investigating the explosion. Apparently you know more about it than they do."

"Me?"

"Don't give me that."

"I know where a cave is that Tom thinks might have something to do with the explosion. That's all. I'll be there at nine."

I didn't know who exactly I'd be guiding in but I decided I needed to represent the reserve deputies so I took time to wear a clean, sharp uniform. I curled my hair and wore just a touch of make-up like I thought the female officers probably wore.

Despite the uniform and the gun strapped to my side I was met with skeptical looks at the trailhead.

"Gentlemen, this is Cassidy Callahan. I gave her the day off so let's hope nobody gets lost in the mountains today. Cassidy is normally a tracker and a damn good one. She'll get you to the cave by the quickest and easiest route available."

"Is everybody ready?" I asked. "I just need to grab my pack."

Everybody scattered and met back at the trail a few minutes later. I went to the car, dug out my pack and shouldered it. We set off at a good clip. A few of the group kept pace, but soon there were laggers. Several of them looked as though they'd had their fill of the mountains. A few were enjoying the hike and the novelty of their guide. Then there were those in the middle who were just out doing their job and this time it involved looking for a cave.

The man directly behind me trotted up beside me.

"Dean Quinlan," he said extending his hand.

"It's good to meet you," I answered. "So, you want to see an old cave in the mountains?"

"Maybe, we'll see when we get there, won't we."

"You sound skeptical."

"Oh, I know there are several caves in these mountains. I just think that if the cave were there you'd be more reluctant to bring people in there."

"I am reluctant to go to this cave because the last time I was in it I was bound and beaten. When I became aware of the way the cave was being used, I definitely was not looking forward to going back."

"You expect trouble?"

"No, I expect to find an empty cave or a dead end. No one would stick around up there if investigators were going to knock on their door any minute."

The first two miles went by fairly quickly. We stopped at the bottom of the canyon to regroup.

"Everybody who needs a rest better take it. If you need water, fill up your canteens now. We have a two mile, off trail climb ahead of us. I'll take you up the easiest route but it is still rough. There's water in the canyon but we won't always be near it."

If Chase was as thorough as I expected, there would be a lot of unhappy investigators. The walk under the boulder field would certainly interest the more scientific minded ones. I had wondered how the boulder field came to be when I was walking around down there. Hundreds of boulders from the size of a car to a small house had just been strewn onto a mountaintop. How did that happen?

Men talked in small groups. I assumed they had divided up depending on their area of expertise. Dean Quinlan was grouped with another young man. They looked like graduate students from a large university. Two here, three there, except for one lone man. When everybody appeared rested and attention had turned from the trail to the problems at hand I led the way up the canyon. I took the way up that was predominately hiking. Occasionally we encountered a rock face that had to be climbed. They all seemed to take it in stride. The climb up the canyon was slower, so the group stayed together more easily. When I saw the waterfall go by I sadly reminded myself that the deer wouldn't be in the clearing. There were too many people in the canyon now. I watched the ground as I hiked. There were footprints everywhere. The shoes of the deputies were very recognizable, while the footprints of the investigators were more varied. I turned to keep track of our progress. The groups had remained together on the hike up the canyon, but the lone man was off to the side. He carried his light pack awkwardly, and I wondered why he was here. Some of the men carried packs full of equipment. Several packed food and camping supplies. Teams had divided their loads and seemed to be in good spirits. The lone man watched the scene warily, and stole glances at me. As we neared the turn off to the cave I began watching the ground for signs of Chase. I led the group to the north wall of the canyon, into the small cleft through the rocks, and up to the top of the canyon. The trail was barely recognizable. However, the fact that there was any trail at all meant that many men had walked this way. The small trail went through the woods then started down a hill and into the rocks. This was the spot where I'd turned back the last time I'd been in the area. I followed the trail down into the boulders half expecting Troy to appear from behind some rock. No sign of Chase. The sand down here was impossible to hide tracks in, but if anybody could do it, it would be Chase.

I turned, leading the group beneath the boulders to the entrance of the cave. We wound around under the rocks until I found the way had been blocked solidly by shattered rock and fallen boulders from above. I peeked in the crevices thinking I could worm my way between the boulders but I wasn't sure how stable they had been wedged in there. What if they rolled?

I turned and addressed the group of men. "This is as far as we go unless someone wants to try and get through the rocks. When I was through here last time the walking was easy, like the walking we just did. The ground went down between boulders like this until it gradually turned into a tunnel under the mountain. The tunnel was maybe fifty feet long and ended in a cave. All these boulders weren't here. They have fallen down from above, probably when the explosion occurred."

"These rocks weren't here when you came here before?"

"The ones you see firmly planted in the sand were here. The others have fallen recently."

"How recently?"

"Since the first week in December. That's when I was in the cave."

"But it could have been as recently as the explosion?"

"Yes sir, that's possible. If you look at the lichen on the rocks you can see what direction they were facing before they fell."

They seemed disappointed that there was little to see, so I removed my pack, then looked and prodded, attempting to work my way between the rocks. A spelunker might have gotten further, but I was definitely the smallest person in the group. If I couldn't get in, there was no hope for them.

"Gentlemen, I'll leave you to do your research and I'll be back by three o'clock. We should probably hit the trail by three if we hope to get back to the trailhead by dark."

As they broke up into small groups, I hiked out of the rocks and made my way to the canyon. My goal was to check the hideout, but I wasn't going there first. I was going to guard my back first. I wasn't convinced all those investigators were really researching the explosion. I was particularly suspicious of the solitary man. He didn't fit the pattern somehow and I watched my trail, catching him following me away from the rocks. This guy wasn't too smart. If he was going to follow me, the least he could have done was to stay out of sight. There was no way I was going to lead him to the hideout.

I turned on the radio.

"Strict?"

"Go ahead, Cassidy."

"Who's patrolling the canyon?"

Landon cut in, "That's me and Thez, Cassidy, what's up?"

"Where are you?"

"Comin' down."

"Have you gotten to the big pine tree?"

"Negative. About a quarter mile from there."

"Okay, I'll find you."

"Ten-four."

I started hiking up the canyon purposely ignoring the hideout. I couldn't help but notice, though, that either a big storm had passed through or Chase really had been hacking his way through a jungle. The whole area was littered with branches and rocks. I wasn't sure, but I thought Chase had gone to considerable trouble to make the camp look undesirable to patrols and researchers.

I found Landon and Thez making their way down the canyon, talking, just like everybody did when they were with Thez. Thez looked at me, taking in the uniform. He'd been out of the loop for a while.

"Congratulations on making it through academy," he said.

"Thanks."

"What's up, Cassidy?" Landon asked.

"Ten-twelve," I said, visitors present, be discreet.

They looked around.

I spoke softly. "I led some investigators in to what used to be a cave. One of them is more interested in me than the investigation."

"That doesn't surprise me at all," Landon said with a smirk.

"That's not what I mean. He's tailing me and he thinks I don't know it."

"That doesn't surprise me either. You always know stuff like that."

"There's a guy named Troy after me. Right now he works from a distance and thinks I'm dead. I'd like to keep him thinking that. Problem is he has an interest in this canyon and this cave and now I've got a mysterious guy following me. I don't like it."

"And you want me to know this because?"

"If you run into him, can you talk to him so I can give him the slip?"

"You can give him the slip without us talking to him, so what's up?"

"See if you can get a name out of him."

"Sure."

"Thanks."

I continued up the canyon, still pretending not to notice the man following me. Pretty soon I saw Landon and Thez approaching the guy. They stopped him and spoke to him, so I continued up canyon, then silently slipped into the trees. I then doubled back to where I could keep an eye on my follower. Landon and Thez were still talking to him when I snuck into a hiding place nearby, ready to follow. The tables had turned. They asked him for an ID and not having anything to identify himself as an investigator, he was politely asked to stick to the marked trails just like Rusty and I had done the day before. They escorted him back towards the trail, making small talk on the way. I followed, observing from a distance. When they got to the trail I noticed the guy didn't take the trail back to Creekside. Landon and Thez turned around and continued their patrol back up the canyon.

Hidden in the bushes beside them I said, "He's not going to stay on the trail. He's going to let you get a head start and then come back."

Thez was startled, not used to my quiet ways.

Landon laughed at him. "We need to take Thez out more. He's getting jumpy."

"If he was going to leave, he'd head for the trailhead. Was he armed?"

"Not that I could see. But you're right; he was no investigator. You say he snuck in with the group?"

"I wouldn't say he snuck, he blended in and followed along with the group."

"What made you decide he was different?"

"Like usual, odd behavior. He just didn't blend in enough, and then when all the investigators dug in and got to work he had nothing to do."

"His name is Douglas Thorne. Does the name mean anything to you?"

"No, but it might mean something to Tom. Thanks."

I let them continue their patrol and waited in hiding until my follower snuck by. I followed him up the canyon, taking note of his tracks and mannerisms. I had a hunch any information I could pick up might come in handy. When I had a chance, I tracked Landon and Thez. There was no telling when I might have to distinguish their tracks from a lost person's trail.

The man I had been following hiked up canyon, staying out of sight of Landon and Thez. He'd walked around the vicinity of the hideout without finding it and then wandered back to the same area as the investigators. I wandered from group to group noting their odd ways of investigating. None of it made much sense to me. Three o'clock rolled around, and not one of them looked like they were ready to head for the trail.

"Okay, gentlemen, we have a four mile hike ahead of us before dark. Anybody who wants to hike out with me, gather at the big pine tree in half an hour."

Dean Quinlan looked tempted, but he had a job to do.

Half an hour later one man stood under the tree. I went up to the boulders again and noticed a few pup tents had been set up. Nobody was packing up. Oh great, I thought, now I have a four mile hike with this guy. I didn't like this one bit, but I led him down the canyon to the trail. The man lagged behind me on the way, and I didn't like having my back to him. There was no telling what was in that backpack. After considerable thought I decided the hike down was fairly safe. I had a gun. I had the radio. I had patrols roaming the canyon and the trails. We were also walking into a campground full of deputies. My only worry with this guy was the possibility that he could identify me to Troy, unless this *was* Troy. I studied his features attempting to find any traces of Trent in him. As I had learned during conservation with Tom, people don't always have just one name. I'd never considered the possibility of Troy using two names. It was common enough amongst criminals.

I spotted a patrol ahead and read the trail until I figured out the guys ahead were Victor and someone I hadn't met yet. It wasn't Rosco because I knew his tracks. I got on the radio.

"Victor, wait up," I said.

As I appeared on the trail and grew closer he asked, "How'd you know it was me?"

"One guess."

"Cassidy is our tracker," he told his partner. "Cassidy, this is Barry Oliver."

"Good to meet you. Next time I'll know you by your tracks."

"Who's this?" Victor asked, indicating the man following me.

"I don't know," I replied. "He came in with a group of investigators and he was the only one who wanted to hike out today. Not much to investigate, I guess."

When the man extended his hand, I noticed he had almost no fingerprints, like they'd been sanded many times over the years. "Don Dalton," he said. Red flags waved furiously. I knew where I was going when I got off duty. First I'd write those names in my tracking notebook and then drive straight to the station.

"So," said Victor pointing, "Barry Oliver, Don Dalton, Cassidy Callahan, Victor Gomez. You coming up again tomorrow?"

"Nah," said Don, "I just had to verify something. I'm done here."

We all turned and continued down the trail. I was glad to be hiking with the group and wondered if Don would notice the wheels turning furiously in my brain. What had he come up here to verify? Was it the cave, or me, that needed verifying? I owed Victor for this. Whether he knew it or not he might have just saved me from another trouble attack.

"Cassidy, I hear you've been to hell and back since we went out on a call together."

No! I can't talk about that now! Change the subject, Cass, anything besides the kidnapping.

"Yeah, I got run over by a water skier at the beach. You'd think I could go a couple months without a trip to the hospital, but, *no*."

"I didn't hear about that one."

"That's why I couldn't go out after Big John. I cracked four ribs and had a concussion."

"What are you doing out here then? That wasn't that long ago."

"I've been working on my recovery. Actually being out here with just a light pack has helped a bunch. I've also been practicing my shooting and going to the gym and boxing a bit. I think I'm ready for the summer tourist season. I need to get ready for the wedding, too. If I can just walk down that aisle without bruises I'll be happy. I'll probably have to stay home the two weeks before the wedding to accomplish it but you know I won't do that. I'll be out tracking every week."

"I heard you're going to abandon us for two weeks in the hottest part of summer."

"I am?"

He looked at me like maybe he should have kept quiet. "That's what I heard. But if you don't know, maybe you should keep quiet."

"I have to know something or I won't know what to pack."

"Well, you didn't hear it from me."

Am I going to have fun, I thought. But that isn't something you ask a guy about your honeymoon.

"Have you heard more about Big John? How's he doing?"

"He'll be back. Last I heard he was in physical therapy. The bear did a number on his leg but they expect him to make a full recovery if he works at it."

"That's good news. Did we ever find out what happened?"

"Just what you'd expect, he saw a bear and had never seen one in the wild before, so he followed trying to get a good look at it."

"But you were on that trail for two days. He couldn't have followed a bear for two days."

"It took us two days to follow John's trail. It wasn't very far, just time consuming. You cut our tracking time in half when you got on the radio. You would have found him the first day."

The two miles went quickly. Don kept quiet, and I hoped he wasn't taking too many mental notes.

"Cassidy," Lou called as I went through base camp, "you lost your group."

"None of them wanted to come back today. They had gear."

"Where are you off to in such a hurry?"

I looked around for Don.

"Hold on Lou, I'll be right back."

I searched the parking area for Don/Doug but there was no sign of him. The yellow van was still there. There was movement inside. I approached the van from a non-windowed side then crept around it, noting fresh footprints. I went back to the trail and compared the tracks. Oh damn, Don was now linked to the yellow van, too, and I was in trouble again.

I found Lou and stopped to talk. He could tell there was something on my mind. I told him about the conversation with Tom and why I had been called on to lead the group to the cave. Then I told him about the day, explaining my suspicions.

"I need to go talk to Rusty and Tom before I forget anything."

"Okay, go ahead. I don't think we'll need to patrol tomorrow. It's been pretty quiet."

Half an hour later I was in town. I drove home to see if Rusty was there yet. He was still working, so I changed clothes and then headed for the station. I checked in at the front counter even though I didn't have to anymore. I wanted the girl at the desk to buzz Tom. I really needed to find out his last name.

"I need to talk to Tom," I said, "the new detective."

She buzzed me through and I stopped at Rusty's office on the way through. Knock, knock, a peek in the window. When I saw he was alone I opened the door and poked my head in.

"You busy?"

He brightened up when he saw me, walked around his desk and wrapped his arms around me. I gave him a quick kiss.

"Yeah, what's up?"

"I've got some information for Tom and I thought you'd want to hear it too."

"Is it good information or bad information?"

"It could be both, maybe you and Tom can tell me."

We walked to Tom's office and I knocked on the door. I heard a curt "Come in," and opened the door.

"I've got a new character to add to your kidnapping and explosion story. I need you to look up Douglas Thorne and Don Dalton." I explained about the group I had led to the cave and how this Doug/Don character had followed me around the canyon and was linked to the yellow van. "Douglas Thorne is the name on the driver's license he showed to Landon, and Don Dalton is how he introduced himself to Victor and Barry."

"Who were you working with up there today?" Rusty asked.

"No one, I was just guiding a group in. I guess Lou thought it was a simple job. When I got suspicious about this guy I called to see who was patrolling the canyon. They were never far away."

"If they were in that canyon and on foot they were too far away. It's three miles long and it takes three hours to hike it."

"I won't be out there tomorrow. Lou said things were slowing down enough that we won't have to patrol the area."

I felt a relieved squeeze to my shoulder and felt the hug itching to get out, but he waited until we were alone.

Trouble was taking its toll on Rusty.

Chapter 17

Since I was home and the usual stir crazy feelings were setting in, I thought I'd better make some progress with our wedding plans. I checked with the printer and returned the caterer's call regarding arrangements for the reception. The wedding cake was ordered. I bought a guestbook and a pillow for the ring bearer to carry. The ring bearer, yikes, I forgot. I called Jesse and asked her if Patrick would be my ring bearer. I then ran through the flower girl exercise with Shadow. I was sitting at the dining room table studying my checklist when Rusty burst through the front door startling me. He looked around, finding me quickly, but gave me a glimpse of something. What was it?

He plopped down on the chair next to me and put his head down on his crossed arms. "Cass, why haven't you answered your phone?"

"I must have left it somewhere. It's probably in my pack. I've been out running errands." I found my pack and dug my phone out from the bottom of it. Three missed calls. All from Rusty. "You can't get all bent out of shape just because I don't answer my phone. What if Strict called me? My phone doesn't work most of the time when I'm tracking."

"I know. I probably wouldn't have worried except that we found out who Troy is and I was calling to warn you."

You could have heard a pin drop. Something told me I didn't want to know this particular piece of information. Something told me it was going to mean trouble, and I'd had enough trouble to last a lifetime. Well, major trouble anyway. I could still do with some minor trouble, but I'd placed Troy in the major trouble category.

Rusty took a sheet of paper from a folder he'd carried in. "Does this guy look familiar to you?"

I studied the picture. The guy was familiar to me somehow.

"You're lucky Douglas Thorne has a heart," he said. "Tom brought him in for questioning. On the hike in to the cave he was supposed to find out if you were still alive, and then find the hideout. He had also been working with two other men in the group. They were looking for something specific near the cave. If they didn't find it, Thorne was ordered to bring you in. They thought you'd know where it was."

"What are they looking for?"

"He wouldn't say, only that turning you in to them was too high a price. He wasn't willing to do it. What about this guy?" he said, showing me a second printout.

I put the two pictures together. Now it made more sense. When I saw the third man I placed the pair as part of the group I'd taken to the cave.

"I wonder if they found what they were looking for."

"Not yet, but things got confused when the boulders near the cave were all rearranged. The placement of the boulders were important clues, so they haven't given up yet."

"How could I know where it is? I don't even know *what* it is!"

"Apparently you were the last person to talk to Tyrell Trent and your behavior made him think that you knew something."

"I did? Hell, all I did was run away from him. And he didn't tell me anything."

"I know that, and you know that, but Troy doesn't."

"And why would they take me all the way up north if what they were looking for was down here? That doesn't make sense."

"I didn't say it made sense. I said we knew who Troy is. He's this guy," he said tapping one of the pictures.

"You mean I led Troy to the cave? I need to make cookies."

"Huh? You lost me somewhere."

"That's how I pay back the guys on the team when they accidentally do something to help me. They don't know that's what I'm doing, but I just happen to pack extra cookies on the next call."

"What did the guys do to help you this time?"

"They were just there when I called on them. I was uncomfortable being alone with this Douglas guy following me, so they helped watch out for me."

"I'll make them some, too, then," he said grinning.

"Well, now Troy definitely knows I'm alive. At least I'm worth more to him alive than dead. That's a plus. I just wish I knew what they think I know."

Strict had opened up a real can of worms the day he'd sent me with that group of investigators to the cave. A few days later, however, he sent me on a search that proved to be a very interesting case.

"Some clown got lost on the Pacific Crest Trail," he'd said.

"That's not nice, it takes real talent to get lost on that trail."

"He's not just any clown. This is Bullhorn Brewski. He's a rodeo clown. In his spare time he does stuff like hike the PCT to raise money to buy safety equipment for cowboys just starting out in rodeo. He hikes along telling his story to anyone who will listen, and he accepts whatever they give him. He should be easy to track and easy to spot. He's wearing clown shoes, patched overalls, a loud plaid shirt, and the most beaten up old cowboy hat you ever saw. It's been gored five or six times. His pack is bright purple with hatpins all over it. You should be able to spot him from a mile away."

"There's no way a pair of clown shoes would survive a week on the Pacific Crest Trail."

"He's never been seen without them."

"Where was he last spotted?"

"He stocked up in Wrightwood, spent a day there. Towns like that are handy for his fund raising efforts so he generally spends a day in town before hitting the trail again. Then he didn't show up for a meeting in Agua Dulce."

"Great. So he's somewhere in that ninety mile stretch of trail. Ninety miles is a long ways."

"Could be five, could be ninety."

"I can't leave today. A trip like this takes some planning. I can be ready in the morning, early, the earlier the better."

Dozens of little details had to be considered to be ready for a search as extensive as this one could be. Five days of food was all I could carry. My gas, too, would last about five days, if I was careful. As I prepared for the search, however, something kept niggling at my mind. The Pacific Crest Trail followed the San Gabriel Mountains, and it frequently hit the highway and county roads on its way. I bet I could narrow down my search considerably if I did some homework first. I jumped into the Jeep, taking Shadow with me, and drove up to Wrightwood to find the closest place the PCT hit the highway. I clipped on Shadow's leash and followed the trail, watching for Bullhorn Brewski's big, clown shoe footprints. Several people had been down the trail since Brewski had, but I still made out the clear *heel, slap, heel, slap* of his clown shoes going down the trail. This was good news. I led a disappointed Shadow back to the Jeep and we drove to the next spot a few miles down the highway. I got out and checked the trail again. Whenever Shadow jumped out of the Jeep he was ready for a day out in the hills, but each time I found Brewski's tracks I tugged him back to the waiting Jeep. The trail crossed again at Big Rock Creek and yet again at Eagles Roost Picnic ground. Yes! I was narrowing down my search considerably. Brewski had made it to Eagles Roost, but not to Cloudburst Summit. I'd just narrowed my search from ninety miles to less than ten.

When Rusty returned home there was camping gear scattered all over the living room. I came back home and found him sitting on the couch looking despondent in the midst of all the gear.

"This doesn't look good. You're packing for a week."

"Nope," I replied, "I *was* packing for a week. I've been up in the mountains all afternoon and managed to narrow down the search to a ten mile section of trail. Should I take Shadow to the kennel or do you want to doggy sit?"

"He can stay with me, I don't mind. It's just kind of boring for him."

I checked all my supplies: four backpacker meals, four packets of oatmeal and eight packets of hot chocolate, camp stove, gas, lighter, tent, sleeping bag, two changes of clothes, extra socks, 9 mm, hunting knife, magnesium stick, water, water filter system, and trail mix. I would eventually run out of trail mix, but it was too heavy to weigh down my pack with any more of it. I packed carefully, putting the heavy things at the back of the pack, near the center of gravity, to distribute the weight and make it easier to carry. I zipped everything up and hefted the pack, hoping that my ribs were healed. This was more weight than I'd carried in a long time. I added cookies, knowing they would disappear fast and I wouldn't have to carry them long. Rusty hefted the pack and looked at me. I could see the wheels turning and knew he didn't want me carrying that heavy thing.

"I'll get used to it quick and then it'll feel like a part of me. I've done it before."

Dinner was quiet. I'd made a dish with lots of vegetables because my meals for the next several days would consist of only meat, pasta, oatmeal and trail mix. I always missed vegetables when I was on a long call.

It was one of those moody nights for Rusty and it rubbed off on me too. He always had mixed feelings about long calls and didn't like coming home to an empty house.

In a way I was looking forward to camping again. The tracking would be child's play. How could you miss the prints from a pair of clown shoes? I'd be out in the hills again but I felt the familiar tug. My feet longed for a trail while my heart longed for home. Neither of us were particularly happy about this call, but at least I'd had some warning. Sometimes Rusty came home to a hastily scribbled note saying I got a call and I'd be back ASAP. Sometimes it meant hours, but it could mean days.

Landon and Thez knocked on the door bright and early the next morning. Guess they were serious about Thez not getting out enough. Or maybe some stories had made it back to him and he was just curious. I thought the hike would at least be more entertaining with him along.

"Hold on," I said, "I'm all ready but I need to call Strict before we leave. How many days did you pack for?"

"I just brought as much as my pack would hold."

"Well, you can lighten your load. I know where Brewski is, well I narrowed it down anyway."

It was early, but I knew Lou would be getting ready to start the search.

"Hey, Lou, it's Cassidy."

"What's up?"

"I think we have a change in plans."

The line grew very quiet. He was probably thinking I had another disaster during the night and couldn't go out.

I continued, "We need to start the search at Eagles Roost Picnic Ground."

"What?"

"I spent yesterday afternoon narrowing down the search. I know Brewski got to Eagles Roost but he didn't reach Cloudburst Summit. Just thought you'd want to know."

"You cut a ninety mile trail in half in one afternoon?"

"Yep, and I'm glad I did, too. I didn't want to follow those clown tracks for two useless days. Anyway, Landon, Thez and I are heading out in just a few minutes."

"See you there."

"Okay, bye."

I stuck my pack in the trunk along with Landon's and Thez's packs then ran back in the house and took a bag of cookies from the freezer for Rusty. I left them on the counter where he'd be sure to see them. I bounded up the stairs two at a time and met Rusty getting out of the shower. He toweled off quickly, his damp hair sticking out every which way, his eyes smiling at me in a serious manner. He knew I was ready for this search even if he didn't want me to go. Still smelling like shampoo and soap, he pulled me into a long kiss and a warm, damp hug.

"You take care of yourself out there. Be careful."

"I will. This search is a lot shorter than it was yesterday. I should only be a day or two. The tracking is easy. It's just a matter of following the guy until I find him. I'll be back as soon as I can. I left some cookies out for you."

Another quick kiss and I had to go. Landon was waiting on the front porch.

"Lucky guy," he said. "We're headed for Eagles Roost?"

"Yep, I did a little driving around in the mountains yesterday. He has to be somewhere around there. He didn't make it to Cloudburst Summit."

"Good work. I was prepared for a week out there. Thez will be disappointed. He's been stuck in an office for months."

We got to Eagles Roost and found Strict ready for action, but I didn't think there would be much action this time.

"You're sure about this?" he asked.

"His tracks are unmistakable. I don't think there are two guys in these mountains hiking in clown shoes."

He acknowledged that with a shrug. I shouldered my pack feeling every ounce of the weight until I tightened the shoulder pads and pulled the hip belt snug. Okay, I was ready for action, too.

Landon was lightening his pack. Thez didn't. He either didn't mind the load or he wanted to be prepared for anything, I wasn't sure which.

"Radio?"

"Check."

"GPS?"

"Check."

"Okay, ready?"

"Check."

We headed off to find our clown, out there somewhere wearing a purple backpack full of money. I hoped he hadn't been robbed. I felt for my gun. Yup, it was there. The tracks were as plain as they could be even with tracks on top of his. There was no measuring of his stride. One shoe ended where the next one took off. The trail began across the highway from the picnic ground. It started out as an old fire road but after a mile it hit a little stream. At our first rest stop I pulled out the thawed cookies.

"Here, I brought cookies," I said, "I owe you one."

"Why?"

"Because you saved my butt in the canyon. That guy, Douglas Thorne, was teamed up with two other guys in the group of investigators. They think I know the location of something they're looking for. I'm hoping, whatever it is, they find it so they won't care about finding me. I don't know what it is or where it is but they think I do. If it weren't for all the officers in the area, I might have been in serious trouble."

"We did all that and all we get are cookies?" Landon said jokingly.

"I didn't have to bring them at all. You'd never have known the difference. That reminds me, Thez, if you're still looking for scary stories I've accumulated some more. You'll have to choose a couple that sound interesting. There's the rattlesnake story, the kidnapping, the water skier, the avalanche, the car wreck. Hell, there might be more. A lot has happened since I saw you last."

I checked the ground to verify that Brewski's clown shoe tracks were still visible.

"Hey, I missed the kidnapping one," said Landon.

"That's because it happened recently, and the case is still ongoing at the station."

"Recently? How recently?"

"Recently enough for Douglas Thorne to be part of it. Shortly before the explosion."

"You didn't have anything to do with the explosion did you?"

"No! I didn't even know about it until I saw it on the news."

"Okay, so tell us about the kidnapping."

Hoo boy, okay, I guess I'd asked for it. I started talking and they listened, amazed as always about how I managed to get into so much trouble and then get out of it with so little to show for my efforts. Landon managed to link the kidnapping with the yellow van and Douglas Thorne.

"So the guy that had his goons pick you up the first time is back looking for something near the canyon and they think you know what and where it is?"

"Right, but I don't. Apparently I did something to convince Tyrell Trent that I knew where it was. All I can think of that I did was run away from him. I climbed up a big rock trying to find Rusty and Kelly."

Oh, no. An idea struck me like a bolt of lightning. That rock, the most visible rock in the whole boulder field, it was the first clue! It was split in a big V and when I stood within the V, I could only see in two directions. Trent thought I knew something because I'd chosen that particular landmark. That rock pointed to something, I knew it. Why did I have to think of these things out in the middle of nowhere when I couldn't do anything about it? I was sure that rock would point me to another landmark. What did I see when I was up there? What one landmark had stood out? The big pine tree! My camp. No wonder they thought I knew something. I was camped at the last known clue!

"Earth to Cassidy. Anybody home? Hello, hello?"

"Sorry guys I just figured out a piece to this puzzle. I sure wish I could go back to that canyon, with a group of bodyguards who don't mind going on wild goose chases."

"I don't mind!" said Thez. He must be awfully sick of that office.

"Well, first things first. We need to find this clown."

I took note of the tracks. Brewski was just hiking along, *heel, slap, heel, slap*, as usual. He couldn't be walking two miles an hour like that. I don't know how he expected to hike the whole trail when it was hard enough with the right shoes.

The day was hot but we pressed on, me tracking, the guys asking questions about my latest exploits. I was watching the trail, making sure Brewski stayed on it. I needed to catch any signs of him leaving the trail because it could be the break we were looking for. Every once in a while Brewski's tracks stopped and other tracks would stop too. I assumed he was talking to other hikers. I imagined weary hikers running across a clown on this hot trail, writing in their journals of their trek, adding pictures of their interesting visitor. Brewski, the Cody of the PCT.

We were hiking down a particularly hot and dusty stretch of trail when I heard a familiar whirring rattle. I stepped back, colliding with Landon. I held out my arm so he wouldn't step past me. I identified the rattler beside the trail.

"Just walk a big circle around it. Keep your distance and it'll leave us alone."

"This you say after telling us that rattlesnake story?"

"I couldn't get away from that one. If you give them some space they won't bite you. The rattle is just a warning."

We walked a wide circle around the snake and continued on but every time a lizard moved in the bushes or Thez spotted a crooked stick on the ground he'd leap aside with a startled "Aiyee!" I was glad he wasn't trigger-happy.

After four very amusing leaps off the trail within a mile I asked, "Thez, have you ever eaten snake?"

"No, yuck! How could anybody eat a snake?" he responded. "Is it even safe?"

"Guess you don't want to try it on this trip then?"

"What? Eat snake on this trip? No!"

I laughed at him.

"Why?" he asked skeptically. "Is that something we're likely to do?"

"Not if you're that much against it. It's not that bad though."

The trail divided. Brewski took the right turn. Oh, no. Not the right turn. I got out Strict's map. We sat next to the trail as I studied our options. Obviously we had to follow Brewski's trail, but the hike just got a lot longer. He'd taken the Burkhart trail that led eleven miles to Devil's Punchbowl. Why in the world had he done that? I knew he liked visiting towns and campgrounds to raise money but eleven miles was a long detour, especially when Buckhorn Campground was just a little over a mile south. I looked at the map. From Devil's Punchbowl he could have hitched a ride somewhere, or he could have ended up passing Devil's Punchbowl and hitting the South Fork Trail. Oh gee, I hoped he didn't do that. It circled around and hit the Pacific Crest trail behind Eagles Roost. It was a huge circle. The hike to Buckhorn was a pleasant trail following a shady little canyon. Maybe he thought he was headed that way and ended up taking the wrong turn. Either way our search just got longer.

"It's time to ask Strict for help."

"You do it, you know what you need to know."

"I know, but he just won't talk to me in code. I feel silly just talking to him. I feel like a little kid on a walkie-talkie."

I got on the radio, "Testing, testing, Strict?"

"Gotcha Cassidy, what's up?"

"I got good news and bad news. We're still on the trail and it's still plain. That's the good news. Bad news is that Brewski took the Burkhart trail north. Can you send someone around to confirm whether or not he made it to Devil's Punchbowl? They'll have to get down there quick. I think it closes at dusk. If Brewski went to Devil's Punchbowl I've got an eleven mile hike just to see if he left the trail or took the South Fork trail back around to the PCT. If he made it to Devil's Punchbowl we'd be better off hiking back out and starting again from there. If he knew it was a county park, he'd go talk to the rangers and tourists to raise money. But if he thought he was still on the PCT, he could have just followed the trail on this huge twenty mile circle."

There was a long pause as Strict studied the map.

"Will do," he said. "Stay put. No use getting further away if you need to come back."

"Is Victor handy? He could verify Brewski's tracks on the Punchbowl Trail. They are very recognizable. Victor should be able to handle that."

"Ten-four."

I put the radio down.

"Well, guys, we've got a wait ahead of us."

We all shed our packs and found comfortable places to sit and wait. I passed around the cookies again. Thez got a deck of cards from a pocket of his pack, and we played poker with sticks and rocks. No use carrying lots of cash on an empty trail, which made me wonder how Brewski made any money. Rocks were coins, sticks were bills. I would have lost a fortune to Thez except I kept finding more funds around me whenever I was broke. I just hoped these sticks and rocks didn't represent real money.

The sun sank lower and lower and still no word from Victor. I got out my stove and fired it up. I heated water and added it to a pouch of beef stroganoff. The guys took this as their cue to cook dinner as well. I liked to eat before dark to avoid critters and the inconvenience of trying to clean up in the dark. I'd learned to just eat from the pouches to avoid dirty dishes. One very clean water pot and one licked clean spoon was all I had to deal with. I rolled up the used pouch and stuck it inside the trash bag I carried.

It was nearly dark when the radio crackled.

"Cassidy?"

"Go ahead, Victor."

"No sign of clown shoes on the Punchbowl Trail."

Sigh, okay. "You're sure? Did you check the Burkhart Trail and the Punchbowl Trail?"

"Ten-four."

"Did you question the rangers to see if a clown had made the rounds of the station and picnic grounds?"

"It was all locked up. Nobody home."

"Strict? Any ideas?"

"Sounds like you need to just follow the trail."

"Okay, will do. First thing in the morning. I think this is the only camping place for several miles so we're going to camp here."

"Okay."

We set up camp in the few flat spaces around. Landon took a rope out of his pack.

"Anybody else want to tie up their pack tonight?"

We all tied our packs together and he threw the rope over a branch and pulled it up into a tree. We sat around in the dark for a while.

"Cassidy, tell us another story."

"You're as bad as my nephew. The first thing he wants when I go home to visit my folks is a story, preferably one with animals in it."

"Well, you have lots of interesting stories."

"How about if you help me piece together this puzzle I'm working on?"

"What puzzle?"

"The puzzle about what my kidnappers are after in the canyon."

"Okay, what do we have to go on?"

"I was running from Tyrell Trent and I climbed up this big rock that stuck up from the boulder field. When Trent saw me do that it somehow convinced him I knew where this thing was. So, think back to the canyon. When I was up in the big V of that rock the most prominent landmark was the big pine tree in the canyon. If you stood at the big pine tree and looked for another prominent landmark what comes to mind?"

There was a long silence while they thought. I'd been in the canyon many times but I never thought to look for things like this.

"At the top of the canyon there is a rock like a pillar that is tipped. Maybe it points to something," Thez said.

"There is? Can you see it from the pine tree? I've been up there before but I didn't notice one. Of course the first time I was stalking deer. The second time I was attacked by a dog and the third time I was tracking. So I wasn't really thinking about landmarks. Can you think of what the pillar would be pointing to?"

The speculation went on but that's all it really was. Nothing could be decided for sure without going there and searching the canyon in person. We all turned in with the plan to get up at first light.

"Eleven miles to Devil's Punchbowl. We have a long day tomorrow."

In the night I heard a loud *whuffle* noise and a breathless sounding snort. I heard something moving through the brush. I went back to sleep, thinking it was just curious critters. As soon as I dozed off I heard a piercing "Aiyeeee!" and the hapless critter, whatever it was, ran square over my tent in its rush to flee from Thez's panic. Something hard knocked me over. There was a fearful thrashing as the animal got tangled in my tent fabric. I rolled away from the action, hoping I wouldn't get stepped on or struck. A tent pole snapped and tore through the roof of my tent, nearly skewering me in the process. I heard the animal running off through the brush, then quiet settled in.

"Thez!" I yelled. "You have *got* to learn to be quiet in the woods! I don't know what that was but it was harmless until you scared it half to death."

The guys came out of their tents in a rush. Landon held a flashlight. I saw the beam of light shine over the torn remains of my tent.

"Cassidy? You okay?"

"Yeah, I think so." I unzipped my tent and crawled out from the remains of it. I took the poles off the tent and examined them in the dark. One pole was planted firmly through the tent fabric, through the floor and inches deep into the ground beneath my tent. One section was splintered, so the poles were no good to me anymore. I put my hand through the hole. I yanked the pole out of the dirt and removed all the poles from my tattered tent, then stacked up the poles so they would be easy to pack in the morning.

I shone the light on the ground until I picked up some good tracks.

"Well, from what I see now, I'd say I got run over by a very large elk. Thez, an elk is *not* going to hurt you. Even a bear would be unlikely to hurt you, if you just stay quiet, and you don't have food in your tent. There's nothing up here that you need to be that scared of. If an animal investigates your tent at night just wait for it to lose interest. They will usually just get bored and go away."

"It didn't walk around *your* tent making scary noises," he said defensively.

"It did," I countered, "but I'm used to animals in the night. I knew it was harmless if I just ignored it… Look, I'm not angry about the tent. I'm not angry about getting trampled. I just wish you could be more comfortable in the outdoors. There's no reason to freak out even if you do run into a dangerous animal. In those rare instances, it never helps to panic. You have to keep a calm exterior if you want nature to respond to you in a calm manner. You have to be able to think in the outdoors, not just react. We all need some sleep tonight. Let's all try again, okay?"

"Cassidy, your tent is thrashed."

"It's okay, if we get to Devil's Punchbowl, and I need a new tent, I'll just call Rusty, and he'll bring my old one up."

"But what about tonight?"

"Tonight I'll be fine. I'm only going to be sleeping. I don't even *need* a tent except for you guys insisting on it."

I crawled into my flat tent and found my way into my sleeping bag and curled up on my side so the tent roof wouldn't rub against my face. I lay there quietly waiting for the guys to do likewise. Eventually I heard them both return to their tents, heard their doors zip closed, and sleep finally came.

Morning dawned and I was ready to hit the trail. I heated water and made oatmeal and hot chocolate anyway. I examined the ground as I rolled up the tent and packed it away. I was convinced a large bull elk had run over my tent during the night. I wouldn't have believed it except that the track was unmistakable.

Landon looked at me as though he should get out his medical kit.

"Are you sure you're okay?" he asked me.

"Yeah, why?"

"It looks like I took a baseball bat to you."

"Oh, no, not again. Well, at least he didn't step directly on me. It could have been worse."

I made the rounds making sure everybody was on track. I'd eaten breakfast. My tent was packed up. My pack was all set. I was ready to head out. I passed around the cookies again, hoping they would just finish them off so I wouldn't have to carry them.

"Eleven miles today unless Brewski changes our plans," I said.

"You think we can do eleven miles in one day?" Thez asked.

"I can, unless we find Brewski. If Victor was right, we should find him today. Are you ready to give it a try? Thez, something's wrong. What's up?"

"I just can't believe one wrong reaction could result in all those bruises."

"Hey, if you were around more you'd know this is normal. Ask Landon to tell you about when I rolled my BMW. That's his story to tell anyway. I should expect these things to happen by now. But you really do need to guard your reactions when you are in the outdoors. I'm not getting after you, just offering you some practical advice. You will get along better in the woods if you keep a level head. Just work on it, not for my sake, but so you can learn to enjoy it more. For the most part nature is friendly. So don't worry so much."

We hit the trail again and Thez didn't go through theatrics every time he saw a stick. Either he'd forgotten about the rattler or he was making an effort to stay calm. Either way I was glad.

It was a very hot, dusty eleven miles. Brewski stuck to the trail except for brief pit stops. The trail turned rocky and I lost the tracks so we hiked until we reached the end of the rocks. Suddenly, Brewski's tracks were gone. There were still tracks, but no clown tracks. I backtracked to where I'd seen Brewski's trail, then followed the clown shoe prints up to the rocky area. I studied the trail over the rocks. It was plain. He wouldn't have turned off mistaking another way for the right one.

"Okay guys, we need to take a break. Packs off while I figure this out."

I took off my pack so I could move around more easily, and got down on my hands and knees to examine the rock. I looked down the rock face. There were bits of color down there. I climbed down the rock to more closely examine the colorful objects at the bottom. It was like thick foam rubber. I picked up several pieces, looked them over and tried to decide what they were. They had a smooth side and a rough side, like they'd been torn off something larger. I climbed back up the rock and showed the pieces to the guys.

"Do you think these used to be part of a pair of clown shoes?" I asked.

"Who knows?" Thez responded.

"Brewski's footprints disappear on the other side of these rocks. If his shoes were falling apart, he could have changed them. I thought they'd have fallen apart miles ago, but why did they have to do it where I can't be certain? Either we lost Brewski or he changed shoes. The tennis shoe tracks on the other side are easy to track, but I don't know if they belong to him. If he changed shoes it would explain why Victor didn't find any clown shoe tracks at Devil's Punchbowl. Shoot, I don't like these delays when we are trying to make eleven miles in one day. I need to go back and examine the clown shoe prints. Maybe I can find signs of cracking. I was only verifying that they were still there so they could have been giving him trouble for some time."

The guys sat on the rocks while I backtracked, examining the clown shoe tracks for wear and stress points.

Rattlesnakes, elk tramplings, magic disappearing shoes; this search was turning into a three ring circus. All we needed was a clown.

Sure enough, when I got down and examined the prints closely I was able to make out a definite crack right across where the ball of his foot would have been. I went back to the rocks and climbed down again to make sure Brewski hadn't taken a tumble. There was no sign of him down there, no footprints, just little bits of colorful foam rubber. I climbed to the trail again and looked up. There was no way Brewski would tackle a climb like that in his clown get up. There was one more check I needed to make before deciding that Brewski had changed shoes. I went to the tennis shoe tracks and examined them closely, then I went to the clown shoe tracks and looked for any signs of tennis shoe tracks. I backtracked several hundred feet. No tennis shoe tracks.

"Okay, decision time," I said. I then presented the facts. "The clown shoe tracks end at the rocks. The tennis shoe tracks start after the rocks. Worn, cracked clown shoe prints coming in. New tennis shoe tracks going out. No sign of Brewski or his tracks at the bottom of the rocks. No way he'd climb to the top of the rocks. What do you think? I'm about ready to decide he ditched the clown shoes."

There was silence. None of us liked making assumptions. Facts, just give us facts. Facts, however minute, we could deal with.

I continued, "We can't ask Strict. He can't see what we see. He can't tell us anything. The only thing calling Strict accomplishes is a shift in blame if we fail. If we fail it can't be Strict's fault. So we won't call Strict."

Landon looked at the clown shoe tracks carefully then again back at the tennis shoe tracks. They were obviously very new tennis shoes. Even he could see that.

"I say Brewski changed shoes," he said.

"Okay, so we follow the tennis shoes."

We'd wasted a half hour of hiking time on the rocks. I stepped up the pace as we continued on. The tennis shoe prints were very plain, very recognizable, and I liked the tread. It revealed a lot about Brewski's mannerisms that I hadn't been able to read off the clown shoe prints. As we hiked along and I read the footprints, I became more and more convinced that we were still on the right trail. I decided he was an older man than I had first been told but that he was more agile than I had imagined. I had pictured a fiftyish potbellied man, but the person wearing the tennis shoes was not heavy. He was spry and alert and lightweight for a man. I thought when we finally met him we'd instantly like him. Unfortunately, after he gave up on the clown shoes his pace increased proportionally. Walking was easier. Brewski was agile, so the miles went by fast for him. No more slapping along at two miles per hour. I also got the feeling that he wasn't too concerned about getting off the Pacific Crest Trail. A hike was a hike. I just hoped he had enough water to cover the trail to Devil's Punchbowl. Tracking was uneventful that day. We followed Bullhorn Brewski up over Burkhart Saddle and headed down to Devil's Punchbowl. A few miles away I could see the communities of the high desert below so I tried calling Rusty.

"Hey there!" he answered cheerfully. "I sure hope this means you're waiting for me at home."

"No, sorry, I'm following a trail into Devil's Punchbowl but we need a few supplies if you can bring them up here. I'm guessing I'm two miles out."

"Sure, what do you need?"

"My old tent, and any backpacker food we have on hand. This is turning out to be longer than I thought it would be. Brewski didn't stay on the PCT and now it looks like he's started a twenty mile loop. I'll know by the time I see you. If you get to Devil's Punchbowl before I do ask around and see if anybody talked to a rodeo clown within the past week."

"Okay, now tell me what happened to your new tent."

"It had a small mishap."

"And what happened in this small mishap?"

"It got run over by a frightened elk."

"I don't suppose you were *outside* of the tent when this happened."

"No, I was in it. I got tripped over, but not stepped on. The tent got the worst of it. The poles are useless, and there's a hole through it, so I could really use my old tent."

"Okay, I'll see you in a few hours."

"Thanks, it'll be good to see you. I miss you."

"I miss you, too, babe. I'll see you soon."

I put my phone away and kept tracking. Just a few more miles, I kept telling myself.

The turn off to South Fork Campground came up and I saw that Brewski had gone into Devil's Punchbowl, then had come back out and headed for South Fork. Our search wasn't over yet.

Walking around the picnic grounds I noticed Brewski's old broken down clown shoes had been tossed into a trashcan. The material on the shoes matched the pieces I'd found beside the trail.

We discovered a picnic spot that had room for three tents. I opened the map and looked over our route as I was waiting for Rusty to come with my supplies. Hey! I thought, we could drive around to South Fork Campground and I could check the trail there the easy way. We might be able to shave some more time off the search.

"Hey guys, don't set up camp yet," I called out. "Let's camp at South Fork Campground. Rusty can take us there. If Brewski's tracks take off from there, we'll have saved two hot desert miles, and if they don't we'll know he's between Devil's Punchbowl and South Fork Campground."

Making one little observation sure can change my attitude quickly. I was ready to go and happy to be seeing Rusty again. I couldn't wait for him to arrive. I needed something to do so I found some clean clothes and my hairbrush and went to the public restrooms to freshen up as much as I could. I took a sponge bath and brushed my hair then changed into clean clothes. I headed back to our picnic table feeling much better. As I was walking along I saw the Explorer coming up the road. Yes! I took the dirty bundle of clothes and stuffed it into a compartment of my pack. Rusty's eyes were smiling as he stepped out of the Explorer. The worried look almost appeared until he saw me jogging over smiling wide, happy to see him. He wrapped me in his joyful hug.

"I couldn't wait for you to get here. It's so good to see you."

"How about if I just steal you away. You could come back in the morning."

"That wouldn't be very fair to the guys. I wish I were finished with this search, but the tracks continue on to the next campground. You can save us a few miles if you'll give us a ride. Every little bit helps. We can camp there tonight and decide in the morning which direction Brewski went."

"Let's eat dinner first. I thought you'd be ready for some real food so I stopped and picked something up."

He opened the door and the aroma of warm pizza wafted out. He handed me the two pizzas and pulled out a cooler. We took them to the picnic table.

"Hey guys! We have real food tonight!"

Landon's eyes were on the cooler.

Rusty said, "We have a guy's pizza and a girl's pizza. But of course you can decide which is which. I just know Cassidy always orders Hawaiian pizza for herself. So we have a medium Hawaiian with ham, pineapple, and extra cheese. And we have an extra large all meat deluxe pizza. Yes, Wilson, there's a beer in the cooler, but I didn't think you'd want anything heavy after hiking all day so it's just light. There's beer, sodas, and a couple of coolers."

"Ah, the great pineapple debate," said Thez. "Is it real pizza if it's got pineapple on it?"

"What is it if it's not pizza?" I asked.

We all dug in, hungry after a long, hot day on the trail. We didn't have plates and ended up with long, stringy cheese trailing from our droopy pieces of pizza, but it didn't matter. It was a good time with good company. Who cared if we dripped cheese from here to town and back, or that we couldn't put down the pizza to get a drink because the table had three years worth of dust and grime on it? We were having a great time. It was like a party.

I got out the map and showed Rusty what we were up against.

"You know, if we follow these tracks all the way back to the PCT and find out that the other hiker that went over the clown shoe tracks was Bullhorn Brewski, I am going to kick myself royally," I said.

"How could you know he changed shoes?" Thez said trying to be supportive.

"I couldn't. It would be funny to see Strict's face if we tracked Brewski all the way back to Eagles Roost though. No, come to think of it, it wouldn't be funny."

"So," said Rusty, "you want a lift to South Fork Campground?"

"If you don't mind. Everybody throw away the trash you've accumulated so you don't have to haul it around tomorrow."

I found my little bit of trash and threw it away. Then I threw away the damaged tent and made sure the old one was secured to my pack. I offered cookies to everyone, which finished off the bag, so it was thrown out too. I put my dirty clothes in a bag and stuffed it in the back of the Explorer so I could wash them when I got home. I was set: lighter pack, new tent, good pizza, Rusty was here. Everything was looking brighter. We all piled into the Explorer and Rusty drove us to the South Fork Campground. We immediately set up camp before it got too dark. Rusty helped me with my tent, then we went to the trail to see if Brewski had passed that way. I quickly picked up his brand new tennis shoe tracks and saw they led out of the campground and onto the trail.

"That's the next segment," I said pointing up trail. "Five and a half miles to the highway. If we make it to the highway we'll basically be back to square one."

"I tell you what. Make a sketch of the track and I'll drive up to Eagles Roost and hand it over to Strict. He can compare it to tracks they see on the Pacific Crest and radio you if they match up. If they do you can get a lift back up there and save you the hike."

Rusty went back to the Explorer and pulled a blank page from a folder. I then went down to the tracks to sketch it in the fading light. I looked through the backpacker food Rusty had brought up and traded out some of the ones from my pack for meals I liked more. I also added a few more meals to my pack just in case the search went on longer.

He gave me a pleading look as he got back into the Explorer. "Are you sure you don't want to come home with me? I'd have you back here by first light."

I smiled, "Yes, I'm sure I want to go home with you. But I better stay instead. If Landon and Thez aren't going to take the easy way out I shouldn't either, although I bet Thez would take you up on it if you offered. He's the one that scared the elk so bad it took off right over my tent, and all it did was sniff around. You should have seen him after he saw a rattlesnake. I really wish you could have seen that. It was funny."

His eyes laughed as he saw me enjoying myself outdoors.

"I'll swing by Eagles Roost and give the sketch to Strict. Hopefully you can pin it down and find this guy."

"Thanks for coming up here. I feel so much better now. I don't feel all worn out anymore. I just want to finish this so I can go home. Don't forget to tell Strict we're not at Devil's Punchbowl, that we have verified tracks coming out of South Fork Campground."

"Okay, take care of yourself. No more rattlesnakes, or getting run over."

"Okay," I said, leaning in through the open window and giving him a kiss.

It was nice sleeping in my old tent. The new one had packed easier. It was a little lighter, and much more compact, but it didn't compare to my comfortable old tent. It was like being in the hideout except much brighter. I fell asleep hoping to spend the next night in my own bed. My own bed, that was funny. It wasn't my bed but it had earned that distinction in my mind. Rusty's home was my home. Now Rusty's bed was my bed. We really needed to get married. Once I was back home I planned to concentrate on wedding arrangements. I started going through the list of things to do, but it all got confusing as I grew drowsy and fell asleep.

I was up at first light but there wasn't much use in hurrying. We didn't want to hit the trail until Strict called so I let the guys sleep in a bit while I lay awake listening to the birds. I always loved waking up in campgrounds to the sounds of birds in the trees. I never minded when jays raided my backpack. I enjoyed their antics, watching them figure out how to open a bag of chips or trail mix and picking out their favorite treats. One of the reasons I carried trail mix was because so many small animals liked it.

When I thought it was time I rattled the guy's tents and started heating water for oatmeal and hot chocolate. As it heated, I stuffed my sleeping bag in its sack and collapsed my tent. I set out hot chocolate packets and mixed up my oatmeal, eating it just so I could say I'd eaten breakfast. I rinsed out my cup, then made hot chocolate in it. I was pacing camp waiting for the chocolate to cool when I heard the radio crackle.

"Cassidy?"

"Go ahead Strict."

"It's a negative on the sketch. We've looked up and down the trail here and it doesn't match."

"Okay, we'll head out soon. We ought to either find Brewski or meet you back at Eagles Roost today."

"Okay."

The hike from South Fork Campground to the Pacific Crest Trail was a slow and steady upward climb. After cleaning our camp we started up the trail knowing this would be either a very rewarding or a very disappointing day. The hike was pleasant, the trail easy to track on. Many people had gone over the trail after Brewski, but his footprints were recognizable enough that I made do with partial tracks. He only left the trail briefly. We were making our way up the trail through a shady little canyon when we knew we'd found Bullhorn Bob Brewski. No wonder he got the name Bullhorn. We heard him from nearly a mile away singing at the top of his lungs. He'd made up new lyrics to an old, slow rock song, belting out his woes for all the world to hear.

> Sittin' on the mountain side
> Lookin' at my poooor leg bone
> Sittin' on the mountain side
> An' I'm prayin' that the hikers come
> Sittin' on the mountain side
> Waitin' for a handy ride
> Oooo, I'm just sittin' on the mountainside
> Biding my time

As we got closer we realized he was also playing the ukulele. How he managed to still be there after three days was a mystery. You couldn't miss the guy. He was about twenty feet off trail with one leg bent in a position that must have been very painful. But despite being injured he had a whole camp set up around him: a cook stove to one side, sleeping bag to the other, backpack open nearby, and a half empty flask of 90 proof whiskey close at hand. I wished I had a camera. He broke into singing *Amazing Grace* to the tune of *Gilligan's Island* but stopped when he saw us approaching.

"Well halleluiah! I'm saved!" he shouted to the heavens.

"Bullhorn Brewski?" Landon asked.

"That's me," he said thickly.

"What did you do to yourself?"

"It was the snake's fault! Crazy rattler! I was walking along and heard it on the side of the trail and I did what any old rodeo cowboy would do... I dived in a barrel! Only there wasn't a barrel there, and I come down wrong on my leg."

"I can identify with that," said Thez.

I started packing up his camp while Landon and Thez took care of the technical aspects. They called Strict. Brewski reached for the flask and Landon snatched it away and handed it up to me.

"No more of that. You've had plenty."

"It was that or die of dehydration. That stuff kept me alive!"

"Yeah, and happy. You're lucky you're a happy drunk."

"I am not drunk. A minister of the gospel doesn't get drunk. At least not drunk enough to quit ministering."

That caught my attention.

"You're a minister?" I asked.

"Surely am, why? You wouldn't happen to need ministering to, would you?" he asked mischievously.

"No, I'm looking for someone to perform a wedding ceremony in July."

Landon and Thez gave me a warning look, but I felt like this was the right thing to do.

"Now why would I want to do that? I'm hittin' the trail as soon as I can."

"You're going to be laid up for a couple of months. Plus, I think there's going to be TV coverage. If you'll dress like a minister for the ceremony, you can wear the clown getup for the reception. You can even hand out wedding balloons and I bet you catch a few minutes of time on the news."

"Now why would the TV networks care about your wedding?"

"Because of a big mishap I had involving a rescue in a mine."

He squinted at me, "Well, I'll be, it *is* you!"

"If I can swing the wedding for the day the reporters are expecting, I bet they come knocking on my door to do a follow up."

Things got real busy as we got Brewski ready for his trip to the hospital. I kept finding little things that he'd dug out of his pack to entertain himself while he was waiting for help; his ukulele, a deck of magic cards, a disappearing coin trick, a novel, a puzzle book, Mad Libs. How he could carry all that stuff and his necessary backpacking gear I'd never guess. I barely got it all packed into his purple backpack. I didn't try to fit the ukulele inside.

As he was being pulled up into the helicopter he bellowed out, "Onward and upward! Geronimo! Or should I say Ominoreg?"

"Ominoreg?" I asked.

"Yeah, that's the opposite of Geronimo, right?"

I turned to Landon, "I'm going to make a fast hike to Eagles Roost. I'll pick up the paperwork from Strict. You don't need me up there."

"You just want to get home faster. You know what a pain it is to get home from L.A."

"You caught me."

"Be careful."

"I will. Take care of Brewski."

I pulled on my backpack and headed out at a fast walk up the trail to join the PCT and find Eagles Roost on the side of the highway. It was early evening by the time the picnic grounds came into view. South Fork Trail had been an easy hike, then the Pacific Crest Trail added a few more miles to my walk. I was weary, but happy when I entered the picnic grounds and found base camp nearly packed up. Lou had waited for me, and I felt guilty holding him up. He looked me over noting the bruises.

"What happened this time?" he asked.

"Just a minor mishap."

"Thez?"

"Yeah, but don't worry about it. He just needs to get out more. Actually, he was very entertaining."

"But was he a help, or a hindrance?"

"He was very professional once we found Brewski and a real help to Landon."

"And all this," he said pointing to the bruises, "was just a minor mishap?"

"Yeah."

"Okay."

"Do you need a ride back to town?"

"Landon had a car. Do I need to return it?"

We looked around, no car. I guess they took care of that.

"Yeah, I guess I could use a ride if you're headed that way."

Lou dropped me off at the condo. Shadow barreled into me at the door and I spent some time wrestling with him on the floor. That made him hyper and he started racing all over the condo. I was glad to get home before Rusty. I quickly showered, then dressed. I was happy, and perky, and wanted to surprise Rusty, so I put on a dress, curled my hair, and put on make-up.

I was in Rusty's office checking my email when I heard the front door open. I peeked around the doorway to see Rusty drag himself into the condo and wearily glance around the room. Shadow raced up to him and he petted him briefly. His attitude, expressions, even the way he walked exuded a gloom that seemed to fill the room. Shadow walked calmly by his side as Rusty headed for the dog food bin to feed him before letting him out. Silently I crept down the stairs while Rusty's attention was diverted. Shadow took a whole five seconds to eat and then Rusty let him out. I made it to the kitchen just as he turned around to go upstairs and change. When he saw me it was like someone suddenly turned all the lights in the condo on at the same time. Did I really do that to him? His smile lit up the room and he quickly put all his things down on the kitchen counter and opened his arms.

I got lost in the folds of his old brown sports coat, the familiar scent wrapping around me.

"Oh, Cass, my girl is home," he said softly, "my girl is home. And look at you, all dressed up."

"I wanted to surprise you," I said.

"You did that," he admitted. "When I didn't see you I started thinking where you'd be by now, what it meant for the search if you'd completed the circle and still not found Brewski. I didn't want to think about dinner. I don't care what's for dinner when it's just me. But here you are. You're home and

I can care again."

"So, now that you care, what do you want for dinner?"

"Time, just a little time with you. Let's go get you some real food. Let's go some place with cheesecake. You will eat dinner first this time, won't you?"

"If you insist," I said, smiling. "I had more real food on this search than I normally do. I had pizza last night, remember?"

"The days all run together while you are gone. It all just feels like forever."

As we were sitting in a restaurant over steaming plates of real food we laughed and talked while I filled him in on the rest of the search.

"It must have gone well, you're home happy. That's always a good sign."

"Yeah, we found Brewski halfway up the South Fork Trail. He's a real character. If he shows up at the station asking weird questions it's because he's interested in performing our wedding ceremony."

"You're kidding. He's qualified?"

"Well, that's one thing we need to make sure of. He was qualified when he was drunk. We need to make sure he's still qualified when he's sober. I don't think he'd show up at the station drunk, though, and I can't imagine a rodeo clown surviving long if he was drunk often."

"What have you gotten us into?" he asked skeptically.

"You'll like him when you meet him. I need to find a helium tank and some balloons in wedding colors."

"This wedding is getting more and more interesting all the time," Rusty replied.

Chapter 18

For some reason I came back from the Brewski search charged and ready for action. Maybe it was because I wasn't in survival mode. During this last search I was always close to civilization and while I enjoyed the woods, they didn't encroach on my city life this time. Maybe Thez's citified ways had helped to keep me from falling into the lure of the outdoors. Whatever the reason, I was now ready to take on *the wedding*. I went around to several photography studios and looked at their work, compared their prices, and chose a photographer. I picked up the invitations from the printer and started addressing the envelopes to our guests. I also asked Landon and Victor to be the last two ushers. Steve and Randy would come down from the ranch while Zack and Old Frank earned extra pay to keep the place running by themselves. I went to a tuxedo shop to select tuxes and colors. Things were on track.

Rusty and I were relaxing at home watching TV one evening when Shadow walked up to us carrying a basket in his mouth.

"Why does he do that?" Rusty asked.

"He wants to work. Actually, if you don't mind working with him a little it might make the wedding go a little smoother."

He looked at me like I'd pulled another trick on him.

"He's going to be the flower girl," I explained. "I've been teaching him to carry the basket so he can carry it down the aisle at the wedding. The only problem is that I'll need someone at the altar to give him commands. He knows the hand signals but I don't know if he will obey anyone besides me."

"Show me," Rusty said.

I got up and put Shadow in a sit/stay at one end of the condo. I walked across the room, turned to face him, and gave him the signal to pick up the basket. He picked it up and then I gave him the come signal. He started trotting towards me, carrying the basket, so I gave him the slow signal. Shadow slowed to a walk. When he got to me I gave him the sit signal and he sat, putting the basket down.

"You taught him all that?"

"Sure, he likes to work and, since we aren't able to do agility here, we practice obedience instead. He likes going up and down the stairs. Shadow! Go up!" I said sharply. Shadow raced to the top then sat, waiting for the next command. "Shadow, come down!" He raced down the stairs. "Good boy!

What a good dog!" I said, praising him for a job well done. "I just need someone at the altar to give him the commands since I'm not sure he'll be able to follow through on his own. It would have to be you, Kelly or the minister, but you are in a position to work with him so he'd be more likely to obey you. I won't let him do it unless he'll obey. People like dogs, though, and if he's able to carry through, I bet everyone will enjoy watching him play flower girl, well, actually, flower boy. I'm going to have him wear a bow tie if I decide he's able to do it."

"Show me the commands again."

As I demonstrated the commands a second time Rusty took mental notes.

"I'll practice with him and see what happens. We can work on it if you get called out again. What should I do if he doesn't obey me?"

"If it's just a misunderstanding snap your fingers to get his attention, then repeat the command, and if necessary add a voice command. That helps, too. If he chooses to disobey, then you have to physically place him in the correct position and it will make it easier for him to obey, then try again with a reward. The only one he may have trouble with is the slow down command. He wants to work but has to be paying attention to notice the slow down command. If he's going along well and suddenly stops, then go *ah,ah*, in a gruff way and he'll rethink his actions. Just don't praise him too much or he'll get riled up. We don't need a hyper sheltie running all over the wedding. Just praise him enough that he knows his job is done."

Several days later I returned home from grocery shopping to find a For Sale sign in the yard. At the sight of it, I was hit with a sudden stab of sorrow. Change was coming. I knew we'd have to sell the condo, but it had truly become home to me. The new house was still just a vague idea in my mind and it left me feeling unsettled. Rusty came home from work to find me in the hammock trying to come to terms with the upcoming changes. Even while preparing dinner the odd feeling followed me. As a result I went about my preparations in a distracted manner.

Rusty went up to work in his office, but occasionally returned to the kitchen to check on dinner's progress.

"Cassidy, what's wrong?" he finally asked.

"Nothing. Nothing's wrong," I replied.

"Something's bugging you, I can tell."

"It's the sign. It means things are changing and I was comfortable with the way things were. That's all. It'll pass."

"I'm glad you are finally comfortable here. And the new house will become comfortable to you, too. You can make it into the home you want. It won't just be living in a place somebody else calls home. You know we'll be moving in just over a month. It's time we sold this place."

Wow, time had sure flown by. I hadn't even thought about the house except for wishing I could go out there to get an idea about table placement and seating arrangements for the ceremony. Wedding plans had taken over everything except searches. We planned to move June first, and that would start a new frenzy of wedding activity.

"Rusty, something's been bothering me and I should ask you about it before I run off and get kidnapped again."

"That sounds like a good idea," he said warily. "I mean, to ask me about it. What's been bothering you?"

"I was talking to Landon and Thez about this on the Brewski search. I haven't followed up on it but I'd like to. My theory is that I did something when I was with Tyrell Trent that made him think that I know where something is. We don't know what it is, or where it is, but I did something that convinced him I know. Is that right?"

"Yeah, I think so," he answered, his voice still guarded.

"I was told that the placement of the boulders had something to do with finding this thing. The 'investigators' seemed disappointed that the boulders had changed positions during the explosion. So that means they were counting on the boulders to give them some clue about where this thing is."

"Okay," he said, his voice now even more wary.

"When I ran away from Tyrell Trent I climbed up that big rock with the V cut into it. It's the highest landmark in the whole boulder field. And it's the only one I can think of that would point the way to someplace else. When I climbed up that rock, the most prominent landmark I could see from that location was the big pine tree. So I'm thinking that maybe one landmark points to another until whatever it is up there is found. I asked Landon and Thez what they thought the big pine tree might be pointing to and Thez said the plainest landmark he could remember, besides the big pine tree, was a leaning rock pillar. That pillar could be pointing to something, too. It all sounds plausible, but there's only one way to find out if it's true."

"And that is to go up there and check it out?"

"Yeah. What do you think?"

"No."

"No? No what?"

"I don't want you up there on some wild goose chase through the woods with violent criminals after you."

"That's what I thought you'd say."

"So why are you asking?"

"I'm worried about what they'll do if it's not found. If I went up there and found it first, then there wouldn't be any reason for them to keep looking, and they would go away. If they can't find it, they're likely to try finding me again."

"Cass…you don't know how dangerous this is."

"Yes, I do. Well, I know there's a potential for danger. But if they don't know I am up there then how dangerous can it be? And I bet whatever those guys are looking for is illegal as can be. I bet finding it would solve some old outstanding case. Got any old, outstanding cases you need solved?"

"Not that one."

"So you're not going to let me go up there?"

"Not without a whole posse of backup and a bullet proof vest."

"That's all?"

He gave me a gruff look. I backed up two steps.

"What if I came up with the backup and the bullet proof vest? You know I'll have no trouble getting anyone I want to go up there with me. All I need to do is threaten to go alone and anybody I talk to will volunteer to go with me. But I don't need just anybody. A bunch of guys with guns won't be able to hack it. I need Chase. That's who I need. We both know how to get in there and through the woods without being seen. Could I go if Chase goes with me? He would be able to spot places that have been disturbed a long time ago, too, like if they buried the thing. He's used to older trails and older sign. He's got more experience."

"No."

"It would only take one day in there to convince me one way or the other. Either I'd find it in one day of searching or I'm never going to find it. What if I only had one day in the area? I wouldn't even have to camp in the canyon. I could camp before the canyon by the creek or at the top of the canyon at the deer clearing. What do you think?"

"No."

"I'm thinking that if I don't go up there and discover what this is all about then I'll be dragged up there at gunpoint to try and figure it out. I don't want to find whatever it is for them. It must be worth a lot for them to go to all this trouble. They think they are going to get rich off of this and I don't want to make a bunch of criminals rich."

"You're talking like you can find this thing."

"I don't know if I can or not, but I'd like to test the one theory I have."

"And you think you can talk Chase into this wild goose chase?"

"If I can talk you into letting me talk to Chase, I know I can talk him into going with me."

He shook his head, knowing I was right. Chase wouldn't let me go by myself. All I had to do was threaten to go alone and I could get any kind of backup I wanted. And he seemed to know that firepower wasn't the way to go. A group of deputies up there would not accomplish what Chase and I could do alone.

"Cassidy, are you really going up there whether I let you go or not?"

I had to think about that one.

"If I ask you, from the bottom of my heart, to drop this, would you do it?" he asked.

He was only doing it for my own good. We hadn't seen any sign of Troy or his partner since the patrol, so he was thinking this would blow over.

"I want to know if my hideout is safe for camping… And I need to know that Troy is out of the picture so I'll stop worrying about him. I'd drop it if we hiked the Creekside Trail and there wasn't any sign of them being up the canyon. Then I'd be convinced and drop it."

"So, just the two mile hike to the canyon would convince you one way or the other?"

"Yes, but if the yellow van is sitting in the parking lot I'd know that they are still out there."

"If we went there and the yellow van was gone and you couldn't track anybody to the canyon, you'd drop this?"

"Yes."

"What are we going to do if they *are* up there?"

"If they are still up there I'd consider it too dangerous to continue."

"Wait a minute, first you are talking about sneaking in, and figuring this out. Now it is too dangerous. What changed your mind?"

"I thought they might be gone or at least be distracted by their own searching. I wouldn't go into the canyon if they were there and you were with me."

"Oh, but you'd go by yourself?"

"When you can sneak up on me without me knowing it, then I'll take you with me. For now, I won't risk it."

He seemed amused that I was watching out for him, but I was serious. This kind of an operation needed stealth. Rusty had a quick gun and street smarts but you could see him coming from a mile away.

"Okay," I said, "Let's drop it. I don't want this to turn into an argument. We've never quarreled and I don't want to start now. I promise not to go to the canyon. I can't promise what I'll do if Troy shows up, but I won't go up there on my own."

"And I'll work on sneaking up on you without getting caught."

"Good luck."

Watching Rusty try and sneak up on me was amusing. He would have had better luck if he started sneaking without assessing the situation first. He would come home from work and notice I was upstairs, so he would go about his normal activities and suddenly get very quiet when he got to the stairs. I'd be out of sight in the office checking email and call out, "You're four stairs up. Keep practicing."

If I was in the kitchen I'd hear the front door and then things would get very quiet so I'd wait just inside the kitchen for him to sneak around the wall and then I'd catch him. He'd know I was waiting for him and get embarrassed.

If he was serious about this sneaking thing he should have been trying it outdoors, too. Indoors it was easy to walk silently. I wouldn't take him with me unless he was able to get through the woods without being seen or heard and hide his tracks at the same time. That was a tall order to ask a grown man to learn. It was much easier to just grow into the practice like I had. I'd been sneaking ever since I was old enough to walk.

"What am I doing wrong?" he finally asked one day.

"When you come home from work, decide right at that moment to be in stealth mode. You can't just come in and then focus on being sneaky. It tips me off right away. Even go to the trouble of closing the truck door quietly, walk quietly, open the front door without a scrape or a rattle. If you start out from the very beginning in stealth mode, you'll have better luck."

He did have better luck after that but I still caught him. I even caught him on the stairs while I was still in the shower and he didn't understand that at all. Shadow didn't help. Sometimes I made a point of putting Shadow in the backyard just to give Rusty a break from him. He was fighting a losing battle, though. The harder he tried to sneak up on me the more tuned I became to his approach.

"I had a visitor at the station," Rusty said one day after sneaking in and being caught beside the kitchen wall. "A very nice man, dressed in Wrangler jeans, purple western shirt, and half a cowboy hat. He had a broken leg. And he wanted to know when the wedding was. He didn't know my name, or your name, but the officer at the front desk called me. Any idea who that might have been?"

"Bullhorn Brewski," I said with a smile.

"He said to call him Bob. We had a long talk, and he told me all about his hike up the Pacific Crest Trail."

"Is he going to do the wedding ceremony?"

"It's all set for July 27th. I asked him if he was really qualified to do weddings, and he assured me he was. He didn't think it was unusual at all for a rodeo clown to be a minister. He thought of himself as kind of a chaplain to the cowboys. He said cowboys go through lots of rough times. They get beat up and broken, and they see good friends get beat up and broken. They need someone handy to talk to."

"That sounds like him. I'll be glad to meet him when he's sober."

I was happy with this new turn of events, and reminded myself to buy wedding balloons and a helium tank.

Chapter 19

I was walking around a furniture store, trying to get some ideas about how to furnish the new house. A salesperson was tagging along, asking all kinds of questions, hoping for a sale, but he wasn't going to make one until I had a house to put the furniture in. What style was I interested in? What color? How big a room was it? I was relieved when my cell phone rang.

"Cassidy?" It was Strict.

"Hey, Lou," I answered.

"I have a search for you. Should be easy for you. Two guys went off on a one hour hike and have been gone overnight. Their buddy stayed at camp feeling ill. Any chance you can get away?"

"Sure, I need to go home and make sure my pack is ready. Where am I going?"

"Springside Campground, do you know where it is?"

"Yeah," I hesitated, "this doesn't involve the canyon where the cave is does it?"

"Not that I know of."

"I promised Rusty I'd stay out of that canyon except at gun point."

"It's just a couple of lost hikers. That's all I know. Springside is eight miles from Creekside so it's six miles from the canyon."

"Okay, who am I going with? Please, not Thez, not this time." I don't trust him with a gun, I thought.

"Wilson is available, Victor might be by the time you get up here."

"Okay, sounds good. If we are searching for two guys maybe they'd both want to go. I'll be up there in a few hours."

I hung up and slid the phone back into my pack.

"I gotta go to work," I told the salesman. "I'll be back when I have a house to put this stuff in."

"Here, here's my card," he said running after me. "If you come back just ask for me."

I hurriedly grabbed the card, dropped it in my pack, and jumped in the Jeep. I made a quick stop at the station but didn't bother to check in at the counter. After passing through the door and down the hall, I turned left and walked two doors down to Rusty's office. I peeked in the window. Nobody home. I proceeded two doors further down and then peeked into Tom's office. Nobody home. I called Rusty's cell phone. No answer. I hated just taking off without talking to him first. I wrote a note and taped it to Rusty's office door. He'd at least know I tried to talk to him. I didn't come to the station often so the fact that I stopped by would tell him something.

I got back in the Jeep and took off for the condo. Once I was back home, I checked both packs for supplies, checked my 9mm, changed clothes into camouflage, and strapped on my hunting knife. I then wrote a second note to Rusty just in case he didn't go back to the station. Next I drove to the compound to pick up a rescue car, but Landon was just getting out of his Mustang. It was white with black racing stripes running up the hood and down the spoiler, and it matched him perfectly. I always felt more comfortable letting the guys drive to searches. I felt as if those cars weren't mine and I thought the guys preferred to drive rather than be driven so it worked out well for all of us. We arrived at the campground to find a very serious Strict pacing back and forth at base camp. This was rare for him. Usually he was the calm in the midst of chaos and yet this was not an unusual search. It was often a friend or family member who stayed behind and called when someone went missing. I always appreciated being contacted sooner rather than later. The tracks were fresh and there was a higher survival rate when people called sooner. When they waited days before making the call it then became a constant worry that we wouldn't reach them in time. I expected to lead two hungry, thirsty hikers back to their camp later this evening. Strict looked me up and down. He was back in grandfather mode. I saw concern in his eyes and wondered if he knew the missing party. His eyes strayed to my pistol. Or... was his concern for me?

"Cassidy, are you ready for this?"

"Sure. It sounds very straight forward. Two hikers should be easy to track."

"Something isn't adding up here but I can't put my finger on it."

"Why?"

"I don't know. Is your gun loaded?"

"Of course. I wouldn't carry it unless it was cleaned and loaded."

"Good, I don't expect you to need it. I think it'll be just like I said. But something feels off here."

"When something feels off to me I've learned to listen to it. I'll be careful. And thanks for the warning."

A tall man with a beard and mustache approached. I placed his age somewhere over fifty-five. He wore typical camping clothes: tan cargo pants, outdoor t-shirt, and dirty tennis shoes from walking around in ash-filled camp dirt. He needed to shave and was wearing sunglasses, which had left him with a raccoon mask. I couldn't see his eyes and I thought he wore them precisely for that reason.

"Cassidy, this is Sam Johnson."

"It's good to meet you. I hope we can find your friends quickly and easily. What has been done so far to find them?"

"I walked the trail for an hour and a half yesterday afternoon. They were only supposed to be gone an hour one way and an hour back so I thought walking an hour and half ought to tell me something."

"Can you describe your friends to me?"

He described two men, Jake and Doug, who sounded very much like himself except for their height and weight. He couldn't show me the men's shoes because they were wearing the only shoes they had brought along. He watched me as I spoke, and appeared both cunning and amused at the same time. He kept glancing at Landon, but for a different reason than people usually looked at the guys. People in this situation expect the men to be the ones asking all the questions. They weren't used to talking to kid girls about finding lost people in the mountains. This guy was different, though, as he seemed to know I'd be the one in charge, and that made me feel uneasy.

"You're right," I told Lou once we were alone again, "this isn't adding up right. If this search turns bad it'll take Chase to find me. Let's do hourly checks during daylight hours. If we don't answer, get a GPS fix."

"Are you really that worried?"

"Yeah, I've got two men who are looking for something in that canyon. They think I know where it is. If this isn't two lost camping buddies then it is a trap to get me into the area. I'm even tempted to leave Landon behind. I don't want him walking into my trap."

"No, there's safety in numbers."

"Not if he can't disappear. If I were alone I could lose these guys, but I won't abandon Landon to them. For now we need to treat this like the search it is."

As Landon and I set out down the trail, Lou and Sam looked on with worried expressions. I suspected the two had very different reasons for their concern.

I studied the trail and found the footprints of two men but I didn't see any footprints that belonged to Sam Johnson. He hadn't gone looking for his friends. There was no sign of him anywhere near the trail. When we were out of earshot I decided to tell Landon what I knew so far.

"That guy lied to us," I said. "He didn't go looking for his friends. There is something very odd about this search and Johnson was acting very strange."

"How? I didn't notice anything strange about him at all."

"You don't think it was weird that he knew ahead of time that I was the one to talk to about the search? People always think you or Strict are the ones in charge but this guy came directly to me. Don't you think that's odd?"

"Maybe. Maybe he's heard of you. It's not like your identity is a secret. You are getting to be very well known after finding Kelly Green. Then you were on TV twice."

"Three times, but fortunately nobody knew it was me."

"When was that?"

"Never mind."

"Cassidy…"

"You won't tell anyone will you?"

"Not even Thez?"

"Especially not Thez. This is just for your own information."

"It was on TV but this is only for my own information?"

"Yeah."

"Okay."

"Remember the bank robbery at the mall? Some mysterious shopper who brought down a bank robber?"

"That was you?"

"I go to the mall rarely, and the one time I do some guy robs the bank. Go figure. But you don't know that, right?"

"Uh, yeah, right."

"Something just didn't look right at the bank so I was ready for the guy. And now something doesn't seem right about this search. So I have to be on guard again. Are you ready?"

He looked at me as if I was imagining it all, but it was true. Sam Johnson didn't add up. He had lied about the search and now, after reading the tracks of his two buddies, things were not adding up.

"Look at these tracks," I told Landon. "What stands out to you when you look at them?"

"The guy in front is smaller. He isn't very consistent. The bigger guy is more consistent. He's easier to read."

I gave him time to continue but that was all he'd observed.

"The smaller guy is less consistent because he's uncertain. Something is going on here. The bigger guy is more consistent because he is in charge of the situation. I think these guys are up to no good. At least the big guy is."

"And Johnson?"

"Johnson is definitely up to no good and I don't think his name is Sam Johnson."

The notion that Sam Johnson might have another name reminded me of another person who had two names, Douglas Thorne. And Douglas Thorne reminded me of Troy. Rusty said they knew who Troy was and he had shown me a picture. I tried to remember the men in the photos but they were both clean-shaven. If I had a chance I needed to ask Strict to contact Rusty about those photos. If Sam Johnson matched either of the men in those photos then I was in trouble.

I followed the tracks easily until the two men left the trail. Time to buckle down and do some real tracking. I guessed we'd been on the trail for about three miles. I had Landon check our position and it confirmed our location as two point eight miles down the trail. Oh well, I was close. It was going to slow down now that we were off trail. I had to be much more careful here. I soon hit a confusing mess of tracks. When the tracks left the trail the smaller man had turned on the bigger one. A struggle ensued. I paced the ground, trying to make sense of it. Feet had torn into the ground. Plants were trampled. Handprints showed plainly where the men had fallen. The more I read the more I dreaded the end of this trail. I sat down to clear my head.

"Cassidy, what's wrong?" Landon asked.

"Look at the ground," I answered.

He studied the tracks, but it made even less sense to him.

"It's a fight," I explained. "The big guy is beating up on the smaller guy. I know it's different with men and the smaller guy turned on the bigger one, but I get the feeling the smaller guy is being forced down this trail. When I read these things I can't help but remember what it feels like to be pushed around and beaten on. It hurts, more on the inside than the outside, but it hurts anyway."

"Do you want to turn back? If the trail is really the way you read it, we might need help."

"If we go back now we are turning our back on the little guy. We have to keep going for his sake, but we need to cover our bases too. There are a couple of things we can check. And we can get backup. But I don't think backup is what we need yet. First we need information, and for that we should talk to Strict without Sam Johnson around."

"How can we do that? We can't even ask Strict about Johnson over the radio without raising suspicion."

"I know. Strict is supposed to do hourly checks. When you know that Johnson is out of hearing range ask for Rusty's mug shots of Troy. Ask Strict to look at them and tell us if either man matches Johnson. If you know Johnson is there, then that's good news for us. It means his story is more likely to be true. But I expect he'll pull a fast one and disappear on them. Let's keep going. We won't finish this trail unless we keep after them. If they are going where I'm afraid they are going, we've got a little over three miles to hike."

I circled the scene of the fight to find the direction the men had left the area. I had been hoping they might have headed back to the trail, but unfortunately their tracks led deeper into the woods. The tracking was slow off trail because I had to be sure. What I read in the tracks could warn us of dangers ahead, or provide proof of a crime committed.

The forest floor was littered with pine needles, which are notorious for hiding tracks. I examined them to see if the needles had slid underfoot. Sometimes it was obvious when they had. Other times I would look at the bed of needles sideways and I could make out slight foot-shaped indentations in the surface. Sometimes the needles were broken in a pattern that suggested they had been stepped on. It all took careful examination.

The situation weighed on me because of what I read on the trail. It dragged me down. My heart was heavy. My pack was heavy, even though I was only carrying the bare essentials. The trail was slow and I worried that we were walking into a trap. I argued with myself about whether to turn back or press on, but we had to press on for the smaller man. I had been in his shoes enough times to know he needed someone to not give up on him.

The radio crackled and this time I let Landon talk to Strict since he knew what we needed. I left it to him to figure out how to get it while I continued to read the trail.

"Ten-twelve?" Landon said into the radio.

"Ten-twelve." I heard back. Johnson was still there. Good news in a way. Bad news, though, because we couldn't ask for the information we needed. Then Landon updated Strict on the search. Strict was happy with our progress. I wished I was. It was slow going even when the bed of pine needles ended. The needles gave way to vegetation, the vegetation gave way to rocky soil, and the rocky soil gave way to more vegetation. Something was always hiding the tracks which made me wonder if anybody would be able to find us if we ran into trouble. I quit hiding my tracks and started marking them instead. I began by breaking off plant tips as I passed, leaving the ends dangling in odd ways to catch the eye of any help trying to find us. I wouldn't have marked the trail if I'd been alone. When I'm alone I go for invisibility, but I knew that wasn't an option for Landon so I did what I thought he should have been doing.

The tracks led onward and upward but at least they didn't go straight up the mountain. As they trekked diagonally up the mountain I imagined where they were heading and my dread deepened. As they went upward I was relieved that their tracks became easier to read because their footsteps slid and bit into the mountain with each step.

A mile and a half of off trail tracking brought another call from Strict. One and a half miles an hour. That was slow going. But tracking wasn't a fast process. It took patience. Still, I wished we could close in, no matter what this trail ended in, I wished we could close in.

"Ten-twelve?" I heard Landon ask.

"Negative," Strict said matter of factly.

A quick conversation resulted. Landon asked about the photos, and there was a long pause while Strict processed the meaning behind our request. I concentrated on tracking. The trail was still disturbing. Little scuffles marked the way, places where the smaller guy had made a dash to get away or tried to push the larger man down the mountain.

"Cassidy, wait up."

I stopped while Landon caught up to me.

"Sam Johnson wasn't there. I asked Strict about the photos so he'll call Michaels. He almost canceled the search, but we'll wait for the pictures to be sure. If the police records match Johnson you can count on Strict calling us back."

"I don't know where Rusty was today. I tried to talk to him before I left but he wasn't at the station or at home. He didn't answer his phone. I hope Strict can get through."

"Strict has ways. He can go through Schroeder and find a way."

I was getting worried. Puzzling this trail together with what I knew of the area, I decided Landon needed more puzzle pieces, too. He needed to know his options. I spoke to him seriously, "I need to tell you about something, just in case this turns nasty. These guys think I know something, so they won't hurt me until they are convinced they've gotten as much information out of me as they can. If we meet up with them, I can buy time. I can lead them on. There's a place that's safe and defendable that I need to tell you about." I knelt in a sandy spot and made a quick sketch in the dirt. It showed the rock, the big pine tree, and the hideout with the two trees sticking up. "Remember the big pine tree in the canyon?"

"Yeah."

"Look for two fallen trees. When you find the two fallen trees look directly down at the ground. Kick the ground around there and you will find a tarp. Lift the tarp and crawl under it. Nobody knows about this place except me, Rusty, and Kelly Green. But I want you to know about it because you can be safe there, and if I am forced to lead these guys to find what they are looking for it will involve stopping at the big pine tree. If you are in that hideout, and I can bring those people to the pine tree, you can use the hideout as a blind. Leave your rifle in plain sight and put your side arm someplace where they won't think about it. They will take away your rifle and not think about the pistol."

"You act like you've been through these things before."

"Sort of, I've thought about what I should have done when things like this have happened to me before. I don't like rifles so I prefer not to carry one. Maybe I'll get into the habit... Do you understand what I'm telling you?"

"Yeah, if things get rough you want me to ditch you."

"That's not what I said."

"Yes it is."

"Okay, I want you to ditch me for a better plan. I know this canyon. That hideout I told you about has been there for two years. It's my favorite camping spot. I've explored the canyon on foot for two years. I know what I'm talking about and if these guys turn out to be who I'm expecting them to be the plan will work."

The trail topped out and we followed the tracks across the top of the mountaintop ridge. I'd always wondered what was up here, but I hadn't finished exploring the canyon so I hadn't hiked this far from the hideout. I discovered more clearings where deer might be found in the summer. I pushed exploration from my mind and focused again on the tracks. The larger man was pushing the smaller man. There was more desperation in the smaller man's tracks, more force put into the larger man's tracks. I was reading along, focusing on individual tracks when Landon jerked me back. I backed off, instantly wary.

"Wait here," he ordered.

He crept forward and knelt near a bush just ahead. I looked and realized what Landon had seen, a man's foot and beyond it the sprawled out body of Douglas Thorne.

No! I thought, not him. He'd tried to protect me and look what he got for his trouble. Then I also wondered about the identity of the bigger man and if he was linked to Thorne. Troy. The big man could be Troy. I stood, shock rooting my feet to the mountain. Landon reached for the radio, but before he was able to do anything we heard the click of a gun and a voice nearby said, "I wouldn't do that if I was you."

Chapter 20

We froze. Landon looked to me. I was more worried about him than I was about myself. I, at least, had some time on my hands. They wanted me alive. They thought I knew something. If I could just lead them on I could buy some time, but I wasn't sure Landon could.

"Hand over the radio," he said, gun poised.

Landon turned off the radio and handed it over. The man turned and launched the radio into the brush to the north of us. I tried to watch where it landed in case I could get away. I was actually glad to see it go because in an hour Strict would know something was wrong.

"Now the gun," the man said evenly, "you, too."

Landon handed over the rifle. I unstrapped the 9 mm and surrendered it. Landon looked at me, clearly worried. He still had his pistol hidden away somewhere on him while I was defenseless. I still had my hunting knife strapped to my calf, but Landon didn't know that. That knife had saved my life so many times that I now counted on it. Parts of the handle still had bloodstains from my car wreck. They would never come out. That knife and I were linked in some odd way and I wasn't going to give it up easily. Guns come and go. They get stolen, wear out and get old, but not so the knife. I kept it sharp and it was always there.

The man slung the rifle across his back. He tried to strap on my holster and gun, but the belt was too small. He took the 9 mm and stuck it in his pocket, the handle of it sticking out, ready for quick use.

"Now walk," he demanded. "You know where we're going and I don't want any trouble out of you."

"I *don't* know where we're going. Maybe you should tell me."

"You know what we're looking for. So take me there."

"I *don't* know what you are looking for. Trent just assumed I did because of something he saw me do. But it was a coincidence. What I did had nothing to do with what you are looking for. I was just trying to get away from him. I thought he was going to kill me, so I ran away in the only direction I knew."

He grabbed me by the back of my shirt and spun me around. Landon almost made a grab for his gun but decided this wasn't his break. "I don't believe you. You're lying to me. But I don't know why you would. As soon as you're useless you're dead so you better start thinking about where this thing is."

"I *have* been thinking about where it is. Ever since I found out you have been looking for something I was curious, too. I don't know what it is you're looking for and I only have one clue how to find it, but my one clue might lead to another."

"That's more like it. I'm sick and tired of these woods. I'd dearly love to be quit of them for good. Now march. Wherever it is that tipped Trent off, head there."

"It's at least a mile and a half away…"

"March!"

So we marched. I was grateful he was letting Landon tag along but worried that when I hit a dead end they would use Landon against me, to try and pry more information from me. For now though, things seemed to be going as well as could be expected. When we got to the canyon the guy seemed to be encouraged. It confirmed to him that they'd been in the right area. When I headed for the boulder field and Trent's cave, he seemed even more convinced. I stopped under the boulders.

"I was in Trent's cave," I explained. "I ran out with Trent on my tail. I was just trying to stay out of sight. My hands were tied up so I was really only searching for a way out of the rocks that I could climb without using my hands. I found a rock with a big V-shaped crack in it and climbed up the V."

"Without using your hands?"

"I didn't say it was easy. It ought to be easier today, with hands. But you're going to have to let me climb up there. My theory is, that rock is a very prominent landmark. Maybe it points to another prominent landmark. My idea was to climb up it to see what other landmark stands out. Something about me being up there tipped off Trent so maybe, just maybe it'll give us an idea, too."

It took another half hour to find the right rock. It was a huge rock and the guy looked at it, obviously doubting I could climb it.

"You're going to climb way up there?"

"I did it without hands. I'm sure it'll be easier with hands."

"Don't try anything. I'll shoot before I ask questions."

"What could I possibly do up there?" I asked.

I scrambled up into the V and braced myself, ready for the climb. It was an easy climb as long as I kept outward pressure. I was wedged in securely the whole way up. I noticed the gun tip following me as I climbed, so I took my time. The longer I could draw this out the more time Strict had to figure out something was wrong. As soon as he became overly suspicious back up would be sent.

I announced from the top, "The most prominent landmark I can see, just like I thought it would be, is the pine tree in the canyon. I can't see any other landmark that stands out."

As I climbed back down the V I looked at the men below. They wanted me alive. Would they really shoot me? I worked my way closer to the edge of the crack. I needed to give Landon a break. Any kind of a distraction would let him slip away. But would he do it?

I took a deep breath and launched myself at the big man. A shot went off barely missing me, zinging off the rock behind me. We came crashing down in a tangled heap.

"Landon! Go!" I yelled.

He stood his ground.

"Go! You know what to do!"

I saw him dash around the boulder. Would he go to the hideout? I had no way of knowing. The big man clamped an arm around my neck and got up, dragging me with him. When he stood up my feet were no longer on the ground. He tightened his grip, looking around for Landon. I was relieved that I couldn't see him, but I knew he was near.

"Looks like your chicken boyfriend skipped out on you," the big man laughed, then he threw me into the face of the rock. I hit the hard surface and slid to the ground landing feet first.

"Let him go, he doesn't know anything!"

"But you do," he said, closing in. "If you want to live to see tomorrow I suggest you lead me to that stash."

A stash? A stash of what?

"I told you, this is just a theory. I'm just looking, same as you."

He grabbed me by the shirtfront and pointed the gun at my head. "Then start looking!" he growled.

"Why? Why should I help you?"

I was just buying time. Every second Landon had to get to the hideout would give him a better chance of finding his way inside.

"You give me a hard time and it's going to get much worse for you. I don't have to be nice about this."

The gun swept sideways, knocking me on the head. A fist came up connecting with my shoulder. I was prepared to take a lot of bruises before leading these guys to this stash. I was also buying time for me, for Landon, for Strict, and for Rusty. A lot of things needed to happen to get me out of this. Time was my friend, even time spent being beaten was time I could use. I was convinced they wouldn't kill me yet. Pain in the ass I might be, but I still might be useful. I just hoped Landon wasn't watching this.

"Move it!" he growled, shoving me toward the canyon. I stood defiant. He shoved me again. I saw a movement off to the side. Landon stepped around a rock and fired, hitting the man square in the chest. I stood, paralyzed in shock.

"Landon? How could you? How could you? I wouldn't have. I couldn't have. He could have been brought in. This wasn't hopeless."

"Cassidy, he was beating you!"

"I asked for it. I was stalling. I knew he'd hit me. So I asked for it. To buy time. To give backup a chance to find us. They could have brought him in. He didn't have to die."

Sam Johnson stepped up behind Landon.

"Thank you," he said. "You saved me the trouble. I was just wishing you'd done it a little closer to our goal. Hand over the gun."

Landon looked like he was going to hand over more than the gun, but Johnson had a gun on us too.

"Now that you are really disarmed and Doug and Jake are out of the picture I'm ready to finish this. Where is it?"

"We don't know yet," I told him.

"I suggest you start looking then," he said, holding the gun to Landon's head.

"I want to know something first," I said.

He cocked the gun. "Yeah? What?"

"Are you Troy?"

He smiled. "I see your brain works. Has it figured out *this* little puzzle?"

"I don't know. I guess we'll see. You're pretty good at letting other people do your dirty work."

"And you're pretty good at shaking them. I gotta give you credit for that. Somebody needs to tell you there's a very fine line between bravery and stupidity. I'm not sure which side of the line you're on yet. We ought to know by the end of the day. Now move! You know what I want. Put that brain to work or have it blown to bits."

"Let Landon go first. He doesn't know anything. He can't do anything unarmed. He'll just make things difficult for you if you take him along. So let him go. Handcuff him to a tree or something. Handcuff him to Jake. He can't go far with Jake in tow."

Troy took the rifle and the 45 off Jake's dead body. He frisked Landon, finding the handcuffs in a pocket. He put one cuff on Landon and the other cuff on Jake.

As a tracker I never saw a use for handcuffs, but the deputies carried them religiously. Funny, I still didn't think of myself as a deputy. I hoped Landon remembered that Jake had three guns. My 9mm was still somewhere on him.

I headed for the big pine tree. Just me and Troy. Looking for something, but I didn't know what. All I could do was follow my instincts, and right now they said to head for the big pine tree.

"Bet you didn't know my gun has a timer on it. It fires a bullet every hour on the hour. The more it shoots the more accurate it gets. You might want to find the stash before you catch too many bullets."

"Then I hope you can hike fast. I expect to do a lot of walking to find this thing." I explained my theory to him as we stood at the pine tree looking for a landmark. I found the rock pillar Thez had told me about. How had I missed noticing that during all my trips up here? Admittedly, it blended in with the trees, but it should have caught my eye long ago. "I say the next landmark is the pillar. Can you find anything else it might be?"

"You better be right, you know. Your life depends on it."

"It's all I know to try."

We headed up canyon. Where was a rattlesnake when I could use one? Any kind of a distraction would be a help right now. I could slip into the woods and disappear if I just had a little space. I thought I could get away if I had five seconds of distraction. This was my canyon. I could escape in this canyon. Just a few seconds was all I needed, but it never happened. We walked up-canyon until we got to the rock pillar.

"I'm hoping it points to something," I said. "It's what makes the most sense. If someone were going to hide something, and needed to find it again, they might use a landmark as a pointer."

Troy and I looked up canyon and down, across the ridge in both directions, but nothing stood out.

"I had to climb the boulder by Trent's cave to see the next landmark. Let me climb the pillar and see what I find from up there."

"Can you climb that thing?" he asked, although he didn't seem very concerned about my safety.

"There's only one way to find out. I've climbed rocks before. It slants so I should be able to get up the top side of it."

"Just remember, one wrong move and you're dead."

"One wrong move up there and you won't have to shoot me. The fall will do it."

I approached the pillar cautiously. To be honest, I didn't know if I could climb this rock or not. It was well over the eight to ten foot limit that I usually placed on rocks that I took on. I was guessing the height at around fifty feet. I should be able to see a lot from up there.

I found a handhold and a foothold, and started up. I decided right away I needed to take a technical rock climbing class. This rock was really a climb intended for ropes and I shouldn't have been attempting it. One good thing about it, you can't rush a climb. I could take as long as I wanted to climb this rock. Troy couldn't find fault with my actions as long as I was trying, or it looked like I was trying.

Every few feet I would stop to look around. As I pretended to examine the rock face I was actually studying my surroundings. I could see men making their way up canyon and others making their way across the ridge. My heart raced. They were walking into gunfire. How could I stop them? Did they see me up here? I didn't know what to do. They were still a good ways off. I decided to continue climbing, continue to keep Troy distracted. I noted his gun barrel still following me up the rock, as if I could try anything except killing myself from up here. The fall would do more damage than a bullet at this point.

The men on the ridge were close enough to see me now. I stepped up my climbing pace, then very carefully pulled myself up onto the top of the pillar. There were only a few feet of space up there and looking down made me feel uneasy.

I scanned the area around the pillar, but couldn't find a landmark that stood out. I examined the walls of the canyon, looking for anything unusual. This was what I was good at, right? Finding things out of place. So I studied the area around the rock pillar, and something finally caught my eye. I wasn't sure.

"Troy?"

"Yeah?"

"How big is this thing you are looking for?"

"It's in pieces. Shoebox-sized pieces, and I hear there's about fifty of them, but I can't be sure. What do you see?"

I looked over the spot carefully. What I saw appeared to be a small cave, or possibly an animal's den. The opening had been blocked by rocks. Purposely placed rocks. It was very well hidden between two curves of the canyon wall and would only have been seen from up on the pillar.

"If I climb down I won't be able to see it. I'm not even sure this is it. It just looks like a possibility. I can guide you to it."

"No, you show me."

"We'll use up the rest of the day if you wait for me to climb down. Plus I can't see it from down there. If you want to know the location, then follow my instructions."

He aimed the gun at me and pulled the trigger. A bullet zipped past my ear. I stood still. Hitting the ground was not an option up here. I noticed several men dash forward and then check themselves. Take your time guys, we need Troy good and distracted.

"Okay, you're brave *and* stupid," he said.

"Walk south until you have to stop," I instructed pointing in the direction he should go. I thought pointing would also tip off the men closing in where to search for Troy. This dangerous rock pillar was turning out to be quite advantageous.

Troy walked cautiously to the south, trying to keep an eye on his destination and on me at the same time. When he hit brush I told him to stop.

"Now go around the brush to your right. See the rock against the canyon wall?" I called out, pointing.

The men were closing in quickly. I could make out faces now as they crouched in the forest, closing in as quietly as they knew how. Troy suddenly caught a glimpse of a black swat team uniform moving through the bushes.

"Damn you!" Troy yelled, and in a panic he raised the gun at me and fired. There was nowhere to go! I was standing on a pillar, a rough three-foot square area of rock. It was slanted. It was hard. Two more shots followed and a sharp sting in my side made me dive for the rock anyway. I hit the rock hard and began sliding. As I felt my feet slide over the edge I spread out, creating as much friction as possible. The sliding slowed, then stopped, so I felt cautiously for something to grip.

Be small, Cass, just be small. The end of the pillar faced Troy but there wasn't much I could do about that at first. After the initial shock wore off I began to inch my way to the far side of the pillar and away from him. This put me in line for my descent but I didn't think I could do it. I clung to the rock noting the red smear from the wound on my side. It burned and stung.

Please, don't fire! I thought, I can't stand any more killing today. Please don't fire! I clung to the rock, dreading the sharp sounds of violence I expected. I heard the men below. Rifles readying. Was Rusty down there? Was Troy set to fire on Rusty? I looked around the rock and another bullet zipped by my head.

"Cass, don't move!" I heard shouted from below. Rusty. Rusty was here.

It was a standoff. The police wouldn't shoot unless forced, but Troy was hell bent on putting a bullet in me. Guess he was mad at losing his stash. As the standoff continued, though, I felt a trickle of blood down my side. I couldn't stay up here forever. If I let myself grow weak, I'd never make it down.

"Rusty?" I called out, "I need to climb down. I need help."

"Cass, no! Just wait! We'll get you down."

"I can't. It's either climb down or fall down. I can't wait that long."

I began my descent, carefully feeling for footholds and handholds, lowering myself slowly, ever so slowly. I looked down. It was a long way. I noticed blood dripping off my shoe to the forest floor below, Rusty's worried face gazing up at me. All of a sudden there was a skirmish below but I couldn't let it distract me. My legs were starting to get shaky. I had to stop. I needed a stable place to stop but there were no footholds big enough for me to rest on. Keep climbing, Cass, even if you don't make it, you want to be closer to the ground. I kept going but every move was getting harder, harder to find, harder to focus. I felt with my foot for a crack or a bump to use, thought I had one but slipped as I put my weight on it! I dug in with my fingers, leaned into the rock. Where was it? Where was the foothold? Please, I need a foothold! My right leg didn't want to work right. I needed that foothold now! Anything! I felt this way and that on the rock face, the red smear on the rock growing. At last I found one, but the tension of the moment had drained me. I leaned into the rock. Stop. Rest. Just a short rest and I could make it. I felt for the next foothold and the next, getting shakier as I descended. I looked down again. If I could just make it five more feet Rusty could give me footholds. Please, just five more feet. I felt my way down. I was shaking so badly I thought I'd shake myself right off the rock. Just keep climbing, Cass. Just keep on… and then I felt Rusty's hands pluck me off the rock. He held me tightly as he ran away from the scene behind us.

"Victor! Where's Victor?" he yelled.

I felt Rusty stop, sink to the ground. Victor jogged over.

"Michaels, you have to let go," Victor said. "Come on, man, I can't do anything till you let her go."

But he couldn't. He needed his few minutes; just a few minutes of closeness to prove I was still there, still with him. I didn't fight it but I was fading, and I needed to tell them some things before it was too late.

"Someone go find Landon. He's okay, but he's down by the big rock with the crack in it. And Douglas Thorne, his body is…"

"Up on the ridge, we found it."

"Rusty, I found it. I found what they were looking for. We need to go get it. Troy needs to see it's found so word gets around. The canyon won't be safe until that thing is removed and they know it's gone. I'll go. I know where it is."

"You're not going anywhere."

"Please Rusty, it's important. I need to know the canyon is safe. The hiding place looks like an animal den covered with rocks. It's above where Troy was standing. And somebody go help Landon."

"I thought you said Landon was okay."

"He is, he's not hurt, but he's handcuffed to a corpse, and he's going to be mad as hell. He can't move until someone goes down there and unlocks him."

Victor laughed. "How'd he get handcuffed to a corpse?"

"I knew Landon would try something and that Troy wouldn't hesitate to kill him, so I talked Troy into leaving Landon behind. I knew Landon had handcuffs on him, so Troy cuffed him to Jake."

Rosco hurried in to help Victor.

Victor was more persistent and said, "Michaels, let go. Cassidy?"

"Rusty, I don't know how bad it is but it's bleeding like crazy. Victor should probably have a look. Troy got me in the side. One shot out of four and he only hit me once. He's a lousy shot. Come on. This needs to be done or I'm likely to scare you even worse." I struggled to get up, stood shakily, and found a place to lie back down. Victor opened his pack and went to work. Triage. Examination. Their expressions grew grim. I heard the two men consult each other quietly.

I heard codes fly around the scene. A call for a coroner for Douglas and Jake. A code for 'officer down'. Who? Who would that be? It hurt to hear that code. A condition code. Serious.

"Victor, go help them. Please. It's okay."

"Cassidy, they're talking about you. Lay still." Me? I still didn't feel like a deputy. I was just me, trying to stay out of trouble while I helped the real deputies. Sometimes it backfired.

We heard a high-pitched shot way off in the distance. Everybody stopped in their tracks wondering what it meant.

"It's okay," I said, "I think that was just Landon figuring out my 9mm was still on Jake. Maybe he shot through the chain."

An officer wearing rubber gloves handed Rusty a parcel. Rusty put rubber gloves on, too, and opened the top. He took out stacks of bills. Twenties, fifties and hundred dollar bills.

"Troy said there were around fifty bags like that... So, I did find it. My theory panned out. That's good to know. Did they get him? Troy. Did they get Troy?"

"Yeah, babe, they got him. I just wish they'd gotten him before he got you."

Tom rushed up. He wasn't dressed in his usual sports coat and slacks. He was ready for action in swat team black.

"Guess you weren't kidding when you said you kept the station hopping."

"I don't mean to. Trouble just seems to follow me."

"You going to tell me about it?"

"Sure, as long as Landon is there. I didn't understand his actions and he didn't understand mine, so we need to hash this out."

"Where is he?"

"I hope he's not still handcuffed to that body. I left him down by the cave."

Since the standoff was at the top of the canyon, the helicopter was able to land in the clearing where the deer graze. They trundled me off to the helicopter and it clattered away. I closed my eyes, waiting for the familiar weightless feeling to hit my stomach and then go away.

Rusty rode along stoically. I knew he was angry that I had gone on such a dangerous search. I should have turned back once I realized it was no longer a search and rescue operation. But I couldn't turn my back on Douglas Thorne, and when I could it was just a few seconds too late. The trap had been sprung.

"Cassidy, you there?" Victor asked.

"Yeah, I'm okay. I still don't understand what the big fuss is about. I'm fine."

"You always think you're fine. You said you were fine right before you passed out last time I rode to the hospital with you."

"I'd rather pass out. I hate hospitals, especially emergency rooms. Just stitch me up and toss me out."

"Can't do that. You're in for a tough night. You up for it?"

"Can't be worse than the first part of my day."

Victor was halfway joking, trying to keep my spirits up, but when I got to the hospital they were doing anything but joking. This time Victor didn't go off and do paperwork like he usually did after delivering me into the hands of the hospital staff. Something about this case had touched him in a different way. He'd seen me cut up, bruised, battered, and scarred. Why was getting shot any different?

Some quick scans and tests and I was whisked off to surgery. Rusty managed to sneak in a quick, worried kiss as I was wheeled away.

I woke up slowly. Sounds made their way in first. A quiet conversation by the bed. People walking in the halls. The stitches felt uncomfortable. A shot to the side. If I was lucky it just meant a lot of bleeding. If I was unlucky it hit something important. I'd know pretty quickly. One look at Rusty's face would speak volumes.

"I need to walk around a bit," a voice in the room said. Lou's voice. I heard him get up and walk out of the room.

Why was Lou here? Where was Rusty? I reached out, looking for that familiar hand. Rusty leaned forward, found my hand and gave it a squeeze. I opened my eyes slowly.

"Hey," he said. Smiling eyes. That was good news. "Be still, babe. You okay? Are you all here?"

No, I was groggy, uncomfortable and sleepy, but I also wanted to stick around.

"I think so. Guess surgery went okay?"

"Yeah, it went okay."

"Why is Lou here?"

"He was just worried. Everybody was. Victor waited for word after the surgery. Lou arrived about an hour ago. Landon was here after he finished on the mountain. He said he'd be back in the morning."

"Is he still mad at me?"

"Only because he cares about you."

"You think Kelly would like to climb that pillar?"

"No. I don't think he could. I couldn't. Not knowing whose blood is all over it. I just couldn't."

"That's too bad. It's a challenging climb."

"Maybe in a year or so, when the memories have faded and the rock has been rained on several times. Maybe then."

"Okay. Can I go too?"

"You can show us how it's done."

"It's easier at gun point. I didn't think I could do it, but I had to."

Lou stood in the doorway. When our conversation ended he entered the room.

"Looks like we are out of the woods," he said.

"Yeah," I said. "Let's go back."

"Not for a while, you're not. And next time a search feels off to you I want to know about it. You knew within a mile of base camp that something was wrong. You could have turned back any time and no one would have faulted you for it."

"I couldn't. I knew Douglas Thorne was in trouble."

"Douglas Thorne was a lying, thieving, no good crook."

"He was a man who happened to have a soft spot for little blonde trackers. He let me go when he was supposed to capture me. Then he was killed because of it."

In the morning, after breakfast, I was dozing peacefully, hoping for word that they would let me go home. I must have fallen asleep because Landon was there when I woke up. At first I worried and just lay there, patiently waiting for the tirade, but it never came. The expression on his face was calm. That was good. He scooted his chair over closer to the bed so he could speak in a quiet, gentle voice.

He looked me square in the eye. "*Never*," he said, "never do that to me again."

"I'm sorry, but I did it for your own good. He would have killed you without thinking twice about it. Douglas and Jake are dead because of him. He would have killed you, too. He needed me to find that money."

"*Never* put yourself in danger to protect me."

"I didn't. My chances were about the same either way. It's your chances I was worried about, and I'm sorry I got after you about shooting Jake. Later I realized that if you had followed my plan you would have ended up shooting him anyway. It was just a shock to see him fall at my feet when I was expecting him to slug me."

"Never, ever take a hit for me."

"Landon…it was worth it. If it gave you time to get to the hideout, or gave Strict and Rusty time to call in backup, then it was worth it. That's not what put me here."

"It could have. I'm starting to worry about Michaels. I have a better idea of what he goes through now. Do you know how hard it was, knowing you were out there with a killer, hearing all those shots, unable to do anything? You can't possibly know, or you wouldn't have done it."

"If you could have talked Troy into leaving me behind, would you have done it? If you knew he only wanted some information and you could supply it, and that I could only be used against you, or killed while you watched, would you try and get me out of the picture?"

"I can't honestly answer that. But I can see where you are coming from."

"I'm just glad he shot me where he did. I have to wear a strapless gown for my wedding. I didn't even think about getting shot at when I bought a strapless gown."

"Oh yeah? You know, I've never even seen you in a dress. Do you ever dress up?"

"Only for Rusty."

"Rats."

"I'll probably wear a dress to the rehearsal dinner."

"I'll be there," he said with a wink, and I knew I was in the clear.

Chapter 21

I walked slowly and stiffly into the condo. Shadow rushed up excitedly, but Rusty grabbed him before he was able to jump on me. I had some recuperating to do. I'd appeared to be fine in the hospital, but that had been a requirement for being discharged. I had kept up the pretense long enough to be released. Now, at home, I let my guard down and felt very uncomfortable. It was hard to move around with staples in my side and I tired easily.

Why did this always happen when I needed to be physically active? I needed to start packing and hauling boxes around, and I wasn't allowed to lift anything. Rusty didn't appear concerned about the packing, though.

"Don't even start yet. Just rest. You'll know when you're ready."

So I rested. I rested and was bored stiff. I needed to get out and work on something to improve myself, then I'd start to feel better. Progress always seemed to encourage me, but progress was a long time coming. The first few days just the stairs were a challenge. I'd get downstairs then be unable to make it back up. When Rusty came home from work I'd be asleep on the couch with no energy left to even climb the stairs. Once I fell asleep in the hammock and it sent Rusty into a panic. He searched the condo, checked the Jeep. Had I tried to go out? What had happened? I finally awoke and sleepily came in the back door. The sudden sound of the door opening caught his attention and he rushed down the stairs and through the kitchen.

"Cass, I looked all over for you! Don't do this to me," he said, wrapping me in his usual home-from-work hug.

I thought it was amusing that he could keep his head while I was being shot at but my sleeping in the hammock had scared him.

A week went by and my strength started returning. Rusty brought home some boxes with strict orders that I was not to carry them. I slowly filled the boxes with nonessentials and Rusty carried them downstairs, stacking them in the garage.

June first was just around the corner and I was determined to be ready for moving day. I started walking, and when that became easier I went to the gym, working my way back by strengthening my body. I couldn't run without hurting my side, but as long as I took things slowly my strength increased. I began carrying my pack around the house again, until Rusty walked in after work and caught me wearing it.

"No," he said, "I don't care what Strict says. You're not going yet."

"I'm just practicing. I've been wearing this around the house just to get used to the weight again. Strict didn't call. I'm beginning to think he's not going to... Rusty, why was this time so different? It feels like everybody has backed off. Everyone is treating me like I'm going to break. I don't get it," I said, taking my pack off and setting it aside.

We sat together on the couch where we could be close and talk.

"Babe, I think you finally convinced them you're human." He paused. "When you heard the officer-down code up on the mountain it hit you differently, too. Remember? You assumed the code was about somebody else? You instantly felt for that person, didn't you?"

"Of course."

"Why?"

"Knowing someone got shot makes me feel helpless for that person."

"And you think it affects the guys any different?"

"I can't tell by looking at them. You're the only one I can read in a tense situation."

"It's a self defense mechanism. We have to concentrate on business, so emotions get shoved aside. But they are still there, especially when you are involved. It didn't take you long to work your way into their hearts."

"I wouldn't make a good cop. I can't shove things aside. I see things for what they are. I feel it all."

"You don't always see things for what they are or you wouldn't do half the things that get you in trouble."

I gradually filled boxes and Rusty carried them down to the garage. The condo became even more bare, and June first crept up.

We sat across a table from Mrs. Morgan and a smartly dressed real estate agent to go over the paperwork and sign the loan documents. Mrs. Morgan smiled pleasantly, although she seemed a bit melancholy. I guess I would have felt the same way myself if I were in her shoes. She was leaving the home that her husband had built and would be moving to a small apartment in town. It was a reminder that time never stands still.

"I received your beautiful wedding invitation," she said pleasantly. "It will be good to see such a wonderful beginning to your time in this house. I'm glad it's going to see some life and happy times."

"Me, too. Now that we can move in, I am excited to start planning the rest of the wedding. We'll have family and friends and half the police force here. I was thinking of putting a gazebo in the yard for the wedding."

"Oh," she said, "I always wanted a gazebo. They look so romantic. I hope you do it."

We talked and signed papers, and then she reluctantly handed over the keys to the house.

The next day Kelly and Rhonda showed up at the condo bright and early. I hadn't been expecting them, although I'd been wondering how Rusty and I would manage moving the furniture and heavy boxes by ourselves.

"Don't lift," admonished Rusty.

Kelly looked at me sternly. "What did you do this time?"

"I haven't done anything for weeks," I answered truthfully.

"She went and got herself shot," Rusty said grimly.

"It's no fun to get shot," Kelly said. "I know. Where'd you get shot?"

"On a rock pillar at the top of the canyon," I answered, trying to make light of the situation.

"You know what I mean."

"Oh, all right, in the side. But the guy was a lousy shot. It took him four tries to hit me once."

Rusty broke in, "You can vacuum or clean if you need to do something. When we get the first load to the new house you can unpack boxes while we go for the next load. We'll be moved in before too long if you unpack while we haul the furniture and boxes."

There was no sense in arguing, so I went upstairs and started cleaning. The condo would sell faster if everything was clean and shiny. I started at the back of the condo, away from the guys so I'd be out of their way. I found the box of cleaning supplies and told everyone not to load it. I sprayed and cleaned, mopped and scrubbed. While cleaning the bathroom I remembered the shower in the new house. Hoo boy, the shower. Rhonda vacuumed Rusty's office then started on the stairs. I worked my way out to the bedroom, vacuumed the carpet, washed the windows, then the baseboards, and finally the walls. Shadow followed me around and lay down close by, watching me work. I was glad that he'd chosen to follow me instead of the guys going in and out the front door.

"Cass? Are you ready?" Rusty called up to me.

I came downstairs, Shadow in tow. The guys piled into the truck. Rhonda and I took their shiny, Kelly green 1968 Dodge Charger so their car would end up at the new house. I put Shadow in the backseat. We drove out of town following the truck up into the hills, winding around from one road to the next. When we turned onto our new street I caught the name on the signpost. Lost Hills Road. How appropriate was that? We followed the road around until finally Mrs. Morgan's house, our new home, came into view. The flowers were still on the porch and the welcome sign remained next to the front door. But other than that the house appeared empty and lonely looking. I was hoping to fix that little problem real quick.

We walked Kelly and Rhonda from room to room, showing them the house. Rhonda loved the kitchen cupboards. Kelly liked the fireplace in the den.

"And what did you say your favorite part of the house was?" Kelly asked.

I blushed. "This is embarrassing," I said.

Rusty grinned broadly. He seemed to be enjoying my predicament.

"If Rusty knew what my favorite part of the house was, he never would have asked me that question in front of you two."

"Oh yeah?" Rusty said.

"I hope you wouldn't."

"Oh."

I took them to the master bedroom and opened the door on the bathroom.

"There you go, the shower. The shower is my favorite part of the house."

And there it stood in all its shiny brass glory, the big, tile bench sitting there behind clear glass doors, two shower heads, room for two. It reminded me of the stage in a risqué bar with pole dancers. I blushed again.

"I'll leave you to think what you will."

I went outside and opened up the back of the truck, looking around for a lightweight box. I found one that I thought had pots and pans in it. It wasn't heavy, just bulky. Kelly pulled it out of my hands and walked into the house.

"Nice shower!" he quipped as he went by.

"Yeah," said Rusty, "I'm glad she likes the shower, too."

I looked for another light box. I found one that I thought had towels in it. I picked it up and Rusty quickly jerked it out of my hands.

"Why don't you go inside and unpack the boxes?" he suggested.

Oh, all right. I went inside to the kitchen and popped open the box holding our pots and pans. After washing and drying them, I decided which cupboard I wanted to store them in and started putting them away. As the rooms gradually filled with boxes, I wandered from room to room unpacking.

When the furniture arrived and was being placed in the various rooms I watched as the house began to fill up.

"The couch goes in the den," I called out as it came through the front door. The computer desk followed, then the bed and dresser.

"Anything we need to move before we go back for another load?" Rusty asked.

"Umm, it's up to you. Are you sure you want your office next to the living room? Wouldn't you rather have it at the end of the hall?"

"Why?"

I took him to the master bedroom. I was embarrassed again but hopefully it would only be in front of Rusty. I pointed to the wall with the bed against it. "What's on the other side of that wall?"

"The guest room."

"Now, which room would you rather company stay in? The room on the other side of the wall from our bed? Or the room a little further away down the hall?"

He paused, scratching his head. "Okay. We'll move it. I thought the guest room should be the bigger one. I don't need much room for an office."

"It's up to you. You can use the smaller room for your office."

"No, no, you're right."

I smiled. He'd never had his parents visit before or he would have thought of that for himself.

"Kelly? Grab the end of this desk," he called out.

The guys hauled furniture and boxes while Rhonda and I unpacked. Rusty was right, we were nearly moved in by the end of the day. We all sat together in the den and shared a satisfied sigh of relief.

After returning the truck, we went out to dinner at Trujillo's, a Mexican restaurant just off the downtown area. Canned mariachi music blared, the food was good, and we were so tired that everyone just sat back to enjoy the atmosphere. Waitresses in peasant blouses and multicolored skirts waited on us and brought steaming plates of enchiladas and chile rellenos. Rhonda ordered tacos, gringo Mexican food. They fell apart as soon as she bit into them.

After dinner we thanked Kelly and Rhonda for all their help and they drove off to their little house in the mountains. Rusty and I took a moment and walked through our box-filled home. At least now most of the boxes were empty. Rusty hadn't accumulated many possessions during his bachelorhood and I hadn't owned much when we'd moved in together, so moving had been fairly easy. I gathered up empty boxes, nesting as many as possible, and took them to the garage. Rusty stopped me in the middle of my box gathering.

"Enough. You don't have to do it all today. The wedding isn't for two months."

"I know. I just don't have anything else to do, so I might as well gather boxes."

"But there is something else for you to do. And you need to do it before you wear yourself out," he said, pulling me close.

"Oh, I do, do I?"

"Yes, and it's important. If we don't do this I'm going to go nuts."

"Oh, you are?" I said, laughing at him.

He grabbed my hand and tugged me gently towards the bedroom. "You know, I really hadn't noticed the shower when we first looked at the house. Why did you have to show it to me so early in the day?"

"Umm, because you and Kelly asked for it?"

"I didn't know it was *that kind* of a shower. You've had me thinking about this shower all day. And I've been stuck hauling furniture and carrying boxes and trying to have patience with friends when all I really wanted to do was boot them out the door and turn the water on."

"You can turn the water on," I said, teasing.

"It's not just the water I want turned on."

"Show me."

His eyes softened. I was his and he knew it. He ran his fingers around the neckline of my shirt and kissed me deeply. He pulled my t-shirt up over my head and my breath quickened just thinking about what was ahead. He wrapped his arms around me, hands straying, fingers hitting the scar on my side. He pulled his hands back.

"No, don't stop, Rusty, just ignore it."

"Babe, please, if I ever hurt you, you'd tell me, wouldn't you?"

"Don't stop…"

"I have to know, promise me you'll say something."

"I promise. Don't stop."

"Why?" he said, grinning.

"Don't stop!"

"Why?" he said, teasing. "Show me."

I launched myself at him. That scoundrel! He'd driven me to it and I had to have him. He caught me in an embrace and we tumbled down onto the bed.

"Because I love you," I said between kisses. "Because I want you. I want you. You drive me crazy… Don't stop…"

Why did clothes have to be so darned complicated? Men's belts, stiff buttons… Each piece of clothing brought a new wave of touches. My bra came off and his hands found my breasts. Then his lips, teasing. Clothes slid off the bed as we fumbled and laughed at each other. Then they were gone and we were free. Free to touch and play. We started out laughing and playing in the bedroom and ended in steamy, slithery embraces, the water pulsing around us in the shower. Soapy bodies sliding and caressing, tensions building and waning and building again.

The next day I thought, if Rusty and I just showered together each morning we could cancel our gym membership.

Chapter 22

I went outside and threw the barn doors open, taking care to watch out for snakes. To ensure the barn was really empty I shined a flashlight around inside, then opened the back doors to air the place out.

Weeds were taking over the dirt areas of the backyard, so I began pulling them one by one. The pile grew. Shadow followed me, curious about his new surroundings, so I watched him carefully. He needed to know his boundaries here, so when he began straying too far I called him back in a gruff voice. He was used to unseen boundaries when we visited my parents' ranch, so I was confident I'd soon have him trained to stay close to home.

The weed pile turned into two piles, then three as I made my way around the yard. I was struggling with a weed nearly as tall as me when Rusty appeared.

"What are you doing out here all by yourself? You could have woken me up."

"Why? Just because I feel like working doesn't mean *you* have to."

"Cass, you don't have to do everything on your own. You're allowed to have some help. You might be stubborn enough to weed the whole place by hand but that doesn't mean you have to."

He grabbed the weed and pulled steadily until the roots gave way. I started down the side of the barn, pulling more weeds. The sun rose in the sky and the heat began settling in.

"Enough," he said, "we can do more another day."

"We need to buy some tools if we are going to have a place this big. We need a wheelbarrow or a pushcart for jobs like this. We need a lawn mower, shovels, rakes, a hedge trimmer, a table saw and workbench. We need to start accumulating these things before the yard takes over."

"What do we need a table saw for?"

"To make a new agility course. Since we have room to set one up, I'd like to start building a new one."

"I don't want you using a table saw all by yourself."

"You don't? Where do you think the first agility course came from? I built it myself. I was working on building a new obstacle when you called me to search for Kelly. Work like that keeps my hands and my mind busy. Sometimes I think if I only did what you would allow me to do I'd be sitting in the house crocheting afghans and baking cookies all day. You know I'm not going to do that. I want to clean this place up, plan a wedding on the lawn, put in a gazebo, and set up a woodworking shop in the barn. I want to explore the hills, find some tracks and follow them until I don't know where I am, then track my way home again."

"Cassidy, hold up," he said. "I know. I know you need to do all those things and you will. Just take it one step at a time, that's all I'm asking."

We walked around to the huge lawn on the side of the house.

"If we put a gazebo up near the house we can set up chairs through the middle of the lawn and place tables around the outside edges."

Making plans brought on ideas, ideas led to purchases, and purchases led to work. It was good creative work, though, and I was really getting into it. I dismayed Rusty time and again when he came home to find large projects in the making. In the area where the gazebo was planned, I'd tilled up and carted the dirt and grass away in wheelbarrow loads to a pile behind the barn. When the area was lowered and raked level, I went and bought truckloads of flagstone, hauled it piece by piece, and laid them down to make a patio for the gazebo to rest on.

There were so many things we needed. I had to buy a ladder, lawnmower, and wheelbarrow. I was glad we had a barn to store everything.

I bought furniture for the living room and guest room.

I wanted to create a visual separation between the lawn and the corral area so I bought tall posts, put eyebolts near the tops, and sunk them in concrete. The decorating of them would come later.

"Cass, what in the world are you doing out there?" Rusty asked at dinner.

"You'll see when the wedding gets closer. The posts are only temporary. I'll take them down after the wedding."

I went to the fabric store and bought bolts of tulle, spools of ribbon, and armloads of silk flowers.

After ordering a big, iron gazebo, I waited excitedly until it was delivered and set up on the flagstones. Yes! We were getting closer. Time was growing shorter, too.

I checked with the guys to make sure they had their tuxes reserved, then checked in with the photographer, florist, and caterer. I also called Bullhorn Brewski to make sure we were still on for the 27th, and he reminded me about the rehearsal.

As the wedding day grew closer I was a bundle of nerves, which translated into plenty of nervous energy. There were too many details running through my mind.

"Cass, please, sit down, you're making me nervous," Rusty finally asked.

I sat down, but stilling my pacing didn't slow my thoughts. "I can't help it, there are too many things to remember."

"And pacing the house is going to help you remember?"

"No, but I feel like I can keep up with my head if I'm pacing."

"You know, I bet if you forget a few things nobody will notice."

"Maybe not, but I don't want to be walking down the aisle and suddenly think, oh no! I forgot to lock the pantry. Now Cody's going to take all the labels off the cans. Although, I already decided what to do if he tries that."

Rusty laughed. "What's that?"

"I'm just going to make him a big casserole using nothing but canned goods. I might even go out and buy some really weird things in cans to add to it. I picture a mush of vegetable soup, tuna, various canned fruits and some odd meats that would look weird, like anchovies or smelt. Creamed corn and caviar would really muck it up. Pie filling and fish, how does that sound? Weird combinations work well too. Prunes and black olives and creamed corn and anchovies."

"Okay, I get the picture. You really think he would eat it?"

"It doesn't matter, just watching him try and get out of it would be worth the trouble."

"I don't think you have anything to worry about. Cody won't do anything to ruin your wedding day. He isn't spiteful and he won't have fun at your expense. He might take all the labels off the cans but he won't do anything you need to worry about like set the sprinkler system to come on during the wedding vows."

"Oh, I better make a note to remind myself to turn the sprinklers to rain that day!"

And so off I'd go, the wheels in my head turning and spinning. I was glad the group from the ranch showed up. The busyness kept me focused. I gave them all a tour of the house. My mother loved the master bedroom with its big bay window. I only had the one guestroom but other arrangements had already been made for everyone else. It was decided that the bridesmaids would use the guestroom and the groomsmen would take over the office.

As soon as it was tactful I put my mom and Jesse to work.

"I need these flowers arranged in bouquets. They need to be seen from below, so keep that in mind. Here, I'll show you what I am thinking."

I brought them outside and showed them the posts.

"I'm going to hang tulle between the posts and I want a bouquet at the top of each scallop."

"Cassidy! Do you know how much tulle you're going to need to pull that off?" my mother exclaimed.

"Do you think a hundred yards will do it?" I asked.

"It might. How long is the yard?"

"A hundred and twenty feet, so it's less than fifty yards. And I have a hundred yards of each color, so if we run out we can always just get creative with arranging the colors. Or we can cut the tulle in half and have twice the length. The goal is to break up the view of the corrals and barn. I weeded back there but I haven't had time to paint and fix it up."

I showed them the boxes of flowers and spools of ribbon. This was Jesse's department. She loved doing anything creative and I knew she would keep at it until she had something she liked.

When the big truck arrived, the men started unloading the tables and chairs. As planned, the chairs were set up in rows and the tables placed along the outside of the freshly cut lawn.

I climbed a ladder to start hanging tulle from the posts, which prompted Jesse to rush out from the house.

"Cass, use the white tulle for the longer drapes," she advised.

"Okay, why?" I asked.

"Because I have a plan for using the extra tulle in your wedding colors."

It sounded fine to me. Jesse usually had good ideas. I started hanging the light blue first, then made a slightly longer drape with the light green and ended with the white. I tied each drape to the eye bolt at the top of the posts with wedding color ribbon then stepped back to admire the effect.

Once I had finished, Jesse came back outside to inspect my work.

"You better pray for no wind tonight! How much tulle do you have left? If you fill in one section with tulle and we staple flowers onto the posts it'll make a nice picture taking spot. If we run out of flowers you can staple up small pine branches and pine cones for a more outdoorsy look."

"Jesse, you're a genius. I hadn't thought of that," I said. I had to give her credit, she was a master at being crafty. She'd always been the crafty one and I was the sneaky one. Only problem was that a wedding wasn't exactly a sneaky occasion. She chose a section and started hanging more drapes of tulle between the two posts. Then she stapled up the leftover flowers to hide the edges of the tulle and made little ribbon bows to fill in spots that looked like they needed help. After running out of flowers just short of the bottom we went to the front porch and brought the pots of real flowers that Mrs. Morgan had left behind and stood one at each post.

"Do you have any spray paint in wedding colors?" Jesse asked.

"Now, why would I think to buy spray paint?" I asked. Spray paint didn't seem like a wedding necessity to me.

"I just thought it would be romantic to spray hearts across the tulle. Spray paint doesn't have to look like graffiti. You can use it in lots of ways."

"Nope, sorry, no spray paint."

The seating was arranged. The tulle and flowers were hung. The tables were arranged. All I needed were tablecloths, and for all my hired help to be reliable.

Rusty's parents arrived with Cody early in the afternoon. There were hugs and introductions all around.

Shadow was having a ball. He thought of people as sheep, and had never seen so many sheep in all his life. I wondered how he'd react tomorrow when a couple hundred people would be invading his domain.

Rehearsal time was getting closer so I slipped off to change clothes. Although everyone was casually dressed I felt a need to dress up a little. I decided to wear my birthday dress, which was still my favorite, and lately had been begging to be worn. It fit just right and made me feel pretty, exactly what I needed for my rehearsal. I carefully curled and styled my hair and put on a little make-up, wanting to save the real makeover for tomorrow. I then put on the necklace and earrings my mom had given me last year for my birthday. The doorbell rang and somebody answered the door. I heard a lull in the conversation and then listened as it picked up again as introductions were exchanged. I slipped on some pumps and went to join the growing crowd. Landon had joined the group and he turned as I entered the room. He stood a moment, appraising. His reaction caused me to hesitate and I almost turned to see if Jesse was down the hall. I wasn't used to being looked at that way. He walked over.

"Hi, I'm Landon Wilson, I work with Cassidy," he said.

"I think I'd better go change," I answered uncomfortably.

"No, don't," he said a little too quickly.

"Who haven't you met already? I'll take you around. I think the only guests left to arrive are Kelly and Rhonda, Victor, and Bullhorn Brewski."

"You're kidding. You really got him to perform the ceremony?"

"Yeah, he contacted Rusty at the station and set everything up."

We approached the group by the front door.

"You met Rusty's parents, Bill and Beverly; his brother, Cody; and my sister, Jesse."

"Yeah."

"Okay, then let's head for the kitchen." We rounded the breakfast bar. "This is my mom, you can call her Betty. Mom, this is Landon Wilson. We do a lot of searches together. I'm the tracker and he's the patcher. He's an EMT. I don't know what he does for his regular job. Do you have a regular job? How is it you are *always* available when Lou calls?"

"I really am an EMT. It runs in the family. My dad owns an ambulance company and I work for him. We have more ambulances than calls, so that leaves me free to work for Strict."

Schroeder walked in from the backyard.

"You know Schroeder."

It took Schroeder a second to place me. Okay, so I looked different, I'd admit it.

Landon said, "Hi."

Schroeder acknowledged the terse greeting with a nod.

"Is everyone out back?" I asked him.

"A bunch of them are. I'm not sure who they all are."

I took Landon out the back door and showed him the corrals and barn.

"I have a horse on my parents' ranch and I'm debating on whether or not to bring him down. I have the room but I won't move him down here unless I know I can take care of him. If I get called out on a search that takes days, I need to know he's being fed, but I hate to saddle Rusty with that job. I am waiting to see how willing he's going to be with the horses. Shasta is fine at the ranch. They work him there and keep him trained. So, I'm debating."

Rusty walked over and joined our conversation. "She wants to put a table saw in the barn and set up a woodworking shop," he said.

"Since when do you do woodworking?" Landon asked Rusty.

"I don't," he answered, "Cassidy does. She makes obstacles to add to an agility course and then she trains her dog to run the course. I'm not so sure about the table saw though."

"You'd rather I saw all that plywood by hand? I can, it's just a pain and it's not as accurate. Anyway, that hasn't been decided yet. Come on," I said, leading Landon around to the wedding section of the yard. "This is my dad, his name is Wayne but everybody calls him Mr. Gordon. This is Steve and Randy. Steve has worked on the ranch as long as I can remember. Randy has been working there since I was sixteen." They were both dressed in their cowboy best, colorful western shirts with string ties and pressed Wranglers. I thought Bullhorn Brewski would feel right at home with Dad and a couple of ranch hands around. I led Landon on further. "This is my brother-in-law, James, and my nephews, Patrick and Wyatt. If there was ever going to be another tracker in the family, Patrick is it. Hey, buddy, have you tagged your first rabbit yet?"

"Nah, but I've gotten closer!"

"I promised to take him stalking deer after he tagged his first rabbit. He has to stalk it until he can touch it. When he can do that, I figure he'll be ready to try it on deer."

"A wild rabbit?"

"Yeah."

"And you've done that?"

"Sure, when I was about eight. I figure I have some time before I need to go stalking with Patrick."

Kelly rounded the corner of the house with Rhonda close on his heels.

"Landon, you've met Kelly Green, haven't you?"

"Nope, I've looked for him but we've never met," he said, extending his hand. Kelly shook hands with Landon and then gave me a quick hug. I always felt uncomfortable whenever Kelly hugged me in front of his wife. I hugged Rhonda, too. Kelly was dressed in his usual faded jeans and t-shirt. The t-shirt advertised a landscaping company. His dark brown, curly hair was down over his collar. I wondered if he planned on getting a haircut before the wedding, but decided it didn't matter. I was curious, though, how he'd look with a haircut.

"This is my wife, Rhonda," he said to Landon.

Shadow bounded up when he heard Kelly's voice.

"And this is Shadow. Today we get to find out if he's going to be the flower girl. No! No hose," I scolded, backing away from his flying paws. "Sit!" Shadow sat. "Now, shake hands with Landon." Shadow held out his paw and Landon shook it gently.

"Hey, shake hands with me too!" said Victor. Shadow shook hands and then Victor shook hands with Kelly and Rhonda too. "Well, well," he said, "we finally get to see another side to our little tracker."

Suddenly we all heard a burst of laughter coming from the house.

"It sounds like Bullhorn Brewski is here. I wonder what we are supposed to call him when he's in minister mode. Guess we'll find out."

My mom came rushing out the back door.

"Cassidy, are you quite sure you want to go ahead with this... this clown for a minister?"

"Mom, this is just the rehearsal. He knows he has to wear a suit tomorrow and he can't be a clown until the reception. Both Rusty and I have talked to him. He knows. Why? He isn't drunk is he?"

"Well, no, he's just, well, a character!"

"He's a very nice man. How's his leg doing? He broke it several weeks ago."

"It's in a cast but he's walking on it."

"That's good to hear. It was a pretty bad break."

We all headed for the living room, which seemed to have shrunk by a good ten feet once everybody got in there. Would there be room to have a wedding here? I reminded myself that the guests would be mingling both inside and outside the house, and there would be plenty of room as the people wandered about.

The rehearsal took a little tweaking. I needed to find someone to be in charge of Shadow until he walked down the aisle.

"Randy, you've worked with Shadow before. All you have to do is heel him over to this spot. Tell him to sit, unclip his leash and then put the basket in front of him. Rusty will do the rest."

Randy walked through the steps and Shadow sat behind his little basket of flower petals. Rusty stood in his place at the gazebo and discreetly gave him the *pickup* signal. Nothing. He called Shadow and tried again. Shadow looked at all the people standing around and shrunk back without moving. Then he studied Rusty with some uncertainty, but picked up the basket. Rusty gave him the *come* signal. Shadow started down the aisle and Rusty gave him the *slow down* signal as a test, then the *come* signal to speed him up again. When Shadow reached the front of the assembly Rusty gave a discreet *sit* signal followed by a *drop it* signal and Shadow put the basket down. Randy called him from the sidelines and Shadow went off to do other doggy things. Patrick picked up the basket on his way up the aisle and set it down out of the way, then took his place beside Kelly.

One glitch taken care of, only one more to go: my father.

"Dad," I said as we were waiting for our turn to walk up the aisle, "I know you didn't have much to do with my first wedding. And I'd be honored to walk down the aisle with you. But I want you to know, I'll be giving myself to Rusty. You and mom aren't doing it. I am. And I want him to know that."

He looked at me seriously, but Wayne Gordon only had serious looks to begin with so it was sometimes a little hard to read him.

"I should've known," he said, resigned to my decision. "You're just as stubborn as your old man, you know that? But I love you anyway."

"I love you too, Dad."

So we walked down the aisle. When Bullborn Brewski asked, "Who giveth this woman to be wed?"

I said, "I do."

And he said, "It ain't your turn yet."

"Well, I still do."

"That's the way it's going to be?"

"Yup."

"Okay, but it just ain't proper."

Rusty was silently laughing at me.

"Nobody ever accused me of being proper before."

Mom shook her head.

The rehearsal went off without a hitch. I was comfortable that everyone knew their role and the right time to arrive the next day. They had also been informed of what they were supposed to say and when; and also what not to say. We all gathered in the living room where Rusty provided directions to the rehearsal dinner. The evening was spent enjoying lively conversation with each side exchanging stories about the bride and groom. It was all taken in good humor and I especially enjoyed listening to the years when Rusty was younger. He had never spoken much about his childhood, which made me wonder if I'd ever really get to know him. So I learned that day to treasure every story his family would share with me.

Chapter 23

My wedding day dawned and I looked out the big bay window of our bedroom as I did every morning, looking for those deer that Mrs. Morgan had promised came down out of the hills. So far I hadn't seen any but perhaps that was because of all the activity around the house of late.

The sky was blue, not a puff of breeze to mess up the tulle. The tulle! Oh no!

"Rusty! Quick! Where are your leather gloves?" I called urgently as I rushed to pull on my jeans and a t-shirt.

"Huh?" he asked sleepily.

"Your leather gloves, where are they?"

"I think they're in the garage. Why?"

"Ooooh. Because! I've got a mess on my hands and I'm going to need the leather or I'll get bit!"

I rushed off to the garage. Leather gloves, leather gloves, where were the stupid leather gloves? I had two hundred people arriving in a few hours and I needed to take care of this *now*!

There they were! Were they thick enough? I hoped so. I put them on and ran to the barn. Throwing the door open I grabbed the ladder which nearly sent me toppling over in my rush. Carrying it to the first post, I positioned the ladder then scrambled up the rungs. Stupid bats! The tulle was full of bats! Aren't bats supposed to know not to run into things in the night? They're supposed to see things in front of them, things as small as mosquitoes. Surely they should have seen a bunch of netting!

"Cassidy? Are you nuts? What's wrong?" Rusty called from the back door.

"I'm not nuts! I'm batty. Just plain batty! Look at this!"

He wandered outside dressed only in boxer pants. I grabbed a bat and gently pulled its claws loose from the fine netting then tossed it up in the air and it flew away.

"Cass! What are you doing? You can't do that! One of them is going to bite you!"

"This isn't a Halloween wedding. I'm not having *bats* in my decorations!"

I tossed another one up into the air. It flapped around disoriented, then took a bearing and flew away. I gently grabbed another bat. After Rusty watched me for a while and was convinced that I wasn't going to kill them, be bitten, or fall off the ladder, he disappeared inside. A short time later he returned with a camera and started snapping pictures.

"What are you doing?!" I cried.

"In a few months we'll look back on this and it'll be funny. Here, let me help you."

"As long as we're making a documentary let's take a close up. Here," I said climbing down the ladder. I held up a bat for the photo, floppy gloves grasping the struggling bat. I spread out its wings for a good picture, then tossed it in the air where it promptly flew right back into the netting. Not knowing whether to laugh or cry, I climbed back up the ladder and started pulling another bat loose. Their small claws were perfect little hooks for the netting. Plus, they had thrashed around in their excitement to escape, so some of them were all bound up as well as snagged.

"Go see if you can borrow another ladder from a neighbor."

I kept working, pulling bats loose, tossing them to their freedom, then going on to the next bat. There must have been fifty of the dumb things. As I pulled them gently loose I arranged the tulle, and when I had one section bat free I climbed down to inspect my work. Whew! I couldn't even tell it had a mishap. Maybe, just maybe. Rusty appeared with another ladder, a second pair of gloves and a very amused neighbor who was roaring with laughter.

"And you say the wedding is when?" he bellowed.

"Ten o'clock!" I wailed back. "Rusty, be careful. Don't squeeze. You can't squeeze them. It's easy to hurt them."

"I know, I'm trying," he said with a puzzled look on his face.

We were still up there pulling bats out of the netting when the first news van rolled up. Oh great! Then my parents arrived.

"Cassidy! What are you doing? You're supposed to be getting ready for your wedding!" my mother lamented.

"I am! I can't have a wedding with my decorations full of bats! I can get ready in fifteen minutes if I have to, but I can't get rid of bats that quickly, so they have to come first! If you want to help out put tablecloths on all the tables. Alternate blue and green around each one, a blue tablecloth with a green runner and vice versa. The florist will be here in a few minutes. There will be an arrangement on each table and they are supposed to decorate the gazebo a little bit too."

"Cassidy! How can you do that? You couldn't get me within a hundred yards of those icky bats," Jesse called out.

"You're within a hundred yards now. They aren't so bad, just like flying mice. Here," I tossed one her way and she flung her arms over her head. The bat flew away to find its normal daytime home. Patrick giggled at his mom.

By eight o'clock the tulle was bat free. Our new neighbor was given a wedding invitation and a thank you for the use of his ladder. Rusty and I looked as if we'd just returned from a three day search and our wedding was starting in two hours. We rushed into the house, took a very unsexy, hurried shower and started getting ready for the ceremony. I got out an arsenal of hair care products. I moussed my hair and dried it, then curled it and sprayed it and curled it some more and finally sprayed it again. I was extra careful with my make-up. Mascara, foundation, blush, a little eye shadow, eyeliner, the works. I wore the diamond earrings and necklace my mom had given to me.

Rusty knocked on the bathroom door. I cracked it open.

"Yeah?"

"I need to get something."

"Umm, okay, I think I'm at the point where Sandy would be horrified if you saw me but come on in." I hid behind the door as he found what he needed. "Anything else? You're about to be banished to the office."

"No, I think I'm fine."

"If only it were that simple," I sighed.

"Oh wait, I need a kiss," he said before I could close the door.

"Okay, close your eyes," I said laughing, and gave him a quick kiss. "Now go wash the lipstick off."

My mom knocked on the door a short while later, relieved to see that everything was back under control.

"The florist is setting up, the cake arrived and they are decorating it now. The photographer is waiting on pins and needles. The caterer is outside wanting to know if they can use your kitchen with the breakfast bar or should they set up a buffet outside."

"Okay, help me with the dress and then we can answer all the questions."

I pulled my dress from the closet and stepped into it, pulling it up and around me. My mom started fastening the buttons up the back.

"Rusty's going to love all these buttons," she said sarcastically.

"I know, but I had to buy it anyway. His sister, Sandy, invoked Rule 642. The other dress I was looking at was cute but I didn't want to look cute. So," I asked turning around, "what do you think?"

"Oh my," she said, drawing in her breath, "you look stunning!"

I looked at myself in the mirror. If ever there was a day to look stunning this was it. I didn't quite agree with Mom's assessment but my heart beat more quickly in anticipation of Rusty's reaction. I turned back and forth watching the dress sparkle with my movements.

"Thanks. Okay, you can send in the photographer. The florist knows what to do. The buffet on the breakfast bar will be good if there is enough room. Tell them to put the wet bar on the patio. The cake will eventually be either at the head table or the gazebo. Gee I hate head tables. I'd rather just be a part of the group."

"Okay, I'll send in the photographer, and I'll pass along the instructions."

"Thanks Mom."

I looked around for my shoes. I bought shoes, didn't I? I must have! I know I bought a veil. I found the veil and pinned it in place. I peeked out the bay window. Oh, man! Look at all the people, and the guests weren't even here yet! I counted three different news crews. I hoped they had enough sense to stay in the background.

The florist came in with our bouquets and looked at the hair and veil configuration. She decided against putting flowers in my hair.

"Is the gazebo decorated?"

"Everything's set. You'll love it."

"Thanks."

Now where are my stupid shoes?

The photographer came in with Jesse and Rhonda, then took a roll of pictures in various staged poses.

"Cass, my beautiful big sister! I can't believe this is you!" Jesse said wistfully. "Have you ever felt more special in all your life?"

No, come to think of it, I hadn't.

Now, where are my stupid shoes!

My mom came in again.

"Do all the groomsmen have boutonnieres? Is there an arrangement on each table? Are the caterers set up? Did the photographer take pictures of the guys? Is Patrick all set? Are the rings tied to the little pillow? Did we put out the guestbook? Has the minister arrived? In a suit? Is he sober?"

"Yes, yes, yes, and more yeses."

"Thanks, Mom."

I found a bow tie and then Jesse brought Shadow into my room so I could brush him and clip it on. Oh gee, I hadn't thought about brushing a black dog while wearing a full white skirt. I gave him a once over then put the bow tie on him and handed the basket and leash to Randy.

Before I knew it I was hearing music coming from the backyard. All I could do now was hope that everyone knew their job.

"Cassidy? Are you ready? It's time," Jesse called.

"I can't find my shoes! I can't wear my moccasins or hiking boots. Oh shoot, let's just go!"

"But..."

"It'll be fine. I walk around in the woods barefoot. Surely a lawn will be fine."

"But..."

"Let's go, no one will even see my feet under this huge dress."

"But..."

I peeked out the door, making sure Rusty was nowhere to be seen, then slipped quickly out the front door and to the side of the house.

How could time go by so fast? Just a few minutes ago I was pulling bats out of the netting and now here I was ready to walk down the aisle! Smile, Cass, don't forget to smile. I peeked around the house. It was no fair. A bride doesn't even get to see her own wedding. She has to hide in the sidelines while it all happens before her entry and then she just steps into it all.

Randy positioned Shadow and unclipped the leash. I watched Rusty give him the pick up signal. Shadow didn't know what to think of all the people. I couldn't blame him, I didn't know what to think about all the guests either! I saw dozens of uniforms. I picked out Ben and Big John, then Tom, Strict, Rosco and Thez. I was happy to see Rusty's brother, Tony, who had traveled here all the way from New York City. I would have to make sure to introduce myself at the reception. He sat between Sandy and another woman. Men in suits, women in dresses, kids dressed up in uncomfortable frills and ties. Rusty snapped his fingers and gave Shadow the pick up signal and this time he paid attention. He picked up the basket and trotted up the aisle, flower petals spilling over the side of the basket. Rusty gave him a slow down signal and he slowed, walking the rest of the way before coming to a stop in front of the minister. Rusty pointed at the ground and Shadow put down the basket and sat. When Rusty tossed him a treat, Shadow leaped into the air to catch it. Rusty blushed. Shadow sat, staring longingly at Rusty, hoping for more. I smiled, enjoying Rusty's predicament. He didn't have another treat but he certainly had Shadow's attention. Patrick started down the aisle. When he reached the front he hauled Shadow away then came back to stand in front with the groomsmen. Patrick stood there proudly in his miniature tuxedo and then Jesse and Rhonda started down the aisle. I heard the clicks from a score of cameras.

Bullhorn Brewski was dressed nicely in a black suit and bow tie. Rusty looked sharp in his black, formal tux, brown cummerbund and bow tie. Schroeder and Kelly stood proudly beside him. I was shocked to see that Kelly had indeed gotten a haircut. Now I'd never recognize him in the pictures. He flashed looks at Rhonda in her bridesmaid dress. Her red hair had been curled and styled off her shoulders. She had gone out of her way to get dolled up, which was very unusual for her. By the way she was standing, I knew she felt both pretty and awkward. I knew that feeling all too well. Jesse had no problem with such things, she'd been born to it and loved dressing up and fussing with her hair, nails and jewelry. She shined.

It was my turn. I hardly heard the music any longer once I stepped out. My dad took my arm and I slowly walked with him down the aisle. I looked at Rusty from the end of the aisle. His eyes were smiling. He squared his shoulders, stood tall, and worked to keep his emotions in check. I thought about Sandy watching her big brother. Slowly, slowly, we walked down the aisle. I took a few quick steps and my dad pulled me back. Rusty gave me the slow signal and I smiled. Why? Why must weddings be slow solemn occasions? I wanted to be up there. I watched Rusty as we made our way, step by very slow step all the way up to the gazebo. Halfway up the aisle I suddenly remembered why I really needed my shoes. The garter! There were going to be a dozen cameras focused on my leg and I didn't have shoes on! I almost laughed. If possible I would have busted out laughing, but I couldn't do that so I just smiled and watched Rusty. His eyes went from wistful to quizzical as I neared the alter.

"Who gives this woman to be wed to this man?"

"I do!" I said, still trying to keep a straight face.

My dad gave me a hug, stepped down and sat with my mom. I stepped forward and took Rusty's arm.

"What is it?" he whispered.

"I couldn't find my shoes!" I whispered back.

His eyes laughed again. "What are you wearing? Not your hiking boots."

"Nothing! I ran out of time! I'm barefoot!" I whispered back.

We turned to Bullhorn Brewski. He thanked the guests for coming and for their support of Rusty and myself. He also thanked the press for their good manners. I noticed a wide wedding-blue ribbon had fenced them off from the guests and wondered who had thought to do that. Brewski then launched into a short speech about the seriousness of wedding vows. Next he told the story of breaking his leg on the South Fork Trail where he had met me, and then about meeting Rusty at the station.

"Just as Rusty and Cassidy worked together in the search for me, I know they will work well together for the rest of their lives. Join me with your support as they follow their hopes and dreams."

I wanted to put my hand in the air and add, "Hey! Landon and Thez were there too." But I knew it wasn't the place.

When it was time to recite our vows, Rusty squared his shoulders, took my hands in his, and looked me in the eye. He waited just long enough to cause people to wonder if he had forgotten what came next. Then he said his vows in a booming bass voice that carried out over the lawn. As he spoke and the words became more personal to him, his voice softened and by the end of his vows he was smiling.

"I, Rusty, take you, Cassidy, to be my lawful wife, my partner in life and my one true love. Forsaking all others, I will be faithful only to you. I will trust you, respect you, and love you faithfully through good times and bad, in sickness and in health, in times of plenty and times of need, regardless of the obstacles we may face together. I give you my hand, my heart, and my love, from this day forward for as long as we both shall live." He slipped the ring over my finger, and with a wink added, "Let this ring be a symbol of my promises to you and a reminder of my devotion to you. I am honored to call you my wife."

It was odd. I could almost feel the devotion he felt for me through his hands. An intensity and longing and hope that trouble would cease as long as he was there. A love beyond words. It humbled me and I fought back the tears. I had to recite my vows, too, so it took me a moment and once again a long pause drifted over the desert lawn. As I recited my vows I couldn't help but think that Rusty sure was promising an awful lot. So far, trouble had not let up just because we were together. I hoped the good times would outweigh the bad ones, but... I fought with myself. Could I really condemn Rusty to troubles like we had seen together? Trouble for the rest of our lives? But I knew he was earnest. He would be there, no matter what happened, so I continued my vows. Only the strongest of men could do what he had done, so I truly felt proud to call him my husband as I slipped the ring over his finger. I took a deep breath, calmed my churning thoughts and stood tall as we faced our friends and family.

Bullhorn Brewski bellowed out for the whole assembly to hear, "By the power vested in me by the State of California, I now pronounce you husband and wife. You may kiss the bride."

We both looked at each other. Despite my second thoughts I was overjoyed. We did it! We finally did it! I leaped into his arms and we kissed like it might be our last. It brought hoots, cheers, and a round of applause from the guests.

"Ladies and gentlemen," the minister bellowed over the cheers of the crowd, "I present to you Mr. and Mrs. Rusty Michaels!"

Rusty and I beamed as we quickly walked back down the aisle. Rusty lifted me up and spun me around as the bridal party followed behind. When we reached the end of the aisle Patrick stood amongst the wedding party, uncertain of what to do next. I knelt down to his level and said, "Keep your suit on until the picture taking is over. Then you can do whatever you want. Go find your dad."

He gave me a high five and ran off to find James.

We quickly formed a receiving line for the guests to pass through before the reception. Usually I'm uncomfortable with receiving lines because I'm never quite sure of what to say. This time, however, I appreciated being able to finally greet the guests we'd invited to our wedding. There were some surprises. Trevor was here. I'd sent him an invitation but I never expected him to attend. I wondered if he came to be on TV again.

I met Rusty's other brother, Tony. He was very much like their father, Bill. He talked like a radio announcer. He stood next to Cody in line, who greeted me with, "Hey, little sis!"

"Hi! I was wondering if you might have anything to do with my disappearing shoes. Cody, you wouldn't happen to know where they are, like *before* we have to do the garter toss?"

He said he didn't know anything and I was pretty sure he was telling me the truth. I was beginning to wonder if I ever bought shoes. Maybe it got put on my to-do list so many times that I assumed it had been done.

The line of people continued. Rusty had several aunts and uncles who had attended but I'd never be able to remember all their names. Mrs. Morgan gave me a tearful hug, declaring that she loved the gazebo. My new neighbor and his wife had quickly changed into their best clothes which, on such short notice, happened to be ten-year-old polyester pantsuits. They introduced themselves as Hazel and Wally. Hazel was a heavyset woman with a quick wit and a firm handshake. Wally appeared to be more easygoing and ready to follow Hazel's lead. They had been married forty-nine years. They apologized for not bringing a gift and I assured them we were just glad to have them there.

"Plus, we will always have a funny story about how we met," I reminded them.

The wedding magically morphed into a reception. The chairs suddenly disappeared from the lawn and appeared around the tables. I assumed the wedding party had helped while we were busy shaking hands and hugging people in the receiving line. I went to the house and brought out packages of light blue and green balloons with wedding bells printed on them. A helium tank had been stationed near the house. I gave Bullhorn Brewski the balloons, ribbons to tie onto them and permission to transform into a clown for the rest of the day. I turned the music track back on softly so our guests were able to mingle while the buffet line started.

The photographer snagged different groups and had us pose in different locations around the property. Jesse's backdrop became a favorite area for picture taking, as was the gazebo and the fireplace in the den. I discovered Mrs. Morgan wandering around in her former house and gave her some privacy to explore the changes we'd made in our new home.

Everything settled down as the reception began. I hadn't assigned seating to allow our guests the freedom to sit with familiar groups. The search and rescue team were seated at one table. There were several tables filled with officers and their families. Our relatives sat together. Everything seemed to be running smoothly when I spotted an uninvited guest, but it was one I was particularly happy to see. Off in the woods just seeming to be investigating the place was a young buck. I quietly left my place at the table and, wedding dress and all, slowly approached the young deer. He was distracted by the crowd which permitted me to quietly approach from a direction he had been ignoring. I was standing about forty feet from the buck when I heard Patrick's loud voice declare from across the yard, "Hey! Look at Aunt Cassidy!"

Silence fell and I suddenly got very self-conscious. I wasn't used to giving stalking demonstrations in the middle of a wedding reception but I couldn't pass this up. I crept closer, hiding behind a tree. I heard my mom say, "Oh, Cassidy," in that tone of voice that told me she was shaking her head in consternation.

I thought this would be a good time for the all the team, the officers, and Patrick to know I could do it. If I could stalk a deer under these conditions I could do it in camouflage. So I put aside my self-conscious feeling and kept at it. The deer turned his head and I crept out from behind the tree. Two steps and I froze. I waited, crept forward, froze. It was a bit awkward. I couldn't get into a real crouch without ruining the dress so I had to rely on patience. Twenty feet and the buck started acting wary.

The picture in the newspaper the next day showed a bride in full wedding attire standing by a tree, holding her hand out towards a young deer, looking as if she was about to pet a horse. He didn't quite allow me to touch him, shying away at the last second. I wished the camera had caught his expression once he realized a hand was reaching for his nose. I'd never seen a cross-eyed deer before. It only lasted for a split second before he sprang up the hillside and into the junipers again. But I was happy knowing he'd eventually be back and probably have a few does with him. I returned to the head table beaming.

"We've got deer!" I said to Rusty enthusiastically.

Chase appeared, hands in the pockets of his jeans. "I never would have thought that was possible," he said.

"I agree. It wasn't exactly ideal stalking conditions. If I had been in camouflage and moccasins it would have been easier."

"I meant, that I didn't think it was possible at all. You've done that before?"

"I don't usually get that close. I touched a deer once but I didn't exactly try and pet it. I just touched her gently on the back. I'd rather just get into a herd and enjoy them being close. They seem to relax if I just lay down in amongst them quietly. That's what I like to do. I want the deer that visit our house to know I won't hurt them. The only way to teach them is to approach them so they can see nothing bad happens. The deer in the canyon were starting to get used to me. They were fairly easy to stalk until they were driven away."

"Have you been up to the canyon lately?"

"I was up there a lot right after that mysterious explosion. They sent patrols up there to keep the public out, and then I had a search that took me to the top of the canyon, but you don't want to hear about that."

He raised an eyebrow.

"Okay, you don't want to hear about it at a wedding reception with most of the cops involved in attendance."

"I'll hold you to it, though."

"Okay."

While I was stalking the deer everyone had been enjoying lunch, so I sat down and hurried through some of the food on my plate. It was time to cut the cake.

We had an unusual cake topper. Martha had it made as a wedding gift to me. It was a fancy branding iron with the brand being R&C. The handle went down through the cake and held the layers together. After the wedding I'd clean it off and hang it up in the house.

We cut the cake and despite chants from some of the guests we refrained from any cake mashing. Martha served wedding cake for everybody while Rusty and I mingled. Bullhorn Brewski was inflating balloons and handing them out to kids first, then to anybody who wanted one. I never saw him pushing for donations but noticed that when he spoke to people they found him interesting. Wyatt ran by with a balloon tied to his wrist. Patrick had lost both his coat and tie and was running around with his shirt untucked like a normal boy.

Schroeder caught up to us and said, "We got a shift of guys fixing to leave. Do you think we can do the bouquet and the garter toss before they take off?"

Oh, golly, here we go. Bullhorn Brewski gathered all the single girls and women in a group and I tossed my bouquet backwards over my head and listened to the scramble. I closed my eyes, turned around, and when I opened them again there stood Sandy, my new sister-in-law, holding my bouquet, looking surprised and happy.

A couple of guys scooted chairs up and I sat down in one of them. The guys started chanting, "With your teeth, with your teeth!" and Rusty looked at me. I couldn't decide if he was embarrassed or just wanting to know how far I was willing to go. Heck, after the shoes I wasn't worried about much else. He pulled the hem of my dress up high enough to show a little thigh, then he reached up underneath and pulled off the garter. He held it up for all to see. Red? I didn't have a red garter! He reached up again. Green! Then blue! He gave me a mischievous look and smiled. Out came the light blue one I remembered. He slid it all the way down my leg and over my outstretched bare foot.

The guys started whistling and making remarks about the bare feet.

"Hey, Cassidy, you going to be barefoot and pregnant tonight?"

"I lost my shoes!" I said in defense but they would have none of it. I let them have their fun.

"This one's the real one," Rusty called out. "Where are all the single guys?"

There were lots of bachelors and half of them were in uniform. Rusty shot the light blue one up and Landon leaped to snatch it out of the air. Rusty shot about a half dozen other garters into the group and they dived for them, even though they were all fakes.

"So," Landon asked me afterwards, "who is that girl?"

"Right there? The one who caught the bouquet?"

"Yeah."

"That's Sandy, Rusty's sister."

"Oh yeah? How old is she?"

"Twenty-five or twenty-six."

"Thanks." He made his way over and introduced himself. I smiled, then thought, oh man, that's just what I don't need, Landon for a brother-in-law, but I silently wished him luck anyway.

"Where did all the extra garters come from?" I asked Rusty.

"Guess."

I thought for a second. "Brewski?"

"I think he has a bunch more in his pockets."

"Interesting minister."

"Yeah."

People started leaving a few at a time. A group of officers disappeared, next shift, I figured. It was now time to talk to the press. I found Bullhorn Brewski.

"Shall we see what the reporters are curious about? Maybe they will ask about the search and rescue work and it'll give you a chance to tell your story."

We came across Trevor on the way.

"Who put up the press tape?" I asked.

"That would be me," answered Brewski. "You don't know what a news crew can do to a wedding if you just turn them loose. They'd have tried to invade the gazebo if I hadn't made them stay out of the way."

"How has life been treating you since the avalanche?" a reporter asked.

"It's been one big adventure after another. Some I can tell you about, some I can't. This is Bullhorn Brewski. He's one of my rescues who doesn't mind telling you his story. I tracked him when he went missing from the Pacific Crest Trail earlier this summer. Landon Wilson, Thez Brockman and I searched for him for two days and two nights."

I looked to Brewski, glad to let him use up airtime for his cause. He told the reporters about why he was out on the PCT, about the rattlesnake, and then about being found and flown out. I was able to add a plug about the search and rescue operations and how they are volunteer efforts. I explained what is involved in the process and told of the commitment of those involved. I used Brewski as an example since he was a willing participant.

Trevor told the press about arriving back in Texas and telling his friends about his trip to California.

"Nobody wanted to hear about the beach and the roller coasters," he said. "They all wanted to hear about the earthquake. None of my friends can even imagine an earthquake and when I told them I had felt one and gotten trapped in the mine it was like I was an instant celebrity at school. My teacher let me write a report about it for extra credit. The only bad thing about it was I had to look up what an earthquake really is and that stunk, but I liked writing about what it felt like. She said it was good for my writing skills and she would like to read about it. So I wrote a report and at the end of school I got an A in English."

He went on and on. If there was one thing Trevor could do it was talk, and he wasn't afraid of the cameras so I let him have all the airtime he wanted.

"Mrs. Michaels?"

Now, that sounded weird. I'd never been called Mrs. Michaels before. Even when I was a Callahan people assumed I was Miss Callahan.

"Everything is going great. I've had my ups and downs since the avalanche but today topped it all."

"What kinds of ups and downs?"

"Searches, accidents, adventures, meeting my new in-laws, buying a house, planning a wedding. It's been one thing after another for me. I can say I've never been happier."

"Where are you going on your honeymoon?"

My honeymoon? I hadn't forgotten, but just didn't pressure Rusty about it. Now here we were on our wedding day and I still didn't know. "That is privileged information," I told them. "Only two people know that but I'm not one of them. Guess I ought to go find out."

Chapter 24

I slipped up behind Rusty while he was talking to a group of guys in the backyard. Most of the wedding guests had departed and we were down to the faithful few. They could be here for hours. I waited for a lull in the conversation, then addressed Rusty, "I have some reporters who want to know what we are doing for our honeymoon."

"Did you tell them it's a secret?"

"Yeah."

"And?"

"Rusty, I at least need to know what to pack."

"No you don't. You're already packed."

"You packed my suitcase?"

"I had some help."

"A man cannot pack a suitcase for a woman. You don't know what I need."

"Okay, well, go check it over. But I'm warning you it will only make you more curious."

Who could have helped Rusty pack my suitcase? Only Jesse or Mom. So off I trotted to find them. Jesse and Rhonda were straightening up the kitchen, enjoying girl talk when I flew in the backdoor. I almost caught the train of my dress in the sliding glass door.

"Jesse, did you help Rusty pack my suitcase for our honeymoon?"

"No, where are you going? I've been dying of curiosity!"

Okay, this was getting more and more curious.

"Me, too! I asked Rusty and he said it was a secret. When I told him I needed to pack he said I was already packed, that somebody had helped him with my suitcase. It had to be you or Mom. I'm going to find Mom."

I found Mom talking to Rusty's parents in the living room.

"It wasn't me," Mom said as I rounded the corner.

Arg! Who was it? Who would Rusty allow to go through my personal things?

Maybe the suitcase would hold some clues. I went to the bedroom. No suitcases. I checked the closet. No suitcases. I then noticed that about half my clothes were missing from the closet so I started opening drawers and found them half empty as well. The bathroom revealed that it had to be a woman. Sandy? A quick survey of the house and yard revealed we were down to just family and friends so I changed into my birthday dress so I could poke around without getting grease on my wedding dress. The backpacks were missing from the garage but most of the contents were still there. Only the stove seemed to be with the packs. Hmmm. A quick walk through the house revealed that the suitcases were not hidden away in the guestroom, office, or closets. I checked the Explorer. No suitcases. There was only one place left. The barn. All the guys watched me as I trotted across the lawn and behind the tulle. I opened the barn door and looked around inside. There were no suitcases, but there was a brand new table saw. My emotions suddenly became jumbled up. I wanted to sneak out the back door of the barn and go up into the hills to let things settle down. But, no, Rusty needed to know my real reaction. So I found the same group of guys still standing, waiting for me to come out of the barn. I clasped Rusty in a tight hug. I swallowed a big lump in my throat. "Is it from you?" I asked hesitantly.

He nodded, his eyes confirming.

"I don't know what to say, thank you."

"Just don't cut off any fingers and I'll be happy," he said.

"Why would you get your wife a table saw?" Tony asked.

"Come visit when you have time to stay," Rusty answered. "You'll see."

"Where are the suitcases?" I asked Rusty.

"At the hotel."

"You just told me to check my suitcase so I'd find the table saw?"

"Yeah. You'll just have to trust me on the suitcases."

"You sneak."

"Nope, not me, you still won't take me stalking because I can't sneak up on you. You're the sneak."

"I will, too, take you stalking. I don't mind you scaring the animals. I won't take you scouting. Staying out of sight of armed men is a whole different story."

"And you're telling this to a detective?" Tony asked.

"Yeah," I said, "it's not something you can understand unless you've known us a while. Ask Lou, Landon, Victor, or Jacobsen. There aren't too many people I will scout with. Maybe Chase."

Tony shook his head in dismay, but most men did when first meeting me. Rusty certainly had. I glanced around looking for Chase, knowing he had arrived with Rusty's parents. He had to be around here somewhere. I spotted him in the woods tracking the area where I had stalked the deer. I saw the familiar headshake and he finally walked over.

"Cassidy, did you really spend your whole wedding day barefoot?"

Embarrassed, I admitted, "I couldn't find my shoes and ran out of time. I'm convinced I forgot to buy them. It was no big deal, until I remembered the garter toss. I almost busted out laughing halfway up the aisle when I remembered the garter toss and my lack of shoes."

"After watching you with the deer, I'd like to propose a little contest. Did you know that even with fifty cops in attendance I bet none of them could find your tracks from when you were stalking that deer?" Chase said.

That didn't surprise me but the idea of a contest was intriguing. "What kind of a contest?"

"Something to test both our skills in leaving a trail and in tracking."

"Sounds like fun. Can you throw in some scouting? We were just talking about that before you walked up."

"Scouting?"

"Yeah, the guys don't like me to do scouting. They think I'm going to get myself shot. The one time I did get shot I wasn't scouting. So I'd like to test myself against someone who knows what to watch for. If I can sneak up on you, surely I can sneak up on some unsuspecting criminal."

"I don't like the sounds of that. If you beat me then you'll use that against the guys. I'll think of something and we can give it a try after you get back."

The next month of my life sounded like it would be interesting. Two weeks on some mystery honeymoon trip and a contest with Chase. This sounded like fun.

And so I'd like to say I lived happily ever after, but things didn't turn out that way. Trouble did not give up and go away just because I had a wonderful wedding and a fun plan. Nope, no way. Trouble was still after me, but I'll leave that for another story.